MISTS
over the
CHANNEL
ISLANDS

Books by Sarah Sundin

When Twilight Breaks
Until Leaves Fall in Paris
The Sound of Light
Embers in the London Sky
Midnight on the Scottish Shore
Mists over the Channel Islands

SUNRISE AT NORMANDY SERIES

The Sea Before Us
The Sky Above Us
The Land Beneath Us

WINGS OF GLORY SERIES

A Distant Melody
A Memory Between Us
Blue Skies Tomorrow

WINGS OF THE NIGHTINGALE SERIES

With Every Letter
On Distant Shores
In Perfect Time

WAVES OF FREEDOM SERIES

Through Waters Deep
Anchor in the Storm
When Tides Turn

MISTS
over the
CHANNEL ISLANDS

a NOVEL *of* WORLD WAR II

SARAH SUNDIN

Revell

a division of Baker Publishing Group
Grand Rapids, Michigan

© 2026 by D & S Enterprises

Published by Revell
a division of Baker Publishing Group
Grand Rapids, Michigan
RevellBooks.com

Printed in the United States of America

Library of Congress Cataloging-in-Publication Data
Names: Sundin, Sarah author
Title: Mists over the Channel Islands : a novel of World War II / Sarah Sundin.
Description: Grand Rapids : Revell, 2026.
Identifiers: LCCN 2025023843 | ISBN 9780800741877 paperback | ISBN
    9780800747978 casebound | ISBN 9781493452804 ebook
Subjects: LCSH: Young women--Fiction | World War, 1939-1945—Channel Islands—
    Fiction | Channel Islands—History—German occupation, 1940-1945—Fiction |
    LCGFT: Fiction
Classification: LCC PS3619.U5626 M55 2026 | DDC undefined—dc23/eng/20250612
LC record available at https://lccn.loc.gov/2025023843

Cover design by Laura Klynstra.

Photograph of woman © Magdalena Russocka / Trevillion Images.

Published in association with Books & Such Literary Management, www.BooksAndSuch.com.

Baker Publishing Group publications use paper produced from sustainable forestry practices and postconsumer waste whenever possible.

26 27 28 29 30 31 32   7 6 5 4 3 2 1

In loving memory
of my mother-in-law,
Diane Sundin,
who shone the light of Jesus
to all who knew her.

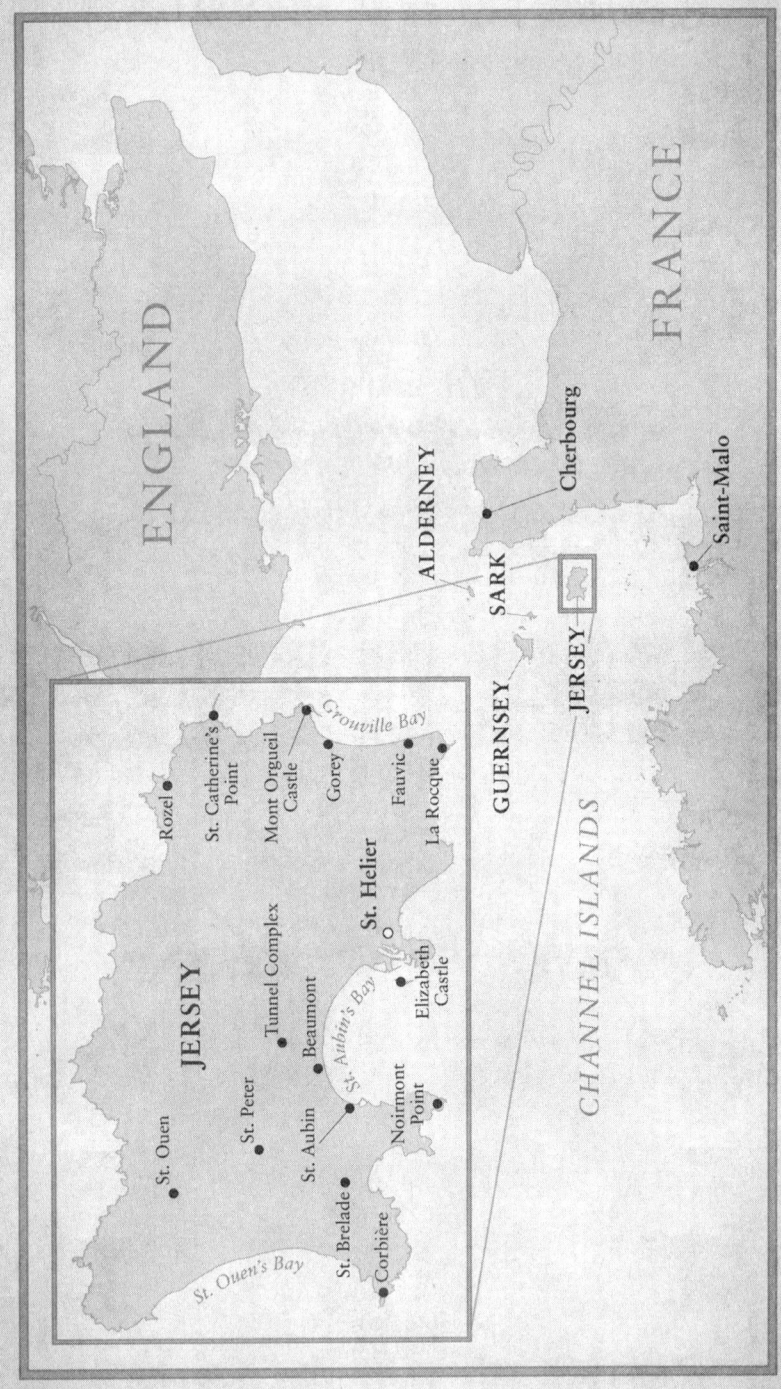

ENGLAND

FRANCE

Cherbourg

ALDERNEY

Saint-Malo

SARK

GUERNSEY

JERSEY

CHANNEL ISLANDS

Grouville Bay

Rozel

St. Catherine's
Point

Mont Orgueil
Castle

Gorey

Fauvic

La Rocque

St. Helier

Tunnel Complex

Beaumont

St. Aubin's Bay

Elizabeth
Castle

St. Ouen

St. Peter

JERSEY

St. Aubin

Noirmont
Point

St. Brelade

Corbière

St. Ouen's Bay

CHAPTER

1

Words failed Dr. Ivy Picot, so she sketched her father with gray-flecked hair, packing to go to war.

In his office, Dad buckled his medical bag. "Have no fear."

"Perhaps I should fear the Germans, but I don't." Ivy drew her father's rounded cheeks and chin, so much like hers. With the fall of France certain and the Channel Islands too distant for Britain to defend, the British troops and Jersey Militia were evacuating. "I'm proud of you. The militia needs their medical officer."

Dad engaged Ivy with a gaze as soft as the black leather of his bag. "I meant you mustn't fear for the medical practice."

Ivy stifled a wince. Since she was a woman and only one year out of university, patients often asked for the "real doctor." Would they trust her without Dad's experience behind her?

"You come from a long line of Doctors Picot, and you may be the finest yet." Dad's brown-eyed gaze drilled into her. "Come along."

Ivy set her sketch pad on Dad's desk—her desk for now. How long until he returned?

Would the Germans invade the Channel Islands or ignore them as inconsequential? Could Hitler resist planting his flag on British soil? What would happen if they came? The horrifying stories from Poland and the Netherlands and Belgium . . .

Ivy shuddered and followed her father into the waiting room of the surgery. Since the Nazis loved to provoke panic and despair, staying calm seemed an appealing act of defiance.

Dad slipped on his overcoat. "Fern will be a good help to you."

"She will." Ivy pinned on her hat. In April, her older sister had taken their mother's place as receptionist when Mum went to England to care for her ill father.

"You're each strong where the other is weak. Don't forget that."

Ivy's only strength lay in medicine. Even then, she relied on her father's wisdom. A fluttery sensation filled her stomach. How could she run the practice without him?

"You're ready, Dad?" Charlie clomped down the hall, his face alight. "I wish I could fight too."

Ivy pulled her twelve-year-old brother to her side, resisting the urge to brush back the shank of black hair hanging over his brow. "Let's finish school first, shall we?"

Charlie screwed up his handsome face. "The war will be over by then."

Ivy certainly hoped so. "Are you sure you don't want to evacuate?"

"I'm not afraid of the Nazis." He pulled himself tall but barely cleared Ivy's shoulder. "Besides, you need a man around the house."

Charlie's voice had yet to change, but Ivy gave his narrow shoulders a squeeze.

"If you evacuated, Ivy . . ." Dad said.

If she evacuated, Charlie would too. "And who would care for our patients?"

"Indeed." A sad wisp of a smile rose. "War makes for difficult choices."

How unfair that Dad should have to make those difficult choices twice in one lifetime. "I know—now I know."

8

Dad's gaze swept the walls of the ground floor of the family home, La Bliue Brise, where he'd been raised, where he'd raised his own family, and where he practiced. "In times of peace, we choose amongst many good and pleasant paths, but in times of war . . ."

Ivy's throat tightened. "No path is good or pleasant."

"Not pleasant, no." He aimed one finger at Ivy. "But you can still choose the good. You must."

She managed a nod. What could possibly be good about Nazi soldiers coming to their beautiful island?

Dad picked up his luggage and led the way out onto Bath Street.

In the skies above, puffy clouds edged with light played in the cool breeze, oblivious to the turmoil below.

Bill and Fern Le Corre came down the road with their twin seven-year-old sons. Billy and Freddy scampered to Dad and hugged him, then Ivy.

"We don't want to go to England." Tears swam in Billy's dark eyes. "Mummy doesn't want us to leave."

"But Daddy says we must," Freddy said.

One look at Fern's quivering chin and Bill's stony chin, and Ivy took her nephews' hands and led them down the street toward the harbor. "What a lovely adventure you'll have. Your grandmother can show you where she played as a girl before she came to Jersey."

Ahead of Ivy, Fern clutched her husband's arm and tipped up her exquisite heart-shaped face. Her eyelashes fluttered over her wide-set eyes. "Please stay, Bill. I need you."

"Then come with me. Stay with your mother."

"I will not leave Jersey. It's my home. And Ivy needs me to run the practice. Right, Ivy?"

Ivy did, but she wanted no part of their discussion, so she told the boys to count the houses they passed to distract them from their parents' ongoing argument.

"I'm in the militia." Bill strode with a military bearing as if to prove his point. "It's my duty to fight for our island."

"How can you fight for our island by leaving it?"

"We already discussed this. I refuse to stay when I can fight for Britain."

"At least let me keep my boys. They're all I have." Fern's voice warbled.

Those boys had reached their limit with counting, so Ivy had them look for their chums on their way to the docks.

So many children. Schoolchildren, like Billy and Freddy, evacuating alone. Younger children with their mothers. Men of military age, off to enlist in the British Army. All jostling each other, hefting luggage, skirting the mass of abandoned cars. Ivy clutched the boys' hands so she wouldn't lose them in the crowd.

Alexander Coutanche, the Bailiff of Jersey, had urged people to stay, but hundreds filled the Weighbridge area by the docks and circled the gardens around the statue of Queen Victoria.

"My decision is final," Bill said to Fern. "The boys are evacuating to England for their safety. Join them or don't. That's your decision."

Fern jerked her head to the side.

"Come now." Bill's voice sweetened. "May I have one lovely smile before I leave?"

Ivy ripped her gaze from their farewell, hugged her nephews, and sent them to Charlie for one last hug from their beloved uncle.

She fell into her father's embrace and absorbed his scent of wool and pipe tobacco and disinfectant, his strength and wisdom and cheer. Somehow she had to make do without him. Somehow she had to relieve his worries, his guilt about leaving. "I'll miss you, but we'll be fine."

"I know you will." Dad's voice went gruff. He spun away to hug Fern, and then he and Bill led the boys down Albert Pier extending over the turquoise waters.

Fern's face wobbled between grief and anger, and Charlie's between grief and stoicism.

Ivy linked arms with them, one on each side. "We'll make do. We will. As long as we look after each other."

Something too manly and resolute crossed Charlie's face. "And choose the good."

The family. The practice. The patients.

"Yes," Ivy said. "We'll choose the good."

AMSTERDAM, THE NETHERLANDS
THURSDAY, JULY 2, 1942

The Gestapo knew how to follow a man far better than Gerrit van der Zee knew how to avoid being followed.

The sensation of being watched heated the back of Gerrit's skull, and he walked right past the door to his own apartment building.

Sixteen months had passed since he and his best friend, Bernardus Kroon, had dissolved their resistance group. Sixteen months since he'd done anything warranting arrest.

Yet that familiar heat persisted. If the Germans had arrested one of his former colleagues, they could have extracted names under torture.

Gerrit's grip tightened on his attaché case. Every time he had turned a corner on his way home from work, he'd discreetly scanned the street behind him. But discretion created blind spots.

His next movements had to be smooth, swift, and innocent. He couldn't afford to step into a Gestapo trap, but he did want to go home.

To still his mind, he counted to ten.

Stopped. Glanced at a house number. Frowned. A quick back-and-forth as if lost.

Spun on his heel and retraced his steps.

What had lain behind him now lay before him. No one on the street stopped. No one ducked into a doorway. No one stood reading a newspaper.

Two businessmen passed, discussing a supplier who owed them a shipment. A young mother carried a bundle on one hip and a baby on the other. An elderly couple leaned on each other as they shuffled over the flagstones.

The back of Gerrit's skull cooled, and he strode on, casually surveying the neighborhood.

When he reached his building, he studied the house number while checking out the side of his eye in case anyone had doubled back.

No one had. He exhaled, slipped inside, and shut the door behind him.

A man stood by the staircase, a gray homburg shielding his lowered head.

Gerrit's heart seized, and he groped for the door handle. He'd walked into a trap after all.

The man lifted the brim of his hat, revealing Bernardus Kroon's pale blue eyes and ruddy complexion.

The air rushed from Gerrit's lungs. "Ber—"

Bernardus pressed one finger to his lips, then pointed upstairs.

Only the most important of reasons would compel Bernardus to break their silence, so Gerrit led his friend up to his flat.

In early 1941, Dutch Nazi thugs had murdered Dirk de Vos, the editor of their underground newspaper. With the Germans cracking down on the Dutch resistance with arrests and executions, Gerrit and Bernardus had shut down the group and parted ways.

Inside the flat, Bernardus tossed his hat on the coatrack, went to Gerrit's phonograph, and lowered the needle. Strains of Mozart's Clarinet Concerto in A Major frolicked in the air.

Bernardus's shoulders slumped, and he rolled his eyes at Gerrit as he sat in one of the two armchairs by the stove. "You need better records."

"You need better taste." Gerrit allowed a little smile and pulled the second chair closer to his oldest friend. "You're alive."

"So are you. No mean feat nowadays."

"Which is why we aren't supposed to meet."

Bernardus flicked up the smile he always gave when he disregarded Gerrit's advice. "Have you joined another resistance group?"

Gerrit stilled, his hands clasped on his knees. In the resistance, no one asked or answered questions about his work. The less everyone knew, the better. In case of arrest and torture.

But this was Bernardus, so he swallowed hard. "No."

"I'm involved again."

Gerrit raised one hand to hush his friend.

Bernardus raised one hand to hush Gerrit's reservations. "In France."

"France?"

"Something's wrong here in the Netherlands." Bernardus mashed his lips together. "Too many arrests. I think the Gestapo has infiltrated the resistance groups."

Gerrit groaned. Thank goodness he'd retired from that line of work.

Bernardus fiddled with the tin model of a catapult on the side table. "Remember Pierre Lavoie from university?"

"Yes."

"His construction firm in Paris needed a geologist, so they hired me last summer. The job allows me to travel all over France. To meet people. I've met men drawing maps and diagrams of German fortifications to send to the Allies."

Gerrit's stomach hardened. "You shouldn't tell me this."

"Yes, I should. We need you to—"

"Absolutely not."

Bernardus raised one eyebrow of pale blond. "You didn't let me finish."

"I don't need to." Conviction kept his voice low. "I won't get involved again."

"It's time."

One shake of his head. "Look at all we did, all we risked—for nothing. We spoke out against the Germans, and they're still here, stronger than ever, more oppressive than ever. We spoke up for the Jews, and the Germans are deporting them by the trainload to camps in the east—men, women, little children."

"Yes, but—"

"All those good men and women on our side—they're dead. They're in concentration camps. They're in hiding."

Bernardus's gaze narrowed to a pinprick. "Or they're too scared to lift their heads."

Gerrit drew back his chin. "I'm willing to risk my life. But only if some good will come of it."

"Which is why I'm here." Bernardus set his elbows on his knees. "We want your experience as a civil engineer to draw diagrams and maps."

Gerrit let out a scoffing chuckle. "I doubt the Germans would let me close enough to their fortifications."

"They would if we were employed by a firm contracted with Organisation Todt."

"Org—absolutely not." The German quasi-military organization built gun emplacements and defensive works along the Atlantic coast.

Bernardus shifted in his seat. "My French firm doesn't qualify for a subcontract with a German OT firm, but the German firms are desperate. Most of their men are in the military, so they need men like us."

Gerrit stared at his friend, but Bernardus still stared back. "You want us to work for—I'd never."

"I know this sounds like a wild plan, but—"

"Wild, yes. Helping the Germans build fortifications that prevent the Allies from invading? When an Allied invasion is the only thing that can save us from the Nazis?"

Bernardus sat back and rubbed his hand over his chin. "They're building them with or without us. And very possibly with us as forced labor. At some point they'll conscript us to dig ditches or work in a factory in Germany—where we could do no good whatsoever. Or we can use our professional skills and my resistance network to send intelligence to the Allies."

Gerrit's mouth tightened. "While wearing a German uniform."

Bernardus rubbed his chin over and over. "Everyone thinks the Allies will invade next spring."

"I certainly hope so."

"The Germans are strong and entrenched and growing stronger. The Allies need all the information they can get. You and I can—"

"You." Gerrit jabbed a finger at his friend. "You alone. I will not be a part of this."

Bernardus glanced down to the side table, to Gerrit's collection of tin and cast-iron gadgets. He picked up a scrap of paper, filled with Gerrit's diagrams of those gadgets. "This is why we need you. I have the connections. I have skills the Germans need. But I don't have your knowledge of engineering, your skill in precision drawing."

Something strange stirred in Gerrit's head. Yes, he could make precision drawings and maps—enjoyed doing so. But not for the Germans, and he shook the stirring out of his head.

"I need you for another reason too." Bernardus picked up a cast-iron mechanical bank and fingered the lever. "The Germans trust the Dutch in general, which is why the firm is willing to consider us. But they said I don't have the right political affiliations."

Gerrit murmured in sympathy, even as an odd note of disappointment twanged in his chest. Neither of them belonged to Nazi organizations. Quest finished.

Iron clinked on iron as Bernardus played with the bank. "The firm needs civil engineers more than they need geologists. They agreed to hire me if I recruited an engineer with the proper affiliations."

"I don't—"

"You do." Pain rippled across Bernardus's face. "I heard about Cilla."

Gerrit slammed his eyes shut, his mind shut. The recent news of his cousin's death had devastated his family. "I don't believe it."

"That she died?"

"That she died in the service of Germany. She couldn't. She was on our side." Gerrit had recruited Cilla to infiltrate the *Nationaal-Socialistische Beweging*, the Dutch Nazi Party, since Cilla's wayward sister, Hilde, was a member. Cilla had provided vital information for their underground paper at exceptional risk.

Gerrit pried his eyes open. "Cilla could never serve Germany. Something is wrong. It doesn't ring true."

Bernardus huffed out a sigh. "I don't know what to think. She disappeared after Dirk's death, ja? Time passes. People change. Hard times make people do things they ordinarily wouldn't consider. Like joining Organisation Todt." He let out a wry chuckle. "Can you imagine wearing a German uniform?"

"No." Yet that strange stirring resumed, stirring enough to be named.

Purpose.

Gerrit shoved out of his chair. In the past sixteen months, his life had been safer, but it didn't fulfill.

Bernardus set the bank down with a thump of iron on wood. "Regardless of what you think, the Germans think Cilla was on their side. They know Hilde is on their side. And you have no affiliations on any side. The Germans are free to color you Nazi black instead of Dutch orange. They are very interested in you."

Air inflated Gerrit's cheeks, and he strode to the phonograph playing the final intricate scales of the concerto. His left hand flexed and stretched, flexed and stretched. "Can you guarantee the diagrams would aid the Allies?"

"I guarantee."

It was a wild idea. Beyond wild. So why was he considering it?

"How much time do I have?"

"I leave for Paris tomorrow morning. I can give you tonight to think about it. Pray about it. You would need to apply for travel papers straightaway."

Pray about it? Bernardus was a man of prayer. He remembered

Gerrit as a man of prayer. But so much had happened. Or rather, so little had happened.

At the center of the phonograph, the arm bounced and bounced. Without a track to run in, the needle produced no sound, no music.

Gerrit lifted the arm and set it in the track on the outside rim, and music again flowed. "I'll apply for papers in the morning."

CHAPTER

2

At Uncle Arthur and Aunt Opal's dairy farm, Ivy parked her bicycle outside the farmhouse of rosy Jersey granite. "Uncle Arthur? I came to patch you up again."

"It's nothing to bother about." Uncle Arthur emerged from the barn, also of granite. "You shouldn't have come all the way out here. Not that you aren't welcome, mind."

Yet Ivy noticed a hitch in Uncle Arthur's step. "Since I'm here, I might as well look."

"No escape now." Charlie trotted out of the barn. He'd taken a summer job at the farm, mainly because the Germans allowed extra rations for laborers. Regular rations didn't provide enough for a growing fourteen-year-old boy, even with Fern and Ivy surreptitiously slipping him extra portions.

Uncle Arthur pulled off his cap and entered the house. "Opal? Ivy's here. Your doing, I suppose?"

"Of course." Aunt Opal set a plate of potatoes on the table and motioned for Charlie to sit and eat. "Ivy and I are conspiring to keep you alive, cruel and conniving women that we are."

With a dramatic sigh, Uncle Arthur flopped into a wooden

chair at the table. "If only your ravishing beauty hadn't enticed me into marrying into a medical family."

Aunt Opal kissed the top of her husband's head and brought a pot to the table. "Water's been boiled and cooled for you, Ivy, and I have clean bandages. I'm afraid I have only a sliver of that awful green French soap."

"It'll do." Jersey had run out of soap in the early months of the occupation, and the Germans sent a low-quality soap that didn't even lather. After Ivy washed her hands at the sink, she sat at the table and opened her bag. "No use hiding. Show me."

Much grumbling emanated from Uncle Arthur's square face, but he rolled up his trouser leg and propped his foot on an empty chair.

An unbandaged, three-inch laceration cut across his calf. Ivy palpated the red, raised edges. "As soon as you get a cut, you must cleanse it with water and soap if you have it. Then bandage it to keep it clean. With our poor diets, we can't fend off infections as we ought. Simple cuts are taking six weeks to heal."

Uncle Arthur groaned, this time closer to acceptance.

Ivy cleansed the wound with soap and water. Over the past two years of the German occupation, the Jersey Medical Society had met monthly to discuss the worsening health situation. The "occupation ulcers" developing from simple cuts. The cases of life-threatening sepsis. And the scarcity of medications.

"This will sting." Ivy opened a bottle of iodine and painted the wound area.

Uncle Arthur hissed through his teeth.

"I'll visit again tomorrow. In the meantime, keep the wound clean and bandaged." She glanced up to Aunt Opal.

Aunt Opal patted Charlie's shoulder. "Charlie and I will tie him up if we must."

Charlie swallowed a bite of potato, pan-fried without any fat. "May I, please?"

Uncle Arthur gave his nephew a mock glare. "Cheeky lad."

Charlie pinched his own cheek. "The cheekiest."

Ivy chuckled and pinned a strip of fabric around her uncle's calf. Uncle Arthur would surely miss Charlie when the boy returned to school at Victoria College in a few weeks.

Uncle Arthur tugged down his trouser leg. "Would you like to hear the latest news?"

In June, the Germans had confiscated ten thousand wireless sets in Jersey. Losing the news on the BBC made the islanders feel more isolated than ever, with only censored news allowed in the *Jersey Evening Post*.

Ivy didn't want to know where Uncle Arthur had hidden his wireless, but she did want the news.

Uncle Arthur rested his sturdy forearms on the table. "The Germans have already told us about their advances on Stalingrad."

"Of course." German victories received full coverage.

"But they didn't tell us American pilots are arriving in England. The BBC did."

Charlie's dark eyes darted around. "Then they can send soldiers. Then they can invade."

"Someday," Uncle Arthur said. "And soon."

Ivy managed to smile. Although the Channel Islands had surrendered to the Germans without bloodshed—other than a couple dozen poor souls killed in Luftwaffe air raids to Jersey and Guernsey—the Germans certainly wouldn't allow the Allies to land at so low a cost.

Aunt Opal cleared away the extra bandages. "Remember not to spread the news. If you must, speak in Jèrriais."

"*Oui, ma bouonnefemme,*" Uncle Arthur said in the local patois. Before the war, Jèrriais had fallen into disuse, but it was regaining popularity. Since it was descended from an ancient Norman tongue, it sounded a bit like French—but not enough for a French speaker to follow.

"*Mêfie-té,*" Aunt Opal said.

"I'm always careful." Uncle Arthur clapped his hands to his knees. "Come, young Charlie. Let's see to those cows."

"Thank you." Charlie handed Aunt Opal his plate. "Ivy, tell Fern I'll be home in an hour."

"I will." Ivy glanced at her wristwatch. How had she lost track of time again? "Oh no. I'm late. I told Fern I was low on iodine solution, so she rang Carter's Chemist's. They were to have a bottle ready for me an hour ago."

"Carter's?" Aunt Opal washed Charlie's dish. "The Picots have always used Island Drugs."

"Mr. Johnson retired and closed his shop last week." Ivy packed the empty iodine bottle in her medical bag next to her sketch pad. If only she hadn't stopped to draw that sweet patch of bell heather. "I must rush. Fern scheduled two appointments in the surgery late this afternoon."

Charlie rolled his eyes. "Without Bill and the boys, Fern has only us to boss around."

"Oh, hush. She's trying to keep the practice afloat. And I *am* always late." Ivy kissed her aunt and uncle goodbye and rushed outside.

She pedaled hard down narrow roads bound on each side by unforgiving granite walls. If only she could drive to save time.

Not long after the Germans arrived, they'd requisitioned Ivy's brand-new car. As a physician, she'd been allowed to keep Dad's older-model car and to receive a petrol ration, but a small one, best reserved for night calls and emergencies.

She turned left onto Route de Beaumont, cutting close to the corner.

A lorry came straight at her. Ivy veered to the left and rammed sideways into the wall. She cried out, planted her feet, and grabbed her left wrist.

"Watch where you're going," a soldier shouted in a German accent from the lorry. "Stupid girl."

21

Ivy knew better than to tell him to drive slower. Far too many islanders had died due to reckless German drivers.

She palpated her throbbing wrist. Nothing broken—except her wristwatch.

"Oh no." She'd never be able to get it repaired. The jewelers' shops had closed long before, with no stock and no spare parts. Now punctuality would be even more difficult.

Ivy mounted her bicycle and crossed the road. The previous summer, the Germans had switched traffic from the left to the right.

She coasted downhill through verdant hills, lightly forested, bright with sunshine and flowers and begging to be sketched.

Around the bend came the sound of harsh voices and tramping feet.

Ivy slowed down.

Ahead of her, men trudged along the road, five abreast, some wearing civilian clothes, some wearing an unfamiliar army uniform. Torn. Ragged. Colors muted by filth.

A filth that penetrated Ivy's nostrils. The smell of unwashed bodies and dirt and bodily fluids—and disease.

A pudgy German soldier marched up to Ivy, waving a truncheon.

Ivy gasped and yanked her bicycle off the road, onto a drive heading into the valley.

The motley column marched past her, dozens upon dozens of men.

The guards wore the brown uniform of Germany's Organisation Todt, which built the hideous fortifications marring Jersey's landscape. They'd brought in hundreds of foreign workers, mainly Spaniards and Frenchmen, but these men now marching up Route de Beaumont had a Slavic look about them. And the uniforms—they were Soviet.

Ivy's breath snagged. The Nazis considered the Slavic peoples to be "subhuman," and from the condition of these men, they treated them accordingly.

But these were human beings created in God's image, and she refused to let revulsion or pity warp her face, only concern.

One man, with wheat-colored hair and a scar across his cheek and brow, met her gaze with a desperate look. "Please, miss. Can you spare any food?"

She had none. "I'm sorry. I have—"

A truncheon slammed down on the Russian's shoulder, and he stumbled.

Ivy cried out.

A guard shook his victim's arm and barked at him in German, waving the truncheon in Ivy's direction.

The Russian wore red epaulettes on his double-breasted smock—an officer, most likely. With his head bowed, he glanced at Ivy from under a strong brow. "He says to tell you, to tell your comrades, that if you feed us, you must be prepared to join us."

Somehow Ivy nodded. "I am so sorry, sir."

The guard scowled at her and shoved the officer back into formation.

The formation that kept marching. Dozens—no, hundreds of men. Many with makeshift bandages. With rags in place of shoes.

Ivy kept her chin high, kept giving the men the same look of sorrow mixed with respect, even as tears tingled on her cheeks.

She'd been trained to soothe suffering. And now she could do nothing at all.

Ivy turned onto King Street, delayed by who knew how long, aching from the memory of the bedraggled Todt workers.

In the once-thriving shopping area, too many shops were boarded up—those that sold goods that were no longer attainable. Most other shops were open only three days a week, with queues to buy the weekly ration of six ounces of meat and three ounces of sugar and two ounces of butter.

After King Street turned to Queen Street, Ivy locked her bicycle to a bench, a necessity with rampant thefts, and she removed her medical bag. Losing that would be even worse than losing her bicycle. She could never replace the instruments.

Inside Carter's Chemist's, Miss de Ferrers was working today, rather than Mr. Carter.

Ivy approached the counter. "Good afternoon. I'm Dr. Picot."

"I'll bring your iodine as soon as I finish compounding this ointment." On a marble slab, Miss de Ferrers wielded a skinny spatula in a figure-eight motion through the clump of ointment. She wore her curly auburn hair tucked up in rolls, and lines of concentration radiated around her mouth. Not a pretty face, but intriguing with deep-set eyes and a pointed chin.

Ivy resisted the urge to fetch her sketch pad. "I'm glad I could finally meet you."

Miss de Ferrers cut her a quick glance, revealing hazel in her eyes. "Why? Because I'm the only lady chemist in Jersey and you're the only lady doctor?"

"Well . . . yes." Why did Ivy feel that was the incorrect answer?

A huff of a chuckle. Miss de Ferrers scooped the ointment into a squat glass jar and swirled the tip of her spatula inside, creating a tiny peak. "I apologize, but I have no taste for feminine friendships."

Ivy's jaw froze open, and she guided it closed. Pain pinged in her chest for the woman who must have seen only the ugly side of feminine friendship—and for herself, because she missed the beautiful side.

At Oxford, there were only twelve women in Ivy's year of medical school. They'd banded together to support and help each other. They'd become lifelong friends.

The chemist set down the ointment jar, picked up a bottle of brown-black iodine solution, and handed it to Ivy. "That will be two shillings, please."

Concealing her sigh, Ivy paid Miss de Ferrers with the new two-shilling banknote printed in Jersey due to a shortage of coins.

After saying goodbye, she cycled along Queen Street. Yes, she had lifelong friends, but they were in England. She couldn't see them, couldn't talk to them, couldn't even write them. And her childhood friends in Jersey? Whilst Ivy had been away at university, they'd married and had children and formed new circles with no room for her.

How she missed Dad and Mum. Messages passed between them through the Red Cross, but only about twice a year, with a limit of twenty-five words, and delayed by several months.

At least Ivy had her aunts, uncles, sister, and brother.

Ivy pedaled up Bath Street to La Bliue Brise, painted white with peacock-blue shutters and door.

Fern had saved the home—and the medical practice.

The Germans had requisitioned La Bliue Brise, as they had many other homes in Jersey. But Fern had marched up to the German *Feldkommandantur*'s office at Victoria College House and offered her home instead. Not as large, but with a lovely view of the ocean from the top floor. She'd also made the case that preserving the medical practice would keep the islanders healthy, which would keep the occupiers healthy too.

The field commander had accepted Fern's offer, and Fern had moved back into her childhood room. Ivy enjoyed both her sister's company and her help with the housekeeping.

Ivy pushed her bicycle through the back door and locked it in the supply room. Sounds emanated from the kitchen. "Fern? I'm sorry I'm late. I—"

"Charlie told me about the foreign workers blocking the road," Fern called. "He's washing up. I sent your patients home. I only hope they'll understand."

"I hope so too." Ivy entered the kitchen.

Over two years had passed since Mum had last fried Jersey Wonders in this kitchen. Now with butter and cream and flour rationed, Wonders were only a memory. Yet Ivy could almost smell the twisted loops of sweet dough, could almost hear her mother humming.

At the table, Fern chopped vegetables. "The Jersey grapevine says over one thousand workers arrived today. They're from Ukraine. Some were captured fighting with the Red Army, some are partisan fighters, and some are conscripts."

Ivy picked up a knife and peeled a pretty little Jersey Royal potato. "Many are no older than Charlie, and all are in the most pitiable state."

"I doubt that." Fern smiled at her and dropped the vegetables into the pot on the stove. "That soft heart of yours."

"Ivy's right." Charlie leaned against the doorjamb. "I saw them too."

"Make yourself useful, young man." Fern tossed him a potato.

Instead of peeling it, he studied it with a pensive look. "I enjoyed being useful this summer, making wages and helping the family."

Fern smoothed a sable curl back from her cheek. "Much appreciated with the practice doing so poorly."

Ivy's shoulders stiffened as she diced the potato. What more could she do? She couldn't force patients to trust a young lady doctor. At least the flood of patients leaving the practice in the first weeks after Dad left had stopped.

"It made me determined to do my bit." Charlie puffed out his thin chest. "When I'm in school, not only do I not earn money, but my school fees add another burden."

Ivy's cheeks tingled as the blood drained from her face. "It's never a burden."

Charlie's lower jaw jutted out. "As the man of the house, I need to contribute, not take. Yesterday I was hired as a deckhand on the SS *Ormer*."

Ivy's knife clattered to the table. "A deckhand!"

"The *Ormer*?" Fern stared at Charlie with her lovely mouth hanging open.

Charlie strode to the table and peeled his potato, but his dark lashes fluttered. "It's a cargo boat. It carries Jersey potatoes to

SARAH SUNDIN

Saint-Malo and returns with food and supplies from France. Not only will I earn money, but I'll help the people of the Channel Islands."

"Oh, Charlie." Ivy waved her hand toward Victoria College, the finest boys' school in Jersey, where Charlie was a top pupil. "You can't leave school. You have three more years."

"In a fortnight I turn fifteen, the school-leaving age."

"That's for other boys," Fern said. "Not boys like you."

Charlie's knuckles protruded as his grip on the knife intensified. "Why should boys like me lounge around learning Latin when other boys my age are helping their families? It isn't right that Ivy's supporting the three of us."

Fern gasped. "I work too."

"You work for Ivy. She's the only one bringing in money."

"We don't mind. We get by." A horrible spinning sensation, and Ivy pressed her hand to her stomach. "Charlie, please don't give up your dream. You want to be a doctor. You've always wanted—"

"How can I?" He thumped the potato on the table. "Most of the boys and masters from the college evacuated. We have a shell of a school. And where can I study medicine? There are no universities in the Channel Islands. This war—it's never going to end. I might as well work."

"Please don't." Ivy's vision blurred. "We've always dreamed . . . Dad and you and I—"

"I know. I'm sorry." Charlie's gaze softened. "We'd always planned that I'd join the practice, and when you had children, you could practice part-time."

Fern turned back to her stew and clucked her tongue. "You needn't worry about that. Ivy isn't having children."

Ivy gaped at her older sister. "I'm only twenty-five. I'm hardly a spinster."

"All the eligible men abandoned the island." Fern lifted one dainty shoulder. "Unless you want to marry a Ger—"

"Never!" Women who dated enemy soldiers might have new

27

clothes and extra food, but they were shunned and despised for good reason.

One corner of Fern's mouth buckled. "You had your chance at Oxford. Such a shame."

Warmth rose up Ivy's neck, and she averted her gaze.

"The more I think about it . . ." Fern stirred the stew. "Charlie is right."

"Fern!" Ivy said.

A triumphant smile rose on Charlie's face. "Of course, I'm right."

"Yes." Fern gave a sharp nod. "I've been concerned about Victoria College all summer, ever since the Germans took five of the masters as hostages. They wouldn't have done so unless the men were subversive."

"Subversive?" The Germans had arrested prominent citizens to force the surrender of two brothers who criticized the German seizure of wireless sets.

"They're not subversive," Charlie said with a sigh. "That's not why I'm leaving school."

"For the money." Fern's spoon banged around in the pot. "Not only will we save his school fees and add his wages, but he'll travel to France. He can buy goods we can't buy here, like medical supplies. You always complain about shortages, Ivy."

Ivy didn't care about that. She cared about Charlie. "What would Dad and Mum say? They'd be heartbroken. What would you do if one of your boys left school?"

"My boys aren't here." Each word a pointed barb. "Neither are Dad and Mum. I'm the eldest, and I say Charlie takes the job."

Charlie's expression—instead of brightening at Fern's support—darkened. "It isn't your decision. Either of you. It's mine. I'm old enough to leave school. I'm old enough to take a job. And I've done so."

With Dad gone, Ivy was the caretaker of the family dream. And it was slipping through her fingers.

CHAPTER
3

The hotel room door opened, and Bernardus sauntered in.

Gerrit sprang up from his chair. "Where have you been all night? We're leaving in ten minutes."

With a sly smile, Bernardus adjusted the black "Organisation Todt" armband around the sleeve of the despised brown uniform. "Becoming reacquainted with an old girlfriend here in Saint-Malo." He held Gerrit's gaze hard.

Gerrit blinked. Bernardus had memorized a list of contacts along the French coast provided by his resistance network. Since OT hadn't informed them of their destination before their month-long training near Frankfurt, Bernardus had come prepared for many possibilities, apparently including this "girlfriend."

Gerrit beckoned to the middle of the room and lowered his voice. "And?"

"All is well."

"Do they know where we'll go? This area seems unlikely." Saint-Malo lay at the base of a deep bay bound by Normandy to the east and Brittany to the west, with the approach guarded by the Channel

Islands. If Gerrit were a British general, he wouldn't invade at Saint-Malo. Erecting fortifications would be wasteful.

Bernardus shrugged. "Since they gave us travel orders to Saint-Malo, we'll be nearby. At least I can visit my girlfriend. She is rather lovely." An impish gleam brightened his light eyes.

Gerrit chuckled. For a woman in the resistance to be seen with a man in a German uniform might protect the network from scrutiny.

Footsteps sounded in the hallway.

"Come. It's time." Gerrit picked up his kit bag, already packed.

Bernardus grabbed his bag, never unpacked, and the men headed down to the hotel lobby, where two middle-aged men waited, wearing OT uniforms with officer's insignia. One stood tall and thin with a thin face, the other short and thick with a thick face to match.

Since almost all German men of military age served in the armed forces, only older men or those with infirmities remained to serve in OT.

Gerrit and Bernardus raised traditional military salutes. Thank goodness, as Dutch nationals they were not required to give the "Heil, Hitler" salute used by the Germans in OT.

The tall man did raise that salute in reply. "I am Oberbauführer Ernst Schmeling, the commander of the technical section for our region."

"Haupttruppführer Bernardus Kroon," Bernardus said.

"Haupttruppführer Gerrit van der Zee."

"*Sehr gut.*" Schmeling dipped his narrow chin. "My Dutch geologist, my Dutch engineer, and my Czech armaments—"

"I am not Czech, Herr Oberbauführer." The thickset man's cheeks reddened. "I am Sudeten German, proud to be a citizen of Greater Germany."

"Excellent." Schmeling cracked a smile as thin as everything else about him. "I understand you worked for Skoda. Your knowledge of armaments will be useful."

"Thank you." The man offered handshakes to Gerrit and Bernardus. "I'm Bauführer Wilhelm Riedel. Call me Willy."

Gerrit shook his hand, but Riedel was an officer. Since only Germans were granted officers' commissions, Gerrit and Bernardus were noncommissioned officers, despite their qualifications. He would not be calling the man "Willy."

"Come along." Schmeling led the way out of the quayside hotel.

The tang of sea air filled Gerrit's nostrils, and the busy sounds of the docks hit his ears.

No staff car waited, and Schmeling headed onto a pier, where German soldiers trailed up the gangway of a troopship.

Gerrit shot Bernardus a confused look. "Where are we going, Herr Oberbauführer?"

Schmeling flipped a hand to silence him. "Not until we're underway. The French are not to be trusted."

Underway? Gerrit's breath came shallow and shallower. Why would they board a ship? Why not drive along the coast?

Bernardus followed Riedel and Schmeling up the gangway and glanced over his shoulder at Gerrit with a pointedly fake smile.

Although his insides churned, Gerrit needed to assume a pleasant expression.

On board, they stashed their kit bags where indicated, then Schmeling led them through the pressing crowd of troops in the stifling heat.

At the bow, Gerrit gripped the railing and struggled to keep his breath even. Why a ship? They could take trains to every city in France. They could drive to smaller towns.

The engines rumbled to life, and the ship pulled away from the dock. Gerrit tucked his overseas cap into his pocket so it wouldn't be lost in the wind.

Schmeling removed his own cap, revealing scant gray hair. "I am pleased to inform you that you will be serving with me in *Bauleitung* Julius."

A Bauleitung was a smaller administrative unit in Organisation

Todt, usually a city. But Gerrit knew of no French city named Julius.

A smirk played on Schmeling's lips. "I see I have confused you all. Julius is the code for Jersey in the *Kanalinseln*."

Kanalinseln . . . Channel Islands. An island. They were going to an island, and Gerrit's breath grew erratic. Transporting diagrams from an island to Saint-Malo would be difficult.

"How far?" A strain infected Bernardus's voice.

"Sixty-six kilometers." Schmeling gestured to the north. "If you look hard, you can see. Jersey is the southernmost of the Channel Islands, closest to us."

"The Channel Islands?" Riedel frowned. "I am not familiar with that term."

"A most pleasant posting." Schmeling leaned one elbow on the railing. "A thousand years ago, the islands belonged to the Duchy of Normandy. When William the Conqueror became King of England, his lands became English lands. Over the centuries, the French liberated all their territory except the Channel Islands. Now we Germans have liberated them from English rule and returned them to their native France."

Gerrit clenched his hands behind his back, where his clenching couldn't be noticed.

The creases in Riedel's cheeks deepened. "I do not speak French well."

"The natives speak English," Schmeling said. "Their culture is an unnatural blend. Many of the natives have French surnames and English given names. The place names are French but pronounced as if by an uneducated English tourist. The name of the island's only town of any note is pronounced 'Saint HEL-ee-er' rather than 'Sahn El-ee-ay.' Very unnatural. Yet it is a land of great beauty."

Gerrit didn't want a lesson in culture and history. He wanted a reason to justify wearing the uniform of his enemy.

"We have fortifications there?" Bernardus sounded cool, curious, calm.

If Gerrit were to speak, he could never feign the same demeanor.

"Many fortifications." Schmeling turned his face to the buffeting wind. "The English consider the islands English soil. It is a matter of pride for Churchill to take them back, and a matter of pride for Hitler to keep them. Also, the islands guard this bay. No English vessels or aircraft can cross these waters without encountering a great many guns."

Riedel chuckled. "And more to come."

"We won't be far from the mainland." Bernardus swept his arm to the south. "We shall be able to visit often? I have a girl—"

"You are members of Organisation Todt." Schmeling's grayish eyes became steely daggers. "As volunteers, you will have freedom on the island, even though you are foreigners. But you will not qualify for leave for six months. I'm sure you learned that in training."

Six months. Gerrit swayed and grabbed the rail.

Another chuckle jiggled Riedel's ample belly. "Never fear. You are sure to meet girls in Jersey."

"Indeed," Schmeling said. "Their young men left before our men arrived."

"Cowards." Riedel wrinkled his broad nose.

"Misled by English propaganda to fight for Churchill, but not cowards. Regardless, their absence has left the women lonesome. However, we will comport ourselves like gentlemen." Schmeling added a scowl for emphasis.

"Ja, Herr Oberbauführer," Gerrit said with Bernardus and Riedel.

Meeting women was the least of his worries—and impossible. Any good woman would reject him for the loathsome uniform, and he wouldn't want the sort of woman who liked it.

"I shall miss her." Bernardus swept his gaze south as if longing for his girlfriend, but when he met Gerrit's gaze in passing, it was with a mix of alarm and apology.

Gerrit faced the green island rising from the blue waters. They wouldn't be able to pass intelligence to the resistance for six months. Useless.

His stomach tumbled in a green mess. He'd be building fortifications for the Nazis without the consolation of aiding the Allies. Since he and Bernardus wouldn't get leave until late March, his maps and diagrams wouldn't arrive in England in time to provide intelligence for a spring invasion. Why even bother to draw them?

A groan rolled out into the wind.

"Seasick?" Riedel asked with a teasing grin.

Gerrit nodded. He could honestly say he felt sick to his stomach.

CHAPTER

4

Ivy slipped her stethoscope into her medical bag and smiled at Thelma Galais. "You're as healthy as ever."

"I keep telling Edna." Mrs. Galais sent a fond smile to her daughter sitting on the sofa beside her, a smile beautified by lines born of laughter.

Edna Walters gripped her mother's gnarled hand. "I won't take any chances."

"Neither will I." Which was why Ivy made monthly visits to the cozy home in St. Helier.

Mrs. Galais waved her free hand at her daughter. "I only let you make these appointments so we can see our Ivy."

"Our *Dr. Picot*, Mum."

For the sweet woman she'd known all her life, Ivy would gladly make an exception. "You can always call me Ivy."

Determination pursed Mrs. Galais's lips. "Edna's right. You're a physician and a fine one. Whenever one of my friends tells me to switch doctors, I tell them no. A Dr. Picot brought me into this world, and a Dr. Picot will see me into the next one."

"Mum, you mustn't talk that way."

Mrs. Galais heaved a mock sigh. "Let's change the subject so we don't grieve my dear Edna. Do you have a drawing for me, Iv—Dr. Picot?"

"Oh yes." She pulled out her sketch pad and flipped through. With care, she tore out a drawing and handed it to Mrs. Galais.

She gasped. "Oh, isn't he precious? Look at that precious rabbit."

Ivy chuckled. "I doubt Mrs. Nicolle would have called him precious if she spotted him chewing her carrots."

Edna tapped the drawing. "Nice and plump. He'd make a good stew."

Another gasp from Mrs. Galais. "How you vex me."

The doorbell rang.

"Excuse me, please." Edna left the drawing room.

Mrs. Galais traced the rabbit's penciled lines with a gleam in her hazel eyes. "Precious. Simply precious."

Warmth swirled in Ivy's stomach, empty though it was. She drew because she loved to draw, because her fingers needed to record what her eyes saw. But bringing a bit of joy to her patients brought joy to her heart too.

Out in the hallway, Edna's voice grew louder, strident and worried, trading sentences with a man's voice, consoling but firm.

Ivy frowned and met Mrs. Galais's concerned gaze. What was happening?

In a few minutes, Edna entered the drawing room, staring at a sheet of paper, her face pale. "We—we—Frank and I—we're being deported to Germany."

"Deported?" Ivy said, echoed by Mrs. Galais.

Edna fumbled for the chair arm and lowered herself to sitting. "The Germans are deporting all men born in England, not the Channel Islands. Frank—Frank is from London. Wives and children too, even if Jersey-born."

The warmth in Ivy's stomach turned to ice. "What? How can

they . . ." Thousands of Englishmen lived in Jersey, including many of the island's seventeen physicians.

"I don't understand." Mrs. Galais's voice wavered. "You've done nothing wrong."

"Oh, Mum." The order shook in Edna's hands. "What should we do? You—you don't fall under the order, but you're allowed to come with us. I can't bear to leave you alone, but—but they won't tell us where we're going, what conditions—they say we'll be treated well, but I don't trust—" Her face crumpled, and she lowered her chin.

Ivy pressed her hand over her mouth. Edna didn't trust the Nazis, and neither did Ivy, especially after she'd seen those slave workers. Surely they wouldn't send innocent civilians to their horrid concentration camps—but they did. They did send innocent Jewish civilians to those camps. Would they do the same to the English?

Mrs. Galais placed a fluttering hand on her chest. "You're my only family here."

Edna gave a jerking nod of her lowered head. Her two sons had evacuated in 1940 to fight with the British, along with Dad and Bill and four of Ivy's cousins.

Ivy's gaze bounced between mother and daughter, who faced no good nor pleasant paths. Mrs. Galais could stay in her home, but alone, with worsening living conditions. Or she could leave with her daughter, but to unknown—perhaps horrific—conditions. At eighty years of age.

Edna raised hazel eyes like her mother's, now rimmed with red. "Mum? I'll let you decide."

"How long?"

"Tomorrow at four o'clock. We must report to the garage at the Weighbridge." Edna rubbed her temple. "I need to find Frank. The shop. He'll have to—Oh dear. It's already five o'clock. We need to pack. Only what we can carry. Oh my."

Mrs. Galais drew in a long breath, and her gaze cleared and

steadied. "I'll stay here in my home. You needn't worry about me. I have everything I need. I have friends to keep an eye on me, keep me out of mischief."

"And me," Ivy said in a soft voice. "You have me."

"See, I'll be fine." Mrs. Galais pushed herself to standing. "Find Frank. I'll start gathering your belongings."

Edna stood and flung the order down to her chair. "If only Frank and I weren't so healthy. We could get a medical exemption."

Medical exemption? Ivy rose. If all the Englishmen in Jersey had received deportation orders, how many might be seeking exemptions? "I need to return to the surgery."

"Oh my. Yes, you do."

Ivy said goodbye, dashed outside, and cycled home. The streets prickled with anxious activity. A pair of German soldiers knocked on a door a few houses up from La Bliue Brise.

She shoved her bicycle through the garden, through the back door, and into the supply room.

Fern ran to her. "Where have you been? The Germans—"

"I heard." Ivy strode down the hallway.

"Dr. McKinstry rang—the Medical Officer of Health himself." Fern kept pace with Ivy. "A board of doctors will meet at the Weighbridge garage tomorrow to decide on exemptions. They want you to write brief but thorough reports."

"Thank you." What would Ivy do without her efficient sister?

A dozen patients filled the waiting room. So many dear and familiar faces, and she gave them each a soothing look. "Good evening. I'm so sorry to hear about the orders. I'll see you as quickly as possible."

A middle-aged man rose with a lift to his square chin. "You'll see me first."

Mr. Sanderson huffed. "I was here long before him. We all were."

"Mrs. Le Corre?" Ivy sent a taut smile to her sister, who recorded who came and when.

Fern nodded to the square-jawed gentleman. "Come on through, sir."

"Fern," Ivy said in a fierce whisper.

"He's important," she whispered back.

Ivy snatched her white coat from a hook. "His chart?"

"He doesn't have one. He isn't one of our patients." She whisked an empty folder from her desk as they passed. "His name is Anthony Sloan-Huntington. Yes, *the* Anthony Sloan-Huntington."

Ivy didn't know the name, but she hadn't time to set things to rights. She had a full waiting room. Those who qualified for exemptions deserved relief from their fears. Those who didn't qualify needed time to pack and make provisions.

In the examination room, she straightened her white coat, greeted Mr. Sloan-Huntington, and motioned him to the examination table. "I understand you're new to our practice. Who is your usual physician?"

Gray-blue eyes narrowed. "Dr. Tipton will no longer be my physician. He refused to write a medical exemption for me, but you will, young lady."

Of all the doctors in Jersey, he'd chosen Ivy. Did he assume a young lady would be easier to intimidate? With a mild smile, she motioned again to the table. "Please be seated."

"An examination is most unnecessary. But an exemption is most necessary."

Ivy concealed her sigh and sat at a desk with the empty chart. "What is your ailment?"

Mr. Sloan-Huntington gave her a tepid smile. "Whichever ailment will grant me an exemption."

Ivy set down her pen. "You are perfectly healthy."

"Say that I'm a diabetic taking insulin."

"Sir, we have no more insulin in Jersey. All the diabetics are now in hospital so we can control their diet and activity." Where they lived in a horrid state of slow starvation.

"A heart condition, perhaps." He gestured to the chart in an impatient manner.

This was why Dr. Tipton had refused. Ivy sat back and gave the man a sympathetic look. "I can understand how alarming the order must be, but I cannot write a false report."

"You can, and you will. I own one of the largest banks in Jersey. If I were deported, it would lead to financial catastrophe."

Surely the man had competent employees, and Ivy tucked her pen in her pocket. "If the Germans discovered I wrote a false report, not only would they dismiss your case but those of all my patients. If they were deported, it might lead to medical catastrophe. I cannot allow that."

"Enough of this nonsense." His square chin hiked up. "Get on with it."

Ivy stood and extended her hand. "Good evening, Mr. Sloan-Huntington. I wish you all the best in finding a more compliant doctor."

"The nerve." He shook a finger at her. "I'll do so, and then I'll see this practice ruined."

Ivy opened the door for him, and he marched out.

Fern ducked in. "Oh no. What happened?"

"Perfectly healthy."

Fern winced and glanced after the man, who was slamming the front door. "Oh dear. He would have been a great asset to the practice."

"If I were caught writing a false report, the practice would be destroyed." It still might be if Mr. Sloan-Huntington bent another doctor to his will and took his revenge. She blew out a sharp breath. "Who's next?"

Fern ushered in Joe Sanderson, only thirty years old but with a weak heart from rheumatic fever and a pregnant wife on bed rest.

"I don't know what to do." Mr. Sanderson sat on the examination table and twisted his cap in his hands. "Alice can't manage without me, not with the little ones."

Ivy was already writing a list of all the reasons deporting this man and his family would be injurious to the health of man, wife, and baby. "If anyone deserves an exemption, you do. I'll do my best."

"What if they don't accept it?" More twisting of his cap. "How will I get my medication? They won't even tell me where we're going."

"I'll write a prescription for several months' supply, just in case. Take it to Carter's Chemist's. They're nearby."

"Mr. Carter got a deportation order too."

Ivy snapped up her head. "He did?"

"His shop's next door to mine." Mr. Sanderson waved to the imaginary shopfront. "He's busy with his own matters tonight, but Miss de Ferrers promised to keep the shop open all night if necessary."

She would. Beneath Miss de Ferrers's prickly edges lay a soft core. Ivy referred patients to their pharmacy whenever possible.

Ivy scanned the report and the prescription. "I'll come to the Weighbridge tomorrow in case my patients need assistance with the board. Please don't worry. Surely . . ."

Surely the Germans wouldn't be so cruel as to deport the Sanderson family?

Ivy forced a smile and handed the papers to Mr. Sanderson. The Nazis specialized in cruelty and in erasing all goodness from the island. Why did God do nothing to stop them?

~

WEDNESDAY, SEPTEMBER 16, 1942

Fighting her heavy eyelids, Ivy stood with Fern in the crowd at the Weighbridge. She'd stayed up late the night before, writing as many exemptions as possible, consoling those who didn't qualify, and writing prescriptions for the journey.

All morning, she'd sat with her patients before the board of physicians—three Jersey doctors and three German. Some exemptions, like Mr. Sanderson's, had been accepted. Some had not. The German doctors at least had the grace to apologize for the deportations.

A queue of several hundred deportees snaked past the crowd and onto Albert Pier, where two ships awaited to carry them away. Charlie and the *Ormer* had left for France yesterday, so he wouldn't have to witness the travesty.

Frank and Edna Walters passed, and Ivy managed a quivering smile and wave. Like all the deportees, they carried bulging suitcases and wore as much clothing as possible, despite the excessive heat.

Mr. Sloan-Huntington passed with his wife. Officiousness hardly qualified the man for deportation, and sympathy rippled through Ivy's chest, but accompanied by a ripple of appreciation for her fellow doctors for refusing to bend to his demands. The island's physicians might treat her dismissively, but they were men of principle.

Then came Mr. and Mrs. Carter and their two nearly grown daughters.

Fern sniffed. "At least the Germans allow families to stay together."

"Oh?" Ivy ripped her gaze from the poignant scene to her sister's stony face. "I imagine most of these men would prefer for their wives and children to stay at home."

One shake of Fern's lovely head. "Families should be together, even if Bill disagrees. How can that man think a husband should abandon his wife and tear little boys from their mother?"

Ivy suppressed a sigh and patted her sister's arm. How often had she tried to help Fern see that Bill had to fight for his country, that he wanted his boys to be safe, that he'd begged Fern to join them? But Fern saw what she wanted to see.

A sound arose, melodic and rhythmic, floating down from Mount Bingham on the east side of the marina, where boys in school blazers lined the hill. As their song flowed downhill, it gathered voices in its wake.

They sang "There'll Always Be an England," and Ivy's breath caught.

An ardently pro-English song.

By deporting the English, the Germans hoped to widen the existing divide between those born in Jersey and those born in England, to curry favor with the locals.

The song grew in strength and volume and fervency, enveloping the crowd, and Ivy joined in.

"Ivy!" Fern nudged her. "Hush. You'll get in trouble."

The song would indeed anger the Germans, and Ivy sang louder, her voice snagging on her throat, swollen by tears.

Tears for those being deported to an unknown fate, simply because of the place of their birth. Tears for a world rent by war and occupation and oppression. And tears of pride for her fellow Jersey folk.

Today they were all Jersey folk, and they were all English folk. In this, the Germans had failed.

CHAPTER
5

Bernardus and Gerrit walked from one massive naval gun platform to another, along a path among yellow gorse bushes.

"We should quit," Bernardus said in Dutch.

"Kalm aan!" Gerrit pressed a finger to his lips and whipped his gaze around. About fifty meters behind them, Oberbauführer Ernst Schmeling stood chatting with the naval commander of Batterie Lothringen, but the warm wind blew the Dutchmen's words down the steep rocky cliffs of Noirmont Point and into the sea.

"We need to quit." Bernardus's voice dropped in tone but not intensity. "We can't do this."

"I want to quit too." Gerrit slowed his pace so they wouldn't reach the gun platform—and its German crew—too quickly. "I want to go home to my family and my job, but we cannot quit."

"We're volunteers. We can quit. And we must." Bernardus stopped, and his hands fisted at his sides. "You only agreed to do this if we could help the Allies. I promised you. And now..."

Gerrit gave him a slow nod without breaking his gaze. "We may be volunteers, but we signed a contract. Even if we could quit, what would we tell Schmeling? Why would we want to quit three days after arriving on what they call an island paradise?"

Any excuse would arouse suspicion. Questioning. Perhaps interrogation. Under interrogation, the strongest men broke, and Bernardus's entire network could be shattered.

Horror flicked through the blue of Bernardus's eyes.

Gerrit shared his rage at the situation, at their entrapment, and at the breach of faith—unintended on Bernardus's part. But God knew what would happen, and he'd allowed them to join OT anyway. Once again, Gerrit had done his part, had done something brave and noble. Why wouldn't God do his part?

Bernardus stomped one foot and thrust his arm toward the nearest concrete platform, topped by an imposing 15-centimeter gun. "If we must stay, let's commit sabotage."

Gerrit shielded his eyes from the sun and glanced back toward their commander. "This island measures only fourteen kilometers by eight kilometers. How many dozens of batteries and bunkers has Schmeling shown us the past two days? How many more are under construction?"

"He expects us to help build a command bunker right here. To modify German plans to make it better, stronger, so they can fend off an invasion. Fine. Let's build it, then destroy it."

Gerrit folded his arms, encased in the vile brown uniform. "If we did so, it would decrease German strength in Jersey by less than one percent, and they would quickly rebuild."

"I have to do something." Bernardus's voice hissed through his clenched teeth. "I'll do my job poorly, lead them to build on unstable soil. And you—you can—"

"If they discovered what we'd done, we'd be tortured and shot, and your contacts would be in danger."

Bernardus's head sagged back. "Why do you always have to be logical?"

Since they'd met as schoolboys, Bernardus had always been the accelerator and Gerrit the brakes. Both necessary.

"Kroon!" Schmeling beckoned to them. "Van der Zee!"

"On to the next fortification," Bernardus mumbled.

Gerrit sent a wry smile. "Every day spent sightseeing means a day we aren't building."

Schmeling led them back to his dark green Bentley, which had once been some wealthy Jerseyman's prized possession. The car, like the hotel where Gerrit was billeted, had been requisitioned by the Germans. Schmeling had explained that since the islanders didn't receive a petrol ration, they had no need for cars anyway.

Gerrit's mouth tightened as he slid into the backseat.

Schmeling drove north up Noirmont Point, through the village of St. Aubin, and followed the coastal road east along St. Aubin's Bay. The tide was in, isolating two forts on either end of the bay. When the tide was out, one could walk to the forts along the seafloor.

"It is beautiful here, *nicht wahr*?" Schmeling gestured to the sweep of golden sand beside brilliant blue waters. "When we've won this war, this shall be a holiday spot for the German people."

Gerrit gave a noncommittal murmur. The Germans weren't building resorts. They were building "resistance nests," evenly spaced around the bay, with machine guns and anti-tank guns poking from concealed concrete bunkers. Any Allied landing force would be decimated.

Schmeling drove into the town of St. Helier with its handsome homes. "As you can imagine, we require vast quantities of materials, especially cement. Van der Zee, one of your roles will be to inspect shipments to ensure the materials haven't been sabotaged by French terrorists."

Bernardus clucked his tongue. "I'm sorry to hear not everyone appreciates the benefits of German rule."

Gerrit resisted the urge to whack his friend. Overplaying Nazi zeal was as dangerous as underplaying it.

Soon they crossed a railway line ringing the harbor.

"We built this railway," Schmeling said with pride. "We dedicated it this summer. The local children have been a bit of a nuisance, I'm afraid, laying rocks on the rails. They shall learn their lesson."

Gerrit's fingers coiled around his knees. He knew all too well how the Nazis taught those lessons.

Schmeling turned the car toward the docks. "I see our workers are here to unload."

Gerrit's heart wrenched as it had yesterday when he'd seen the prisoners at work on a construction site, poorly fed and clad and shod.

"You needn't mind them." Schmeling parked the car at the foot of a pier, where two dozen workers huddled. "Their *Schutzkommando* guards keep them in line."

Kept them in line with harsh voices and truncheons.

Schmeling led Gerrit and Bernardus onto the pier and aboard a small cargo ship. "This ship has just arrived from Saint-Malo with a load of cement. An English boat with an English crew."

"We're not English. We're Jerseymen." A young man coiled a line. He had dark hair and eyes paired with a light complexion, a common combination on the island.

Schmeling nodded at the boy, not dismissive, but not accepting, and he strode across the deck toward the captain.

Bernardus approached the boy—yes, still a boy—with gangly limbs and spots on his chin and nose. "We are new to the Channel Islands. Please explain the difference."

The boy looped the line in a figure eight around two metal cleats on the deck. "The States of Jersey are a crown dependency—as is Guernsey. We are part of Britain, but not part of the United Kingdom, not part of England. We have our own currency, our own states chamber—similar to parliament—our own courts, and our own laws. We were quite independent. Until your lot came."

"We are not German," Bernardus said. "We are Dutch."

The boy glanced at the swastika armband around the sleeve of Bernardus's uniform jacket. "You serve the Germans."

"So do you."

"Bernardus," Gerrit grumbled. What was he doing?

"I do not." The boy stood straight, several centimeters shorter than Bernardus. "This is a Jersey boat."

"Carrying supplies for the Germans."

The boy's eyelids twitched.

Bernardus stepped closer to the young man. "We who live under occupation have few choices, yes? We must work for them on our terms—or on theirs." He jerked his head toward the slave workers waiting to unload the ship.

The boy followed Bernardus's line of sight, then gave him a look of shock.

Bernardus leaned his head close to the boy's shoulder. "You don't like the Nazis, do you?"

Gerrit glanced toward Schmeling in conversation with the captain—too far away to hear, but never far enough. "Bernardus," he said through gritted teeth. "You'll get him arrested."

The boy's gaze flicked around the deck, between Gerrit and Bernardus and Schmeling. Then he met Bernardus's gaze with a blaze of defiance. "I do not," he whispered.

"Neither do we," Bernardus whispered back. Then he grinned and extended his hand. "I am Bernardus Kroon, and this is my friend Gerrit van der Zee." His voice returned to normal volume.

"Charlie . . . Charlie Picot."

"How do you do, Mr. Picot?" Bernardus crossed his arms over his barrel chest. "Do you make this run often?"

"Yes." Charlie shot a glance at the captain and resumed coiling the line.

"It'll be a pleasure to work with you. I'm a geologist, and Gerrit is a civil engineer. Gerrit will be inspecting your cargo."

Charlie jerked up his head. "You—you'll find nothing amiss."

Bernardus ducked down to the boy. "A shame."

"Come along, van der Zee, Kroon." Schmeling beckoned them to the hatch. "Jersey customs officials have already checked for contraband. They found none." He led the way through the hatch.

Gerrit climbed down a ladder into the hold.

"You were issued pocketknives, ja?" Schmeling pulled one from his trousers and turned to the neat stacks of bags. "Select a few random bags and cut them open near the top. Make sure they contain cement. It is better to discover sabotage here on the docks, where we might be able to trace the source, than on the worksite."

Bernardus flashed Gerrit a mischievous look, accelerating.

Gerrit slammed on the brakes with a quick scowl. A possible way to commit sabotage, but it would require careful thought.

He wrestled a bag from the top of the pile and slashed it open. The familiar feel and scent of cement met his fingertips and nostrils.

Schmeling scooted a bag to the side. "Set the opened bags here. They must be placed upright in the lorry."

"Yes, Herr Oberbauführer." Gerrit shoved his opened bag to join the other.

"Excellent so far." Schmeling brushed his hands together and climbed the ladder. "I shall tell the guard to bring in the workers. As they unload, check a few more bags."

When he disappeared through the hatch, Gerrit stood close to Bernardus and lowered his voice to the deck. "You could have gotten the boy arrested. Killed."

"He's smart. Well spoken."

True. Charlie Picot spoke with the vocabulary and diction provided by an expensive school. But at his age, he should still be at that expensive school.

"He's cautious," Bernardus murmured.

"Impetuous."

"He's young. He could learn."

Gerrit pulled back enough to pin his friend under his gaze. "Don't."

Bernardus shrugged. "Just making acquaintances."

"Contacts."

Bernardus shrugged again and glanced around the hold. The hold of a ship that frequently ran to Saint-Malo.

Gerrit's blood chilled. No. Too many variables. Too many unseen factors.

"I'm only thinking," Bernardus said. "First, we have a great deal to learn."

As much as Gerrit longed to redeem his decision to join Organisation Todt, he refused to endanger lives to do so. "A very great deal."

CHAPTER
6

A breeze flipped the curled ends of Ivy's hair as she walked down Hill Street with Fern and Charlie to church on Sunday. The one day a week she let herself don a pretty floral dress and wear her hair down.

The one day a week she didn't need to convince everyone she was actually a doctor.

Fern's shoes clicked on the flagstones as they passed the Town Hall, the elegant pale pink Victorian building bloodied by the swastika flag. "I've come up with a solution for your rounds."

"Oh?" Ivy didn't want to talk about work on a warm sunny day.

Fern's smile tipped toward her high cheekbones. "I run the morning surgery like clockwork."

"Yes, you do." She moved patients in and out of the examination room faster than Ivy liked, but the waiting room never overflowed.

"However, when you go on rounds, I lose all control."

Charlie peeked around from Fern's other side and grinned. "Lucky Ivy."

51

"Oh, you." Fern chuckled and elbowed their little brother. "For the past few weeks, I've analyzed your rounds. Every day, you travel all over the island in a most inefficient manner."

"It can't be helped," Ivy said as they turned onto Church Street.

"That was fine when you had plenty of petrol, but not on bicycle. I've divided the island into five sectors and designed five routes. Each day you'll take one route."

Ivy shook her head. "Some patients need to be seen more than once a week."

"If you follow the route, you'll finish in late afternoon and have an hour or two to visit patients on other routes. But to do so, you must be disciplined. No more than twenty minutes per patient, and no dawdling to sketch on the way."

A breeze swept through, and Charlie grasped the brim of his homburg, formerly Dad's homburg. "Ivy's watch is broken. How can she keep time?"

Fern frowned. "It's obvious when twenty minutes have passed."

Obvious to Fern, but not Ivy. And though parts of Fern's plan made sense, others didn't. However, a pleased look brightened Fern's face, so Ivy smiled at her. "I'll do my best."

"You will." Fern looped her arm through Ivy's. "And now that you'll no longer sketch on your rounds, I know you can keep this schedule."

With effort, Ivy held her smile aloft. The day before, Fern had plucked Ivy's sketch pad out of her medical bag and declared it unnecessary equipment.

They passed through the wrought iron gate surrounding the red granite Parish Church of St. Helier. Inside the church, organ music and colorful stained glass windows enlivened the whitewashed interior.

Thelma Galais sat on the left near the front, wearing a gray hat above her low silver chignon.

Ivy slid into the pew beside her, with Fern and Charlie following. Sitting with a family friend eased some of the pain of not sitting with her own parents. "Good morning, Mrs. Galais. How are you?"

Mrs. Galais had good color in her round cheeks and a light in her hazel eyes. "You precious girl. Don't you look pretty?"

"You look pretty too. Any word from . . ." No, it was far too early.

The light faded. "Edna and Frank? No."

Ivy murmured in sympathy. Over the past few days, over six hundred people had been shipped from Jersey to Germany, and several hundred more still awaited deportation. Rumors said the deportees would be subject to forced labor, but the Germans said they were being sent to internment camps, just as German subjects had been interned in England.

"The Lord is good." Mrs. Galais smiled and restored some of the light. "He will sustain Edna and Frank, and he will sustain me."

If the Lord was good, why did he allow innocents to be ripped from their homes? Ivy winced. A horrible thought to have, especially in church.

Many of the deportees had lived in St. Helier, and holes darkened the pews. The Carters, who always sat in the second row on the left. The Yorks, who always sat in the same row as the Picots on the right.

Behind the Yorks' customary pew, Doris des Forges Mollet met Ivy's gaze, gave her a polite nod, and turned to her husband and children.

Ivy's chest sank in. Doris and Dulcie des Forges had been Ivy's best friends—until diphtheria struck. Ivy and Dulcie had been quarantined together, both deathly ill. But Ivy alone had survived.

A sense of being watched, and Ivy glanced back to find the source.

Three rows behind her sat a young man with golden-blond hair, his face framed between the hats of the ladies in the row before him.

Not quite a handsome face, but his gaze held hers, full of gentle strength, of kindly intelligence, and her gaze entwined with his, knit with his, and she saw . . . she knew . . . knew she was meant to spend her life with him.

Ivy sucked in a breath and spun to face the altar, severing the cord of connection.

She struggled to breathe. She'd never met the man, never seen him before.

The rector of the church, the Very Reverend Matthew Le Marinel, stood at the pulpit, and Ivy rose with the congregation. She fumbled to help Mrs. Galais hold the hymnal, forced herself to sing.

She'd heard of love at first sight, but this was different. Not love. Just knowing. What was she to do with it?

Dizziness swept through her, and she gripped the pew in front of her with her free hand.

Finally, the rector began his message, and Ivy pulled her little notepad from her purse to sketch as she always did, a quirk the congregation had come to accept from her. But this time she sketched the golden-haired man.

Who was he? Was this simply a silly longing from her lonely heart? And what on earth should she do after the service?

The image filled in, her pencil shading in dimension, capturing the bend of his mouth, the curve of his hairline, the radiance in his eyes.

At the end of the message, Ivy stuffed her notepad in her purse, and she bumbled her way through the closing hymn. But now what? The thought of seeing him again . . .

Instead, she faced Mrs. Galais and asked about her plans for the day. Mrs. Galais chatted about having dinner with Mrs. Le Huquet, and Fern slipped into the aisle to talk to a friend. Ivy simply needed to stay in the pew long enough for the golden-haired man to leave.

"Good morning, Mr. Picot," a man said from the aisle.

Mr. Picot? Charlie was only fifteen.

Ivy glanced behind her. Over Charlie's shoulder, she saw a man with white-blond hair. And beside him . . . her golden-haired man.

His gaze pulled her closer. His eyes shimmered in the most arresting shade of aquamarine, the same shade as the waters in St. Aubin's Bay, not far from shore. How often had she tried to capture that color but failed? She could duplicate the shade, but not the luminous translucence. Now that same color shone in this man's eyes.

Charlie was talking to the two men, but the words slipped by. Then Charlie glanced back at her. "Ivy, I'd like you to meet Bernardus Kroon and Gerrit van der Zee."

Gerrit was his name. Gerrit, and the cord entwined once more.

"Gentlemen, this is my sister, Dr. Ivy Picot." Charlie stepped into the aisle to allow the shaking of hands.

Gerrit van der Zee wore a uniform. A brown uniform with a khaki shirt and a black tie and a black belt. With black shoulder straps piped in red.

With a red swastika armband and another armband below it that read "Org. Todt."

The organization that enslaved and beat and starved its workers. The cord of connection snapped, recoiled, tangled into a knot. Ivy stifled a gasp. The sting of it.

"It's a pleasure to meet you." The first man extended a hand to her.

Something sad swam in the sea of Gerrit's eyes, and he did not reach out to her. "It is indeed a pleasure, Dr. Picot."

Ivy hated to be rude, but she refused to shake hands with German soldiers. She gave them a tight-lipped hint of a smile. "Come along, Charlie."

"But Fern isn't—"

"We'll meet her at home." She gripped Charlie's arm and steered him past the two Nazis.

"Ivy, what are you doing? Don't be rude."

"They're Germans," she muttered.

"They're Dutch."

In the clear air outside, Ivy hauled in long breaths to cleanse her mind. Yes, van der Zee sounded Dutch. She continued her march home. "They wear German uniforms. You shouldn't talk to them."

Charlie wrested his arm free. "They come to my boat for inspections. I like them. They aren't like the others."

"No." Ivy gave her head a series of tiny shakes to dislodge the stubborn sensation of connection. "No, they're worse. Only volunteers are allowed to wear German uniforms. They're collaborating with the enemy that occupied their country—and ours. Worse than collaborators. They're traitors."

"They're not like—"

"I don't want to hear another word about them." Her voice sounded shrill. "You mustn't talk to them unless it's absolutely necessary."

"I'm not a little boy." His upper lip curled.

Ivy took slow breaths to calm down, to tease out her emotions from Charlie's situation. "No, you aren't. You're a young man, and young men must be extra careful."

"I understand." Charlie's expression melted into rueful resignation. "If I'm seen as a friend to them, the Picots will be seen as collaborators. That would be bad for the practice."

"Oh, Charlie." Ivy gripped his arm again, with affection rather than alarm. "The practice concerns me far less than your safety. You know how many people have been sentenced to prison simply for making jokes about the Germans, for insulting them. You mustn't let your guard down around those men."

Charlie sighed and glanced away.

Ivy steadied her breath. Whatever attraction she'd felt, she could never associate with a man who had betrayed his country, a man who condoned the abuse of his fellow man.

She mustn't let her guard down either.

CHAPTER
7

In the hold of the SS *Ormer*, Gerrit braced his feet wide as the ship rocked in rough weather. He tore off a bit of bread, sliced a sliver of cheese, and handed it to the next worker in the queue.

The man's craggy face lit up, and joyful words burst forth.

"Nyet," Gerrit whispered. "Nein." He slammed a finger to his lips, then mimed chewing, swallowing, and frowning.

But excitement bubbled among the bags of cement.

Although Bernardus had insisted this was a bad idea, he'd sweet-talked a lady in the hotel kitchen into giving him the bread and cheese, supposedly for his own lunch, and now he stood on deck, chatting with Charlie Picot, ready to call "Ahoy there!" if an OT officer approached.

Gerrit passed bread and cheese to the next man and repeated his miming.

A wicked scar slashed through the worker's cheek and eyebrow. "You would like us to finish this before returning to deck, yes?" He spoke in fluent German.

Gerrit blinked in surprise. "Yes, thank you. They must be quiet, must not discuss this, even amongst themselves, must not look pleased."

"Understood." The worker glanced around with quick intelligent eyes. "One each?"

Gerrit turned his shoulder to the press of men so he could keep distributing food. "Yes. This is all I have—one loaf of bread, one block of cheese."

The worker spoke to the men in a Slavic tongue, and the men responded with murmurs of understanding.

"I will stay with you, explain, help."

"Thank you." Gerrit held out the cheese and knife.

"Nein!" He flung up both hands. "If the guards catch me with a weapon . . ."

Gerrit winced. He'd seen what the guards did at the smallest offense, and he handed his helper the loaf of bread instead.

Together, they distributed the feeble snack.

"You are from Russia?" Gerrit asked.

"Ukraine. All the men in this squad are." He wore a Soviet officer's uniform, knees worn through, one sleeve hanging loose, one red epaulette dangling. He repeated instructions in Ukrainian in a firm tone.

Grateful gazes met Gerrit's, but the workers assumed a neutral expression, obeying the officer as they stuffed the morsels into their dirty mouths.

"I cannot do this every day," Gerrit said. "I may never be able to do this again. But I'll do what I can."

"If we are discovered, the consequences would be bad for all of us. Even you."

"My friend is keeping watch."

The officer cast a glance up the ladder. "You are new, yes? You still seem surprised by the actions of your people."

"I'm not German. I'm Dutch. My name is Gerrit van der Zee. And I'm no Nazi."

"Lt. Demyan Marchenko." He scanned Gerrit's uniform, not

58

with the repugnance Dr. Ivy Picot had shown but with detachment, as if making allowance for compromise in times of war.

The latter cut as deeply as the former.

Marchenko passed out the last piece of bread. "Whoever you are, you are our comrade, and we thank you."

With his lips pressed tight, Gerrit passed out the final slivers of cheese.

Marchenko brushed crumbs from his fingers into his palm and cupped his hand to his mouth.

Not one crumb littered the deck of the hold, and that wrenched through Gerrit.

Marchenko shouldered the last bag of concrete, gave Gerrit a strong nod, and climbed out of the hold.

Gerrit pulled in a breath over his roughened throat and checked the hold for any evidence. With his clipboard and the empty bread bag in hand, he returned to the deck, where Bernardus and Charlie were laughing about something.

Bernardus raised a pale eyebrow at Gerrit. "Your inspection went well?"

"Indeed."

"Come along, then. Goodbye, Charlie." Bernardus shook the boy's hand. "We're going out to Elizabeth Castle."

Charlie sent a wistful smile toward the bay. He shared his sister's striking coloring. "I used to love running around the castle, pretending to be a soldier."

Now the Germans had taken over the castle's original fortifications and added modern ones.

Gerrit and Bernardus said goodbye and strolled down the pier and onto the Esplanade, staying within the wire fencing that kept the civilians away from the harbor and beaches. Clouds darkened the southwest horizon, and wind tossed the clouds closer to the island.

Bernardus went down the steps to the beach.

Gerrit gestured over his shoulder with his thumb. "Riedel's supposed to meet us here."

"He'll catch up." Bernardus kept walking, sand kicking out from under his black boots.

Gerrit trotted down the steps and crossed the gentle slope of beach to the narrow concrete causeway that led to the castle at low tide.

Ahead of them, the castle rose in a stony mound with a mixture of Elizabethan and Napoleonic era architecture. The Germans were adding sleek modern concrete batteries and observation posts that didn't belong.

Wind heavy with sea spray tugged at Gerrit's overseas cap. Although tempted to allow it to steal the bit of brown cloth with red piping that labeled him as a Nazi, Gerrit stuffed it in his pocket.

Holding his own cap in hand, Bernardus looked back over his shoulder. "Charlie Picot is doing us a favor."

"Yes?"

"He's delivering a letter to my girlfriend in Saint-Malo."

Gerrit stopped in his tracks. "What?"

"Keep walking. After Riedel joins us, we'll no longer be able to talk."

Gerrit jogged to catch up over the damp sand on the causeway. "Civilians aren't allowed to carry mail to France. I read it in the local newspaper."

"Charlie knows. He doesn't mind."

"You didn't tell him what the letter is about, did—"

"Of course not."

"Then you're involving him unwittingly." Gerrit's arms swung hard. "Even worse. He won't know what he's walking into. If he's caught with a letter—you could get him killed."

"The letter is innocuous. I told my girlfriend I was posted to Jersey, not near Saint-Malo as I'd hoped, and I won't have leave for six months. I said she's free to find someone new."

Air puffed out Gerrit's cheeks, and he blew it out. "Letting the network know why they haven't heard from us. And never will."

"Yes."

"Send it by post. Leave Charlie out of it."

"I don't want the censors reading it in case they suspect my contact."

A groan rumbled in Gerrit's throat. "All the more reason not to involve Charlie. He can't even be sixteen."

"He's fifteen. I told him I didn't want the censors reading my letter because it was sappy and sentimental, and I made it as sappy and sentimental as I could stomach."

"He's fifteen." Gerrit glared at his friend. "Fifteen, Bernardus."

"Which makes him look innocent." Bernardus kept his square face trained on the castle. "But he's smart. He was one of the top boys at Victoria College, the best boys' school on the island, but he quit to help his family. His parents evacuated to England, and the elder Dr. Picot left the practice in his daughter's hands. It isn't doing well, and Charlie wants to help."

A kind and selfless boy. Yet another reason not to risk his safety.

Bernardus's mouth puckered on one side. "I have some sad news about the family though. Charlie's sister is married."

A kick to Gerrit's chest, which made no sense. Despite the strange and wonderful affinity he'd felt with Ivy Picot, she was appropriately disgusted by his uniform. "Dr. Picot is married? But she uses her maiden name."

Bernardus gave Gerrit's arm a light whack. "The other sister. The stunner."

"Oh, that one." Gerrit had seen her first, of course. A face that could grace the cover of any magazine.

Bernardus chatted about what Charlie had told him about that sister, the older sister—Fern was her name—and her husband and sons.

Gerrit's thoughts trailed to the younger sister with the sweet face that had drawn him. She'd been talking to the elderly lady beside her, not with the condescension of youth or even the oversight of a physician, but with genuine interest and affection.

Which had drawn Gerrit even more. Then she'd turned to him

with those large dark eyes set in a face that was all softness—round cheeks and chin and a little round mouth. And she'd kept looking at him, and he'd wanted to keep looking at her forever.

Dr. Ivy Picot. To become a physician, strength and determination and courage had to lie behind all that sweetness and softness. And he'd liked her very much.

Then she'd recoiled at the sight of his uniform, and he'd gained deep respect for her, even as he'd resigned himself to the fact that she'd never again direct that sweetness his way.

"Kroon!" A man's voice rose from behind them. "Van der Zee!"

"Don't look," Bernardus said in a sharp tone. "Anything else to discuss?"

The letter had already been given to Charlie, so Gerrit sighed and shook his head. With that letter passed their last hope of helping the Allies. He and Bernardus had gone from brave freedom fighters infiltrating the enemy stronghold to sniveling collaborators building that stronghold.

Nothing could be done. Quitting was impossible. Escape even more so. And sabotage would lead to torture and death with nothing to show for it.

"Kroon!" Riedel called, closer now. "Van der Zee."

Bernardus turned and waved at the officer. "There you are, Herr Bauführer. I thought you'd gone on before us."

At least Bernardus hadn't included Gerrit in his lie.

Riedel jogged up, breathing hard, his belly shaking. He wiped sweat from under his nose, then shielded his eyes to study the castle. "What a sight, ja? Not as magnificent as the castles in Germany, but it's still impressive."

Even more so up close.

The men climbed the stone ramp from the seabed to the wall of rough granite blocks, mottled with golden lichen.

Two German guards in the gateway examined each man's *Dienstbuch*—paybook—that served as identification papers and service documentation and more.

Once admitted, the men passed through a narrow ward bound by granite walls interspersed with arched openings filled with guns. The wind picked up as they went, ruffling clumps of grass in the mud beside the path.

They passed through a stone gateway stamped with a royal coat of arms.

On the other side, a crew of OT workers was setting up wooden framing in preparation for the pouring of concrete for yet another bunker.

As soon as Schmeling arrived, Gerrit, Bernardus, and Riedel would review the plans for the bunker and start calculations for any changes that needed to be made.

Unlike the Ukrainian workers on the docks, these men had meat on their bones and adequate clothing. Oddly enough, most of them wore bowler hats.

They were speaking Spanish. After the Spanish Civil War, many of the communist Spanish Republicans had fled for their lives to France, where they'd been interned. When the Germans invaded France, the Spaniards were given a choice—return to Spain, where they would be executed—or volunteer with Organisation Todt.

At least their classification as volunteers granted them more freedom and benefits than the slave workers.

Organisation Todt treated their fellow Germans best. Those they considered Aryans—like the Dutch and Scandinavians— were treated fairly well. Those from western Europe were treated with moderation. And Jews and those from eastern Europe were abused.

The wrongness of it all. The cruelty. It grated and swelled in his chest.

Schmeling had yet to arrive at the construction site, so Gerrit, Bernardus, and Riedel waited to the side. And Gerrit observed. Observed the men working hard and with good cheer.

He could no longer contain it, so he assumed an innocent air. "These men work harder than the Ukrainians and Russians."

"Ja, even though this castle serves as a penal colony for our workers." Riedel wrinkled his broad nose. "But then these men are not lazy Slavs."

"They are also well-fed and properly clothed." Gerrit closed his mouth before mentioning how they weren't being beaten. "That must help them work harder."

Riedel's eyes narrowed in thought, but Bernardus shot Gerrit a look of death.

"Possibly," Riedel said. "But it isn't our concern. The guards and camp commandants know what's best. They know how to work with Slavs."

Gerrit sniffed and fiddled with the cuff of his jacket. "I heard a guard say they're little better than beasts."

"They would know."

Gerrit tugged at that cuff. "If you want good milk and eggs and pork, you treat your beasts with care."

A sharp inhalation, and understanding glimmered in Riedel's brown eyes.

"Gerrit, come see the view." Bernardus strode across to the far wall.

"Excuse me," Gerrit said to Riedel, and he joined his friend by the wall facing east, toward the docks, not the most outstanding of views.

"What are you doing?" Bernardus glared at him. "Stop it."

"I can't stand by while—"

"We can fight only one battle at a time."

Gerrit's sigh tumbled in the darkening air. "We aren't fighting even one battle."

The starch went out of Bernardus's spine. "I know. I—I'm sorry."

Bernardus didn't need more guilt, so Gerrit offered a slight smile. "I understand. No use dying in a battle we can't begin to win."

"Yes."

Across the narrow grounds, Riedel crossed his arms and studied the Spanish workers.

"I may have swayed Riedel's thinking."

"Don't trust him, Gerrit. He's a Nazi."

"I'll be careful." But careful words could still sway hearts.

CHAPTER
8

Chemists often rang Ivy with questions about prescriptions, but not with summons to their shops.

Regardless, Ivy entered Carter's Chemist's. At the counter, Miss de Ferrers handed a bottle to an elderly woman.

After the patient left, Miss de Ferrers locked the front door, flipped the sign to "closed," and strode back toward the counter. "Please come with me, Dr. Picot."

Ivy suppressed a smile and a "good afternoon to you too." The chemist certainly didn't waste time on pleasantries.

"Come on through." Miss de Ferrers led Ivy behind the counter and into a small office with a desk strewn with books and jars of what looked like dried herbs and flowers.

Ivy read the title of the top book, "*Pharmacognosy.*"

The chemist crossed her arms. "The study of deriving pharmaceutical compounds from plants. We can no longer purchase most commercial medications, but Jersey has a wealth of plants, many of which were formerly used for treatment."

Ivy leaned down and smiled at a jar of foxglove flowers, a source of digitalis, used for treating coronary disease. "Reviving the ancient arts."

"You must wonder why I rang." Miss de Ferrers cleared a pile of books from a wooden chair. "I want you to examine a patient."

Ivy's eyebrows arched high. What an odd inquiry from a chemist.

"I needed to ask in person, because the Gestapo are known to listen to telephone conversations." Miss de Ferrers motioned Ivy toward the vacated chair.

Ivy lowered herself to sitting. The Gestapo hadn't come to Jersey, but the German *Geheime Feldpolizei* employed the Gestapo's plainclothes spying tactics—and their cruelty. "Why . . ."

Miss de Ferrers perched on the side of her desk, threatening a stack of papers. "Some patients do not wish to be found."

"Oh." Lately, the *Evening Post* printed German demands to turn in escaped foreign workers. The poor men often sneaked out of their camps in search of food, and some islanders were known to shelter them.

Ivy swallowed hard. "Is he sick? Injured?"

"Are you willing to risk prison?"

Ivy folded her arms across the thinning green wool of her coat. She would be risking not only her own freedom, but her family's as well. The Germans arrested first and asked questions later.

But Dad wouldn't hesitate to relieve suffering. And Jesus had healed the leper and the lame, the rich and the poor, the Jew and the Gentile. He'd broken the law to heal on the Sabbath.

Ivy drew in a slow, steadying breath. "I'm willing."

Miss de Ferrers leaned forward, and one tiny auburn curl defied the hairpins over her ear. "Can we trust you? Many lives are at stake."

The escapee, the family sheltering him, Miss de Ferrers, and whoever else composed the "we" she referred to.

"I would speak of it to no one, and I'd keep no charts or records."

Miss de Ferrers studied her with an incising gaze. "If we are satisfied, would you be willing to see more such patients?"

For months, Ivy had ached to help the bedraggled workers. "I would. But why ask me?"

The chemist's gaze skittered away, and her jaw shifted to the side. "I . . . was not kind to you. Yet you've been persistent in your kindness to me. After Mr. Carter was deported, the shop lost many patients. A woman in charge, you know."

"I know, but my referrals to your shop have been earned."

Miss de Ferrers jerked one shoulder. "You'd best move along. Here's the address, in St. Brelade. Please burn this." She handed Ivy a slip of paper.

"Thank you."

Miss de Ferrers strode out toward the counter. "If we should need you again, I'll ring. I'll speak only to you, not your receptionist."

"I understand." Fern would too, since she couldn't answer questions about prescriptions.

"I will tell you Mrs. Smith—or a similar name, it matters not— told me you were making a home visit, and would you please pick up her prescription on your way." Miss de Ferrers swung open a half door in the counter and led Ivy through the shop. "When you arrive here, I'll tell you the actual name and address, and I'll give you a medication to take with you as cover."

"Very clever."

"Good day to you." Miss de Ferrers flipped the sign back to "open."

"Good day to you too." Ivy smiled, but the chemist was already halfway across the shop.

Outside, Ivy mounted her bicycle and headed west out of town. Miss de Ferrers might never be a friend, but at least Ivy had earned her respect—and that was a cherished gift.

A mist hung over St. Aubin's Bay, obscuring the horizon. If Ivy were to treat escaped workers on a regular basis, she'd have an even greater need to follow Fern's plans to simplify her rounds.

Yet the waves called to her to be sketched. The tiny flowers that would emerge if she stopped to look. The curlews hopping on the sand, ignoring the barbed wire and the German signs warning of mines.

She loved caring for patients, but without her sketch pad, she felt . . . diminished.

When she reached St. Aubin's village, she turned right, then found the road leading to the Bullard home.

Mrs. Bullard, a thin woman in her forties, rushed Ivy inside and upstairs to a bedroom, where the curtains were drawn.

A paraffin lamp revealed a young man lying on the bed, wild-eyed, his wrists tied to a bedpost. A streak of red stained his tattered trousers.

"I—I didn't mean to hurt him." Mr. Bullard stood at the foot of the bed, rubbing the back of his neck, his face contorted. "He was in my rabbit hutch, had my best breeder by the throat. I—I didn't think. I clobbered him with a piece of lumber. But there was a nail." His voice broke.

"It's all right. I understand." Ivy stepped closer to the bed. "I'm Dr. Picot, and I'm here to help you."

"He doesn't speak English," Mrs. Bullard said.

"We had to tie him up." Mr. Bullard gestured to the bed. "He keeps trying to run away, but if they catch him—"

"He's just a boy." Mrs. Bullard clapped a hand over her mouth.

He was indeed a boy, no older than Charlie, and he shrank back from Ivy, chattering in Russian or Ukrainian.

Ivy knelt a few feet away from the bed. "I'm a doctor." She displayed her medical bag, then removed her stethoscope and showed it to the boy. "Doctor."

"Our neighbor came by," Mrs. Bullard said. "He told us to ring—"

"Hush, Mabel."

"But Dr. Picot is part of the—"

"No one," Mr. Bullard said. "No one. Remember?"

Ivy edged closer to her patient, lifting her stethoscope and a gentle smile. The details of the ring—or whatever it was—that she now belonged to concerned her far less than the deep gash on the boy's thigh. As filthy and malnourished as he was, the risk of sepsis was high. And tetanus as well.

Gerrit van der Zee's face flashed in her mind. He and his friend had attended church the past three Sundays in a row, despite the cool reception from the congregation. When Ivy had overheard Gerrit chatting with Charlie, he'd sounded thoughtful and mild. But had he beaten young boys like the one before her? Or stood by whilst others did? Approved of depriving them of food, driving them to the dangers of escape and theft?

Ivy inhaled a quick breath to clear her mind. "Mrs. Bullard, please boil some water, add soap, and bring me cloth for bandaging."

"Here you are." She brought over a basin from the bureau. "I tried to bandage the wound myself, but he won't let me near."

The boy's pale blue eyes still stretched wide, but he'd stopped pulling against his restraints.

Ivy moved up to the bedside and lifted the bell of her stethoscope. "May I?" She wasn't worried about his heart, but she needed to establish trust.

His breathing quieted.

Murmuring softly, Ivy pressed her stethoscope to the boy's thin chest. His heartbeat hammered her eardrums.

"Very good," she said with a smile, and she pointed to his leg. "May I?"

Ever so slightly, he scooted his leg closer.

"Very good." She shifted the remnants of his trousers away from the wound and examined it. After she tested the water temperature, she began cleansing the wound.

The boy grunted in pain, but he allowed her to work.

"Has he had anything to eat or drink?" Ivy asked.

"He won't let us near," Mrs. Bullard said.

"He may now. Mrs. Bullard, please bring him some food. Mr.

Bullard, offer him something to drink and untie his restraints. Then he'll know you mean him no harm."

"But I'm the one who hurt him." His voice choked off.

Ivy gave Mr. Bullard a reassuring smile. "It's clear in any language how sorry you feel."

He nodded rapidly. "I'll fetch some tea."

"Thank you." Ivy resumed cleaning the wound. If they could hold off infection—and the Germans—the young man might stand a chance.

∽

ST. HELIER
TUESDAY, OCTOBER 20, 1942

Ivy's stomach growled after the meager dinner of limpet stew and rough rationed bread, and she set the last patient chart on the sofa beside her and stretched.

Most of the day had been spent visiting patients in Jersey General Hospital and Overdale Isolation Hospital. A diphtheria epidemic had taken hold, ravaging adults as well as children. Ghastly disease, and the doctors in Jersey hadn't enough serum to treat the ill.

She'd also visited the Ukrainian boy the Bullards had nicknamed Henry. He was recovering well, even though two days had passed before he'd allowed her to inject tetanus antitoxin. Surely he had received more and better food from the Bullards than if he'd succeeded in killing their prized rabbit.

But how long could the Bullards keep him hidden?

Fern sat sewing in an armchair next to Ivy, and Charlie played the piano across the room.

It was good to have him home, even if foul weather was the reason for it.

Ivy lifted a sketch pad and pencil from her basket by the sofa. Evenings had always been her favorite, but the warm blanket of family felt as thin and frayed as Ivy's tweed skirt. She shivered in the cold as she sketched her sister's profile.

For October, the Picot household received two hundredweights of wood and one of coal. Since the surgery on the ground floor needed to be kept warm for patient appointments, little remained to heat the family quarters on the first and second floors.

The piano music stopped, and Charlie put a record on the phonograph. Soon a lively tune filled the room.

Charlie waltzed around the room, and he stretched out his hands to his oldest sister. "Dance with me, Fernie."

She snipped the thread with her scissors. "I don't have time. I'm hemming Bill's trousers for you." A savage smile flickered in the lamplight. "If he ever comes home, he shan't have a stitch to wear."

Ivy's pencil whispered over the paper. She hadn't heard a kind word about her brother-in-law for months. "I can't imagine how difficult this is for you. I know how you miss him." Especially since messages came through the Red Cross only twice a year, limited to twenty-five words.

Fern's mouth opened and shut, and she shook her head, not as if about to cry but as if swallowing words best left unsaid.

"So dance with me and cheer up." Charlie swayed to the tune, smiling, reaching, utterly charming.

"I don't have time." Fern spooled out thread. "I have too much work, and Ivy isn't helping at all."

Ivy's pencil paused midstroke. "Pardon?"

Fern flicked her chin at Ivy. "How can you sit there drawing when you see me hard at work, all day, every day?"

"Be fair, Fern." Charlie set his hands low on his hips. "Ivy and I work all day too. We have evenings off. You have afternoons off and visit your friends."

Fern sent Charlie a dark look, but Charlie was right. Aunt Ruby came in every afternoon to clean the surgery and answer the telephone. But reminding Fern would shred more threads from the family blanket.

Fern took a stabbing little stitch. "Regardless, it's rude of her to draw when I'm working."

Ivy's chest tightened. Fern's timetables made Ivy feel pumped up with adrenaline. No time to breathe. Never to record on paper the sights that captured her imagination. Before rounds, Fern checked Ivy's medical bag to make sure she hadn't packed her sketch pad, as if Ivy were a sneaky, errant child.

Now Fern wanted to take away her evening drawing time as well?

Something sparked in her chest. She never talked back to Fern, but she couldn't lose yet another thing that fed her soul. "When I agreed not to draw on my rounds, you promised to allow me to sketch in the evenings."

"Allow?" Charlie stepped closer. "Ivy, she isn't your boss. You're her boss."

Fern gasped. "She is not my boss. I'm the eldest."

"She's the doctor."

Tension whirled, destructive as a gale, and Ivy sprang to her feet. "Come, Charlie. I'll dance with you."

A grin dug into one cheek. "You're a lousy dancer."

"But a willing one."

Charlie tipped his head in grudging acceptance, and he swept her into his arms and twirled her around.

What an appealing boy he was, with Mum's good looks and Dad's congeniality. Soon he'd be a most attractive young man.

Her heart twisted as it did each day when she saw boys in the smart blazers of Victoria College. What would become of Charlie now that he'd sacrificed his education? Yet she had to honor his decision and the heart behind it, the heart to help his family.

"What is this?" Fern stood by the sofa, the trousers draped over one arm, the sketch pad shaking in her fist. "Is this supposed to be me?"

Ivy's steps faltered. "Yes." She hadn't paid much attention to her sketching.

Fern's chin quivered. "I never would have thought you to be so cruel."

"Cruel?" Ivy stepped away from Charlie and took the sketch pad.

Her breath caught. The lines of Fern's face always called Ivy's pencil to soft shading and gentle curves. Tonight she'd drawn pointed corners and blunt edges.

In the sketch, Fern's eyes held the sharp darkness of a knife of flint.

Ivy met the point of that flinty knife. "I—I—"

The knife plunged deep. "You always say you draw what you see, you draw what's underneath. Is this what you see? This is ugly!"

"I—I'm sorry."

"You're so cruel." Fern sobbed, dropped the trousers, and ran from the room.

"Never mind her." Charlie patted Ivy's shoulder and returned to the piano. "She's been nothing but cross lately."

Ivy couldn't stop staring at her drawing. Was that truly what she'd seen inside her sister? Yes, Fern had been cross and bitter of late, but this . . .

As Charlie's wistful tune arose, Ivy ripped out her drawing, crumpled it, and stuffed it behind the grate into the fire. It curled and blackened and fed the flames.

What had Ivy done?

Even when cross, Fern cared. She worked hard, all for the family. She'd sacrificed her own house for the family. Even Ivy's restrictive schedule had been created for the benefit of the practice, of the family.

And Ivy had hurt her with the jagged lines of a mindless drawing.

Her chest ached, and she reached for the sketch pad cover to close it.

The next page—a drawing of Gerrit van der Zee.

Last Sunday, he'd sat two rows ahead of her, where Ivy couldn't help but see him. Her pencil had defied her and traced his likeness.

74

If she truly saw what lay underneath, why hadn't she drawn the sickly evil of a collaborating heart? Instead, the image showed a gaze intent on the rector, an innate goodness about the mouth, and lines strong but gentle.

Not a face for the cinema screen, but for the drawing room.

Ivy tore it from the sketch pad. She wouldn't burn it as she had the sketch of Fern—she'd hurt her sister by it. This sketch of the Dutch traitor would join the one she'd drawn the day she met him, hidden in the back of her desk drawer.

She should burn it. Burn both of them.

Why couldn't she?

CHAPTER
9

ST. HELIER
SUNDAY, NOVEMBER 1, 1942

Gerrit matched Bernardus's brisk pace along the Esplanade through St. Helier. Zeal for the Lord had once propelled Gerrit to church, as it now propelled Bernardus. Gerrit's zeal had cooled, but he kept attending church and doing the right things, as if to show the Lord that he wasn't the one who had slacked.

Still, church wasn't without its appeal. Last week, Bernardus had chosen the pew behind the Picot family so he could chat with Charlie, leaving Gerrit behind Dr. Ivy Picot with her shiny black hair curling beneath the rim of her dark green hat.

Ivy had been deep in conversation with Mrs. Galais—who had been shockingly friendly with Gerrit and Bernardus since Charlie had introduced them as his friends.

On Sunday, Ivy had handed the older woman a pencil drawing of a house.

Not as Gerrit would have drawn it. Not unless that house truly had walls bowed out like cheeks or a roof tilted like a hat worn at a saucy angle or an open door like a smiling mouth or light in the windows like sparkling eyes.

"How precious." Mrs. Galais had held the drawing over the pew. "Look, Gerrit. Ivy drew my house."

"It's very nice. I like it." The whimsy of it did appeal to him. "I would have drawn simply what I saw."

"I did draw what I saw." Ivy didn't face him, and her tone chilled.

"Then you see far more than I do."

Mrs. Galais's eyes sparkled like the windows in Ivy's drawing. "She's a marvel, our Ivy. Isn't she?"

From what little Gerrit had seen of her, she was indeed, but his tongue turned to stone. The rector had relieved his discomfort by starting the service.

In the blustery autumn air, Gerrit and Bernardus passed the elegant Pomme d'Or Hotel. Red swastika flags marked the building as requisitioned for use as German naval headquarters.

In front of the Southampton Hotel next door, Charlie Picot stood on the damp pavement in a homburg and a gray overcoat two sizes too big.

He marched up to Gerrit and Bernardus. "Come with me to the *Ormer*."

"Now?" Gerrit frowned at the boy. "We're on our way to church."

"You won't mind being late when you see." Excitement danced in Charlie's dark brown eyes. "Please come."

Bernardus shrugged at Gerrit, inquiring. Gerrit shrugged back, accepting.

"You'll be glad." Charlie strode toward the harbor. "You have your passes, yes?"

"Yes." They couldn't go anywhere without their paybooks.

Guards ringed the harbor, but when the three men showed their papers, they were admitted.

"No one's on board." Charlie led them up the gangplank onto the *Ormer* and into the cabin, where he sat on a wooden bench. "About a month ago, you gave me a letter for your girlfriend in Saint-Malo. A few days later, I delivered it."

"Thank you." Bernardus lowered himself to the bench across from Charlie.

With his insides squirming, Gerrit joined his friend and schooled his face to neutral.

Charlie clasped his hands together between his knees. "On Friday, we docked in Saint-Malo. A girl greeted me at the pier with a . . . a kiss." His cheeks darkened to pink.

Gerrit smiled. "It is the French way."

"No. Here." Charlie tapped his own lips, and the pink turned to red.

Bernardus chuckled. "A pleasant surprise, yes?"

Charlie bobbled a nod. "She took me by the arm—I was too stunned to protest—and she led me to a house. Not the same house as before, but the same lady was there. Your girlfriend, Bernardus."

The resistance contact. Gerrit held his breath. With great effort, he avoided glancing at Bernardus.

Charlie pulled an envelope from inside his coat. "She asked me to deliver this to you."

"Thank you." Bernardus stretched across for the letter.

Charlie didn't surrender it. "She said you were to hold it to the light but not too close."

A frown pulled at Gerrit's lips, but he resisted. Why would they need to hold it to the light?

Charlie pressed the envelope into Bernardus's hand. "She made me repeat it, but she refused to answer my questions."

"Thank you. I'll do as she asked." Bernardus tucked the envelope into his greatcoat, but a stiffness to his tone said he didn't understand the instructions either.

"You know what I think?" Charlie grinned and leaned closer. "It's in secret ink."

Gerrit sucked in a breath. "Secret—"

"When you were boys, did you ever write a message in lemon juice? You could read it by holding it close to a flame. Here."

Charlie pulled a matchbox and a candle stub from his pocket. "Let's see what it says."

Bernardus shot Gerrit an alarmed look. "Thank you, but it isn't nearly that exciting. My girlfriend uses paper with a watermark. You can see it if you hold it to the light."

Charlie let out a scoffing sound. "Nonsense. The meeting was very hush-hush. Your girlfriend is in the resistance, and so are you."

Gerrit's blood chilled, crackled.

"You're mistaken," Bernardus said in a measured tone. "You mustn't say things like that in public, or you'll get yourself killed."

"It all makes sense now." Charlie struck the match. "You aren't like the others. Bernardus, you just warned me. A real Nazi would have had me arrested."

No color remained in Bernardus's cheeks. "I don't care to see young men come to—"

"And Gerrit." Charlie held the match to the blackened wick. "You fed the Todt workers."

"I . . ." Truth clogged his throat.

A flame wiggled above the stub of the candle. "Your sack was full when you went into the hold and empty when you came out, and the hold smelled of Camembert. You're good men, both of you. Why did you join OT?"

"We already told you." Bernardus scooted forward to stand.

Charlie's face lit up. "I think you joined to spy. It's fantastic. And I think your resistance friends want me to be your courier."

Absolutely not, and Gerrit's muscles clenched. He should leave. They should both leave. But Bernardus had also frozen in place, halfway out of his seat.

Charlie waved his hand toward shore. "Whatever you're spying on, you have no way to send the information off the island, do you? But I do. And I want to do so."

A million arguments swarmed in Gerrit's mind.

"You think I'm too young." Charlie's smile hardened. "But it makes me look innocent. Same reason they sent Marie to fetch me. Simply a pretty girl meeting her boyfriend at the docks."

"That's quite enough." Bernardus stood. "Please don't spin stories. You'll land in prison, and you'll get us arrested too."

Gerrit also stood. "We're late to church."

Charlie didn't rise, and he huffed. "You can trust me. I'm smart, and I'm discreet. I brought you somewhere private to deliver the letter, yes? And I'm a physician's son. I've watched my father and sister discuss patients whilst guarding their privacy. And the three of us—we're already known to be acquainted. We even have a place to meet—at church."

Bernardus stepped toward the cabin door. "Speaking of church, we are indeed late."

Charlie bolted to his feet, and the flame in his eyes matched the candle in his hand. "I know you're worried about me getting arrested, tortured, killed. I understand. But I want to do something that matters. My friends—they play pranks on the Germans. They slash tires and siphon petrol, but it doesn't truly matter. They could get arrested and killed for something of no account. But this—this would matter."

Bernardus opened the cabin door. "For your sake, we will forget we ever had this conversation, yes, Gerrit?"

"Yes. You should too," he said to Charlie.

The boy's upper lip curled in frustration. "I want to help. I hate how the Germans treat people—the Todt workers, the Jews, the deportees. Please let me help."

Gerrit's chest hurt for Charlie. He also wanted to do something that mattered. More than anything, he wanted to draw those maps and send them to the Allies. But not at the expense of a young man's life.

Gerrit stepped closer. "Your sisters need you alive."

The flame died in Charlie's eyes.

With one breath, Gerrit blew out the candle.

The Very Reverend Matthew Le Marinel spoke the final words of the benediction, and Ivy opened her eyes.

"Oh, good." Thelma Galais beamed her smile toward the back of the sanctuary. "Our nice young men came. It isn't like them to miss church."

Nice young men? Surely she didn't mean . . .

Ivy followed her line of sight to the back pew on the right, where that Mr. van der Zee was looking straight at her.

She whirled to face front and gathered her Bible and purse. Nothing nice about a man in Organisation Todt, but she held her tongue so she wouldn't disillusion the sweet woman who saw good in everyone.

"Your brother came too."

"He did?" Charlie had been away with the SS *Ormer* for several days.

Charlie made his way down the aisle, with an unusual element of restraint in his smile.

"I'm glad you're home again." Fern stood and pecked him on the cheek.

Ivy did likewise. "What's wrong, Charlie?"

"Wrong? Nothing." He widened his smile, most surely to prove his point, but actually disproving it. Disappointment or frustration flickered in the background.

The little boy who'd poured out his heart to her was becoming a man, so she managed a smile in return.

"Excuse me." Fern slipped past Charlie to chat with her friends.

"And I see Bertie Nicolle." Charlie gave Ivy a polite nod and joined one of his friends from Victoria College in the back pew on the left. He passed the two Dutchmen without even a glance.

Good. Perhaps he'd seen their true nature. Had that caused her brother's disappointment?

If it didn't require meeting the collaborator's gaze, she'd glare at him.

"Did I tell you?" Mrs. Galais adjusted her eyeglasses. "I received a postcard from Frank and Edna."

"You did? How are they?" About a month before, the International Red Cross had promised to watch over the welfare of the deportees from the Channel Islands—over a thousand from Jersey and nearly a thousand from Guernsey and Sark.

"They're doing well, from what I can tell." In her dark blue coat, Mrs. Galais led the way up the aisle. "They're at an internment camp in southern Germany, as the Red Cross said. They're comfortable and well-fed but asked me to send their warm clothes."

"They could take so few possessions. I'm glad you're allowed to send more now." Outside, the dove-gray clouds had parted, and sunshine poured through the ragged hole and dripped liquid light on the churchyard. The scent of damp flagstone and moss filled the air.

"Oh!" A flurry of dark blue, a leg swinging up in the air, a thump.

"Mrs. Galais!" Ivy dropped to her knees beside her friend. "Are you hurt?"

Mrs. Galais lay sprawled on her back, her hat askew. "Oh dear."

"Where do you hurt?" Ivy felt behind her head—no blood, thank goodness. "Did you hit your head?"

"No, no." Her left hand fumbled for her right shoulder.

A man knelt on Mrs. Galais's other side. "May I help you up?"

"Oh, you dear man." Mrs. Galais stretched her hand to him.

To Gerrit van der Zee—who took that hand.

Ivy's stomach contracted, and she raised an arm. Not to shove him away—if only she could!—but to delay the assistance. "I need to examine her first."

"Yes, Dr. Picot." A light Dutch accent—and respect—lilted in his deep voice.

And respect radiated from the clear blue-green of his eyes, so clear she could see straight through.

Ivy wrenched her gaze back to Mrs. Galais, and she gently palpated her right shoulder. "Tell me when it hurts. Are you feeling pain anywhere else?"

"Only in my dignity." Mrs. Galais felt around her face. "Oh dear. My glasses."

"Here they are, ma'am. I'll get your purse." Mr. van der Zee handed her the glasses and pushed up to standing on long, lanky legs, with a stumble as if a youth still unaccustomed to the length of those legs.

Ivy huffed. Those legs were encased in Nazi brown.

Parishioners gathered about, all eager to help their beloved Mrs. Galais.

"Such a fuss for nothing." Mrs. Galais tutted her tongue.

Nothing felt amiss in the woman's shoulder, so Ivy—and Charlie—helped her to sitting.

"I took most of the fall in my bum." Mrs. Galais spoke low and close, with amusement in her hazel eyes. "Despite rationing, it's still amply padded."

Ivy chuckled. "You may have some bruising tomorrow, but don't hesitate to ring for—"

"For any reason at all, precious Ivy." Mrs. Galais sat taller and stretched out one hand. "Dearest Gerrit, will you and Charlie please help me to my feet? What a blessing to have strong young men at my beck and call."

Ivy's jaw dangled, but what could she do? The Dutch collaborator and Ivy's darling brother helped the Jerseywoman to her feet.

Then Mr. van der Zee handed over the purse with a slight bow. "May I escort you home?"

"That would be—"

"Most unnecessary." Ivy scrambled to her feet and hooked her arm through Mrs. Galais's. "We thank you for your help, but Charlie and I will see her home."

"I will too." From behind, Fern brushed off Mrs. Galais's coat.

"Very well." Mr. van der Zee picked up Ivy's own purse and

Bible—at least she'd thought to place her Bible on top of her purse—and handed them to her. "I understand."

After a moment's hesitation, Ivy took her belongings.

Her hand brushed his. Her gaze locked with his.

Warmth. Connection.

Ivy screwed her eyes shut and wiped her hand on her coat. "Come along, Mrs. Galais."

On Hill Street, the pavement allowed only two to walk abreast. Since Mrs. Galais's gait and pace had returned to normal, Ivy dropped behind Charlie and Mrs. Galais.

"What happened in the churchyard?" Fern walked close to Ivy's side with an inquisitive spark in her eyes.

"Mrs. Galais slipped on—"

"No, no. With you and Gerrit van der Zee."

"With . . . ?" Ivy's jaw drifted open, and she snapped it shut. "Nothing. He insisted on helping, and I couldn't stop him."

A little laugh danced in the air. "Oh, sweet Ivy. Can't you see? He's smitten with you."

"Smitten!"

Charlie and Mrs. Galais glanced back at her.

Ivy assumed an unassuming smile until they faced forward again. "That's utter rubbish," she whispered to her sister.

"No, *that* is rubbish. He can't take his eyes off you in church. Now, he may not be the handsomest of men and he's rather un- gainly, but he'd provide well for you."

Ivy's feet glued to the pavement. "Fern! He wears a German uniform."

"Charlie thinks well of him. And isn't it time we looked past the uniforms? The Germans are here to stay."

In her mind, Ivy saw a veil of inky black descend over the oak- brown of Fern's eyes.

Ivy blew out a breath and strode after Charlie and Mrs. Galais.

Why was she suddenly seeing darkness in her own sister and light in the enemy? Perhaps Ivy was the one who needed eyeglasses.

84

CHAPTER
10

Uncle Arthur greeted them at the farmhouse door, wearing his good suit from attending church in St. Peter. "Happy birthday, Ivy."

"Thank you." She stepped inside to see Leo and Ruby Bissell. "Uncle Leo! Aunt Ruby! I'm so happy to see you."

Aunt Ruby, Dad's youngest sister, gave Ivy a hug. "We see each other every day, silly goose. Where's Fern?"

Ivy leaned closer to lower her voice. "Occupation Disease." The increased roughage in the rationed diet brought frequent bouts of dysentery, even as it reduced cardiac disease and gout.

"Poor Fernie."

Ivy murmured her sympathy. Her sister's misery was compounded by the arrival of Billy and Freddy's birthday, which they shared with Ivy. The boys were now ten years old, and Fern couldn't hug them or bake for them or tease them about how tall they were. Only twice-yearly messages from Dad, Mum, and Bill informed her of the boys' growth.

Ivy hung her coat on a peg. The Jouny farmhouse was as cold

85

as all Jersey homes nowadays, but heat radiated from the kitchen. "Is Aunt Opal in the kitchen?"

"She's running behind." Aunt Ruby settled into a wooden chair and adjusted her glasses. "But she won't let me help."

Aunt Opal peeked out of the kitchen, her cheeks flushed. "I won't let you help either, Ivy." Her voice rasped a bit. "What a pretty dress."

"Thank you." Ivy fingered the burgundy wool gabardine. "It's Fern's birthday gift. She remade one of Mum's old dresses she found in the attic. She's so talented."

"Want to hear the latest news?" Uncle Arthur gestured for Ivy and Charlie to sit on the sofa with Uncle Leo, and he sat in an armchair.

"I would." Charlie's eyes gleamed. "The *Evening Post* isn't allowed to publish much, but it's clear the British and the Americans are sweeping the Germans out of North Africa."

Uncle Leo chuckled. "The Huns here are as skittish as newborn calves."

"They should be." Uncle Arthur leaned forward. "The Vichy French surrendered in Morocco and Algeria, and our boys are chasing the Germans back through Libya."

"Remember not to repeat this on the docks. There are informers everywhere." Uncle Leo stabbed a finger in Charlie's direction. "If you must tell your friends, speak in Jèrriais. It confounds the Germans."

Ivy creased the gabardine in her fingers. The prison on Gloucester Street, next door to the General Hospital, teemed with men and women arrested for owning a wireless set or for spreading news from the BBC. "Do be careful, especially around those Todt men."

Charlie kept his chin low. "Bernardus and Gerrit aren't what you think."

A slow sigh leached from her lungs. They weren't what Charlie thought either, despite Gerrit's chivalry to elderly women.

"They feed the Todt workers. The Russians. On the sly." Charlie lifted his chin, and the disappointment or frustration Ivy had observed the past fortnight washed away in a sea of conviction.

They fed the workers? That seemed unlikely. Why would men in an organization that beat its workers show kindness to them? Ivy had now treated two men who had escaped Nazi deprivation and abuse. "Regardless, don't—"

"I don't. I know better." An edge crept into his voice, a reminder to all that he was no longer a child. Then he brightened. "But it's your birthday. I have presents."

"You shouldn't have done." The shops were practically empty, and any remaining goods were dear. "Having all of you together is the best present I could receive."

"Good." Uncle Arthur clapped his hands on his knees. "That's all we're giving you."

Ivy joined in the laughter.

"This didn't cost much at all." Charlie handed Ivy her own wristwatch—ticking.

She gasped and buckled it around her wrist. "Thank you. How—"

"A watchmaker in Saint-Malo fixed it. Now Fern can stop harassing you."

"Harassing?" Uncle Arthur said.

"It isn't that bad." Ivy held the watch to her ear and savored the sound. "She sets timetables for me, but I'm hopeless without a watch. I have no sense of time."

Aunt Ruby sniffed. "I've seen those timetables. Our dear Fern does run a tight ship."

"I couldn't do it without her."

Aunt Ruby crossed her arms, clad in a dark blue jumper. "She'd have no ship to run without you."

"Oh, Fern would find something to run," Uncle Leo said.

Charlie snickered.

"Charlie!" Ivy said.

"Uncle Leo said it." He pointed at his uncle, whose shoulders jiggled with laughter.

Correct or not, Ivy didn't like talking about someone who wasn't present.

"She is efficient, our Fern. An excellent quality." Aunt Ruby's dark eyes turned serious. "But you mustn't let her talk down to you, especially in front of the patients. It undermines their respect for you. I've spoken to her about that."

Aunt Ruby had spoken to Fern? Ivy wrestled up a little smile. "It isn't that bad. And I know Fern is unhappy, which makes her crosser than usual. Not only is she separated from her family, but she's working for her younger sister."

"She's jealous," Charlie said. "You're a doctor, and she isn't."

Ivy's shoulders squirmed. "She never wanted to be a doctor." If anything, Ivy was the one who ought to be jealous of her gorgeous sister with her gaggle of friends.

"You depend on your sister, just as you always depended on your father." Aunt Ruby tipped her head, her gray-streaked hair rolled on the sides and coiled in the back. "It's time you depended on God alone and trust the skills he gave you."

"Thank you. I'll try." Ivy edged forward in her seat. "I should check with Aunt Opal."

"I'm waiting for the blancmange to set," Aunt Opal called, followed by a cough.

"It's worth the wait." Uncle Arthur rubbed his belly, far leaner than it had been two years earlier. "She does wonders with carrageen moss."

Joan de Ferrers and the other island chemists did quite a business turning the reddish seaweed into a powder that became gelatinous when boiled. Miss de Ferrers used it to make syrups more palatable, and Aunt Opal used it to make a splendid dessert.

"I have another gift for you," Charlie said.

"You shouldn't have done. This is all I need." Ivy stroked the brown leather of her watchstrap.

"You'll like this." Charlie fiddled with something under the wing of his jacket. "The real reason you hate the timetables is because you can't draw."

Ivy sighed. She could draw only in the evenings, and only the same subjects over and over. When she saw something breathtaking on her rounds, she was powerless. "I understand why it's necessary. When I draw, I get caught up, and hours pass. That isn't fair to my patients."

"All right, Dr. Picot." Charlie leveled a fatherly look at her. "When Uncle Arthur had a cut on his leg, did you amputate?"

"Of course not." Ivy slid her uncle a smile. "Perhaps I should have done."

Uncle Arthur gave her a mock scowl.

"Well, Fern amputated your drawing, when all you needed was some ointment. Or a kitchen timer." Charlie lifted a little steel timer and a big grin. "I obtained it through the 'Exchange and Mart' column in the *Evening Post*, traded for some of Dad's tobacco."

Ivy turned the dial, and it started ticking. The loud ding would break into Ivy's dreamworld when she was drawing. In fifteen minutes, she could sketch an outline, the essence of what had attracted her. Then she could finish the drawing in the evening.

She clasped the timer to her chest. "Charlie, you're brilliant. And so thoughtful."

He flapped a hand at her, and his cheeks reddened.

"Speaking of kitchens and timing..." Aunt Ruby frowned at the kitchen door.

"I'll check." Ivy stood and set the timer on the sofa. "I didn't greet Aunt Opal properly anyway."

Aunt Opal sat at the kitchen table. She sprang to her feet and to the stove. "It's almost ready."

Aunt Opal never sat when cooking. And her color was high. Her voice rasped.

"Are you all right?" Ivy asked.

"Of course." Her neck contorted as she swallowed, and she wobbled as she stirred the pan on the stove.

"Let me see your throat."

"Nonsense. It's nothing to—"

"Dad always says doctors make the worst patients. Must I add doctors' daughters to the list? Let me see." Ivy came beside her aunt.

"It's nothing." Her sigh released a foul odor. A familiar odor.

Ivy gagged. The odor of the sickroom where she'd watched Dulcie des Forges die. The odor of Overdale Isolation Hospital right now.

She set her fingers on her aunt's chin and turned her toward the light from the kitchen window. "Open wide."

Ivy needed no torch to see the gray membrane on her aunt's tonsils, no thermometer to detect her aunt's fever.

She moved the pan off the stove. "It looks like diphtheria."

"Diphtheria? That's a children's disease." Aunt Opal groped for the pan handle.

Ivy stilled her aunt's hand. "This epidemic is hitting adults too. We're all weakened by our poor diets. I'll send you to Overdale straightaway."

"Right now?" Bleariness dulled Aunt Opal's dark brown eyes. "But dinner—"

"We'll make do." Ivy went to the kitchen door. "I'm afraid we have a change in plans. Aunt Opal might have diphtheria."

"Diphtheria?" The cry circled the room.

"Uncle Leo and Aunt Ruby, please go home," Ivy said. "Even if you had the disease as children, we mustn't take chances. Uncle Arthur, please pack a bag of necessities for Aunt Opal. Charlie, please go to the telephone box on the road and ring for an ambulance—then go home straightaway. You never had diphtheria."

"An ambulance?" Aunt Opal said from behind Ivy. "That's hardly necessary."

"It's quite necessary." Ivy leveled a firm gaze at her aunt. "The

Germans requisitioned your car, and you mustn't exert yourself by bicycling. Charlie?"

"On my way." Footsteps pounded to the door.

"Diphtheria?" Aunt Opal sank into a kitchen chair, and her eyebrows tented.

"We caught it early. That makes for a good prognosis." Ivy gave her the most comforting, most confident smile she could muster.

Even as fear wrenched through her gut.

CHAPTER
11

Rocks weighted down the blueprint on a table at the construction site, but Gerrit wouldn't mind if the wind flung his detailed drawings into Rozel Bay.

To Gerrit's left, Schmidt, the site foreman, folded his thick arms. "You modified the design of the Type 670 casemate?"

To Gerrit's right, Bernardus toed the ground, softened by a persistent mist. "The Rozel conglomerate in the area lies on a graded base of mudstones, siltstones, and microbreccias."

The foreman's heavy gray brows rose over protruding eyes.

Gerrit gave the man his most serious nod. "It means the rocky soil isn't stable. I needed to compensate for that and design features to support the casemate so it can bear the weight of the gun."

Schmidt huffed. "When plans are modified, they must be approved by headquarters, by bureaucrats in Paris. That could take weeks. Months."

So Gerrit hoped. "I'm afraid so, but it's necessary."

"Quite," Bernardus said.

A muttered curse, and the foreman waved his hand over the

blueprint. "That will delay my work. My supervisor will not be pleased."

Gerrit managed a sympathetic murmur. "He'd be even less pleased if you finished construction quickly and the casemate tumbled into the bay."

A quieter curse, and Schmidt settled his hands on his hips.

Gerrit shifted the rocks off the blueprint and rolled it up. "While you wait, you can do the preparatory work we discussed. But how much work can you complete in winter anyway?"

Schmidt glared at the rough gray clouds overhead. "The weather favors the English."

Gerrit slid the rolled blueprint into a tube. For once, something did favor the Allies—and Gerrit and Bernardus's goals.

Outright sabotage would be futile and fatal, but conscientiousness offered a subtle form of sabotage. Painstaking attention to detail. Investigating every potential problem. Performing soil studies. Modifying plans and drafting new sets of blueprints. Such actions had allowed them to delay a handful of projects until winter. Then winter caused its own delays.

It wasn't much. In fact, it was pathetically little. But it was all they had.

Gerrit and Bernardus bid the foreman farewell and left the construction site, passing a squad of workers huddled in thin clothing.

"We should give them our coats," Gerrit said.

"They'd be presumed guilty of theft and punished." Bernardus whacked Gerrit in the arm. "Come on. I have the wild plans. You're the voice of reason. Don't mix up our roles."

Gerrit gave his friend half a smile. When they reached the road, they mounted the bicycles they'd propped against a tree and pedaled east along La Grande Route de Rozel.

On occasion, Gerrit saw Demyan Marchenko and passed on packets of food, but with over five thousand foreign workers in Jersey, the problem was too large for one man to solve.

Those workers were making their own solutions, breaking out of their camps at night and begging for food from local farmers—or stealing it. Dozens of workers were missing.

Two days earlier, a Jerseyman had been killed while protecting his shop from theft, and the Germans were searching house by house for escapees.

The narrow road curved around a promontory, opening a vista over the sea to the east.

Bernardus hopped off his bicycle, rested it against the hedges on the landward side of the road, and crossed to the seaward side. "Beautiful land, ja?" Bernardus said in Dutch.

"Ja." Gerrit parked his own bicycle and followed his friend down a footpath until they reached the point. A veil of mist concealed France, lying about thirty kilometers to the east. If only he could sail the tube with the blueprints across the waters, under the mist, and to the resistance.

"I saw Charlie Picot on the docks this morning. He gave me this." From the pocket of his greatcoat, Bernardus pulled out a—lemon.

Gerrit hadn't seen a lemon since the Nazis invaded the Netherlands in May 1940. He'd forgotten the brilliance of yellow, the tangy smell. "How . . . ?"

"He said he got it in France. Black market, no doubt." Bernardus rotated the fruit in his gloved hand. "Enterprising lad."

He was. "Why did he give it to you?"

A slight smile creased Bernardus's cheeks. "He only said, 'I hope you find it of use.'"

Gerrit could still see the candle flame reflecting in Charlie's bright eyes as he talked about secret messages in lemon juice.

He scowled at Bernardus. "No."

Bernardus shrugged, and his smile deepened.

Gerrit took one step closer. "You didn't tell him about the letter, did you?"

"No. Did you?"

"Of course not." When held to the light, the secret ink in the letter from Saint-Malo had revealed the resistance suggestion to use Charlie as a courier, to smuggle pieces of Gerrit's maps folded inside the boy's shoes.

Gerrit and Bernardus had not replied to that letter, their silence serving as refusal. Sending maps of German military installations in plain ink would be foolish. If Charlie were searched for any reason—like buying lemons on the black market—and they removed his shoes in the search, he would be tortured and shot, and during torture might condemn countless others to death.

Bernardus tossed the lemon up and down. "Charlie has never repeated his offer. Until now."

The yellow orb rose and fell and rose again. With one gesture, with few and carefully chosen words, Charlie had indeed repeated his offer—and his willingness to participate.

Bernardus snatched the lemon from the air and held it in his fist toward Gerrit. "We should do it."

"No. This changes nothing."

"This changes everything."

"He's still a fifteen-year-old boy. I won't risk his life." The lovely face of Ivy Picot flashed through his mind. How she doted on her little brother. How she protected him.

"He's willing to risk his own life." Bernardus shook his fist. "Trace the maps in lemon juice, and I'll write a florid love letter in regular ink on the other side. It'll work. We have the network's instructions on how Charlie should transfer the maps in Saint-Malo, his 'cutout,' they call it."

Gerrit shut his eyes against all that yellow. "How can we trust those instructions? That cutout? It's too far out of our hands, out of our sight, out of our control. We can't guarantee the maps will reach the Allies."

Bernardus fell silent, then sighed. "Could we ever?"

"No, we couldn't." Heavy though they were, Gerrit's eyelids lifted. "We can't do it. I refuse to be responsible for more deaths."

"More?"

Gerrit's mouth twitched. He'd said too much. He turned for the footpath. "We should go. Dinner."

"Deaths? Whose deaths are you responsible for?"

Gerrit forged his way up the path. Didn't Bernardus know? Of course not. How could he? Gerrit had certainly never told him.

"What are you saying?" Bernardus's tone pierced Gerrit's back like a sword.

"Dirk," Gerrit said. "Cilla."

"Dirk? Cilla?" Bernardus grabbed Gerrit's arm and jerked him around. "What did you do?"

"Nothing!" Gerrit tried to wrest his arm free, failed. Tried to wrest his gaze from Bernardus's gaze—even more piercing than his tone. Failed again.

"I did nothing." Gerrit's voice deflated. "Or not enough. I don't know."

Bernardus's fingers dug into Gerrit's bicep. "What did you do to Dirk? Tell me."

Gerrit lowered his head and yanked his arm free. "He told me he was going to confront that mob attacking the Jews. I told him not to. I said his work with the underground newspaper was too valuable to risk. He—he asked me to go with him. I refused." His voice caught, and he jerked his head to the side. Away.

A deep groan from Bernardus. "What could you have done? You're no fighter."

"No." Gerrit's left hand ached, and he rubbed it. "But I might have been able to—"

"To what? Negotiate? With a violent Nazi mob?" Bernardus sank down to sit on a boulder. "You're no more responsible for Dirk's death than I am. I didn't go with him either."

No, he hadn't, but Gerrit kept rubbing his hand.

"What about Cilla?" No sharpness remained in Bernardus's tone.

"The day Dirk died—she saw him die, remember?—she asked me to help her escape to England. I told her it was impossible."

"I'll say. We didn't have escape lines to help people flee back then. Even now, it's dangerous and difficult."

"I didn't even try. Didn't even investigate the possibility." Gerrit waved his arm toward the sea, toward home. "I said her work was too important to the resistance group—the same group we dissolved only a few weeks later. And she—I don't know what she did."

"We'll never know. But she did it. Not you." Bernardus rose from the boulder and handed Gerrit the lemon. "Only you can make this decision. Charlie is willing to be a courier. I have the contacts, the knowledge of the resistance network. But only you can draw the diagrams."

The lemon shone with freshness in Gerrit's hand. "He's so young."

"So eager. A boy like that will find a way."

Gerrit winced. If they turned Charlie away, he might find an even more perilous path. "So many ways for boys to die nowadays."

"What about us? Dying a bit each day, building for the enemy, closing our eyes to suffering, our brave decision to join Organisation Todt in vain." Echoing Gerrit's own thoughts.

With the lemon in his right hand, Gerrit flexed his left hand over and over. They'd joined OT to send diagrams and maps to the Allies. Charlie had offered them a means to do just that, to make everything worthwhile. "If only I could know the maps would arrive in England."

Bernardus's eyes grew as gray as the clouds. "I was wrong to give you a guarantee before. Arrogant, even. Only God knows the future. We have to trust him."

Gerrit sniffed.

Bernardus let out a wry chuckle. "Ah, that's it, ja? You're willing to risk your life, but trusting God? That takes far more courage."

Gerrit wanted to trust again, needed to trust again, but how?

He frowned at the fruit in his hand. Somewhere in Spain,

God had made the lemon. He'd guided it north to Saint-Malo, to Charlie Picot, and across the waters to Gerrit.

If God could orchestrate that—and he had.

And if God was good—and he was.

And if he knew the future—and he did.

Then Gerrit had to trust.

CHAPTER
12

Ivy stroked Penny Surcouf's little pink cheek. "Her color's returned," she said to Penny's mother, "and her eyes are bright. She's made a full recovery from the diphtheria."

Aunt Opal had also come through the worst of it, but she would remain in Overdale Isolation Hospital for a few more weeks. If Ivy hadn't sent her to hospital when she had . . .

A tiny shudder, and she worked up a smile for her three-year-old patient. "Be sure to drink all your milk, Penny, so you grow big and strong."

A knock on the examination room door. "Another patient, Ivy."

The third time Fern had interrupted, and Ivy stiffened. "In a minute, Mrs. Le Corre."

"I'm sorry to be such a bother." Mary Surcouf wrestled her daughter's arms into a tiny blanket coat. She blinked rapidly, her eyes red.

Ivy settled a hand on Mary's arm. "You are never a bother. You love your daughter, and you've been worried about her."

She nodded a trembling chin. "I—I thought I was going to lose her."

They'd come dangerously close. "Look how much better she is."

"Thank you." With a watery smile, Mary departed with her daughter on her hip.

Out in the surgery's waiting room, Fern stood before a seated young man. "I do apologize. Ivy is running late again. I'm afraid she's rather easily distracted."

Ivy gaped at her sister. Aunt Ruby said she'd talked to Fern about this. All Ivy wanted was harmony in the family, but Fern kept striking discordant notes.

The young man stared at Ivy. "I—I'll come back another day." He dashed out the front door.

Fern clucked her tongue as she returned to the receptionist's desk. "We can't afford to keep losing patients due to your tardiness."

Struggling for words, Ivy glanced at her wristwatch. "I'm only ten minutes behind."

Fern sat and wrote in the appointment book. "He didn't want to wait."

Ivy squeezed her eyes shut. After she prayed, she smoothed her white coat and approached her sister's desk. Fern had styled her sable hair in a fashionable roll framing her lovely face, and Ivy unstuck her tongue from the back of her teeth. "He didn't leave because he had to wait. He left because you made me sound unprofessional."

Fern's mouth puckered on one side as if to say that Ivy had brought it on herself.

No, she hadn't. "You called me 'Ivy,' not 'Dr. Picot,' although I've reminded you not to do so—and although I always call you 'Mrs. Le Corre.'"

Long black eyelashes fluttered. "It's hardly—"

"You said I was easily distracted. That doesn't inspire confidence in me as a doctor."

"Then make a better effort."

Ivy's hands coiled at her sides. "I am never distracted when seeing patients. They have my full attention, which is why I took longer with Mrs. Surcouf. She needed reassurance after her little girl almost died."

"You have more than one patient." Fern waved a hand toward the door. "Well, you did until Mr. Wilson left."

All her life, Fern had sloughed blame off her own back and onto Ivy's. Not today. Ivy wiggled her shoulders to release the weight. "He left because you belittled me."

Fern gasped. "How can you speak to me like that?"

"How can you speak *about* me like that?" Ivy's voice strengthened.

"We don't have time for this." Fern shoved back her chair and stood. "You need to start your rounds."

Ivy braced herself against the desk. She'd seen patients in the surgery for four hours straight. "After lunch."

"You'll have to eat on the way." Fern handed Ivy her timetable and marched toward the kitchen. "I prepared your lunch."

Ivy scanned the timetable as she walked. This was all wrong. She'd told Fern home visits required thirty minutes. With all the niceties, they took longer than appointments in the surgery, with the offer of tea and the polite refusal, the decision on where to sit, and the "never mind the cat."

And this timetable? Twenty minutes per visit, precisely enough travel time, without even fifteen minutes for sketching—much less eating lunch. All the way to Gorey to see . . .

Ivy paused in the kitchen door. "Didn't you ask these three patients in Gorey to make appointments here in the surgery?"

"I couldn't possibly." Fern bustled about the kitchen. "One is the wife of a jurat. She's far too important."

Ivy forced herself to breathe, to sort her thoughts into words. "She isn't an invalid, and I often see her in town."

Fern closed a cabinet and gave Ivy a pointed look. "Dad never refused a request for a home visit."

Dad had plenty of petrol. "I told you to change my timetables and to ask these patients to come to town. You haven't done so."

Fern curled her upper lip. "How disrespectful of you. Dad would be appalled."

Why couldn't Ivy take her words back into her mouth? Restore peace?

But why should she take back truthful words, gently spoken?

Because she wanted to return to the way things once were, when she'd leaned on Fern, leaned on Dad.

But to lean on God? What would the Lord have her do? Wouldn't he want what was best for the patients—not for their convenience but for their health and peace of mind? If Ivy's own health and peace of mind suffered, her patients would suffer too.

"Ivy!" Fern stood in front of her, shaking a lunch basket. "You're daydreaming again."

Ivy stared at her sister and stretched herself tall and straight. "I love you, and I respect you, but you need to respect me too. I will see the patients in Gorey today, but whilst I'm away, please ring the patients I mentioned before and redo tomorrow's timetable as we discussed."

"Discussed?" Flinty sparks flashed in Fern's eyes. "We discussed nothing. You laid out orders as if I were your servant."

"Please. I need you to—"

"Yes. You need me." Fern shoved the basket into Ivy's hand. "Don't forget that."

"We need each other. Without you, I can't practice medicine. But without me, there would be no practice at all."

Fern dropped a curtsy. "Yes, Your Highness. I'll return to scrubbing the scullery." She stormed out of the room.

Ivy groaned and braced her shoulder against the doorjamb. Leaning on the Lord might be right, but it was far more difficult.

OVERDALE ISOLATION HOSPITAL
TUESDAY, DECEMBER 22, 1942

Ivy reviewed Aunt Opal's chart at Overdale Isolation Hospital with Dr. Noel McKinstry, Jersey's jovial Medical Officer of Health. "When can she be discharged, Dr. McKinstry? Before Christmas?"

"Perhaps. She's making excellent progress," Dr. McKinstry said in his Irish accent. "Thank goodness you made the diagnosis so early."

"Are you talking about me, Doctors?" Although thin, Aunt Opal's voice no longer rasped.

Ivy smiled at her aunt. "It's called consultation."

"Gossip."

Ivy smiled to see her aunt's sense of humor returning. For over a dozen islanders, diphtheria had led to a miserable death. "Dr. McKinstry and I are deciding when to send you home and bring relief to these poor nursing sisters."

A nursing sister in her crisp white apron pushed a cart down the aisle of the crowded ward. "We all adore Mrs. Jouny."

Even so, the nursing sisters were working horrific hours during the epidemic—which was worsening in the damp weather.

Dr. McKinstry returned the chart to its hook on the footboard. "A few more days, Mrs. Jouny. Good day, Dr. Picot." He moved to the patient in the next bed.

Aunt Opal rolled the top of her blanket in her hands. "I so worry about Arthur."

He was rather pathetic without his wife. "Fern and Aunt Ruby take turns bringing him dinner, and Charlie and I visit whenever we can."

"I know, but Christmas."

Ivy patted her aunt's blanketed knee. "Aunt Ruby will host a lovely holiday."

"Your sister too." Aunt Opal's pale lips spread in a smile. "Arthur said she's hosting her own dinner this year."

"She is." Fern's dark mood had passed, and she hummed and sang as she made La Bliue Brise festive. "She invited several people who have nowhere else to go."

"How kind of her."

"Yes, and mysterious." Ivy lowered her voice to a conspiratorial whisper. "She won't tell us whom she's invited."

"What would we do without our Fern?"

"Indeed, what?" Ivy's smile twitched. She said goodbye to her aunt and made her way outside. After she brushed leaves off her bicycle seat, she coasted downhill along Westmount Road, then pedaled along The Parade toward King Street.

Despite her improved mood, Fern hadn't made any of Ivy's requested changes and blithely switched subjects if Ivy made inquiries.

Recently, when Ivy visited her more ambulatory patients, she explained her situation and asked whether they'd be willing to come to town in the future. Almost all agreed, some with apologies for their lack of consideration, which Ivy defused. Only a few insisted on home visits, and Ivy would continue to oblige them.

Over time, her rounds would become less frenzied.

The streets of St. Helier teemed with shoppers even though the shops were all but empty, including the elegant de Gruchy department store, which had once sold the finest suits and dresses. Now clothing was rationed and scarce. Long queues trailed from the grocers as people waited to purchase their extra Christmas rations of four ounces of chocolate and four ounces of sugar, a delight since rationing provided only three ounces of sugar a week.

Ivy cycled past Carter's Chemist's. Miss de Ferrers hadn't summoned her for a clandestine medical visit in weeks. Did any escapees even remain in hiding?

In the past few weeks, the Germans had rounded up two dozen escaped Russian workers. Although they promised the escapees would not receive severe punishment, only closer confinement and the loss of certain privileges, no one believed them.

Ivy longed to know if Henry and the other two patients she'd treated had evaded arrest. But inquiring about such matters would yield no answers.

A young man with honed features strolled down the pavement, and his gaze pierced Ivy as if he'd heard her thoughts. His shiny new shoes and crisp new civilian coat announced his German nationality, his membership in the secret police.

Ivy's bicycle wobbled, but she kept her expression blank.

Since when did caring for the oppressed become a crime?

CHAPTER
13

Gerrit paused on the doorstep holding the box of Dutch chocolates his mother had sent him. The bright blue door signaled welcome, but only two-thirds of the home's inhabitants would actually welcome him.

Bernardus would have no qualms ringing the bell, but Bernardus had caught the flu.

Only Charlie's insistence that Ivy Picot was celebrating Christmas with Mrs. Galais had persuaded Gerrit and Bernardus to accept the invitation. That and the anticipation of spending the day with their bright young friend.

Their courier.

Gerrit had used every drop of lemon juice to draw a map, and over the course of two weeks, Bernardus had sent sections of that map to his contacts, folded inside Charlie's shoes. Charlie had promised to be discreet over Christmas dinner, and Gerrit trusted him.

But what if the sweet-faced physician learned Gerrit had entered her home?

He stepped back down to the street. He'd leave the chocolates on the stoop and join the OT men in the hotel dining room.

The blue door flew open, and Charlie grinned at him, wearing a dark gray suit. "Gerrit! Thank you for coming. Where's Bernardus?"

The decision had been made for him. "I'm afraid he's ill. He sends his regrets. I brought chocolates from the Netherlands. Happy Christmas."

"Smashing." Charlie took the box. "Come on through."

Behind Charlie, Fern Le Corre greeted Gerrit in a dark red dress and a smile that would liquify the knees of most men.

Gerrit's knees held firm as he crossed the threshold and removed his cap. "Happy Christmas, Mrs. Le Corre. Thank you for inviting me."

"We're honored to have a dear friend of Charlie's in our home. But since we'll be spending Christmas together, you must call me Fern. And you're Gerrit, yes?"

"Yes." Gerrit hung his greatcoat where indicated and followed his hosts past an office, a waiting room, and examination rooms.

Fern led him up a narrow staircase. "The surgery's on the ground floor. The family quarters are upstairs on the first and second floors."

"I see." On the stairway wall hung framed pencil sketches highlighted with splashes of watercolor. Several of Fern and Charlie, of two older adults—their parents, most likely—and of two little boys with Fern's looks.

"This is Ivy's art," Charlie said.

"I thought it might be." Gerrit smiled at the drawings. Upstairs, more of her art graced the hallway—rabbits and kestrels and toads and wildflowers—as well as family photographs.

The dining room was decorated with conventional oil paintings of seascapes and sailing ships, but Gerrit preferred the intimate charm of Ivy's art.

At one end of the table, Fern swept her hand to her right, toward a bank of windows overlooking the street. "You'll sit here, Gerrit. And, Charlie, as the man of the house . . ." She motioned to the head of the table.

In one instant, Charlie transitioned to that man, standing taller, his chest fuller, and he stroked the back of the dark wood chair.

Gerrit pulled out Fern's chair for her and took his own seat. One empty chair stood to his right and two across the table. "Who else is coming?"

A soft thud downstairs as the front door shut.

Fern grinned. "That will be them now."

Charlie chuckled. "Fern won't tell me who the other guests are."

"Surprises are such fun." Fern clasped her hands in front of her chest.

Gerrit murmured his agreement out of politeness, but he'd never been fond of surprises. They were too . . . surprising.

Why wasn't Fern rushing downstairs to greet her guests? Two feminine voices floated up the stairs and down the hall, laughing and familiar.

"Fern!" Charlie glared down the table at his sister. "You told me—"

"Hush, now." Fern rose and fixed a smile on the door.

Gerrit rose too, even as a dark pit formed in his stomach. What had he done?

Mrs. Galais entered the dining room—with Ivy. "Gerrit!" Mrs. Galais beamed at him. "You darling boy. What a lovely surprise. Ivy didn't tell me you'd be here."

Because Ivy didn't know, but Gerrit wrestled up a smile for the elderly woman. "Happy Christmas, Mrs. Galais."

"What is the meaning of this?" Ivy's voice wavered, dark and low.

"I'm sorry." Charlie stretched a hand toward Ivy, his face agitated. "Fern told me to invite Gerrit and Bernardus. I never would have done, but she said you were dining with Mrs. Galais."

"Dear, oh dear." Fern pressed a hand to her chest. "I said Ivy

108

was *bringing* Mrs. Galais. You must listen with more care. Please have a seat, Mrs. Galais, right here next to me."

Ivy still stood, her hands in stiff knobs at her sides.

Gerrit's insides contracted to a writhing lump. "I apologize, Dr. Picot. I wouldn't have accepted the invitation if I'd known."

Charlie's face approached the shade of Fern's dress. "I promise, I didn't—"

"I know, Charlie." Ivy didn't remove her stony gaze from her sister's face.

Charlie huffed. "Fern, why would you do such a—"

"Oh dear." Fern lowered herself to her chair with a flat smile. "We mustn't argue in front of guests, Charlie. Please do be seated."

What had Gerrit walked into? Had Fern arranged this behind her sister's back? For what reason? Well, he wouldn't be a part of it.

He directed a polite smile to his hostess. "Thank you again for the invitation, but I must decline."

"Nonsense." Fern patted the table. "Charlie is allowed to invite his friends, isn't he, Ivy? Dad and Mum loved to show hospitality to strangers, and we couldn't turn away a guest on Christmas Day. Poor Gerrit has nowhere else to go."

Gerrit's left foot edged toward the door. "Actually, I could—"

"Please be seated, Gerrit." Fern patted the table again. "Ivy, doesn't the rector say we should love our enemies and pray for those who persecute us?"

Gerrit winced and stiffened.

Ivy's mouth formed a taut little circle, and spots of red darkened her round cheeks. A quick intake of air, and she thumped down into her chair.

For months, Gerrit had longed to spend time with Ivy. But not like this.

He sat, but inside he erected a wall facing Fern Le Corre, a woman who bent words and people. He'd been bent and so had Charlie, but something told him Ivy was the intended target.

"Please excuse the informality. Charlie, would you please pass

109

the roast pork?" Fern picked up a bowl of parsnips and carrots. "I'm afraid this is simple fare. Although I was able to purchase the traditional pork, I couldn't make the *podin d'Noué*—the Christmas pudding. However, I made a rather nice blancmange."

When the dishes came Gerrit's way, he took small portions. The islanders faced strict rationing, while he was fed well at his billet. Besides, the fuming tension in the room stole his appetite.

After Charlie spoke a blessing, Mrs. Galais sliced her pork and sent Gerrit a sweet smile. "I am glad you're here, dear Gerrit. I've wanted to become better acquainted, but Sunday mornings fly by."

"They do." He didn't have to force a smile. Mrs. Galais and Bernardus were the only people on this island who made him feel like his old self. Not the resistance warrior Charlie saw, nor the dutiful Nazi the OT men saw, nor the slimy collaborator everyone else saw. Just himself.

"Where are you from in the Netherlands?" Mrs. Galais asked. "Do you have family?"

Gerrit swallowed a bite of potato, appropriately salted, even though salt was rationed. "Amsterdam. My parents live there with my two younger sisters. Fine girls. I miss them."

"I can see." Mrs. Galais wore her silver hair back in a knot. "Do you have a wife? Children? A sweetheart?"

"None, I'm afraid." That wouldn't change anytime soon, if ever, and he sliced his pork with more vigor than required. "How about you, Mrs. Galais? Have you always lived in Jersey?"

"Oh yes. Like the Picots, I come from old Norman stock."

"And your family?"

"My precious husband passed away ten years ago. I have one daughter, Edna, and two grandsons. They're away fighting for England."

"You must be proud." Gerrit lifted a forkful of parsnip and paused. He hadn't seen Mrs. Galais with a woman Edna's age. "Does your daughter live in Jersey?"

A shadow passed over Mrs. Galais's hazel eyes. "I'm afraid she and her husband were deported to Germany in September. Frank was born in England."

"Oh no. I'm sorry to hear that." Silence pressed hard over the table, and Gerrit didn't know how to lift it.

"I have a question, Mr. van der Zee." Ivy had spoken. To him. Although her gaze was intent on the rhythm of fork and knife on her plate.

Gerrit lowered his fork so he wouldn't drop it. "Yes, Dr. Picot?"

Fern chuckled. "Such formality on Christmas Day. That'll never do. Ivy, you shall call him Gerrit. Gerrit, please call her Ivy."

He'd do no such thing. For the sake of peace, he wouldn't call her Dr. Picot. But out of respect, he wouldn't call her Ivy. "What is your question?"

Ivy kept slicing, and her tiny chin jutted forward. "As a Dutchman, how can you work for the nation that invaded your country? And build military installations for them?"

Gasps sprang from both ends of the table, objecting to such a question—of a guest!—on Christmas!

"No, no." Gerrit raised a hand and his voice. "It's all right."

Fern and Charlie quieted.

Ivy stilled her knife, and a blush flooded her cheeks. Quite becomingly.

"It's a good question, a fair question." If only he could give a full and honest answer. "In the Netherlands, men between the ages of eighteen and twenty-three must register for labor. But the German labor shortage only worsens. They've called for volunteers throughout the Netherlands, France, even in the Channel Islands, yes?"

"Yes," Charlie said. "But few volunteer."

"It's only a matter of time until the Germans conscript men my age as well. Now, I am a civil engineer and Bernardus a geologist. We'd rather work in our professions than be forced to dig ditches here in Jersey or to assemble weapons in a German factory under Allied bombardment."

Charlie clucked his tongue. "It's more than—"

Gerrit shot him a quick sidelong glance. Better to be thought a collaborator than to endanger the resistance network, which now included young Charlie.

"Well." Charlie straightened his necktie. "I would do the same thing."

Ivy met Gerrit's gaze for the first time, her eyes as hard as onyx. "I wouldn't. And if conscripted, I'd refuse."

Gerrit gave her a slow nod. "Then you are braver than I. But it's easy to know what you'd do when you aren't actually faced with that choice."

Something gray smudged Ivy's gaze.

And something strange bubbled in Gerrit's throat. Words he'd never dream of saying to a woman with such a gentle spirit. Yet he released them. "The Dutch resistance publishes underground newspapers. They sabotage railways and telephone lines. They smuggle military intelligence to the Allies. Dozens in the resistance have been executed. If a member of the Dutch resistance came here, he might wonder why the people of Jersey don't do the same."

A gasp from Charlie. "We do—"

"You do what you can, yes." He held up a hand to silence Charlie, while never moving his gaze from his sister. "But what would he see here? Schoolboy pranks. People hiding wireless sets so they can listen to the BBC. Sheltering escaped Todt workers. Nothing to truly harm the German war effort, not like we see in the Netherlands. But would that Dutchman be right to say the people of Jersey are complacent? Cowardly?"

"We aren't cowardly." Indignation colored Charlie's voice.

The same protest twitched around Ivy's dark eyes.

"I agree," Gerrit said. "You are not. Your island is small, and everyone knows everyone. You have no mountains to hide in, no forests, no large anonymous cities. The ratio of German soldiers to locals is far higher than in any other occupied land. To resist would be to die. So the assumption the Dutchman made would be incomplete."

Fern laughed, light and airy. "One can tell from your speech that you're an engineer. So much logic. Oh my. How did you come to be an engineer?"

Gerrit couldn't break his gaze with Ivy, nor did he want to.

Her eyelids fluttered, and her mouth relaxed. "I do not agree with your decision, but—but I do see it may not be as simple as I thought."

Gerrit gave a single nod in gratitude.

Fern gestured to Gerrit's plate. "How *did* you come to be an engineer?"

Gerrit shrugged and lifted his fork of vegetables again. "My father and uncles own an engineering firm, and I've always loved to build. Not terribly exciting. I'm more interested in hearing how an artistic Jersey girl became a physician."

Ivy fiddled with her fork for a long moment. "I come from a long line of physicians, and I've always wanted to heal." Some of the chill left her voice.

"She's good." Charlie leaned his elbows on the table in a way that would have excited parental protests, had parents been present. "She simply senses when someone is ill or in pain."

"Oh yes." Mrs. Galais patted her belly. "A few years ago, Ivy knew I needed my gallbladder removed when I thought I had only mild indigestion."

"It isn't that unusual of a skill." Ivy swirled a potato in a circle on her plate. "I could tell by the way you moved, the way you held yourself."

"Dad always said it was a gift." Charlie hefted his chin with brotherly pride. "You see beyond the seen."

Fern tutted. "We're embarrassing our Ivy. Tell me, Gerrit. What do you think of our island?"

"It's lovely." And the embarrassed, sensitive, talented healer sitting across from him was the loveliest sight of all.

CHAPTER
14

Across Queen Street, Fern stood in a queue. Ivy angled her umbrella to shield her face, and she ducked down Halkett Place.

How childish to avoid her own sister, but she still smarted from Fern's mean trick on Christmas Day.

Ivy shook out her umbrella and entered the Central Market, lit by windows in the peaked ceiling and enlivened by ornate Victorian ironwork and the hum of conversations. Dozens of vendors sold vegetables and other goods—what goods were available under German rule.

With a huff, Ivy strode through the main concourse.

Fern had lied to Charlie so he would invite Gerrit and Bernardus. She'd sent Ivy to fetch Mrs. Galais so Ivy would be away when the men arrived.

The Christmas dinner had been planned, not to show hospitality to the lonely, but to embarrass and antagonize Ivy.

Her eyes burned, and she blinked rapidly as she passed the fountain in the middle of the market. A fortnight had passed. Why couldn't she forgive Fern as she always did?

Because she *always* did.

Fern often did little things to addle Ivy, crafted well-worded defenses, sometimes blamed Ivy—and Ivy had always forgiven her, excused her, absorbed the blame.

Ivy passed through the doorway on the far side of the market, lifted her umbrella, and stopped. The rain created a shimmering pattern on the streets, the ugliness of asphalt and potholes and gravel obscured by the loveliness of water.

Everyone praised Ivy for seeing things others didn't, but she'd never let herself see the streak of meanness in Fern, obscured by beauty and cleverness and humor and efficiency and episodes of sacrificial generosity. But the meanness had always been there, and Ivy had ignored it in her quest for family harmony.

Heaviness pressed on her chest, and a sigh did nothing to dislodge it. She headed back toward Queen Street, minding her step with her worn-out shoes newly resoled in wood.

Spending Christmas with a man in a Todt uniform hurt far less than knowing Fern had orchestrated it as revenge for Ivy defying Fern's authority.

Even that man in the Todt uniform had seemed to understand. He'd been anxious to leave, to not impose, to relieve her discomfort. Along with Thelma Galais's cheerful diplomacy and Charlie's righteous indignation, Gerrit's consideration had soothed the sting somewhat.

Over and over, Gerrit's actions spoke of a kindly nature, but kindliness with a spine. He'd been direct in defending his decision. Not that she agreed with him. His decision carried a hint of the mercenary, volunteering for safe and stimulating work, rather than being forced to do dangerous and unpleasant work.

Ivy turned onto Queen Street, one street away from where she'd seen Fern. Gerrit said Ivy wouldn't know what she'd do unless she faced that choice. But she had faced that choice.

She opened the door to Carter's Chemist's.

No one was waiting to see Joan de Ferrers, and within minutes,

Joan handed her a bottle. "Mr. Whistler's digitalis. I understand he's one of your patients, yes? You know where he lives."

"Yes." Ivy's voice held steady, although she'd just received her first assignment for the ring since the Germans had rounded up two dozen escaped workers a month earlier. Apparently Mr. Whistler was sheltering an escapee in need of care. After exchanging pleasantries and shilling notes, Ivy departed the shop.

Two men in German Army uniforms strolled down Queen Street.

Ivy sucked in a breath and jammed the bottle deep in her coat pocket as if the label read "crime against the occupying forces."

Surely a physician picking up a medication wouldn't arouse suspicion, but the Germans had made it a crime not to report infractions of their orders. Ivy was defying the Germans not only by treating these poor men but by not reporting those who sheltered them.

Never in her life had she imagined herself a criminal.

She turned for home to fetch her bicycle and medical bag.

"Ivy!" Charlie loped across the street with a package, grinning, and he ducked under her umbrella. "Look. Fern sent me to the grocer for our special ration for the week—eight ounces of dried beans each."

"Lovely." She resisted the urge to wipe the raindrops from her brother's face.

"I'm supposed to meet Fern at—oh, there she is."

Ivy plastered on a smile.

Her sister approached under her umbrella, and her jaw lowered. "Ivy! You're supposed to be halfway to St. Ouen's village by now."

Ivy waved to the west, toward Gloucester Street. "I was seeing a patient in hospital, then I picked up a medication."

Fern's mouth tilted to the side. "Now you're late again. As always, you disregarded the timetable I made for you, ignored all my hard work."

The sourness in Ivy's stomach dissolved her usual apologies. "I'll be leaving now."

"I'm surprised you're even making rounds. I thought home visits were beneath you." Fern sniffed. "I can't believe how many patients have told me you forced them to come to town."

"Forced?" Ivy couldn't force anyone if she tried. She'd merely explained the situation and offered a choice.

Fern jerked her head to the side. "I've done all I can to save the practice as Dad wanted, but you refuse to cooperate. You've left me with no choice but to take another job."

Ivy gasped. "Another—"

"You can't leave the practice," Charlie said. "Ivy needs a receptionist."

"I already hired a new girl. Aunt Ruby can train her."

Ivy's vision blurred, and no amount of blinking would clear it. "You hired someone without consulting me?"

"It's hardly necessary. The new girl is quite capable."

Ivy's breath accelerated. This couldn't be happening.

"Your new job?" Charlie said in a hard voice. "What is it?"

"Oh." Fern adjusted the parcels in her arm and raised a smile. A twitchy smile. "Do you remember that nice officer who allowed us to keep La Bliue Brise? He was so impressed with me—and my German—that he offered me a job on the spot. Every time I see him in town, he repeats his offer. And this time I accepted. I start Monday."

Ivy's chest hollowed out. "The officer? At the Field Commander's headquarters?"

Charlie scowled at Fern. "You can't work for the Germans."

"Why not? You do."

"I do not. It's a Jersey boat."

"Hired by the Germans." Fern's pretty chin edged high. "You mustn't be self-righteous, you two. We do what we must, and for once, my abilities will be appreciated."

Words clogged Ivy's throat, stung her eyes. How could Fern do such a thing?

Fern released a sigh. "If only it weren't necessary. Bill left me without provision, and you can't keep the practice afloat. But my wages will help. Saving the practice is up to me."

Ivy clutched her purse tight to her stomach. Her family was falling apart, and she couldn't stop it.

ST. CATHERINE'S BAY
MONDAY, JANUARY 18, 1943

Oberbauführer Ernst Schmeling studied the plans Gerrit had drawn for tunnels to be bored behind the artillery bunker at Strongpoint Verclut, guarding St. Catherine's Bay. Bernardus described the challenges with the rock formations in the area, and Schmeling complained about a load of cement lost earlier in the month when a cargo ship struck the rocks off Jersey's Noirmont Point. Over one hundred German soldiers on leave had perished.

Gerrit turned up the collar of his greatcoat against the chilly wind that buffeted around the promontory and frosted blue waves white with foam.

Two dozen foreign workers carried lumber from the breakwater toward the bunker, led by Demyan Marchenko.

Whenever possible, Gerrit slipped Marchenko food to share with his men, as he did with other squad leaders who spoke German or English. Marchenko spoke both well.

On the last portion of the journey, the squad of workers left the road and picked their way over rocky soil, with their feet bound in rags—or nothing.

Inside Gerrit's boots, his toes curled, warm and protected.

A cry, and a man stumbled, struggled to keep the beam of lumber on his shoulder. His companion carrying the other end lost his grip. The beam swung to the side and banged a guard in the leg.

The guard fell, cursed. The beam thudded to the ground.

Those men would be beaten.

Gerrit darted around Schmeling.

"Don't." Schmeling grabbed Gerrit's arm. "The guards will handle this."

That's what Gerrit feared.

The guard rose, cursed, truncheon raised.

Marchenko stepped between the guard and his men, and he lifted his hands. "Let him be. It was a simple accident."

"Out of my way." The guard shook his truncheon. "They are lazy, wicked—"

"They are neither." Marchenko spoke with gentle authority. "They are cold, tired, and have no shoes. They are fed like mice but are expected to work like oxen. Yet see, they are already back at work. And they are sorry." He called to the workers in Ukrainian.

"*Tak! Tak!*" The men wrestled their beam onto a pile near the bunker entrance.

"Yes, they are sorry and promise to work twice as hard. If it happens again, I will say nothing." Marchenko tipped his head toward the truncheon.

The guard growled, but the truncheon lowered. "This time only."

"That is fair. Thank you, comrade." Marchenko headed down toward the breakwater.

A rumble rolled in Schmeling's throat. "That Russian is playing a dangerous game."

"He plays it well." Bernardus gestured to the workers. "Those men will now work harder than if they'd been beaten."

"Nein." Schmeling's pale eyes turned to slits. "He is too proud, stands too tall. He needs more respect for his superiors."

In no way was Marchenko inferior. "I'll talk to him. Excuse me, Herr Oberbauführer." Gerrit jogged down the slope before Schmeling could stop him.

At the base of the breakwater, Marchenko stood in a queue before a lorry stacked with lumber.

"Good afternoon, Marchenko." Gerrit spoke in English, which few on the worksite understood.

"Good afternoon, van der Zee."

Gerrit palmed the wedge of cheese in his greatcoat pocket and extended his hand to the Ukrainian. "Thank you for helping those men."

Marchenko accepted the handshake and slid the cheese into his tunic pocket. "I can't help them all."

"Neither can I. But I'm concerned about you."

Marchenko raised his unscarred eyebrow. "I know which guards listen to reason and which don't. I fight only the battles I can win. This battle was worth fighting. Like Stalingrad." His eyes gleamed.

"Soon to be liberated," Gerrit said in a low voice. The Soviets had surrounded the German-occupied city, each day tightening their stranglehold.

"Someday we shall all be liberated." Marchenko turned to the lorry.

Back at the bunker, Bernardus saluted Schmeling. "Thank you, Herr Oberbauführer. Van der Zee and I are due soon at Rozel."

"Yes." Gerrit saluted Schmeling as well. "I need to finish my periodic progress sheet."

"Very good." Schmeling rolled up the tunnel plans. "I'll see you tomorrow."

Gerrit and Bernardus mounted their bicycles. Petrol was in short supply, even for the occupying forces, and Gerrit preferred to cycle anyway, especially on a brisk winter day.

The road wound along wooded slopes surrounding the bay. Gerrit did indeed need to finish his progress sheet at Rozel, but first they had a more cryptic appointment.

After church the day before, Charlie Picot had mentioned his favorite ramble through St. Catherine's Wood and suggested Gerrit and Bernardus might enjoy it. Then he'd leaned closer and whispered, "Tomorrow. Three o'clock."

With a little creativity, Gerrit and Bernardus had fit it into their workday.

Following Charlie's directions, they turned right at a crossroads, heading inland. What did Charlie want to discuss? After Gerrit's lemony maps had been delivered, a few weeks of silence had followed. Then Marie, the young girl who had greeted Charlie at the docks, told Charlie they should not use lemon juice because it wasn't secure.

Yet plain ink was even less secure. Once again, their plans had come to naught.

The road turned to a muddy path, and the men dismounted and pushed their bicycles deeper into woods of moss-covered oak and ash trees, their bare branches dripping from the recent rains.

About half a kilometer into the woods, Charlie Picot leaned back against a tree. He grinned at the men. "We're in business."

"Pardon?" Bernardus said.

Charlie beckoned them closer. "On Friday, Marie introduced me to a British agent."

Gerrit's bicycle slipped from his hands and clattered to the ground. "A British—"

"He liked your map, Gerrit. He wants more, and he provided a way." Charlie pulled a pen from his pocket. "The end screws off and forms a measuring cap. Inside are crystals to make secret ink. Dilute one capful in one ounce of water. You must use this particular pen nib, he said, with a light touch, and hold it at the smallest angle you can."

"My goodness," Bernardus murmured. "The tool of an actual spy."

An ordinary-looking pen lay in Gerrit's hand, with a turned-up brass nib. His fingers pulsed, not claiming the pen. Not rejecting it.

"We mustn't use paper anymore." Charlie squatted beside a duffel bag and unbuckled it. "We're to use silk."

"Silk?" The shops were stripped bare of wool and cotton, much less silk.

"This should last a while." From the duffel bag, Charlie pulled a large bundle of white.

"Is that a parachute?" Bernardus said.

Charlie tipped up a grin. "I believe it's how our British friend arrived in France."

"Charlie!" Gerrit's fingers clenched around the pen. "Do you know what would happen if the Germans found you with an English parachute?"

Bernardus grabbed the parachute and stuffed it back in the bag. "They'll think you found a downed RAF pilot and didn't report it. The penalty—"

"Is death," Charlie said. "That's why I have a cover story. I bought it in France from a man I don't know in exchange for some of my father's tobacco. I'm bringing it to my sisters so they can make . . . girl clothes."

Underthings, he meant, but the boy's innocence didn't amuse as usual. Instead, a shudder ran up Gerrit's arms.

Bernardus sat back on his haunches and looked up into the bare tree branches with a thoughtful look. "Yes, and when you travel to France, you can say something similar, but you bought it in Jersey and are bringing it to your girlfriend in Saint-Malo. You're young enough. They'll believe you."

"And if they don't?" Gerrit brandished the spy pen. "If this ink is visible in any way—"

"They want your maps." Charlie shot up to his feet. "Need them. It's no more dangerous than carrying them in my shoes."

"I don't like it."

Bernardus gave Gerrit a little smirk, but with a fond look. "You don't like anything."

Gerrit huffed, but he lowered the pen.

"I need to do this," Charlie said in a low, hard voice. "Everyone thinks the Picots are collaborators. Let me prove I'm not like Fern—at least to myself."

Gerrit and Bernardus exchanged a confused look. "Like Fern?" Bernardus asked.

"Haven't you heard?" Charlie knelt to the earth again and buckled the duffel. "She's working as a secretary at the Field Commander's headquarters at College House."

The German civil administration? "Why would she do such a thing?"

"Money, she says." Charlie shrugged, his head lowered to his task. "Pride, I say."

Gerrit's mouth drooped open. If Ivy was appalled to see Gerrit in her dining room . . .

"She says she's trying to save the medical practice, but she's ruining it. Dozens of patients have left." Charlie stretched up to standing, now nearing Bernardus's height, and his gaze firmed. "Let me do this. Let me fight for the Allies in the only way I can."

"And the only way we can," Bernardus said.

Gerrit's left hand opened, then flexed around the spy pen. Every day, he built German defenses. The least he could do, the *best* he could do, was to tell the Allies every detail of those defenses.

Dappled light shimmered through the leaves and onto the brass nib. Mightier than the sword? No, but he could fight with it.

CHAPTER
15

Shielded with tissue paper to satisfy blackout regulations, Ivy's torch cast a faint cone of light onto the damp pavement as she walked along The Parade toward Jersey General Hospital for the medical society meeting.

The doctors always talked over her and looked through her, but if they had heard about Fern's new job, Ivy might be cast out. Then how would she stay abreast of news about public health?

She adjusted the heavy load in her arms. Were her gifts a means of buying their respect? Or was she being honest with herself in saying she was donating for the welfare of the island?

Across the square, a dark silhouette of a man rounded the granite pillar of the Cenotaph. He shined a torch with one arm and braced the other arm over his midsection. A man with an injured hand.

"Dr. Picot?" the man asked.

Ivy's torch illuminated the smiling face of Gerrit van der Zee, and her step hitched. She couldn't avoid him, but she could keep the encounter short.

"You're out late," he said. "On rounds?"

"A medical society meeting at the hospital." She resumed walking. "Good night."

"The hospital? I've been trying to find it. Quite lost."

Ivy winced, but good manners—and medical training—prevailed. "Are you injured?"

"I'm afraid I'm not the most athletic of men. I hit a rough patch of pavement and took a tumble from my bicycle. I didn't think much of it, but my hand is swelling. I broke it as a boy."

Something tender in her moved her feet closer. He had long fingers with square tips, and he held them slightly apart in a rounded position that spoke of pain.

The arm he cradled bore the brassard of Organisation Todt, and she stopped short.

But the man was hurting. To deny him care because of his political ideology would be as wrong as the Germans denying care to the Soviets because of theirs.

Gerrit stood only two feet away, the closest she'd stood to him, his gaze soft in the muted light.

She hauled in a breath and turned west. "I'll show you the way."

"Thank you." He fell in beside her. "If it weren't for my injury, I'd offer to carry your books. Notebooks?"

"Sketch pads." Almost three dozen of them.

"Art night at the medical society?" he said in a humorous tone.

Her lips betrayed her and smiled. She wrestled them into a neutral expression. "We have a serious paper shortage in Jersey. Doctors need paper for patient charts, our notes, even prescriptions. And I have more than my share."

Gerrit nodded toward the stack in her arms. "That's quite a lot of sketch pads."

Ivy didn't want to converse, and she sighed. "When I left Oxford, I ordered six sketch pads from my favorite art shop. The clerk misunderstood me and ordered sixty. The shop owner was furious, and he would have fired the poor girl, so I said I had wanted sixty after all."

Gerrit's smile radiated warmth, as always. "How thoughtful of you."

She shifted her gaze to the park grounds on her right, dark in the moonless night. "A fortuitous mistake, since I haven't been able to buy any during the occupation."

"You're giving them away." His voice lowered in concern. "How many will you have left?"

"Two for my medical practice—same as I'm giving the other doctors, two each. And—and one for drawing." Her throat tightened.

"Only one? That won't last long."

No, it wouldn't, and she couldn't speak.

"You must keep more." Indignation lifted Gerrit's voice, and he circled his injured arm, almost bumping her. "I draw too, but as a draftsman. I draw buildings and machines, things without life. But you—I saw your art at Christmas—you draw things with life. You draw *with* life. To do so, it must bring you life too, yes? Like food for your mind, your soul."

Never had someone voiced it in such a way. It was true. Drawing nourished her, and when Fern had deprived her of sketching, she'd felt famished.

Her feet slowed and stopped.

Gerrit stopped too, and his gaze settled down on her, earnest, understanding, alive for what made her feel alive.

"Yes." The word tumbled out, laying a bridge between them.

A bridge she couldn't allow.

She whipped her gaze around. They stood at the corner of Gloucester Street. Across the way rose the stately gray hospital.

"Right now," she said, "about two dozen men and women are lying in hospital, dying from diabetes because we have no insulin. Children and adults are dying from diphtheria because we have no antitoxin. Elderly people like Thelma Galais grow weaker due to a lack of food. Sacrificing my sketch pads for the sake of the medical community—well, it's no sacrifice. It's a mere inconvenience."

"I'm sorry." Gerrit's voice dived low in sympathy—not only for her inconvenience but for the suffering of the islanders.

The bridge remained intact.

"Good evening, Dr. Picot." A man passed—a physician—and he eyed Gerrit.

"Is that the hospital, miss?" Gerrit asked. "Thank you for showing me the way."

He was helping her save face, and she lifted her eyebrows at him.

Gerrit glanced over Ivy's shoulder for a moment, then leaned closer. "You shouldn't be seen talking with me, especially with what your sister's done. Charlie told me."

Ivy's mouth pursed. She'd need to talk to Charlie about discussing private family matters. Except Fern's actions were hardly private.

"This way." She strode toward the hospital, where the Germans had requisitioned the best of the facilities.

"Charlie is quite unhappy about it." Gerrit caught up with her. "How are you managing without Fern? Isn't she your receptionist?"

Wasn't he worried about her being seen talking with him? Yet, sympathy had a strong appeal. "She hired a new girl, but the girl left after only one week." The poor thing didn't understand how to take a telephone message much less handle the appointment book.

"I'm sorry to hear that."

The arched doorway to the hospital neared. "My Aunt Ruby is helping more, and we have adverts in the *Evening Post*—when they have enough paper to print, that is."

"I hope you find someone soon."

"Thank you. And I hope your hand feels better soon. The German clinic is on the ground floor." She pointed the way.

Gerrit gave her a slight smile, a slight bow. "Thank you for your help, Fräulein."

Sure enough, another physician was right behind her.

Ivy spun away and marched inside toward the stairs.

Gerrit's understanding was sweet on the tongue, soothing in the belly, warm in the veins. It . . . nourished.

She wriggled and groaned. She had to rid herself of the sensation. Even if his character were as it appeared, friendship would be wrong and ruinous.

And his lack of honor in joining Organisation Todt cast a dark shadow on that character.

ST. HELIER
SATURDAY, FEBRUARY 27, 1943

Drawing maps on silk in secret ink sounded great until Gerrit tried to do it.

Silk, being silky, wanted to slip. And secret ink, being invisible, made marking his position difficult.

This afternoon, he'd furtively borrowed a detailed map of Jersey from OT Headquarters in St. Helier, to be furtively returned tomorrow morning.

Clamps and weights braced the paper map and a piece of parachute silk on a pane of glass. On his desk in the hotel room he shared with Bernardus, he'd elevated the glass on books and boxes and laid his desk lamp on its side underneath, all to illuminate the lines on the map through the silk.

Holding a pin from his mending kit to where his last pen stroke ended, Gerrit dipped the brass nib in the secret ink and resumed tracing. This master map of the island, marked in a numbered grid, would be used to orient the Allies to future smaller-scale maps of various grid sectors.

Gerrit needed to finish in one sitting, since perfectly realigning the silk over the paper map would be impossible.

The OT men had gone to see a film at the Forum theater and to visit the pubs, and Bernardus had accompanied them to maintain the appearance of loyalty. Without interruptions, Gerrit could finish by eleven o'clock when the electricity in Jersey was cut off each night.

His pen dragged as the ink ran low. With his right hand, he marked his position with the sewing pin, and he took a moment to stretch out the soreness in his left hand. It had never quite healed from his boyhood injury, and the sprain almost three weeks ago had increased the soreness.

Warmth filled his chest from the memory of Ivy's upturned face in the dim light and from the evidence of her generosity, her thoughtfulness, and her spirit.

In different times, he would have done everything possible to spend more time with her. Instead, he avoided her company to protect her reputation.

With great restraint, he had waited a full week before sending Charlie home with a ream of paper from OT Headquarters and with strict instructions not to tell Ivy the source.

The glass grew warm in the northwest sector of the map, so Gerrit slid the lamp to the southeast, dipped his pen in the ink, and guided the nib around the smooth curve of St. Ouen's Bay on the west coast, a shoreline teeming with guns to prevent an Allied landing.

Time pressed, not only on the clock but on the calendar. Spring and any Allied operations loomed before him. The more information he could provide the Allies, the better.

Tomorrow after church, he'd pass this map to Charlie.

Discretion was more vital than ever. Schmeling had said the German secret field police were screening mail arriving in Jersey, especially mail to foreign workers, as they suspected the presence of the French resistance on the island.

Their suspicions were correct.

Gerrit gritted his teeth. Charlie's cover story of buying the parachute silk from a Jersey farmer rang false. On a small and well-populated island, every farmer could be identified. Every downed plane or airman was accounted for. Every parachute.

His pen rounded the point at Corbière, his starting position. With great care not to disturb the layering of silk and paper and glass, he laid his T square along the first grid line running north to south. This part of the map would be easier, and his pen traced a clean line.

If only Charlie's part were as easy. If only Gerrit could guide each step of the operation as cleanly.

He couldn't. A fifteen-year-old boy, intelligent though he was, had to carry contraband past customs officials, inspectors, crewmen with unknown loyalties, and through the streets of Saint-Malo to his cutout, who might be tailed by the Gestapo.

Gerrit had no control over the results. Only God did. But if God controlled the results, why did things keep falling apart?

Gerrit grimaced and drew another vertical line. He could finally name his doubts. He doubted God's faithfulness, and that made him squirm inside. Either God was faithful by nature, or he was not. If God was faithful, Gerrit had made serious errors in his thinking. Where had his logic failed?

After investing his talents, reputation, and life, was it wrong to want good results? It didn't seem wrong.

Yet the squirming intensified. He didn't simply *want* good results. He *expected* them.

Gerrit leaned back in his chair, and his gaze shifted from the brightness of the lamp to the dimness of the room around him.

He expected God to produce good results, but the Lord had never promised such a thing. That was where his logic had failed, where his faith had failed, where his trust had failed.

With a deep groan, Gerrit resumed his work and prayed for forgiveness and understanding and the courage to trust.

He finished the vertical grid lines, then the horizontal lines, and he penned "A1" in the first sector, "A2" in the second.

A knock on the door. "Van der Zee? Are you here?"

Willy Riedel? Gerrit sucked in a breath. Hadn't he gone to the Forum?

The doorknob turned.

Gerrit had forgotten to lock his door?

He bolted across the room.

The door opened wider and wider, and Gerrit had to fill the space before Riedel could see his desk—his work—his crime.

Without showing panic.

He grabbed the inner doorknob, gripped the doorjamb, thrust his body into the gap, and schooled his expression to mild interest. Despite the flurry in his gut. "Good evening, Herr Bauführer. I thought you went to the Forum."

"Stupid film, and I don't want to go drinking tonight." An expectant smile filled his broad face. "I thought I'd see what you were doing."

Did Gerrit's body block the view of his desk on the far wall under the window? Could he sound benign, as if he weren't tracing maps of German military installations to send to their enemies? Gerrit tilted his head toward his desk. "Writing letters. My sister's birthday is soon. Another time, ja?"

Hope filled Riedel's brown eyes. A social creature, friendly, more refined than most of his OT comrades. "I found some cake in the kitchen. Come join me."

"I'm sorry, but my mother promised bodily harm if I forgot my sister's birthday. Another time?"

Riedel's smile deflated. "Another time. Good night."

"Good night." Gerrit closed the door and leaned back against it. His breath tumbled out.

The only light in the room came from his desk, under the configuration of glass and paper and silk and clamps. Obviously not for writing letters.

Had Riedel seen any of it?

Gerrit threw the lock and returned to his desk, but his heart raced and his hands jittered. He'd have to calm down before resuming work.

He jammed his hands back into his hair. What if Riedel had entered before Gerrit had reached the door?

A groan carved out a hollow in his belly.

Riedel might be friendly, but he was a Nazi.

CHAPTER
16

When Ivy entered the surgical ward of General Hospital, Dr. Harold Tipton stood at a patient's bedside by the window with nursing sister Kitty de Puy, one of Fern's best friends.

At a bed to the right, hospital chaplain Canon Clifford Cohu of St. Saviour's Church prayed with a patient. The canon looked drawn, no doubt due to the arrests of many in his parish on charges of owning a wireless and spreading news from the BBC. Indeed, the canon himself was known for cheering patients with British news.

To the left, Mrs. Le Huquet lay in bed, her leg up in traction. She'd suffered a compound fracture when hit by a speeding German motorcycle. However, the surgeon, Mr. Halliwell, had done a fine bit of work.

Canon Cohu lifted his head and smiled at Ivy, his blue eyes bright. "Good morning, Dr. Picot."

"Don't talk to her." Kitty glared at Ivy. "Her sister works for the Germans."

Ivy's stomach caved in, curling her spine, and she struggled to stand tall. Over the past two months, she'd endured some snubbing, but now a wave of compassion crested over the mortification. Fern had lost one of her oldest friends.

A redheaded physician nearing forty years of age, Dr. Tipton slipped a chart onto a hook on the foot of the bed. "Yes, I'm afraid Dr. Picot can't be trusted."

"Is it true?" Mrs. Le Huquet's voice warbled.

Fern's decision had stirred up a whirlwind in the Picot household. Would it never subside? Dozens had left the practice, but losing Mrs. Le Huquet would hurt deeply, and Ivy made her way to her patient's side. "My sister is indeed working for the Germans, against my advice. I do not approve. However, I'm not her mother but her sister, and her younger sister at that."

Canon Cohu rose and set his hand on Ivy's shoulder. "I trust you."

"Thank you, Reverend." Her voice came out in a whisper, trailing the middle-aged man as he left the room.

Mrs. Le Huquet frowned, and her eyebrows tented. "I'm sorry about your sister. That must be difficult for you."

Ivy picked up the chart, settled into a chair, and set her medical bag beside her. "I'm not here to receive sympathy but to give it. How is your pain?"

The widow fiddled with the braid over her shoulder, of equal parts black and silver. "I won't lie. It hurts, but I'm thankful to be alive."

"I'm thankful too. You'll be in hospital a few weeks, so enjoy the extra rations."

One corner of Mrs. Le Huquet's mouth turned up. "That is indeed a benefit."

"A benefit that'll continue. When you go home, I'll order extra milk rations to help heal the bones." The irony of milk rationing on an island famed for its cows!

Ivy reviewed the chart. All looked well, and Mrs. Le Huquet seemed in good spirits.

"Dr. Picot?" Dr. Tipton stood at the foot of the bed with a stern expression. "May I have a word with you in private?"

How much lower could her heart sink? What if the medical society expelled her? Revoked her hospital privileges? How would she be able to practice medicine?

"Yes, Doctor." She squeezed her patient's hand. "Excuse me, Mrs. Le Huquet. I'm glad to see you recovering so well, and I'll visit in a few days."

Out in the hallway, Dr. Tipton leaned against the wall, his arms crossed over his white coat. He pressed a finger to his lips and watched a nursing sister enter another ward with a tray.

Then he . . . smiled? He leaned closer until his freckles became apparent. "I do hope you can forgive me." His voice barely reached her ears. "Keeping up appearances and all that. You do understand. But I wanted to thank you for your actions and for the paper. Cheerio."

With a swirl of white coat, he marched down the hall.

Ivy stared after the man. First he'd berated her, then thanked her. What on earth had happened?

And men claimed women were difficult to understand.

Ivy shook her head and made her way out of the hospital. She did appreciate the gratitude for the paper. At least once a week now, Charlie brought home a ream, saying, "Don't ask where it came from if you don't want to know."

She did not want to know, didn't want to think of her little brother negotiating France's black market, so she merely warned him to be careful and accepted the gift.

A twofold gift. Not only did she have writing paper for her own practice and to share with the other physicians, but she'd been able to spare three sketch pads—now five, after one of the doctors returned the sketch pads she'd given him.

With care, they could last for months.

She stepped outside to Gloucester Street under a brilliant blue sky, the hospital entrance now imprinted with the memory of

Gerrit van der Zee bowing his goodbye with his arm cradled to his belly, preserving the shreds of her reputation.

Ivy placed her medical bag in her bicycle basket and pedaled down Gloucester Street.

In church, Gerrit and Bernardus no longer conversed with the Picots. Very . . . gallant. Gerrit knew the harm Fern had done to the family, and friendliness with Todt men would only further that harm.

Gerrit did, however, continue to talk to Thelma Galais. Since Thelma had often been ill the past winter, she appreciated his attention when she could attend church. She thought the world of Gerrit van der Zee.

If it weren't for that uniform, Ivy might share her opinion.

Ivy checked her watch, a practice she was trying to make a habit. Still enough time to visit Joan de Ferrers before lunch.

The only benefit Fern's new job provided was more freedom in Ivy's day, and not only from the loss of patients. The daily routes Fern had designed worked well, and Ivy had retained them. But now when patients requested home visits, Aunt Ruby insisted on a visit to the surgery if they were able. With less travel, Ivy could see patients more quickly, and she had more time to treat escapees and to sketch along the way, aided by Charlie's timer.

At Carter's Chemist's, Ivy locked up her bicycle and entered the shop.

"Miss de Ferrers?" Ivy pulled a book from her medical bag and waved it to Joan, far behind the counter. "I brought you a book I found in my father's office."

"Oh?" Joan came to the counter. "What sort of book?"

Ivy handed it to her. "It must go back generations to the first Dr. Picot."

Joan eased the cover open with reverence. "Traditional remedies? Oh my. Look at this. Our modern commercial medications work well, but these—they work too. And look—this grows in the hedgerows."

Ivy knew she'd like it. But she'd soon lose Joan to the pages, so she cleared her throat. "Anything for me?"

Joan's gaze dragged up to Ivy, and she kept one possessive finger in the book. "Oh yes. Yes, I do. Mr. Hooper said you were coming out to his farm tomorrow, and he asked if you could bring his thyroid medicine."

"I'd be glad to." In their code, "tomorrow" meant the case wasn't urgent, and "thyroid" meant a general examination of a new escapee.

Mr. Hooper had sheltered several foreign workers in the past, but they never stayed long, shuttled to other homes by members of the "ring," the name Ivy had given the organization, since no one would tell her about it. Nor should they.

Whoever they were, they trusted her despite everything. Her throat swelled, and she swallowed hard. "You know about my sister's job, don't you?"

Joan's eyes went cool. "Yes."

"Why do you still . . . ?" She knew better than to speak of their work.

Joan's eyelids crimped at the mere allusion to that work. Then she scanned the shop with a languid gaze, took a little steel tray, and poured tablets into it. "I trust you." Her words were almost lost amidst the rat-a-tat of tablets on steel.

Ivy's throat ballooned over the thanks she should have expressed.

With a metal spatula, Joan scooted tablets in families of five into a chute attached to the side of the tray. "Her reputation serves as an excellent decoy."

Decoy? Why, yes. Since the entire Picot family had been smeared as collaborators, no one would suspect Ivy of defying the Nazis.

Joan tipped the tray, and the tablets slid down the chute into a glass vial. She flicked up her gaze to Ivy. "She knows nothing."

Was that a statement or a question?

"Since she no longer works for the practice, I don't discuss patients with her. Even when she did work with me, I only told her what she needed to know for scheduling and billing."

Joan smoothed a label on the vial and handed it to Ivy. "Mr. Hooper will pay me later."

Every word veiled, keeping up the appearances of an ordinary transaction.

Keeping up appearances? Ivy's breath rushed in. Was Dr. Tipton part of the ring? He'd praised her in private for "her actions" but shamed her in public. If he were in the ring, that would make sense.

The question grew in her mouth, but she chewed it to bits. With the Germans, one arrest always led to a dozen. The less each of them knew about the others, the better.

"Is that all for today?" Joan asked.

"Yes." Ivy tucked the vial in her bag. Her fingers brushed her sketch pad, and she pulled it out. "I have something else for you. A little sketch."

She tore out the drawing and handed it to the chemist.

Joan stared at it, completely still, except her lips, which rolled in.

Ivy had drawn Joan at work, intent on turning wildflowers into healing medicine. A wisp of a smile hinted at the chemist's satisfaction and enjoyment. Although Joan kept her hair neat, Ivy had drawn half a dozen curls floating free, and she'd used a splash of watercolor to bring out the auburn in those curls, a stroke of peach on her cheeks, spots of yellow on the flowers.

The drawing showed what Ivy saw in Joan—a woman who cared about her patients, a woman dedicated to her craft, but also a woman who lived outside the expectations of others.

Joan didn't move, and the peach of her cheeks deepened.

Did she hate it? No one would call her a beautiful woman, and Ivy hadn't hidden the pointiness of Joan's chin. Fern had hated Ivy's drawing with similar sharp lines, called it ugly, called Ivy cruel.

"I—I'm—"

"You did this for me?" Joan's voice faltered, her eyelashes fluttered, and her mouth edged up. "It's rather—well, it's rather nice, isn't it?"

She liked it, and Ivy's smile unfurled.

"I need to close shop." Joan hefted her chin and spun away. "I'll see you tomorrow."

Joan de Ferrers, who knew only the poison of feminine relationships, didn't know what to do with the sweetness.

"Yes," Ivy said. "Tomorrow."

Joan shot her a glance over her shoulder, the jerk of an unpracticed smile.

Ivy smiled back and departed. Gerrit had said art brought her life, like food for her mind and soul. Even more so when it nourished others.

CHAPTER
17

In a shed at Charlie's uncle's farm, Charlie handed his work jacket to Gerrit. "Why do you want to see? It's poor quality."

"Is it lined?" Sitting cross-legged, Gerrit turned the jacket inside out. "Yes, thank goodness."

"Fern insisted I buy lined jackets, even for work. They last longer, she said. She also made me buy two, in case one gets wet."

Fern had her flaws, but she'd unwittingly aided Gerrit's plan. He laid the latest silk diagram across the jacket back—it fit. "If we opened the lining, we could insert the diagram, maybe pin it from the shoulders so it doesn't bunch."

Charlie's eyes lit up in the dimness of the shed. "No one could see it."

Bernardus jabbed a finger toward Charlie. "You said you have two jackets. Are they the same color? Same cut?"

"Yes."

Bernardus slapped his knees. "Excellent. You can exchange jackets. One in Jersey, one in France. Your cutout will remove the map and send the jacket back in your next visit."

"That's brilliant," Charlie said.

It would work well. "Do either of you know how to sew? I don't."

"No," Bernardus and Charlie murmured in unison.

Gerrit inspected the seam. "The stitching is so small, I can hardly see it. Even if I could open it, how would I close it again so it looks like this?"

"We'll find someone who sews," Charlie said.

"No." The word shot from Bernardus's mouth. "We can't involve anyone else."

"Ivy sews," Charlie said. "I trust her. But Fern might see."

"No." Gerrit mashed his lips together. He refused to involve Ivy.

"Aunt Opal." Charlie sprang to his feet. "I'll ask her."

"No!" Gerrit said.

Bernardus grabbed for the boy's arm. "Absolutely not."

"She can be trusted." Charlie glared at the men. "Uncle Arthur has a wireless, and the Germans have never found it, never even searched their property."

Gerrit laid the jacket and silk diagram in his lap. "This would put them in danger, and adding someone new would endanger everyone in the network."

"No one else." Bernardus's voice grated like gravel. "We'll learn how to sew."

"Oh?" Charlie set his hands on his hips. "Who'll teach you? What will you tell them?"

What indeed would they tell them? Gerrit fingered the rough wool and smooth silk. "Oh well. It was a good idea."

"It's an excellent idea." Charlie crossed his arms. "In fact, I refuse to serve as your courier unless you enact it. Carrying the maps in my bag is too dangerous. If you want me to be your courier, you'll march over to the farmhouse and ask my aunt."

Gerrit met Bernardus's skeptical gaze. The plan to sew the maps inside the jackets was good. Sending the maps to the Allies was good. And if it was good, he had to act. "You're always telling me to trust the Lord, Bernardus."

"I trust the Lord. I don't trust the Nazis."

"Exactly," Charlie said. "This would protect me from the Nazis."

"It violates every rule." Bernardus groaned and pushed himself to standing. "But what choice do we have? Show us the way, Charlie."

Charlie led them across a field with grasses bright in the chilly sunshine, past Jersey cows, small and russet, and to the granite farmhouse.

After Charlie knocked, he opened the door. "Uncle Arthur? Aunt Opal?"

In a cozy drawing room, a middle-aged couple rose from their armchairs. Stared at their uninvited guests. Turned ashen.

"These are my friends," Charlie said, "Bernardus Kroon and Gerrit van der Zee. Bernardus and Gerrit, may I introduce Arthur and Opal Jouny?"

"Friends." Mr. Jouny's voice rasped, and his cheeks worked. Poor man, trying to conceal his hatred and fear of his enemy.

"Friends indeed. Wait until you hear." Charlie waved Gerrit and Bernardus to the sofa.

Gerrit clenched wool and silk in his hands. "I'm pleased to meet you, Mr. and Mrs. Jouny."

His host and hostess stood stiffly. Mrs. Jouny and Ivy bore a strong family resemblance—Ivy would be an attractive woman in middle age.

Mrs. Jouny shook herself. "Please do have a seat. Would you like some parsnip coffee? It's all I have, I'm afraid."

"No, thank you." Gerrit and Bernardus sat on the sofa with Charlie at one end.

Charlie rested his elbows on his knees. "Gerrit and Bernardus are Dutch, and they're in the resistance."

"Charlie!" Bernardus whacked him in the arm.

"They joined Organisation Todt so they could spy on German fortifications."

"Oh no," Gerrit muttered. What was Charlie doing?

"They can't send their maps and diagrams off the island," Charlie said, "so I've been acting as their courier."

"Charlie Picot!" Mr. Jouny's face turned stonier than the walls of his home. "What on earth are you thinking? It could be a trap."

One shake of Charlie's head. "I've been their courier for several months. If it were a trap, I'd already be in a concentration camp."

"Or dead." His uncle ground out the words, and his aunt slapped her hands over her mouth.

"May I?" Charlie reached across Bernardus and took the silk from Gerrit's lap. "Gerrit draws in secret ink. You can't see, but this is a diagram of a German command bunker about to be built at Noirmont Point—with all the specifications. Think how this will help the Allies."

"What do you two have to say for yourselves?" Mr. Jouny shifted that rock-hard gaze to Gerrit and Bernardus. "How dare you use a fifteen-year-old boy?"

"I volunteered, Uncle Arthur."

Bernardus raised one hand in a calming gesture. "We don't take it lightly, Mr. Jouny. We didn't want to involve Charlie at first."

"You shouldn't have done at all." Mr. Jouny shook his hand toward the silk. "If he's caught with that—"

"I'll be shot," Charlie said. "Which is why I need your help. I've been carrying the maps in my duffel, and I have a cover story about buying silk on the black market for my girlfriend in Saint-Malo or—"

"Oh no." Mrs. Jouny's voice trembled through her fingers. "That won't do."

"No, it won't." Charlie waved to Gerrit. "Tell them your idea."

Gerrit felt as if he were the one facing the firing squad. And for good reason. He cleared his throat and lifted Charlie's jacket. "Charlie's work jacket is lined. If we could open the lining and insert the map, hang it from the shoulders perhaps, and sew it back up."

"None of us knows how to sew." Charlie turned a pleading look to his aunt. "But you do, Aunt Opal. This could save my life."

143

Mrs. Jouny's hands drifted down to her lap. "You want me—"

"Absolutely not." Mr. Jouny slashed his arm through the idea.

"The maps would be out of sight." Bernardus clasped his hands together. "Even if the silk were detected, Charlie could claim he'd added another layer of fabric for warmth. And remember, the maps are invisible."

Mrs. Jouny stretched one hand to Gerrit. "May I see?"

"Opal!" her husband said.

Charlie shrugged. "If Aunt Opal can't help, I'll keep carrying the maps in my bag, using my flimsy cover story."

Gerrit clamped off a laugh. Charlie had told Gerrit and Bernardus he refused to carry them in his bag anymore—and told his aunt the opposite. Perhaps the boy had a future in politics.

He handed the jacket to Mrs. Jouny.

"Opal . . ." Mr. Jouny said, but with a note of resignation.

"Hush, Arthur. I'm only having a look." She opened a hinged wooden box beside her chair and pulled out a tiny metal hook. Two little pokes. "Oh yes. That would be simple."

"Opal . . ." And now full resignation.

"This could save Charlie's life." She picked at stitches. "You know what we Picots are like. He'll keep carrying those maps and putting himself in danger."

Mr. Jouny's head lolled back. "I had to marry a Picot."

A smile tugged at Gerrit's lips. Other than Fern, he liked every Picot he'd met.

Mrs. Jouny kept jabbing with her little hook. "You always say you wish we could do something for the Allies. Well, Charlie is doing just that. Now I can do my bit."

Mr. Jouny huffed out a breath, now with mock aggravation. "Where does that leave me? I'm still not doing my bit."

"Ah, but you could," Charlie said. "I have another idea."

Gerrit snapped his gaze to the youth. What idea?

"Gerrit lives in a hotel with the Todt men. Most are rabid Nazis. One of them almost caught him drawing. He needs a place to work."

"No, no." Gerrit waved one hand. "I'm fine. I'm locking my door now."

"Hmm." Mrs. Jouny frowned at her work. "Our boys are away fighting for Britain. They have a nice big desk in their room upstairs."

"Yes." Mr. Jouny's eyebrows gathered over his dark eyes. "And a large wardrobe. If an agricultural inspector comes, you'd have a place to hide."

"But why would I be here?" Gerrit motioned around him. "I'd be seen coming and going. What excuse could we give?"

Mrs. Jouny lifted the jacket and a smile. "Many of the soldiers hire local women for laundry and mending."

Gerrit closed his eyes, and the ideas tumbled in his mind, tumbled into place.

Tumbled into trust.

Beside him, Bernardus groaned. "This is most unwise."

"It is." Gerrit opened his eyes. "Let's do it."

CHAPTER
18

Ivy knocked on the door of a house in Gorey. Joan had sent her with potassium bromide for Mrs. Renouard, who was "rather in a hurry," which meant an urgent case with a sick escapee.

Mrs. Renouard, a woman in her thirties with curly brown hair, greeted Ivy and led her through the house and into the kitchen.

Dr. Harold Tipton sat at the table, and he rose. "Good afternoon."

Ivy held her breath. Why was Dr. Tipton there? "Good afternoon."

Mrs. Renouard left and shut the kitchen door.

"Please have a seat." Dr. Tipton gestured to a kitchen chair. "Mrs. Renouard prepared blackberry leaf tea for us. And no, a patient is not awaiting your care."

He was indeed involved, and Ivy sank into the chair before her legs gave out.

Dr. Tipton sat and raised his teacup. "You've been working with our ring for six months, and we've decided to bring you in fully."

Air hopped from Ivy's mouth. It was indeed a ring.

"Also . . ." He took a sip, and his lip curled. "Abominable stuff."

Ivy let herself smile. "You brought me here to complain about ersatz tea?"

He laughed, and light from the window glinted off his red hair. Then he sobered. "Given the recent developments in St. Saviour's Parish, we wanted to give you the chance to bow out."

Ivy wrapped her hands around the teacup, and her chest ached. On Friday, eighteen men had been sentenced in the wireless case, including the hospital steward, the hospital secretary—and Canon Clifford Cohu. A devastating blow to the island, with so many beloved and esteemed men given harsh sentences, ranging from two weeks to three years in prison.

Dr. Tipton arched an eyebrow. "If we are caught, the repercussions would be just as severe."

What else could Ivy do? "My father taught me to never turn away someone who is suffering."

"Excellent." Warmth livened his gaze. "Several of us are involved in treating and transporting the escaped workers. We also provide clothing, ration books, and identity papers so they can pass as local farmworkers."

"I see." Ivy sipped the tea, not abominable to her taste. "It's better for the men to perform meaningful work than to stay inside all day."

"Indeed. Boredom drives the men to reckless behavior and must be avoided." Dr. Tipton adjusted his suit jacket, too large on his frame. He'd been rather portly before the occupation. "You and Miss de Ferrers have a clever method of communicating. We need to add a code."

"All right." She primed her memory, since she could write nothing down.

"If an escapee must be moved urgently—for any reason at all— you must ring Miss de Ferrers straightaway with a prescription for the helper. Prescribe a dosage ten times higher than normal. When she corrects you, insist upon it."

"I see. Then she'll know it's a code."

"Yes." Dr. Tipton stood and offered his hand. "We will not speak of this again."

She stood and shook his hand. "Thank you for trusting me to help."

"You've proven discreet and capable. And as unfortunate as your sister's and your brother's associations must be for you, the situation is quite fortunate for us."

A darkness flooded Ivy's heart again. "A decoy."

Dr. Tipton inclined his head in affirmation. "You may leave first, and I'll depart later."

"Thank you." Outside, Ivy rode her bicycle through Gorey under a soft gray sky. For almost three years of the German occupation, the physicians had overlooked and ignored her—although with great politeness. Now she'd earned the respect of Dr. Tipton and others in the ring.

When she reached the Gorey Coast Road, the scenic medieval castle of Mont Orgueil rose to her left on the headlands, keeping watch over a colorful row of shops and a collection of fishing boats.

Ivy headed south, breathing in the scent of spring, of wildflowers and fresh young leaves.

But as she approached Grouville, she smelled dust and oil and filthy men. Here the new Todt railway slashed through greenery and flowers, trampled them, tossed them aside, the bare brown earth scratched with dull steel tracks.

Why did the Germans destroy everything good and beautiful?

"Ivy!" About fifty feet ahead, Charlie flagged her down. "Ivy! I thought it was you."

Ivy coasted up to her brother and hopped from her bicycle. "Hallo, there. What brings you up this way?"

"Gerrit is showing me the new sixty-centimeter gauge railway line. It'll soon connect Gorey to St. Helier. Isn't it fantastic?"

Twenty feet off the road, Gerrit van der Zee stood in his Todt uniform, his face pinched, and he edged away. "Good afternoon, Dr. Picot."

At least he had the grace to know his company wasn't wanted, so she washed some of the starch from her tone. "Good afternoon, Mr. van der Zee."

"Don't leave, Gerrit." Charlie shielded his eyes from the sun. "We can ask Ivy."

"Ask me what?"

Gerrit's face turned pink. "Let's not."

"No, no." Charlie waved him closer. "You see, Ivy, Gerrit's going home on leave next week, and he offered to bring us items."

Ivy's hands tightened around the handlebars. How often had she told Fern she didn't want the food and soap and silk stockings sent home by her German employer? How then could Ivy accept a gift from someone in German uniform?

Gerrit's lips pressed together, and he stepped closer. "I understand your reluctance. But each occupied nation faces different conditions. In Jersey, you have fruit and vegetables and potatoes."

"Potatoes are rationed." Her words came out clipped.

"You receive five pounds weekly, more than my family receives. But in Amsterdam, I may find items that are scarce here."

"A kind offer." Charlie's words carried a challenge.

Kind indeed, but the shortages and rationing existed only because Germany, which Gerrit supported through his labor, occupied most of Europe. So much suffering, so much illness, so much death.

She took Charlie's challenge and directed it at Gerrit. "Insulin."

Two blond eyebrows lifted toward the brown forage cap. "Insulin?"

"To treat diabetes. We have none on the island, and our patients are dying. We've placed them in hospital to control their diet and activity, but it isn't enough. Another died yesterday."

Those golden eyebrows bunched together over sea-blue eyes, and compassion rolled like surf through that sea.

Ivy climbed back onto her bicycle. "The only item I would accept from you would be insulin. Good day, Mr. van der Zee. Goodbye, Charlie."

"Ivy . . ." Charlie's voice followed as she coasted downhill.

Dr. Tipton had referred to Fern's and Charlie's unfortunate associations. Of all the men in Jersey, why did Charlie choose to befriend two collaborators?

SAINT-MALO, FRANCE
TUESDAY, APRIL 27, 1943

Gerrit climbed the gangway onto the SS *Ormer*, his uniform harsh and unwelcome on his limbs. Although required to wear his uniform on leave, Gerrit had changed into a civilian suit upon arrival at the Amsterdam train station and hadn't changed back until the return trip.

His family knew he was working for an engineering firm in Jersey, but not that the firm was contracted to Organisation Todt. How could he explain?

On deck, Charlie Picot coiled a line around his arm.

Gerrit raised a hand and a smile in greeting. "Good afternoon, Charlie."

"Good afternoon." Charlie's smile seemed flat. "Back from leave?"

"I am. I was pleased to see the *Ormer* listed in the convoy."

Charlie set aside the coiled line. "May I put your bags in the cabin?"

"Yes, thank you." Gerrit handed him his duffel bag but patted the satchel over his shoulder. "I'll keep this one. It contains three bottles of insulin."

Charlie's jaw sprang open. "Insulin? How?"

"I explained the situation in Jersey to our family apothecary. He offered to sell me some but said I needed to keep it cold."

Charlie stared at the leather satchel. "How . . ."

"I visited my favorite antique shop." Sadly, the owner's stock of the mechanical metal toys Gerrit collected had been confiscated, to be scrapped for the German war machine. "I bought an apothecary jar, filled it with ice, and packed the insulin inside. Your sister may keep the jar or dash it to pieces."

"This won't be like the reams of paper. She'll know where the insulin came from."

"I think her concern for her patients will overcome her pride." Gerrit held no delusions that this would make Ivy think better of him, nor was that his aim. He only shared her righteous anger at people dying for want of what should be a common medication.

Charlie kept gaping. In his shirtsleeves.

He was never supposed to remove his jacket except when making the exchange.

Gerrit's stomach tensed. "Aren't you . . . chilly?"

"Ripped my jacket, left it in Saint-Malo for mending." Charlie's voice and his gaze dipped low.

Ice crackled in Gerrit's veins. Something must have gone wrong in the exchange. "I have a suit jacket you can wear if you're cold."

"I'm fine. If I'm not busy . . ." He lifted his face, and hesitation cramped his gaze.

"I'll be on the deck." They might be able to speak in private.

He left Charlie to his work and headed to the stern of the cargo boat, where he chose a spot in the corner, out of the way. Dozens of passengers boarded, mostly German soldiers, and Gerrit grumbled. He might have to wait days to find out what had gone wrong.

If only Gerrit or Bernardus could have made the exchange while on the continent on leave. But they couldn't. Only one courier, and only Charlie knew the exchange procedures.

Had Gerrit missed a crucial detail? But how could he control what happened in France? He couldn't. Nor was he meant to, and his groan disappeared in the rumble of engines.

The boat pulled away from the dock and into the harbor, leaving the ancient walled city. Leaving the continent.

Tensions had been high in Amsterdam, but Easter with his

family had been pleasant. Moeder had filled him with his favorite foods—as much as she could with rationing. Vader never once mentioned his disappointment with Gerrit leaving the family firm. And his sisters, Anke and Myrthe, had been in excellent spirits.

Six cargo boats traveled in a close pack, ringed by three German torpedo boats to protect against Allied attack by air or sea.

France shrank to a dark band, and blue seas reflected blue skies, a perfect day for sailing. Despite the fine weather, over time the other passengers abandoned the deck for the cabin.

Two hours out to sea, Charlie joined him at the rail.

Gerrit glanced around in an innocent manner, using his old resistance skills. No one stood in earshot, especially with the racket of the engines.

"Can you tell me what happened?" Gerrit asked in his lowest voice.

"A bit." Charlie clasped his hands on top of the railing. "I went to my usual place, but the jacket wasn't where it should have been. And there was a man—it didn't feel right. After all, what man wears a hat in church?" He winced. "I shouldn't have said that."

"I'll forget it." Surely Saint-Malo had dozens of churches.

Charlie twisted to face Gerrit. "Since I've already said it, a priest is always there lighting candles. He never speaks to anyone. But today, he spoke to the man in the hat, rather louder than necessary, asked if he could light a candle for him. The man looked annoyed, pulled his hat down lower. I think the priest is in the network. I think he was calling my attention to the man, warning me."

Gestapo. Gerrit's fingers dug at the railing. This was why he or Bernardus should have been the ones taking the chances, not a youth. "What happened?"

Charlie hunched his shoulders. "I wanted to run, but that's the worst thing to do. I stayed another fifteen minutes, praying harder than I've ever prayed in my life, and then left. The man in the hat followed me."

"Oh no. Charlie."

The boy's cheeks worked, no longer spotted by blemishes, but still smooth with youth. "I know what to do. I walked at my usual speed, ate lunch at my usual café, strolled back to the docks, never looked back at him. He left me alone halfway through lunch."

"The jacket? Where is it?" The diagram they'd scheduled to send this week was for a giant observation tower under construction at Batterie Lothringen. Since the tower was the first of its kind and the design was unique to the Channel Islands, delivering the diagram to the Allies was essential.

"Marie works in the harbormaster's office. I gave the jacket to her, said I'd ripped it, asked her to mend it. They know what that means."

Now a young girl had the diagram, and Gerrit huffed out a breath. "What next?"

"When I return, I pick up my mending. They'll inform me of my new procedures." His cheeks kept working, paler than usual.

"It isn't too late," Gerrit said. "You can stop at any time. We'll understand."

Charlie gripped his elbows, not quite hugging himself. "Soldiers on the front can't quit when they have a close call. Why should I?"

Because he was too young to be a soldier, too special to die young, too beloved by his family.

And not one of those arguments would hold sway.

"I must do this." Charlie's voice strengthened. "I've been praying all day. I know I must."

Noise built around Gerrit and inside him, engines throbbing, objections shouting, and conviction sizzling like molten steel hitting air. "I know. We all must do this."

Charlie wrenched his gaze to the sky.

The throbbing engines, the shouts. Crewmen scrambled around the deck, up to the antiaircraft gun mounted on top of the cabin. High above, engines whined.

"Oh no," Charlie said. "Another air raid."

"Another?"

153

"Don't tell my sisters." Charlie grabbed Gerrit's arm and dashed to the cabin. "Take cover. Get low."

Inside the cabin, dozens of men crouched on the deck, and Gerrit and Charlie joined them.

Through a porthole, Gerrit saw three fighter planes diving, each with two propellers spinning. The British Royal Air Force.

Part of him wanted to cheer for the RAF. And part of him wanted to scream at the pilots to spare this boat, these men.

Gunfire crackled from on top of the cabin roof.

"Gerrit! Get down." Charlie tugged at his sleeve.

He obeyed, bowing his body around his satchel, around what might be the only insulin bound for Jersey.

"Not this boat, Lord," he muttered. "Not today."

The plane engines and gunfire built to a fever pitch, then faded.

No screams. No shouts. The boat and the men aboard had survived. As had the insulin.

At least this prayer, on behalf of Ivy's patients, the Lord had answered.

CHAPTER
19

In the wooded valley, Gerrit and Bernardus stood with Ernst Schmeling outside *Hohlgangsanlage 8*, a large complex of tunnels being built as an ammunition depot.

The men strode through the arched entrance beside a narrow-gauge railway.

Inside the lantern-lit interior, the temperature dropped.

"Construction is slower than planned." Schmeling's voice reverberated off the plastered walls. "We're low on cement and explosive charges. At least these stubborn islanders are now sharing in our suffering."

Gerrit murmured as if agreeing. A month earlier, on the day he'd returned from leave, the RAF had sunk a supply boat and a German patrol boat. In reprisal, the Germans had reduced the weekly bread ration from four-and-a-half pounds to three pounds and twelve ounces. According to Charlie, this hurt the poor most of all, since the wealthy could afford the high prices for unrationed foods.

Gerrit walled in his words as he turned left, heading deeper into the tunnel complex. If the Germans were suffering due to Allied air raids, what was that compared to the suffering they'd inflicted throughout Europe?

Surely Germany had no lack of medications, no diabetics dying for want of insulin.

Charlie had returned Gerrit's satchel with a note, unaddressed and unsigned, in flowery but strong script, stating, "On behalf of the patients and physicians of Jersey, I thank you."

Not only had Ivy Picot's compassion overcome her pride, so had her manners.

The men passed a squad of workers unloading bags of cement from side-tipping railway wagons while a guard yelled at them. Demyan Marchenko's squad, and the man met Gerrit's eye without showing recognition, which was wise.

Marchenko grew gaunter and gaunter, and Gerrit's hands coiled. How dare the Germans complain about suffering when they treated their workers so inhumanely?

Schmeling led Gerrit and Bernardus down a rough tunnel to the right, where construction had stalled. Foreign workers poked at the roof with poles to knock down loose rock, and they loaded the rubble into railway wagons.

Dangerous work. In April, falling rock had killed two Polish workers in these tunnels, and an accident and explosion in similar tunnels at Grands Vaux had caused multiple casualties.

Water dripped down the rock face, and the scent of damp stone filled the tunnel. Gerrit and Bernardus had come to take measurements and rock samples for the next phase of construction.

Cries rose behind him, from Marchenko's squad. A wagon tipped to the side, and half a dozen bags of cement tumbled to the ground. Split. A powdery cloud rose.

"Imbeciles," Schmeling said. "That's good German cement."

Shouts and cusses emerged from the pale cloud, fists raised to strike, to block.

A glint of steel. The guard raised a rifle, struck a man in the head.

"No!" Gerrit cried. The guard would kill the man, and Gerrit turned to run.

Someone gripped his arm. "Don't," Bernardus said, low and fierce.

"Let the guard do his job." Schmeling wrinkled his nose. "Such carelessness must be punished."

Thuds of blows on bone. Shouts. Screams.

"One thing," Bernardus said with a growl. "One thing only."

What good was Gerrit's one thing of drawing maps if he let a man be beaten to death?

He yanked his arm free and sprinted down the tunnel.

Ahead of him, the guard and Marchenko stood wrestling, the rifle flashing between them.

A shot ricocheted, slammed Gerrit's eardrums.

He dropped to squatting, covered his ears.

The guard staggered backward, crumpled to the ground—his neck, his chest a mess of red.

"No . . ." Gerrit lurched down the tunnel. His ears rang.

Marchenko turned Gerrit's way, his face wide with disbelief and devastation. Then terror contorted his features. He would be executed. No trial. No defense. No mercy.

"Get him!" Schmeling yelled, and footsteps thumped behind him. "Get him!"

Marchenko startled, and he bolted for the entrance.

"Halt!" At the corner, Schmeling shoved past Gerrit and leveled his pistol.

"No." Gerrit's voice strangled in his throat. Another shot pummeled his ears.

Marchenko grabbed at his arm, bounced off the wall, and turned down the tunnel toward the exit.

Schmeling followed.

"Herr Oberbauführer!" Bernardus waved him down, running hard. "Wait! We'll catch him, van der Zee and I. We'll catch him, bring him back. You can make an example of him."

157

"Yes!" Fire crackled in Schmeling's eyes. "Go! Quickly!"

Bernardus had already rounded the corner.

Gerrit shook his head, tried to shake off the ringing, forced his feet to move, to walk, to run.

What was Bernardus thinking? They couldn't bring Marchenko back to be executed. They had to let him escape.

Yes, that was Bernardus's plan—hold Schmeling back, put up a good show, let Marchenko slip away, stall the manhunt.

Gerrit raced down the tunnel.

Outside in drizzly daylight, Marchenko careened up the road to the left, with Bernardus sprinting after him.

Gerrit willed himself to catch up, but why? Gerrit might have been blessed with longer legs than his friend, but Bernardus knew what to do with what the Lord had given him.

Put on a good show. Gerrit drew his pistol from the holster for Schmeling to see.

The road made a sharp right hand turn uphill through dense woodland.

Up ahead, Bernardus gained on Marchenko.

"Let me go!" Marchenko yelled in English. "I'll fight you. I won't go back."

"We want to help," Bernardus said, just loud enough for Marchenko to hear. "Keep going, around the next bend."

Gerrit's breath came hard, and his feet pounded the damp road. Through a break in the trees, he scanned downhill toward the construction site. In a haze of mist, Schmeling and a few others stood in the tunnel entrance. No running, no vehicles.

The road bent to the left.

"Stop," Bernardus said. "We want to help."

"I won't go back." Marchenko gripped his arm, the sleeve tinged deep red, but he slowed to a walk. A halting walk.

Bernardus thumped to a stop and held up both hands. "We want to help."

Help—yes. Gerrit pointed his pistol at the hedgerow. "I'll fire a shot, make them think we're chasing you."

"Good idea," Bernardus said.

Gerrit pulled the trigger. Branches exploded, and leaves flew every which way.

Would his eardrums ever recover?

Marchenko glared at them from under the arching branches of a tree. "How can you help?"

"We know someone," Bernardus said. "I'll take you there."

"Who?" Gerrit said. They knew so few people in Jersey, and who lived in this area? "The Jounys? No."

"They're good people and clever. They'll help him."

"The Germans will send out a manhunt." Gerrit waved toward the Jouny farm.

"We have no time to argue. Marchenko, come with me. Gerrit, pretend to search for ten minutes or so, fire another shot or two, then return. Tell them we split up. And pray."

Gerrit stared at his friend's back as Bernardus jogged up the road with the Ukrainian. What if the Germans searched the Jouny farm in their manhunt? Not only would they find Marchenko, but they might find evidence of Gerrit's work.

One week after his close call, Charlie had picked up his "mending" and new cutout procedures, and Gerrit was sending maps and diagrams—sometimes two or three at a time—sewn with care by Opal Jouny into Charlie's jacket.

Each map drawn at a desk in the farmhouse. Gerrit was careful to clean up, but what if he'd missed something?

Gerrit groaned and ran up the road to continue his fake search.

At the crossroads, Bernardus had turned left, so Gerrit turned right, ran a couple hundred meters, and fired a shot at another innocent hedgerow.

What else would he have Bernardus do? On his own, Marchenko might request assistance from an islander who wasn't discreet, or worse—an informer for the Germans.

This was the only way they could save Marchenko's life.

Pray, Bernardus had said. Gerrit slammed his eyes shut and prayed as if many lives depended on it. Which they did.

ST. HELIER

Thelma Galais pressed a hand over the bandage on her arm, bleeding from a minor injury which should have healed days ago. "Nothing can be done?"

For acute myeloid leukemia? Nothing, and Ivy's jaw quivered. "Oh, these Germans."

Thelma raised her hazel eyes, edged with red. "Sweet Ivy, you mustn't become bitter."

"But if they hadn't come—"

"Would that change your treatment?"

No good treatments existed for the disease. "No, but you'd have better food. You'd be less prone to infection. And Edna and Frank would be here."

Thelma's face buckled, and she glanced around her drawing room, the same room where they'd learned of the deportation order. "I do wish I could say goodbye."

Ivy had promised Edna she'd look after her mother, but she'd failed. Her vision wavered.

"Come now, brave Dr. Picot." Thelma offered a watery smile. "Would your father cry delivering such news?"

Ivy wiped her tears. "For you, he might."

Thelma tutted her tongue. "Do you have a drawing for me?"

With a shaky breath, Ivy collected herself and thumbed through her sketch pad. "You might be the only person on the island who will like this."

Having given up on hiring a receptionist, Ivy had hired a girl as a housekeeper, and Aunt Ruby was serving as receptionist.

The housekeeper had accidentally left out a bag of breakfast meal, and Ivy had found a long-tailed field mouse poking his little brown head from the bag. After sketching him, Ivy had shooed him from the house and given the oats to Uncle Arthur for his livestock.

"Isn't he precious?" Thelma traced the penciled whiskers. "You have a gift. Most people see mice as pests, but you see beauty."

All the frustration and grief and indignation of the past three years frothed inside. "The Germans—they destroy all the beauty in this world, and I—I can't see God's goodness." A sob hiccupped, and she clapped her hand over her mouth, over her horrible words.

Thelma traced the ragged hole in the bag of meal. Her wavy silver hair, pulled in a low chignon, framed her lowered face, her flickering eyelids.

What must she think of Ivy?

Her hazel eyes lifted, shimmering with sadness. "Man's ugliness may destroy the beauty of creation, but we cannot destroy the beauty of God himself. Man's hatred can't destroy God's love. Man's wickedness can't destroy God's goodness. Seeing the Lord amidst all this evil isn't easy, but he's here and he's *good*." The word shook with force.

But why couldn't the Lord give Thelma a few more years? Wait until Edna came home? "He's letting you *die*." Ivy's voice shook with the same force.

"And he is good." A little smile curved. "He will take me home, which is the greatest good I can imagine, and whilst I wait, he will continue to show me his goodness."

All her life, Ivy had seen beyond the seen—but not now.

The telephone rang, and Thelma scooted forward in her armchair.

"Let me." Ivy sprang from her chair and to the telephone. "Galais residence."

"Ivy?" Aunt Ruby said. "I'm glad you're still there. Your Uncle Arthur hurt himself badly, and Opal can't stop the bleeding."

"Oh, dear. I'll go straightaway." She conserved her petrol ration for emergencies like this.

After saying goodbye to Thelma, Ivy ran down the street to La Bliue Brise and unlocked the garage. Ivy drove away, along roads pocked by overweight German lorries, past ancient walls clipped by those lorries, and along the coast spoiled by railways and barbed wire and concrete bunkers.

How could Thelma see God's goodness? Ivy wanted to desperately. Even the purity of her former faith had been destroyed by German recklessness and cruelty.

She swiped another tear from her eye. That was why she couldn't bear to destroy beauty in any form, even the apothecary jar from Gerrit van der Zee.

Everything about his gift was beautiful, especially the insulin. The jar itself was quite old, of white porcelain with intricate vines and flowers of brightest blue.

Considering the source, she didn't want to keep the jar. But if she'd given it to Joan, she would have had to explain where it came from. So Ivy stashed it on the top shelf of the office bookcase. Dad had similar curios, and she hoped no one would notice the newcomer.

But Ivy did. It drew her eyes. Her attention. Her thoughts.

A man who destroyed gave her something beautiful. A man whose organization killed gave the gift of life.

When she arrived at the farm, Uncle Arthur opened the door and pulled her inside.

"Uncle Arthur? I thought you were—"

"Follow me. Hurry." He trotted upstairs, not injured at all.

Ivy blinked and followed. "Is Aunt Opal . . ."

Aunt Opal marched down the upstairs hallway with a stack of linens. "This way."

Uncle Arthur threw open the door to her cousins' bedroom. A man sat on one of the two beds, leaning back against the headboard.

Ivy stopped short. A Russian worker—and she'd seen him before. The wheat-colored hair, the broad face with its distinctive scar.

"Ivy, meet Demyan Marchenko. Mr. Marchenko, this is our niece, Dr. Ivy Picot."

"I believe we've met." His smile twisted from pain. He was stripped to the waist, and the bandage around his arm was dark with blood.

"We have indeed met." Ivy perched on the bed beside him and opened her bag. "What happened?"

Uncle Arthur crossed his arms. "He accidentally killed a guard who was beating one of his men for an innocent mistake. He ran, and a German officer shot him."

Oh no. Ivy unwound the bandage to inspect the wound. The Germans wouldn't stand for that. They'd turn the island upside down.

Aunt Opal knelt before the wardrobe and laid blankets inside. "I'm preparing a hiding place for him when you're done. If the Germans come, he can pull the linens over himself."

"You are kind," Mr. Marchenko said. "I am glad they let me escape and brought me—"

"No!" Uncle Arthur thrust a finger at the patient. "Not a word."

Let him escape? Ivy's gaze darted between the men. What was happening?

The fugitive gave a slow nod. "You are right, comrade."

Her uncle turned that finger toward Ivy. "You know better than to ask questions. You will tell no one what you saw today."

"Of course not." Nor would she tell her uncle that Mr. Marchenko wasn't the first escapee she'd treated.

Aunt Opal fluffed a pillow in the wardrobe. "I cleaned the wound as best I could, but it won't stop bleeding."

Ivy inspected the wound. The bullet had plowed through the bicep, nicking the humerus and a vein. At least the bone wasn't broken, but Ivy plucked out a few bone splinters.

Since her patient spoke excellent English, Ivy switched to Jèrriais. "*Oncl'ye*, you are in danger if he stays here."

"I won't turn him out."

"He should be moved far from here. I'll see what I can do."

"Ivy . . ."

She gave her uncle a firm glance. "You know better than to ask questions."

He murmured in acceptance. "Be careful, *ma nièche*."

Ivy threaded her needle and sutured the nicked vein.

Mr. Marchenko hissed through his teeth. "Do not mind me. Keep working."

"You speak excellent English," Ivy said.

"And you speak very poor French."

Ivy chuckled. "We were speaking Jèrriais, our local language. Where are you from?"

"Kyiv. My parents were in the foreign service when I was a boy—London, Paris."

Now a slave worker, wanted for murder. Intelligence shone in his gray eyes. Defiance. And fear.

CHAPTER
20

A sour chord from the piano jangled through the drawing room, and Ivy flinched.

Charlie started the piece again, but without his usual joking apologies for missed notes, and he'd missed many.

Ivy set aside a patient chart and picked up Thelma Galais's. In the past month, Thelma had declined rapidly, as if the diagnosis had given her permission to go home. Every day, Ivy visited, wanting to boost her spirits. But if anything, Thelma was more peaceful.

Curled up in the armchair by the electric lamp, Ivy finished her chart notes, with the persistent heaviness of grief in her chest.

More sour chords and grumbles from Charlie. His fingers formed taut triangles on the keys.

Ever since the *Ormer* arrived in St. Helier this afternoon, Charlie had acted jumpy.

Ivy capped her pen. "I saw RAF planes today." Charlie had never mentioned any attacks.

"Hmm?" His head notched up, but he didn't meet her gaze.

165

"A hard day at sea?"

A terse shake of his head. "I'm fine."

No, he wasn't. He'd once told her every slight from friends, every accolade in school, every humorous incident. She expected more distance as he became a man, but not like this. Something serious had gnarled his hands.

Ivy filtered her sigh through her lips to conceal her concern. Her chart notes complete, she opened her sketch pad so she could finish her drawing of a horse for Demyan Marchenko.

He was recovering from his injury and had been transferred to the Hooper farm in Trinity Parish in the northeast, which sheltered two other escapees.

When Demyan was healthy enough to work, the ring planned to dye his hair black and issue false papers. In the meantime, his confinement had made him restless, especially after months of slavery. Ivy brought books, but what he loved most was watching the farm horses from his window. He kept threatening to steal away for a ride.

Ivy let her pencil sweep curving lines for the horse's tail. Perhaps her drawing could satisfy his longing and keep him indoors.

The clock chimed eleven o'clock.

Already? Since she liked to go to bed before the electricity turned off, she'd set the clock to chime five minutes beforehand. She hated to waste precious candles and matches, but she lit two candles and placed one on the piano top.

She didn't wish to retire until Fern came home, so Ivy could share the latest Red Cross message. Mum and the boys were safe and sound at Ivy's grandparents' home in the English countryside, and Dad and Bill were busy with their regiment, which trained soldiers somewhere in England.

The electricity flicked off. Eleven o'clock—when curfew started now. The Germans kept changing it. "Fern isn't home yet." She didn't have a curfew pass as Ivy did.

Only a grunt from Charlie.

The front door opened and closed downstairs. Thank goodness. Curfew violators could be arrested and fined.

Ivy shielded her candle as she went to the top of the stairs. "I'm glad you're home. Curfew—"

A giggle bubbled in the darkness downstairs. "I assure you, I was perfectly safe from arrest. I saw a show with my friends from College House."

A building requisitioned from Victoria College that served as the German field commander's headquarters, and another chord from Charlie dripped sour acid in Ivy's gut. But voicing her disdain for her sister's companions would solve nothing. "What show did you see?"

"Show?" Fern emerged from the darkness into the faint glow of Ivy's candle. "Oh, nothing to speak of. A trifle."

Fern climbed the stairs with a sleepy-eyed smile, a smile familiar but from the past, and Ivy couldn't place it.

"Did you enjoy it?" Ivy asked.

"Oh yes." Another giggle bubbled up, bubbled into Ivy's memory to the last time she'd heard that giggle and seen that smile.

When Fern had been falling in love with Bill.

The sour acid chewed into Ivy's stomach, contracted it with pain. No. It couldn't be.

"Oh, dear. Poor Ivy." Fern paused a few steps below Ivy with her hand on the banister. "Look at you in your ratty old dress at home on a Saturday night. You ought to make friends and live life."

Ivy's tongue snagged on her objections. "Not like you." Her words didn't make sense, but she couldn't think well enough to correct them, not when confronted by that dreamy smile.

"Oh yes. You have your scruples." Fern passed Ivy on the landing and headed up the second flight of stairs. "You'll find scruples make rather poor company."

Ivy fumbled for the doorjamb leading to the drawing room, leaned back, covered her mouth. Was Fern falling in love? With a German?

"Excuse me." Charlie edged past Ivy with his candle, his head down.

"Did you—did you hear?" Ivy's words strangled in her throat.

"Mm." Charlie climbed the stairs. "Good night."

Her brother, her sister, her whole family—falling to pieces. No one to turn to. No one to lean on.

Save one. She squeezed her eyes shut. "Lord, help me. Help us."

ST. PETER'S PARISH
SUNDAY, JUNE 27, 1943

"It's over." Charlie leaned against the cabinet in the Jounys' kitchen, his arms crossed tightly across his chest.

After church, Charlie had invited Gerrit and Bernardus to "hike," meaning to meet at the farm, but Gerrit and Bernardus had planned to spend the warm day at the beach with Willy Riedel, part of their campaign to cultivate friendships with their OT colleagues. Something in Charlie's tone had implied this was no Sunday picnic, so they'd split up for the afternoon.

Gerrit sat at the table and motioned to another chair for Charlie. "What's over?"

"Everything." Charlie shoved away from the cabinet and marched toward the oven. "Yesterday, on my way to my meeting place, that man—the man in the hat—he was outside."

Gerrit pulled off his OT cap. "Gestapo."

"He didn't see me." Charlie strode toward the sink and fiddled with the curtains, even though they were already drawn. "I went straight back to the docks. Marie refused to see me—spooked. I forced my way in. Not gentlemanly, but I was worried for her."

And for himself. Gerrit murmured his acknowledgment.

Charlie planted his hands on the rim of the sink and hung his head. "Members of the network have been disappearing, arrested. Marie's afraid she'll be next. I tried to convince her to come here with me, but she won't."

"Oh no." Gerrit set his elbows on the table, set his head in his hands. How many had been arrested? What horrors must they be going through?

What if they had Gerrit's maps? What if the Gestapo suspected the presence of secret ink? They could develop it. Trace the maps to Gerrit—and worse, to Charlie.

"What are we going to do?" Charlie's voice cracked, from terror, from youth.

Gerrit dragged up his head. "What can we do? We must stop sending maps."

"I know. I know." Charlie ruffled his black hair, mussed it up.

The Gestapo might be looking for Charlie. "Don't return to France. Find a new job, go back to school, anything."

"No, no." Charlie trod the kitchen floor and smoothed his hair. "If they suspect me, and I stopped making trips . . ."

Gerrit's eyes slipped shut. "You'd look guilty. They'd know where to find you."

Mumbles and footsteps crossed the kitchen. "I'll have Aunt Opal remove the map in my jacket, and I'll burn it."

"Don't." The quickness of his reply surprised him, and his eyes popped open. "I'll keep making maps."

"Why? It's futile."

"I don't know." Gerrit ran his hands up and down the brown wool of his trousers. "The situation may change. All I know is I must draw maps. I'll keep stashing them in your aunt's fabric basket, keep making them until I run out of silk or ink."

Charlie plopped into the chair, and his body sagged. "Did I do something wrong? Lead the Gestapo to my cutout?"

"No. You did nothing wrong. You followed procedure and—"

"What if I didn't?" Charlie's eyes went wild. "Not on purpose, but what if—"

"Don't." Gerrit thumped his palm on the table in front of the boy. "We can't control everything. We can only do our best, which you did."

On the table, Gerrit's fingers splayed wider and wider. Just as shining his lamp under the glass illuminated maps so he could trace them, shining light on the opposite side of a problem illuminated the truth.

His gaze swam up to Charlie, strengthened, cleared. "Only God knows everything. We don't. We can't control everything, nor should we try. Do your best, yes. Always do your best. But the results . . ."

"Trust in God's good plans." Charlie's face relaxed. "My mum always told me that. She says his plans are ultimately good. Temporarily they may not seem good, but ultimately they are."

"He's faithful." Gerrit ground out the words, ground them into his mind. It was true, but his brain fumbled to fully grasp it. "We have to trust him for the results, and in the meantime keep doing what is good and right."

Charlie gave a half-hearted chuckle. "Even if that means doing nothing?"

A strange peace smoothed out his soul. "Even if."

"Arthur!" Opal Jouny called from out in the drawing room. "Arthur! We have visitors."

Gerrit sat up stiff and straight. The signal to hide, to stash his drawing supplies and slip into the wardrobe. An agricultural inspector must have come.

But where could he hide in the kitchen?

Charlie's gaze darted around in the same quest.

And yet . . . Charlie had reason to be at the farm, and Gerrit wasn't drawing maps, just talking with a known friend over lukewarm blackberry leaf tea.

Gerrit raised one hand to soothe his young friend and lifted his teacup to him.

"Ivy," Opal called. "What a pleasant surprise."

Charlie burst out in a grin, but Gerrit tensed. He did not want to explain his presence—his invasion of her aunt and uncle's home.

"Stay there, Ivy," Opal said. "I'll bring out the tea."

"I'll help."

"No, no. It's already made. I'm afraid it's cold though, since I turned off the fire." Opal opened the kitchen door, shut it, and glared at Gerrit, her finger to her lips. Apparently she didn't want to explain his presence either. She grabbed a scrap of paper and wrote something to Charlie, then assembled her tea tray and returned to the drawing room.

Charlie turned the paper to Gerrit. It read *"Silence! You told her you were hiking."*

Gerrit nodded.

Charlie scribbled on the paper. *"I hope she doesn't stay long. We can't move."*

Indeed not. Even slipping out the back door would make noise from scraping chair legs and creaking hinges. They were trapped—and trapped in the rudeness of eavesdropping.

Yet his ears strained toward Ivy's lilting voice.

"I wasn't expecting you," Opal said. "Your uncle hasn't hurt himself in weeks."

Ivy's laugh stirred something in Gerrit's chest—yet tightness restrained her laugh.

"Are you all right, dear?"

"I'm fine myself," Ivy said, "but I need to talk to someone. I feel quite alone."

Gerrit frowned and resisted the urge to look at Charlie. He thought they were close.

"You're never alone," Opal said.

"I know. I'm trying to lean on God, but God also gives us family and friends. And this—I need to talk to someone, and it needs to stay in the family."

Gerrit winced and glanced at the back door. He wasn't family. He shouldn't listen. But he couldn't leave without making noise, making a scene.

"What's wrong, dear?"

Silence pulsed. Was Ivy speaking in a low voice or not speaking at all? "I'm worried about Charlie and Fern."

Charlie's eyebrows jumped high.

"Oh?" Opal said. "Why are you worried about Charlie?"

"He's been tense since he returned from France yesterday. He won't tell me what happened."

Charlie scrunched up his face. He couldn't tell his sister his resistance contacts had been arrested.

"He's becoming a man," Opal said. "He'll be sixteen soon."

"I know, but I'm afraid something's horribly wrong. I want to help."

Regret pinched Charlie's dark eyes.

Anyone could see how much he loved his sister, and Gerrit picked up the pencil. *Do something nice for her tonight.*

Charlie nodded a few times and wrote *"I'll take her to a Sunday show."*

Gerrit smiled at the boy. If only he could take Ivy to a show and hear her laugh.

Opal was speaking. "And you know he makes wise decisions."

"He does. He's grown up so much. Dad and Mum would be proud. I wish I could trust Fern to make wise decisions too."

"Oh dear." Opal's voice stiffened.

"I don't know how to say this. Fern's been staying out late with—as she says—her friends from College House. Germans."

A flat murmur. "I've heard the rumors."

"Rumors?" Ivy's voice climbed. "Oh no. What have you heard?"

"I'm sure it's nothing."

"It isn't a group, is it? It's one man." A sob.

Gerrit clenched his fists, stopped himself from rushing to Ivy, holding her to his chest. Fern was married. How dare she carry on with another man, much less an enemy soldier?

And Charlie—his face drew long, pale.

"Now, now," Opal said. "Rumors are often wrong."

"Not this one." Ivy sobbed the words. "She's acting as she did when she was falling in love with Bill. Oh, poor Bill. And the boys."

"Three years Bill's been gone. Fern never forgave him for leaving."

"But he had to do his duty. He would have hated himself had he stayed."

Charlie's expression warped with confusion, grief, anger.

Gerrit could no more comfort the brother than he could the sister, and he clamped useless hands together.

"She won't listen to me," Ivy said. "She doesn't respect me."

"She won't listen to me either," Opal said. "If it's true, she's already justified it all—the consequences to her marriage, her reputation, your reputation and Charlie's."

A loud groan from Ivy. "I promised Dad I'd look after the practice, look after the family. I'm failing."

Gerrit's fingers stretched toward the kitchen door. How could she think that?

"Oh, Ivy." Her aunt spoke in a gentle tone. "You care deeply for your patients and your family. Everyone can see. Charlie and Fern are responsible for their own decisions. You are not."

Ivy couldn't control such things.

Neither could Gerrit.

CHAPTER
21

Ivy knocked on Thelma Galais's door, and it was opened by Aunt Opal, who had attended Thelma overnight.

Ivy removed her summer hat. "How is she this morning?"

"It won't be long. She hasn't eaten for three days."

No amount of persuasion helped, and Ivy sighed. She'd seen it with many patients in their final days, but this was Thelma.

"She's sleeping now." Aunt Opal gave her a sympathetic look. "The rector and Ethel de Puy are here, so I'll go home."

"Thank you. I'll see you later." Sleep was a blessing for Thelma—and for Ivy. She needed to ring Joan de Ferrers, and she didn't want to waste even one of Thelma's waking moments.

After Aunt Opal left, Ivy rang the chemist. "I'd like to place a prescription for both Mr. and Mrs. Hooper. Please mix sulfur ointment, 20 percent." Far higher than the usual strength and for two patients, letting her know two fugitives needed to be moved.

"Did you say 20 percent?" Joan asked.

"I insist. They both have a bad case of scabies."

A pause. "Only the two of them?" Joan knew the Hoopers sheltered three fugitives.

"Their farmworkers managed to *escape* the infestation." Ivy placed the slightest stress on the word *escape*, hoping Joan would understand—one of the fugitives had disappeared.

Demyan Marchenko. At dawn, one of the Hoopers' horses had trotted up to the farmhouse, reins hanging loose. Demyan was nowhere to be found.

The Hoopers had summoned Ivy for an emergency visit. They were frantic. If the Germans caught Demyan and he talked, the Hoopers, the two other fugitives, and everyone in the ring would be in danger.

"Sulfur," Joan said. "It'll be ready within the hour."

"Thank you." Ivy hung up.

Joan would ring the next person up the "lifeline," who would see to transferring the two fugitives to another home straightaway.

Ivy gave herself a little shake. She'd done all she could for the escapees. Now to see to Thelma.

Upstairs, deep murmurs rose from Thelma's bedroom.

The Very Reverend Matthew Le Marinel sat by Thelma's bedside, reading a Psalm. Across the room, knitting, sat Ethel de Puy, the mother-in-law of Fern's former friend Kitty.

The rector stood and motioned Ivy to his chair with a gentle smile. As a matter of principle, he refused to use the black market, and he'd lost several stone in body weight.

Thelma lay in bed, her mouth slack, her face pallid, her long silver hair bound in a braid.

Ivy sank into the chair, opened her bag, and removed her stethoscope. Thelma's pulse and respirations were faint and sparse. Death was near.

Ivy's throat throbbed. She draped her stethoscope around her neck and gathered Thelma's chilly fingers in her hand. How could she bear to part with her?

A loud sniff from across the room. "If poor Thelma knew a Picot was in her house."

Ivy's face heated. On a small island, rumors needed little assistance, and yet so many people seemed eager to assist. Like Kitty and Ethel de Puy. In front of the rector, nonetheless.

"Oh?" The rector stood at the foot of the bed. "I can't imagine that to be true, Mrs. de Puy. The Picot and Galais families have been friends for generations."

Mrs. de Puy's knitting needles clacked harder than ever. "There are things you should know, Reverend. Perhaps later, in private."

"Are you referring to the gossip about town?" he asked with an innocent air. "I am quite aware of it. I do hope you haven't played a role in spreading that gossip."

"Oh." Stammering from Mrs. de Puy. A soft thud, and a ball of yarn rolled to Ivy's feet.

Rolling the yarn back to Mrs. de Puy, Ivy lifted her heated face just enough to see the rector.

His demeanor shifted to something more pointed. "Please note the gossip does not concern Dr. Ivy Picot. Indeed, Dr. Picot is regarded by her fellow physicians and by all who know her as a woman of the highest character. Those rumors I trust."

"I—I didn't mean to besmirch—"

"Ah, but that is the way of gossip, is it not?" The pointedness receded into pastoral care. "It poisons all it touches, including—perhaps most of all—those who speak it."

Ivy didn't dare glance at Mrs. de Puy, but the heat of embarrassment flowed from her chair.

"I'll check on Thelma's tea." Mrs. de Puy scrambled from the room.

The rector sent Ivy a tiny smile. "I shall give her a few minutes to feel suitably chastened, then I shall pray with her."

"Thank you. These are difficult days." Not only the gossip and the exodus of even more patients, but losing Thelma. She squeezed her friend's hand as if she could squeeze life back in.

"I shall continue to pray for your sister, and for you and dear Charlie." The rector headed for the bedroom door. "I'll give you some privacy."

"Thank you, Reverend, for—for everything." Her voice came out ragged.

Thelma's fingers twitched in her grasp, and her eyelids fluttered. A rheumy gaze drifted until meeting Ivy's, then cleared. Her lips opened, shut, opened—dry and cracked.

"Would you like some water?" Ivy grabbed a glass from the bedside table and lifted Thelma's head enough to drink.

After two feeble sips, Thelma wrinkled her nose and turned aside.

Ivy eased her head down to the pillow. "You'll feel better if you drink."

"I'm not thirsty." Dry lips bent in a slight smile. "Please don't worry. Soon I'll be with my most precious Savior."

"But I—I'll miss you." Ivy gripped Thelma's hand as if she could hold her back. "You're the last bit of God's goodness I can see."

Something unfamiliar flashed in Thelma's hazel eyes—the same sharpness she'd seen in the reverend's rebuke. "'Why seek ye the living among the dead? He is not here, but is risen.'"

Ivy pulled back her chin. Seeking the living among the dead? Thelma wasn't dead yet.

"The cross . . . oh, Ivy, the cross." Thelma's eyelids fluttered, heavier and heavier, slower and slower, and her hand relaxed in Ivy's grip.

"Please no," Ivy whispered. But Thelma's chest still rose and fell. "Please don't take her, Lord. Not yet."

CHAPTER
22

Standing on the breakwater, Bernardus gazed down into the water, bright turquoise in the afternoon sun. "This would be perfect for sabotage."

Gerrit whipped his gaze in all directions. No one else stood on the breakwater at St. Aubin, but dozens of men worked at the adjacent gun battery. "We've already discussed this."

"Everything's changed." A frenzied look filled Bernardus's light blue eyes. "The network is blown, and we have no way to help."

"I hate it too." Gerrit scanned the bay capped by St. Aubin's Fort on its tiny island. "We have to take comfort in knowing dozens of our maps were delivered."

"Or captured." Bernardus clapped his hands to his hips. "And for what good? The Allies just invaded Sicily. In the Mediterranean. They aren't coming to France."

Not this year, and Gerrit shoved his jaw forward. Would his maps even be relevant when the invasion did come?

"Here we are, building for our enemy." Bernardus jerked his

head toward the gun battery of sand-colored stone. "But I have an idea."

"I don't want to hear about—"

"Listen. On a dark night when the tide is out, we creep along the base of this breakwater, plant explosive charges, and blow up the breakwater. That will wreck this harbor."

"Bernardus." Gerrit bored his gaze into his friend. "You know all the reasons sabotage is a bad idea. We cannot do this."

Bernardus pulled back a bit, and his gaze darkened. "You mean *you* cannot do this."

Down by his side, Gerrit's left hand flexed. Was he trying to control all the details again? Or was this as awful an idea as it seemed? "You're right. I cannot. And you should not, especially alone."

Bernardus wrenched his head to the side. Whatever plan he was concocting, he couldn't do it by himself.

Then Bernardus fixed a fierce gaze on Gerrit. "The Allies will win."

"Yes, thank goodness." Even the Germans seemed to know it.

Bernardus poked a finger at Gerrit's chest. "What will they say about us after the war? They'll call us collaborators, even traitors."

"We're working for the resistance. They'll—"

That poke turned to a shove. "They're all dead. Or will be soon. See if that changes your mind." Bernardus pushed past him and marched up the breakwater.

Gerrit groaned and followed. Surely, some in the network survived. Surely, some of the maps had reached England and would prove their loyalty.

At the base of the breakwater, Gerrit headed for the shed used for construction site headquarters. With RAF raids increasing, the "Aubin Hafen" open casemate was scheduled to be enclosed with reinforced concrete to protect guns and gunners.

In the shed, Ernst Schmeling leaned over a table spread with blueprints. He smiled at Gerrit as he entered. "You'll be pleased to hear we caught the murderer yesterday."

A sickening feeling twined in his gut. "Murderer?"

"That Russian swine we saw murder a German guard."

Not "manslaughter" or "self-defense," but "murder." Marchenko would be executed after all, and Gerrit could no longer help him. "Where—where has he been?" His voice sounded choked, sounded like treason.

The Jounys, everyone who helped Marchenko—all were in danger.

Schmeling pushed back from the table and crossed his arms. "He refused to say who hid him, even though he was questioned all night."

Gerrit fought back a grimace. What had that questioning entailed?

"He insisted he hid in the woods and stole food and clothing." Schmeling released a scoffing sound. "Liar. He was too well fed, too clean, too well healed from his gunshot wound."

With every bit of effort, Gerrit echoed the scoffing sound. "Someone hid him." At least Marchenko hadn't named them yet, but how long until he broke?

"This is our only clue. The swine had it in his pocket. I'm showing it around." Schmeling pulled a square of paper from inside his jacket, unfolded it, and tossed it on the table.

A pencil sketch of a horse, a bright-eyed horse, trotting, his tail high and pluming.

Ivy Picot hadn't signed it. She didn't need to.

Gerrit's stomach roiled, and he pressed his hand over it.

Schmeling jabbed his finger at the horse. "The Russian says he found it on a kitchen table while stealing food. I don't believe him. This could tell us where he was hiding."

And who had treated his gunshot wound.

With quivering fingers, Gerrit picked up the sketch. Ivy was generous with her artwork. If Schmeling showed it around, someone would eventually recognize her hand.

Gerrit moistened his lips. "He—the Russian—he isn't talking?"

"Wasn't. The camp commandant hanged him at dawn at the gate to Lager Schepke."

A punch to Gerrit's gut. Marchenko . . . was dead?

"They made an example of him." Schmeling's thin lips twisted into a smile. "Marched all the workers past his body this morning. They'll march past again this evening."

That punch jabbed deeper. Gerrit gasped from the pain. "He—they left him there? That violates every rule of human decency."

Schmeling's narrow nostrils flared. "He murdered a German. He violated those rules of decency far more."

Gerrit's head shook. He backed up, the drawing in hand.

Turned. Bolted out the door.

He'd be disciplined, but what did it matter?

It was too late for Marchenko to receive justice, but not too late to show him respect.

$\approx$

ST. LAWRENCE'S PARISH

Ivy pedaled along a lane on her way from St. Helier to Beaumont to see a patient. "'Surely goodness and mercy shall follow me all the days of my life.'" The verse hiccuped out of her mouth.

Only an hour before, as Reverend Le Marinel had read the Twenty-third Psalm, Thelma Galais had walked through the valley of the shadow of death, fearing no evil, for the Lord was with her. Now Thelma would dwell in the house of the Lord forever.

But Ivy had lost one of her few friends on the island, one of the few lights of goodness.

"'Why seek ye the living among the dead?'" Thelma had asked Ivy, as the angel had asked the women at the empty tomb.

Ivy cycled past the stump of yet another tree chopped down for fuel. Always she'd seen God's goodness in the world and its people, but both were easily corrupted.

Why did Ivy seek the goodness of the living God in the corruptible world and its corruptible people?

"'He is not here, but is risen,'" she whispered. That was the goodness. The cross. The resurrection.

If every person turned to evil and all creation were destroyed, would God still be good?

He could be no other. The cross was the proof.

Ivy tipped her face to the clear blue sky. "Lord, help me see."

She rounded a slight bend. A tree up ahead poked above the hedgerow. But something was wrong. Too much gray, lines that didn't fit.

She passed the hedges lining the side road, and the sight cleared.

A man hung in the tree. Hung by the neck. His hands bound behind him.

Demyan Marchenko.

A cry birthed in her gut, convulsed her, spewed from her mouth. Guttural. Howling.

She didn't need to take his pulse. The Germans—the brutes!—wouldn't have left him unless certain he was dead.

"Ivy! Don't look!" A male voice. A bicycle bore down on her.

A man in a brown Todt uniform—Gerrit van der Zee—scrambled off the bicycle, his long legs tangling in the frame. He kicked the bicycle aside, lurched toward her. "Don't look, Ivy!"

"You!" The word quaked with fury, and she stumbled off her own bicycle and thrust a finger toward Demyan's body. "You people did this."

Gerrit took her by the shoulders and guided her back to the far side of the hedge.

She wanted to resist, but her feet felt numb, floppy.

"Please don't look." Behind the hedge, Gerrit turned her shoulders away from the body. "I came to cut him down, give him a decent burial. He was a good man."

"I know." She spat the words at him. "I knew him."

Gerrit released her shoulders and removed his cap. Sweat darkened his hairline around his bright red cheeks. "You treated his gunshot wound."

Ivy's face stretched long. "How did you . . . ?" If the Germans knew she had treated Demyan, she would be arrested, Joan, the helpers, maybe even Charlie and Fern.

Gerrit swiped his arm across his forehead and pulled a piece of paper from his trouser pocket. "Marchenko was carrying this when they captured him yesterday."

The horse she'd drawn to cheer him up, and she held it in trembling hands.

"I knew it was yours," Gerrit said. "Marchenko told the Germans he stole it from a farmhouse while stealing food. He was protecting you, protecting those who sheltered him. If the Germans discover you're the artist and question you, tell them you give drawings to many of your patients and can't remember who received this one. Take it home and burn it."

Ivy's gaze rose from the horse to Gerrit's eyes, darkened to teal with concern, his mouth set hard. He—he was protecting her too.

Gerrit tucked in his lips and tapped the paper. "Please be careful who you give your drawings to."

A groaning cry ripped through her, and she crumpled up the drawing. "This—my drawing could get people arrested. Killed. Stupid, frivolous, a waste of paper."

"No." Gerrit clamped his hand around her fist. "It's not a waste. Your art brings joy. It brings light. It brings—hope. Don't ever stop."

Ivy couldn't tear her gaze from the passionate conviction in his eyes, couldn't tear her hand from the warm strength of his grip, couldn't tear her mind from the truth—the truth!—that Gerrit van der Zee was far more than the uniform.

He closed his eyes and stepped away. "You should leave. Quickly. Schmeling—he certainly knows my intentions. He may send men after me. Go that way." He waved to the northeast, back the way she'd come.

Gerrit glanced over her shoulder toward Demyan, and his face buckled.

"What will you do?" she asked. "How will you bury him?"

"I don't know." He stretched his long fingers before him and stared at them. "I have a knife to cut him down. I'll dig with my hands if I must. I can't leave him like that."

With an intake of breath, Ivy pulled herself taller and became Dr. Picot once again. "Cut him down and stay with him. I'll find a telephone and ring for an ambulance to collect the body. The people of Jersey won't stand for this. They'll make sure he has a proper burial."

"Thank you. He was my friend. He—he called me comrade." His voice broke, and he glanced away, his cheeks red and agitated. "Go. Quickly."

"Yes." She turned, picked up her bicycle, and pedaled away. Why would a slave worker call a Todt man his comrade?

She saw—and yet didn't see at all.

CHAPTER
23

Even the extraordinary talent of Germany's propagandists failed to turn the German defeats in Sicily and Ukraine into victories for the newsreel.

Gerrit fidgeted in his seat in the Forum's darkened theater. The film itself was slightly less inane than the newsreel, but watching it—even cheering when the Germans did—soothed suspicions in Organisation Todt.

As his punishment for defying OT and for losing Ivy's sketch on his frenzied bicycle ride—as he had claimed—Gerrit had been deprived of privileges for a month. A pittance of a penalty in comparison to what Marchenko had suffered.

Gerrit clamped his hands over his knees. He could still see his friend's body, hear Ivy's enraged howl. But Marchenko had received a decent burial in the Strangers Cemetery at St. Brelade with dozens of his comrades who had died in the past year. Ivy had been correct—the people of Jersey insisted upon it. The German field commander, eager to be seen as benevolent, had complied.

The praise from the upper echelons of society for Gerrit's humane actions had forced OT into that pittance of a punishment. But Schmeling now watched him with a mix of contempt and suspicion. Gerrit needed to be on his best behavior.

Sitting to Gerrit's left, Willy Riedel laughed at the scene on the cinema screen, and Gerrit joined in. He and Bernardus had increased their social outings with their colleagues, but Bernardus had begged off tonight.

Gerrit would rather be at the Jouny farmhouse, where he'd spent a pleasant afternoon drawing maps while Bernardus and Arthur listened to the BBC. At Bernardus's request, he'd traced a map of land mines along St. Aubin's Bay. Soon he'd run out of silk and secret ink, but until he did, he planned to keep drawing in case a new contact arose.

Two rows ahead of him in the theater, a woman tipped her head, angling her hat higher.

Fern Le Corre, sitting with a German officer.

In public. Unashamed.

The Forum was open to islanders as well as Germans, but the only locals in attendance were women accompanying German soldiers. Women who had earned derisive nicknames from their neighbors.

Didn't Fern care how her decisions affected her sister and brother?

"Gerrit?" A fierce whisper. A tap on his shoulder.

Charlie Picot crouched in the aisle, his eyes frantic in the eerie gray light from the screen. "Come with me. It's an emergency."

"Emer—"

"Come." Charlie marched back up the aisle.

"Excuse me," Gerrit said to Riedel, who gave him a curious look.

Gerrit rushed to catch up. What kind of emergency? How could he help?

Outside in the darkness, Charlie strode to a black car used by OT. "Can you drive?"

"Yes."

"Good." Charlie opened the passenger door. "I can't. It's a miracle I didn't kill anyone driving here."

"What . . . how . . . ?"

"Get in. Drive." Charlie slammed the door shut.

Gerrit climbed behind the wheel, started the car, and pulled into the street. "How did you get an OT car?"

"This way." Charlie pointed west. "I didn't. Bernardus did. He asked me to meet him at your hotel, and we drove to St. Aubin."

St. Aubin—where Bernardus had proposed sabotage over a month ago.

Gerrit pressed the accelerator. "What has he done?"

Charlie sat forward in the seat as if urging the car faster. "He didn't tell me his plans until we arrived. He's committing sabotage. The boot of the car was filled with explosives, and he'd stashed a rowboat in the woods where we parked."

Gerrit slapped the steering wheel. "He involved you?"

"He only wanted me to stand watch. The tide is heading out, and he's using the rowboat to tow his explosives."

"The breakwater." Gerrit huffed. He'd told Bernardus he couldn't do it alone. He never dreamed he'd rope Charlie into his plan. "I told him not to."

"I know. So did I. If he gets caught . . ." His voice broke.

He'd be executed like Marchenko—and the Germans wouldn't stop there. "How many others will get arrested?"

"You must stop him. He listens to you."

Not this time, but Gerrit sped down the Esplanade in the moonless night.

Charlie groaned and pressed his hands to his face. "It's my fault. I lost my cutout."

"It isn't your fault." If anything, Gerrit carried more blame. For once, he had eased up on the brakes, and Bernardus had accelerated over a cliff.

He peered across the inky expanse of St. Aubin's Bay, but he couldn't pick out the blacked-out village on the far side. Gerrit cranked down the window. No sounds of explosions, no fires.

Gerrit's jaw set hard as he raced along the bay. Bernardus had chosen well—a cloudy night with no moon, with favorable tides, and with the Aubin Hafen battery unmanned due to construction.

After Gerrit drove through the seaside village of St. Aubin, Charlie directed him to a wooded area along the shore, where he parked.

"This is where he went down to the water. He was going to cut a passageway through the barbed wire." Charlie led Gerrit through the trees toward the beach.

They stopped inside the tree line, and Gerrit leaned close. "Wait here. If anyone comes, if anything happens, run. Don't take the car—run, get home. If you get caught, tell the truth. Say Bernardus told you to stand watch, and you fetched me to stop him. Say sabotage is wrong, and you don't know why he thought you'd approve."

Gerrit scanned the black sea, the black sky, and the black breakwater dividing them. Where was Bernardus? At least if Gerrit couldn't see him, the guards in St. Aubin's Fort on the island in the bay might not see him either.

"He's wearing black," Charlie said in a low voice. "Soot on his face."

And Gerrit wasn't. Regardless, the breakwater still stood, which meant he had time. Cutting a gap in the barbed wire large enough to accommodate a rowboat must have taken a long while.

Charlie pointed to an indentation in the sand below. "Stay in his footprints. He knows where the mines are."

Bernardus had asked Gerrit to sneak out the map of land mines. For tracing, he'd said. For sabotage, he'd meant.

Gerrit wrestled down a groan and picked his way to the beach. Halfway down the breakwater, a still patch of black disturbed the sea—probably the rowboat.

A muffled boom. A scream. A plume of water, lit up from inside. "Bernardus!" Charlie cried.

Gerrit scrambled back up the bank and clapped a hand over the boy's mouth. He stretched his eyes wide, searching for his friend. What had happened? Was Bernardus hurt? Killed? How long until the Germans came?

Light flashed on in the fort—a searchlight.

Gerrit threw himself flat to the ground, yanking Charlie down beside him.

His heart thumped against the earth, hard and fast. The searchlight panned the bay north to south, blinding Gerrit as it passed, then sweeping back north. The beam paused at the rowboat.

"No," Gerrit whispered. "Please don't let them see."

The beam swept to the end of the breakwater and switched off.

Sparkles filled Gerrit's eyesight—how long until he could see in the dark again?

Had the searchlight turned off because the guards hadn't seen anything? Or because they had? No, if they had, they would have fixed the light on it while they called in troops.

Gerrit nudged Charlie. "I'll see if he's alive."

"I'll go too. If he's hurt, you may need my help to move him."

Objections filled his mouth, but he swallowed them. He might indeed need help. "Stay low. Stay in my footsteps. Stay close to the breakwater—the mines are about a meter out."

Muffled groans rose in the distance. Bernardus was alive!

Gerrit resisted the urge to call to his friend, and he made his way out as fast as he could along the narrow band of sand between breakwater and sea. His feet dipped into damp sand, slipped on wet rocks, and he grasped the lichen-covered stone of the breakwater for support.

Not only did he need to rescue Bernardus, but he needed to remove evidence of his sabotage—or his friend could still face execution. And if caught now, all three of them would be shot.

A figure lay on the sand between the rowboat and the wall.

Gerrit crouched beside Bernardus. "Where are you hurt?"

Bernardus moaned and held his leg, the trousers shredded and shiny in the faint starlight. "Rock. Fell. Mine."

He must have dislodged a rock from the breakwater, which fell and hit a mine. "We'll get you out of here."

Charlie dropped his jacket and ripped off his shirt. "He'll bleed out. I'll apply a tourniquet."

Meanwhile, Gerrit would destroy the evidence. "How many charges did you plant?"

Bernardus shook his head and groaned.

Gerrit leaned over his friend and glared at him. "You're injured. If they find the explosives, you're dead."

"Don't. Care."

"Charlie and I will be dead too." Gerrit spat out the words. "Care about that? How many charges? Where?"

A long moan, and Bernardus waved to the right. "Three."

Gerrit found the first charge in a crevice in the breakwater, pulled it out, followed the detonating cord to the other charges, removed them.

In the rowboat, a canvas tarp covered the remaining explosives. Staying low, Gerrit flung out the canvas—they could use it as a stretcher. Then he placed the charges and detonating cord in the rowboat. They splashed.

Holes pocked the boat, some below the waterline—from the mine explosion, no doubt. Gerrit pried some rocks from the seabed and added them to the rowboat, anything to help it sink.

With a mighty heave, he shoved the boat away from the breakwater. "Please, Lord," he muttered. Might it drift to sea, past the low tide mark, and sink, carrying the evidence with it.

"Ready." Charlie slipped on his jacket.

"Quiet." Gerrit grabbed Bernardus's shoulders and transferred him onto the canvas, while Charlie shifted his hips and legs.

The canvas made a poor stretcher, with Bernardus's body sagging in the middle, but Gerrit and Charlie made their way back.

Gerrit kept his eyes and ears peeled. No torchlight. No shouts. No clicking pistols.

With great effort, they maneuvered Bernardus up the slope and into the backseat of the car.

Gerrit leapt behind the wheel. "To the hospital."

"No!" Bernardus cried.

"Not the hospital," Charlie said. "His injury was obviously caused by a mine."

Gerrit released a long groan and turned onto the road through St. Aubin. "If we missed any evidence, if the boat doesn't sink, they'll realize he was the saboteur." The Germans would torture him. How many names would he spill? "But he needs help."

"Ivy's at home," Charlie said.

"No." With one hand, Gerrit smashed the idea on the car seat. "We can't involve her."

"If he doesn't have surgery soon, he'll bleed to death."

A long, low cry of pain roiled up from the backseat.

Was there another way to explain his injury to the doctors at the hospital? Perhaps Bernardus was walking on the beach. But why would he do so at night? Everyone knew the beaches were mined. He would only be on the beach at night if he were up to no good.

"Fine." Gerrit raced toward St. Helier. "To your house. To Ivy."

"Fern," Bernardus moaned. "What about Fern?"

"She went out with friends," Charlie said.

The film had just started when Gerrit left the cinema. At least Fern's betrayal of family and country had purchased two precious hours before curfew.

CHAPTER
24

The tip of Ivy's pencil didn't move. For the past six weeks since Thelma and Demyan had died, she'd been unable to draw.

"Your art brings joy. It brings light. It brings—hope. Don't ever stop," Gerrit had said to her that day. But her art also sprang from joy and light and hope, and she had none.

"That isn't true," she murmured. She had Charlie. Whatever had been bothering him bothered him no more, and he'd been sweet and attentive, especially after he heard about Thelma. He'd loved Thelma too.

"I have my home." The familiar drawing room, still carrying the warmth of Dad and Mum's love, still echoing the laughter of happier times. "And I have the Lord."

The front door banged open. "Ivy! Hurry! Emergency."

"Charlie?" Ivy tossed aside sketch pad and pencil, and she ran downstairs in her house slippers.

Charlie backed through the front door dragging something heavy on a piece of canvas—no some*one* heavy. Gerrit van der Zee held the other end.

Ivy braced herself against the wall in the hallway. "What on earth?"

"Hurry." Charlie huffed as he carried his end of the canvas. "It's Bernardus. He's badly injured."

Why would they bring him to her? She dashed to the telephone. "I'll ring for an ambulance to take him to casualty at the hospital."

"No," Charlie and Gerrit said together, and Gerrit kicked the front door shut.

"He was injured by a land mine." Charlie entered the treatment room. "They'll know he was committing sabotage."

"Sabotage!" She stared down at the unconscious man, his face blackened, a white tourniquet about his thigh, his leg—what was left of it—stained crimson.

In the treatment room, Charlie and Gerrit hoisted Bernardus onto the examination table.

Ivy flung on her white coat and washed her hands with what little soap she had. "I'm not a surgeon. I don't have proper anesthetics."

"You're his only chance. Our only chance." Charlie grabbed scissors and cut off the remains of Bernardus's boot. "If he goes to hospital, the doctors may save his life, but the Germans will arrest him, torture him, find out he's in the resistance."

"Charlie," Gerrit said with a growl.

"Resistance?" Ivy glanced over her shoulder at the men, who scowled at each other.

Charlie snapped his gaze to Ivy. "If Bernardus talks, they'll find out Gerrit and I are in the resistance too, and they might unravel our whole network."

"Charlie!" Gerrit said. "Silence."

Ivy's hands hung limp under the cold water. Charlie wasn't in the resistance. Impossible. Jersey had no organized resistance. But France did. And Charlie traveled to France. "Charlie? What—"

"Your patient." Charlie snipped away at the tattered trousers. "Bleeding, dying."

Ivy gave her head a shake and scrubbed her hands. "Charlie, you'll serve as my assistant. First, please shave his leg around the wound and place towels under his leg. Gerrit, you'll find blankets in the cabinet on the far left, bottom shelf. Please wrap Bernardus, leaving his injured leg exposed. He's in shock, and we need to warm him."

"Yes, Doctor."

Gerrit was in the resistance too? Not a collaborator?

No, she didn't have time for speculation. She had to save a man's life with her minimal surgical training and the bottle of chloroform Dad kept on hand for emergencies. If he only knew how she'd be using it.

After she dried her hands, she gathered surgical dressings from the cabinet and placed her surgical instruments in a basin filled with disinfectant.

"No. Oh no." Gerrit's voice plummeted deep. He held a folded piece of paper. "The mine map. This should have gone in the boat."

"Burn it," Charlie said.

Gerrit tucked it into his brown uniform jacket. "No, I'll sneak it back into OT Headquarters. They'll never know I took it."

Ivy gaped at him. What was happening?

She gritted her jaw. A grave injury had happened, and Bernardus needed her full attention.

"I finished shaving," Charlie said.

"Thank you." At the sink, she scrubbed her hands again. She hadn't enough time or helpers to prepare a sterile operating theater. "We have less than two hours of electricity. Charlie, fetch the paraffin lamps and all the candles you can find. Matches too." If only she could send Gerrit instead, but he wouldn't know where to find anything.

Charlie ran out of the room.

After Ivy pulled on rubber gloves, she examined her patient. The wounds were indeed grave but seemed limited to his left leg. She might be able to save his leg, but he'd already lost most of his foot.

She draped sheets around the wound and over a table, where she laid out her surgical instruments and prepared some sutures.

Gerrit cleared his throat. "You must have questions for me."

She couldn't look at him. "I do. But not now."

"Understood. May I—can I help in any way?"

Ivy nodded to a large stainless-steel basin. "I need to irrigate the wound, wash out the sand. Please hold that basin under the edge of the table to catch the drainage."

"Yes, Doctor."

She opened a bottle of Dakin's solution and poured it over the wound, and a light smell of chlorine counteracted the scent of sand and seawater and blood.

Liquid tinkled into the basin. "Bernardus will need to go into hiding," Gerrit said. "For the same reason he can't go to hospital."

If he survived. First, Ivy had to stop the bleeding, and she applied clamps to ruptured vessels. "I have a car and some petrol. After I finish the operation, I'll take him to my uncle's farm."

"Yes. That's a good idea. They've hidden someone before. They'll know what to do."

Demyan Marchenko. Ivy's jaw dangled, and she glanced at the Dutchman catching the last dribbles of Dakin's solution. How did he know?

Demyan had mentioned someone helping him escape after he shot the guard. Was it Gerrit? Bernardus?

Gerrit dumped the basin in the sink. "How else can I help?"

All she wanted from him was answers—but she hadn't the time. She dragged her gaze to the table. What could he do? Chloroform? Bernardus was unconscious, but she couldn't have him wake during surgery. "Wash your hands well. I'll put a few drops of chloroform on a cloth mask, and you can tie it over his mouth and nose. I'll have Charlie monitor the anesthesia when he returns."

"Yes, Doctor."

With the main vessels clamped, Ivy chose forceps to pick out bits of fabric and gravel that had evaded the irrigating solution.

"Tomorrow morning." Gerrit paused with his hands under the water. "They'll realize he's gone, send out a manhunt."

Ivy sighed and plucked out a shred of black fabric. "My uncle will hide him well."

"Unless . . . what if they think he escaped? The boat—yes." Gerrit spun to her, and thoughts darted in his green-blue eyes. "The cinema. Charlie. I'll need to—I need to leave. Now. Can you spare me?"

Ivy bobbled a nod. She had no idea what he was talking about.

Charlie entered the room with a box of supplies.

Gerrit scrambled past Charlie to the door. "Charlie, I'm working on a plan. I'll come back later tonight, tell you everything. You'll need to know."

"All right." Charlie stared after his friend, then at Ivy. "What's happening?"

"That's what I'd like to know." Ivy tilted her head to the sink. "Take off your jacket, put on Dad's white coat, and wash your hands."

Charlie shrugged off his jacket, revealing his vest—his shirt must have become the tourniquet. "We'll need to distract Fern when she comes home."

And when they transported Bernardus to the car. Somehow.

Charlie slipped on Dad's coat. "You probably want to know about the resistance."

She did. More than anything. But first, she had to save this man's life.

CHAPTER
25

ST. AUBIN

With gloved hands, Gerrit used his knife to sever the telephone line into the Aubin Hafen gun battery. How ironic that after warning Bernardus against sabotage, Gerrit was committing sabotage himself—to protect half a dozen lives, including his own.

He sheathed his knife, ran along the beach to the wooded area, slid into the car, and drove toward the hotel.

To prevent a manhunt, he had to convince the Germans that Bernardus had escaped—preferably, had died in the attempt. He had to explain why Charlie had fetched him at the Forum, which had been witnessed by Riedel and others. He had to explain why he'd waited so long to alert the Germans. He had to convince them of his own loyalty.

And Gerrit had never been good at lying.

"Start with the truth. Stay as close to the truth as possible." He added a prayer for forgiveness for deviating from the truth—again. But if his story worked, he could save the lives of Bernardus, Charlie, Arthur and Opal Jouny. And Ivy.

Gerrit drove down the darkened road. He could still see Ivy's wide brown eyes staring at him with a mix of confusion and shock and . . . hope. Or maybe he'd seen his own hope in her eyes. He hadn't wanted her to know about his resistance activities, but now she did. Now she knew he wasn't a collaborator looking only to save his own skin.

Now a path had opened between them.

He longed to meet her on that path.

But Bernardus's rash actions had imperiled Ivy, and a romance with Gerrit would imperil her even more. If the Germans found out what Gerrit had done, connected him to her . . .

His jaw clenched. Once again, distance was the best way to protect Ivy. He couldn't bear the thought of that sweet soul being imprisoned, tortured, executed.

At the hotel, Gerrit stashed the mine map in his desk. If the map didn't bear marks of the evening's misadventure, he'd slip it back into the technical section office on Monday.

Gerrit ran upstairs to Ernst Schmeling's room. Being short of breath and disheveled suited his story well. He pounded on the door. "Herr Oberbauführer! Herr Oberbauführer!"

In a few seconds, Schmeling opened the door of his darkened room, pulling a dressing gown over his pajamas. "This had better be important. You disturbed my sleep."

All Gerrit's frustration and anger at Bernardus infused his voice. "It's Kroon—he betrayed us."

"Pardon?" Schmeling blinked heavily. "Betrayed?"

"He tried to commit sabotage. I went to stop him, but I was too late and he was injured and he escaped in a boat but he's so badly injured I don't think he'll survive." Gerrit ran the words together and shook his arm to the west, toward St. Aubin.

"Slow down. Start from the beginning."

Gerrit took a long breath. "I was at the Forum with the other men when Charlie Picot fetched me."

"Charlie . . . ?" Schmeling flicked on his bedside lamp and wrestled off his dressing gown.

Gerrit stepped inside, closed the door, and faced it to give

Schmeling some privacy. "Charlie is a local lad who works on a cargo ship, the *Ormer*. Bernardus and I have befriended him, and he shows us around the island."

Cloth swished. "To the point, van der Zee."

"Yes, Herr Oberbauführer. Bernardus drove Charlie to St. Aubin this evening, told him to stand watch while he blew up the breakwater. I can't believe it! I trusted him!" His voice shook with genuine fury that his friend had endangered so many people.

A curse from Schmeling. "He blew up the breakwater?"

"No, no. Charlie came for me, wanted me to stop Bernardus. I don't understand—why would Bernardus think Charlie would approve of sabotage? One of Charlie's sisters works for the Feldkommandantur. Everyone knows the family is loyal."

"Come." Schmeling flung open the door, wearing his uniform jacket over his pajama pants. "Continue."

Gerrit marched alongside Schmeling. "Charlie brought the OT car Bernardus had taken. I sent the boy home, and I drove to St. Aubin and—"

Another curse, and Schmeling jammed his cap over his rumpled gray hair. "You didn't come for me first? Sound the alarm?"

"I . . ." The truth clogged his throat. "Bernardus is my oldest friend. I thought I could dissuade him. He's a reasonable man."

Schmeling shoved open the door to the stairwell and pounded down the stairs. "He's a traitor."

Gerrit was too, but he had to convince the man otherwise. "I went to the breakwater to stop him. Charlie told me he was using a rowboat to tow the explosives. There was an explosion—Bernardus set off a mine. I heard him scream."

"Good. He'll scream even louder when we catch him."

"I—I don't know if you will. I had to lie low for a few minutes. The searchlight at St. Aubin's Fort switched on. I didn't want them to shoot at me."

On the ground floor, Schmeling opened the door and strode across the lobby to the telephone. "Wise. I'll grant you that."

"After the searchlight turned off, I ran out to him. He was badly injured. So much blood. He'd dragged himself into the boat. He threatened me with his pistol, told me not to follow him. Since he couldn't finish the job, he'd removed the explosives and was sailing for France."

"I'll call for patrol boats." Schmeling grabbed the telephone receiver and started dialing. "Which is what you should have done."

"I tried," Gerrit said. "The telephone line in the battery is cut."

Schmeling cursed yet again, then barked orders into the telephone.

Gerrit still had almost an hour's delay to explain—the gunners at St. Aubin's Fort would have noted the time of the explosion.

Schmeling slammed down the receiver, beckoned to Gerrit, and marched to the door. "Come along."

Gerrit followed him out into the cool night. "I tried to stop him, Herr Oberbauführer. His boat was damaged in the explosion—I saw holes, saw Bernardus bailing water. I took a rowboat from the harbor and followed him."

Schmeling gave him a disgusted look and jerked open the car door.

Gerrit climbed in on the passenger side. "He's my friend. My oldest friend."

"You had no warning that he was about to betray us? None at all?" Schmeling tore down the road.

Gerrit heaved a sigh. "He's been despondent lately. He thinks Germany will lose the war, and he's worried about what will happen to him afterward. Maybe he thought the Allies would look more favorably on him if he was a saboteur." All of it true.

"A dead saboteur if we catch him."

"He's dead either way." A longer sigh from deep in his gut. "Even if the boat wasn't damaged, he couldn't row all the way to France with his injuries. But the boat *was* damaged. I rowed for a while, but I never found him. I had to turn around—I was concerned about our guns at Noirmont Point. Then I fought the tide on the way back."

"The map of mines on the bay." Schmeling swung a glare to Gerrit. "It's missing. He must have taken it."

Gerrit groaned. Now he'd have to burn the map. "How could he?"

Schmeling added yet another curse to the night. "Drowning is too good for him. Bleeding to death is too good for him. He deserves to hang."

Bernardus still might die due to his injuries, during surgery, or if captured. And Gerrit added yet another sigh to the night.

CHAPTER
26

"I'm here to treat Bernardus," Ivy murmured as she knocked on the farmhouse door. Since she had an appointment in the surgery only an hour and a half from now, she should have visited Bernardus on Sunday afternoon. Yet she'd come on Saturday. And she'd taken more care than usual with her hair and had worn her favorite emerald-green blouse under her brown tweed suit.

Because Gerrit often visited Bernardus on Saturday afternoons.

When Charlie had told Ivy about the men's involvement with the resistance, her intuition about Gerrit had been proven correct. However, Ivy hadn't seen him since late on the night of Bernardus's operation, when Gerrit had returned to coordinate stories with Charlie.

Aunt Opal opened the door. "Ivy! How lovely to see you, Ivy," she called, informing Bernardus that he did not need to hide.

Ivy stepped inside. "How is our patient?"

"Physically, he's improving, but his spirits are low. I'm glad Gerrit is here today drawing."

A little trill ran through Ivy's chest. "It's good for him to have friends visit."

After washing her hands in the kitchen, Ivy climbed the stairs. What could she say to Gerrit? Words had never been her strength.

At the top of the stairs, Ivy turned down the hall.

Gerrit was coming from the other direction, and he stopped short, his eyes wide.

Ivy worked up a smile. "Hallo, Gerrit."

"Hallo." He gestured toward the stairs. "I was just—I need to return to my billet. I must go out with the OT men tonight."

It was only two o'clock, but Ivy stepped to the side. "Of course. Will I see you in church tomorrow?"

His gaze skittered past her to the stairs. "I've been attending German-language services. I need to look loyal."

"Oh yes. I see. It must be difficult for you lately. I'm glad they believed you, though, about Bernardus escaping, presumed dead. I saw it in the *Evening Post*."

"Yes. Excuse me." He edged past without meeting her gaze.

The trill sank into a mire of disappointment, but she had more to say. "Thank you for what you're doing. The maps and such."

"Pardon?" He turned back.

She tried for a teasing smile. "I'm glad you're on the right side after all."

He gave her a nod, but his eyebrows pinched together. "I'm sorry we involved Charlie."

"Don't be." She'd given it much consideration over the past few weeks, and her hand fluttered in a dismissive way. "I won't pretend I'm not worried about him. I am. But I'm also extraordinarily proud of him. I told him so. Our father would be proud too."

"We lost our contacts anyway, so . . ." He sidestepped down the hall. "I need to . . ."

"Leave, yes. Goodbye." After he returned her goodbye and headed downstairs, Ivy turned for Bernardus's room. She might have been correct about Gerrit's character, but she'd been mistaken imagining he might be attracted to her. As had Fern.

And that connection she'd sensed when she met him a year earlier. The connection she'd felt each time she'd seen him since. An illusion.

In the bedroom, Bernardus lay in bed with his leg propped up. "How are you today?" she asked.

Bernardus rolled his head away from her toward the wall. "Crippled, bored, chastened."

Ivy pulled up a chair, opened her medical bag, and set the kitchen timer so she'd leave in time for her appointment. Then she unwrapped the bandages. "The crippling is temporary. We saved part of your foot, including the heel, which will aid in walking. And much of the musculature in your calf and thigh will grow back in time. Next week, we'll have you start walking with a crutch."

"I wish the chastening was temporary." He balled up the blanket in his fists.

She raised a soothing smile, but her patient stared at the wall. "I'm glad Gerrit visited. Has he forgiven you?"

"As always, yes. If only I'd learn to give him less to forgive."

What a blessing it must be to have a friendship like Gerrit and Bernardus had.

Ivy examined the surgical incisions—all clean with no signs of redness or infection. Aunt Opal was caring for him well.

"Any word from your contacts?" Bernardus asked.

Dr. Tipton and the others in the ring had balked at adding Bernardus to the lifeline. Although presumed to be dead, Bernardus was far too valuable to the Germans, and his very Dutch looks would make disguise difficult.

But Ivy had pressed her case and prevailed. "They've agreed."

"Perhaps they shouldn't have done. If the Germans learn I'm alive . . ."

Ivy had seen what they'd done to Demyan Marchenko. How much worse would they treat a resistance member who had infiltrated their Todt organization, a man who had fooled them and made a fool of them?

Ivy suppressed a sigh and pinned the bandages back in place. Her job was only to help him heal and to keep him hidden.

Ivy rounded the corner on her bicycle. Up ahead, Mary Surcouf climbed the steps to La Bliue Brise with little Penny on her hip.

Was Ivy late? She'd left the farmhouse even before the kitchen timer dinged. She glanced at her wristwatch—ten minutes early.

A distinctive cough flowed down the street.

Whooping cough, and Ivy cringed. An epidemic was raging amongst Jersey's children, and little Penny had fought off diphtheria less than a year ago.

"Mary!" A woman ran across the street—Doris des Forges Mollet, Ivy's childhood friend.

"Good afternoon, Dor—"

"You're not seeing Dr. Picot, are you? Haven't you heard?"

Oh no. Ivy stopped pedaling, and she set a foot on the ground to brace herself.

"Heard?" Mary turned with one hand on the doorknob.

"They're collaborators, the lot of them," Doris said. "Last Saturday night, my husband and I saw Fern and a German officer in a—shall we say, an *amorous* embrace. Right in the street for all to see."

"Oh, Fern," Ivy whispered.

Mary looked up at the façade of La Bliue Brise, the blue trim peeling now with wartime restrictions on painting. "We've always come to the Picots."

"Suit yourself." Doris hefted her chin. "If you enter that door, we'll all know you're a collaborator too."

Mary lowered her hand and her gaze, and she cradled Penny's whooping little head to her chest and trudged up the street, away from Ivy.

The pain of it slammed Ivy in the chest, punched the breath out of her. Penny Surcouf was the first baby Ivy had delivered in Jersey. Ivy had seen her through diphtheria. Now the Surcouf family had left the practice.

Because of Fern.

Ivy walked her bicycle around the back of the house and into the supply room, praying all the way.

She hated disharmony, but Ivy wasn't sounding the sour notes. Fern was.

Aunt Ruby sat at the receptionist's desk, smiling at Ivy.

Ivy shook her head. "Penny Surcouf won't be coming. The family is leaving the practice."

"Not another one."

"Is Fern home?"

"Yes." Aunt Ruby directed a dark look at the ceiling. "Preparing for her evening out."

With that German officer, and Ivy turned and ascended the stairs. Instead of fury, Ivy felt nothing but sad conviction.

For most of her life, Ivy had adored her sister, leaned on her, and looked up to her. But Fern apparently loved Ivy's dependence and admiration far more than she loved Ivy.

Fern's door stood ajar, and she sat at her dressing table pinning up her sable curls into a fashionable style.

Ivy stood a few feet behind her. "Another family left the practice."

"Dear, oh dear." Fern met her gaze in the mirror. "You were late again?"

"I was ten minutes early." Ivy's voice sounded remarkably calm. "Doris Mollet told my patient she saw you publicly kissing your German lover."

A flash of shame in Fern's brown eyes. A flush of red across her high cheekbones. "Don't be crass." Her voice quivered.

She hadn't denied it, but Ivy's breath still came slow and steady. "You're betraying Bill."

Fern's fingers flew over the pins and curls high on her head.

"Bill abandoned me. He doesn't appreciate me, but Helmut does. Helmut dotes on me."

"You're betraying your country. Bill is fighting for Britain, and you're carrying on with the enemy."

"Enemy?" Fern slapped both hands on the dressing table, and hairpins bounced. "Jersey is governed by Germany. I'm supporting our country."

What a way Fern had for twisting words and ideas to justify her decisions. Yet nothing but sadness filled Ivy's heart. "You've betrayed our family, betrayed the practice. So many patients have left."

Fern gasped. "They've left because you're always late, always daydreaming, always drawing."

"We've lost far more due to your job and your affair. I've been branded as a collaborator because of you."

Fern sprang from her chair and wheeled on Ivy. "Why, you pathetic, priggish little spinster. Just because no one wants you, you can't bear to see me happy."

Ivy's head swung back and forth. "Not when your happiness comes at the expense of everyone you claim to love."

"Get out!" Fern pointed to her door, her arm and her voice shaking in tandem. "Need I remind you of the man who was imprisoned for telling a woman not to step out with German soldiers? Six months in prison."

Ivy studied her sister. Her own sister, who had just threatened her. One half of her hair pinned up and sophisticated, the other half wild and disordered.

Without a word, Ivy left her sister.

CHAPTER
27

For the past two months, Gerrit had become nostalgic for his former life in Amsterdam, confined though it had been. In his current life, he built for Organisation Todt without the consolation of aiding the Allies, without Bernardus's constant companionship, and without the pleasant Sunday services at the Parish Church of St. Helier.

Gerrit climbed the stairs in the Jouny farmhouse. Only on Saturday and Sunday afternoons could he forget he was nothing but a collaborator now.

He opened Bernardus's door. In the sun-dappled room, Bernardus sat in a chair with his foot elevated on a stool—and Ivy and Charlie sat on one of the beds.

"I'm sorry." Gerrit stopped in the doorway. "I'll give you some privacy."

"No, no." Charlie stood and beckoned him in. "I have news about the network, and I wanted to talk to all of you."

Ivy picked up her medical bag from the floor. "I shouldn't be here."

"Agreed," Bernardus said.

She already knew too much for her safety, and Gerrit stepped aside to let her pass.

"Stay, Ivy." Charlie set a hand on her shoulder. "I want your opinion."

"You know the rules," Bernardus said with a growl. "Each person must know as little as possible, must have only one thing. Ivy is already treating fugitives. That's enough."

"No." Charlie fixed a strong gaze on Bernardus. "We're family. In the past few months, I've learned how each person's actions affect the others in the family. I won't proceed without discussing it with Ivy. Not again."

She gazed up at her younger brother with respect and gratitude—and a touch of sadness in her dark eyes.

Gerrit swallowed hard. "That's only fair. If you agree, Ivy, that is."

Ivy nodded and lowered her head, not concealing the pink creeping across her cheeks. She hadn't met his gaze since he'd entered, not that he blamed her. Didn't he skitter away like a rabbit every time he saw her lately?

Bernardus heaved a sigh and banged his crutch on the floorboards beside him. "I call this meeting to order. Charlie, you have the floor."

Gerrit sat on the empty bed.

Charlie settled down beside his sister. "When I was in France yesterday, Marie took me to a safe house. The British agent was there. He's establishing a new network, and he wants us to join him."

"The same agent?" Gerrit exchanged a glance with Bernardus. "How did he escape arrest this summer?"

"He was in England during the rollup."

"Convenient." Bernardus's eyes narrowed.

"No, I trust him." Charlie cupped his hands over his knees. "And they found the informant and liquidated him."

Ivy gasped and covered her mouth.

Charlie nodded to Gerrit. "They want your maps. They know the Todts are leaving the Channel Islands, and they want as much intelligence as possible before you're sent away."

Gerrit winced. Each week, more of the foreign workers were sent to France, and speculation flew about how long the OT technical and headquarters staff would remain.

"Regardless," Bernardus said. "They aren't my contacts, the people I know. I have no connection to them. How can I trust them?"

"I know nothing about such things." Ivy pursed her mouth and gripped her hands in her lap. "However, if the British agent had betrayed the resistance, wouldn't you three have been arrested during this rollup as well?"

Gerrit raised an eyebrow. She had a point. Plenty of time had passed since the arrests. If anyone were to have implicated them under torture, they would have already done so.

"I don't like it," Bernardus said.

Yet Bernardus would be less involved now. The bulk of the work would lie with Gerrit and Charlie.

"Please?" Charlie's brow creased. "The British and Americans are driving up Italy, but everyone knows they must invade in the west to defeat Germany. They need up-to-date information. We can provide it."

Gerrit's foot tapped, eager to stomp on the brakes. His fingers worked, eager to draw, to do something worthwhile. Yet neither impulse was reliable.

On the floor, shadows of branches waved in the sunbeams, void of advice or answers.

Gerrit stood. "I need to think, to pray. I'll return in half an hour."

Downstairs in the drawing room, Arthur and Opal sat reading. Gerrit gave them a polite smile and entered the kitchen. He rested his hands on the rim of the sink. Outside the kitchen window, brown Jersey cows nibbled green grass.

"Lord, help me decide." So many people would be affected. Charlie, Bernardus, Ivy, Arthur, Opal, Marie, the British agent, and others he didn't know by name. Simply because he wanted to aid the Allies and undermine the Germans didn't mean he should.

"Oh, excuse me." Ivy stood in the kitchen doorway, her hand on the knob. "I'm sorry—I didn't mean to disturb you."

"Don't mind me." He waved her in.

"I was fetching tea." She averted her gaze to the stove. "Aunt Opal made a kettle. It may still be warm. It's only beetroot tea, but would you like some too?"

"Yes, please." He couldn't stop watching her as she pulled a tray from a cabinet and set it on the table. For over a year, he'd wanted to converse with her, open and free. His collaboration had stood in the way. Then his resistance work. But now that she was involved . . .

"No sugar, of course, but would you like milk?" She held up a little jug without facing him. "One of the advantages of visiting a dairy farm."

"No, thank you. In the Netherlands, we call tea with milk *kinder thee*—children's tea."

Ivy flashed a little smile over her shoulder. "With only half a pint of milk rationed each day, we islanders are finally growing up."

Gerrit chuckled and ripped his gaze back to the window. He had a decision to make, one that affected the lovely young woman assembling cups and saucers.

China clinked. "Does your hand still hurt? From the sprain?"

"Hmm?" Gerrit's left hand opened and closed. Ached. "It always hurts a bit. I broke it when I was a boy."

"You mentioned that. How did it happen? Climbing trees? Wrestling Bernardus?" A smile pushed up her round cheeks as she fetched the teakettle.

Why was he avoiding her company? Avoiding what he'd longed for? Gerrit turned, leaned back against the sink, and stretched the once-mangled fingers. "A boy lived in my neighborhood. He was a

211

few years younger than I, the son of a servant from the East Indies, quite dark-skinned. The other boys were teasing him, pushing him around, hitting him."

"Oh dear." Ivy's pretty mouth turned down. "Children can be cruel."

Gerrit shrugged. "I didn't know what to do. I was small for my age, and I've never been a fighter."

"I can see that."

Hardly a compliment to his manliness. "The boy caught my eye. I was the only one who could help him. How could I walk away and leave him? So I stepped in, tried to talk the boys out of it. They turned on me."

The teakettle lowered to the table. "Oh no."

Gerrit raised a sheepish smile. "At least I distracted them, and the little boy escaped. But I was beaten up. They stepped on my hand. Stomped on it."

Ivy took a few steps closer, reached one hand toward his. Stopped. Withdrew her hand. "This reminds you of that."

His breath—where was it? "Pardon?"

She shook her head. "I'm sorry. I've never been good with words. I noticed you flexing your hand. Does today's decision remind you of that day?"

"I don't know." He stared at his own hand. "I do that when I'm thinking."

"You needed courage that day." She inclined her head, and soft curls swished to one side. "You need courage today."

Gerrit restrained those fingers from touching those curls. "I do."

"You wanted to protect the little boy that day. Today you want to protect Charlie and Bernardus and everyone in your network." One corner of her mouth dimpled the roundness of her cheek. "That day, protection required action. Today, protection might mean inaction."

Gerrit swallowed hard. "I thought you weren't good with words."

Brown eyes lifted to him, large and warm and wise. "Tell me about your maps. How do they help?"

This he could answer in his sleep, and he rested his hands on the sink behind him. "The maps show the locations of German fortifications—bunkers, gun positions, minefields, anti-tank walls, tunnels. Many are camouflaged so they can't be seen by Allied aircraft. I also send diagrams of those fortifications, showing the entrances, the internal layout, the location of defensive gunnery, ventilation shafts, power lines—anything that could help."

"I see." Dark eyelashes fanned over those enormous eyes. "If the Allies had your maps, they could choose their landing sites well and take the positions more quickly. That would shorten the battle, wouldn't it? Fewer soldiers killed, fewer civilians. You'd be protecting far more than Charlie and Bernardus."

And Ivy. He wanted to protect Ivy. Perhaps helping bring this dreadful war to a quick end would be the best way to protect her and everyone else he cared about.

"You were courageous that day." Ivy nodded at Gerrit's left hand. "You acted to protect."

Gerrit spread his hand before him. "Today I will be courageous again, protect again."

A smile dawned on her face, sweet and strong and bright.

Gerrit had prayed for help making a decision, but he'd never dreamed that help would come through Dr. Ivy Picot.

CHAPTER
28

If not for Bernardus Kroon's build and gait, Ivy would never have recognized him.

Bernardus sat on a stool in the barn milking a cow as Uncle Arthur coached the city boy.

"Like one of your jazz men playing a trumpet." Gerrit demonstrated with his fingers in the air.

"What do you know about milking cows?" Bernardus sent his friend a look as black as his dyed hair. In the three months since his injury, he'd grown longer hair and a mustache as part of his disguise. The ring had taken his photograph and was forging papers and ration cards for him.

"I know a lot." Gerrit frowned in a serious manner, but with a glint in his eyes. "I saw a film once."

Ivy laughed and nudged him with her shoulder, and Charlie and Uncle Arthur joined in the laughter.

At times like this, with Gerrit grinning down at her, surrounded by friends and family, Ivy could almost forget the war.

Almost.

A swastika armband circled Gerrit's brown uniform sleeve. Ivy's stomach protested the thinness of lunch. And Gerrit and Charlie were drawing and delivering maps as quickly as they could.

Yet moments of beauty were meant to be savored, and Ivy filled up at the green-blue font of Gerrit's gaze.

Everything she'd found admirable in him from the start was true, and everything she'd found despicable was false. Thelma Galais had been right about him, and a pang of grief for her precious friend brought up a paradoxical smile. How Thelma would rejoice to see Ivy falling for Gerrit.

From what Ivy could see, he was falling for her too.

Uncle Arthur led the cow to the barn door. "Bring in the next girl, Benny."

Using his crutch—and his anglicized name—Bernardus hauled himself up to standing. His left trouser leg hung loosely, and Aunt Opal had stuffed rags in the cavity inside his left shoe, a wooden-soled pair Uncle Arthur had bought with his own ration book.

Bernardus lost his balance and flung out one arm to right himself.

Ivy reached for him, then clamped her hands in the small of her back. He was doing well, and his stubbornness aided his recovery.

Everyone followed Uncle Arthur and Bernardus out of the barn, and whilst the men trailed into the pasture, Ivy fetched her sketch book, pencil, and a blanket from her bicycle.

The rain of the past few days had departed, and the rinsed-clean landscape called to her. Ivy spread her blanket under a tree and sat with her legs folded to one side and her green coat fanned over her legs for warmth.

Her pencil swept over the paper—the granite blocks of the barn, two cows, Uncle Arthur and Charlie, but not Bernardus or Gerrit.

Since Demyan's death, she no longer gave her sketches to escapees. Her stomach clenched, but her art hadn't caused his capture or execution, and she brushed away the guilt.

At least she now had more time to care for escapees, more time to draw, and more time to visit family. If only that extra time hadn't arisen because the medical practice was ailing.

Ivy brushed away even more guilt. Thanks to Fern's well-designed routes and Charlie's kitchen timer and Aunt Ruby's realistic timetables and Ivy's dedication, she had improved in punctuality. Fern alone bore the blame for the recent decline in the practice.

Heaviness pressed on Ivy's chest. Fern had barely spoken to Ivy in the past month, save to announce when she deposited her wages in the family bank account, as if those wages atoned for adultery.

What would become of her sister? Someday the Allies would win, and Bill would come home with Billy and Freddy, now ten years old.

Footsteps rustled through the grass, and Gerrit approached, smiling at her.

The heaviness melted away, and she smiled back. How hypocritical for Ivy to be falling in love with a man in a German uniform whilst she reprimanded Fern for doing the same. Yet there was no comparison.

Gerrit sat to her right and rested his elbows on his bent knees. "What are you drawing?"

She showed him, and his warmth radiated to her. Here, surrounded by the farm's granite walls and hedgerows, she could lower her own walls.

"Very nice." He gave her a lopsided smile. "Can you draw me?"

Her cheeks warmed, and she added pencil strokes to the barn. If Gerrit only knew how many sketches she'd drawn of him. Then she chuckled. "I never took you to be vain."

He returned the chuckle. "That is one thing I've never been accused of. No, I'm simply being selfish."

"Selfish?" She sketched in more height to Charlie's figure until he matched Uncle Arthur. "I would never accuse you of selfishness. Not the man who sent me reams of paper." Charlie had finally confessed.

Silence beside her, and Gerrit fiddled with his fingers. "This request is selfish. To draw me, you'd need to look at me."

How could she look at him? How could she bear up under the magnitude of his gaze? Yet how could she turn away so sweet a gift?

With a rush of breath and boldness, she flipped the page in her sketchbook and looked Gerrit full in the eye.

His gaze—so tender. His smile—so gentle. His expression—so affectionate.

All the breath rushed right back out of her chest. But not the boldness. Her pencil swished over the paper in her zest to capture the exquisiteness of the moment.

"Why are you not married?" he murmured, then he cringed. "I'm sorry. That was rude."

Less rude than Fern calling her a spinster at twenty-seven, and Ivy drew the curve of Gerrit's ear. "I almost married a boy I met at Oxford. But he loved London more than he loved me, and I loved Jersey more than I loved him."

Gerrit's gaze drifted away to the scenery. "It's beautiful here."

"It was about more than the island." Ivy guided her pencil to convey the length of Gerrit's jaw. "All my life I'd dreamed of practicing medicine with Dad and Charlie."

"Charlie?" A frown twisted the lips she yearned to draw, to touch.

"He wanted to be a physician too." Her mouth turned down as well. "Before the occupation. He left school to help the family."

"He's young," Gerrit said. "The war will be over soon."

Ivy didn't want to talk about the war. Not today. Not with Gerrit sitting so near. She gave him a teasing little smile. "You're twenty-eight, yes? Why are *you* not married?"

"Ah, only fair." A smile flicked up, and he flexed his left hand in front of her. "You know me. In the time it takes me to decide to pursue a woman, she falls in love with someone else."

Yet his slow, deliberate, precise way of thinking made him more attractive to her, and she poured her own affection into her expression.

Gerrit's chest expanded. "If these were normal times, I would be thinking about asking you out to dinner."

"Would you?" The words slipped from her mouth, barely audible. "I'd say yes."

"These aren't normal times. You mustn't be seen with me in public."

"No." Once again he showed as much care for her reputation as for her safety. What a remarkable man.

He gestured to the sketch pad. "You stopped drawing."

The pencil had fallen into her lap. For the first time she could remember, she didn't want to draw what she saw—although she never wanted to forget. "I—I just want to look."

Gerrit dropped his gaze to his hand. He flexed his fingers once, fumbled for her hand, and wrapped his fingers around hers. A hesitant little smile.

Soaring, filling, fulfilling, and she squeezed his hand and leaned into his solidness.

"See?" He lifted their entwined hands. "It took me over a year to hold your hand. I'm hopeless."

Hopelessly adorable. Then a giggle erupted. "I can't believe I'm holding hands with a Todt."

Gerrit wrinkled his nose. "I can't believe you are either. I'm not sure I want to associate with a woman who'd do such a thing."

"Gerrit!" She laughed and nudged him with her shoulder.

He grinned, broad and bright, but then his smile softened. "Thank you for doing so."

She studied the brown wool encasing his long arms and legs. "I can't imagine what it must feel like to wear that uniform."

"Awful." He squirmed his shoulders and legs. "It feels like— have you ever spilled something on yourself in the morning, and you have to spend the day damp, sticky, stained, everyone staring at you? All you can think about is changing your clothes. Well, that's what it feels like. Only worse."

Ivy murmured her sympathy, and she stroked his hand—the bones that had been crushed defending the weak, the muscles that drew enemy fortifications at great risk. Was it possible to fall in love with a man based on his hands?

"Everyone . . ." His voice sounded husky, and he cleared his throat. "They're all in the barn."

The weight of his gaze strengthened as did the pressure of his shoulder against hers, and she glanced up.

His face drew nearer, his eyes took on a smoky haze, his lips parted—and met hers.

Soaring, filling, fulfilling.

She fell completely.

CHAPTER
29

ORGANISATION TODT RECREATION CENTER
BEAUFORT HOTEL, ST. HELIER
FRIDAY, DECEMBER 24, 1943

Candles bedecked a small evergreen tree in the OT recreation center in the Beaufort Hotel, and half a dozen drunken noncommissioned officers sang "O Tannenbaum."

Gerrit sat at a long table eating sausage and potato salad with a vinegary sauce, all well seasoned, although the locals hadn't had a salt ration all month.

Siegfried Meyer brandished a whole sausage on his fork. "We shouldn't celebrate Christmas Eve—only the winter solstice. It's what the Führer wants, purifying us of Jewish influence, returning to our Teutonic roots."

Rolf Hoffman lifted his beer stein. "If it means free beer, I'll celebrate anything."

Raucous laughter circled the table, and Gerrit managed a smile. He'd rather be alone on the holiday than with OT, but he needed to prove his loyalty. His Dutch nationality and his best friend's treachery against the Germans made Gerrit suspect in many eyes. The fact that he'd raised the alarm about Bernardus's sabotage, even if imperfectly, helped in other eyes. Ernst Schmeling kept a close watch on him and checked his work thoroughly.

Gerrit chewed a bite of sausage. Bernardus would spend Christmas Day alone. Arthur and Opal couldn't host Christmas, not with a collaborator for a niece and with Opal's sister, Ruby, unenlightened about their fugitive guest. Instead, Ruby and her husband Leo were hosting the celebration.

Gerrit filled his mouth with potato salad and his mind with thoughts of Ivy. The Picot family would have simple and bland fare, unsalted, but Ivy would be there. The woman he loved.

He hadn't yet told her he loved her. Only four months had passed since she learned he was in the resistance, and only a month since their first kiss.

Gerrit grinned and sliced his sausage. Not their last kiss, not by any means.

"You look happy, van der Zee." Across from Gerrit, Bruno Bauer sopped up sauce with a piece of bread. Bauer, a man nearing sixty who worked in OT Headquarters in St. Helier, lived in the room across from Gerrit.

"The food is good, ja?" Gerrit grinned again, as if delighted with potatoes rather than Ivy.

"I'm surprised you didn't go home for Christmas."

Gerrit shrugged and busied himself with potatoes. Letters from home announced that the Kroon family had been notified of Bernardus's presumed death in the service of Organisation Todt. Now the van der Zee family knew of Gerrit's service as well. Even though Vader and Moeder worded their correspondence with Gestapo censors in mind, their shock and scorn came through.

How could Gerrit go home? How could he watch Mr. and Mrs. Kroon grieve when he could relieve their twofold mourning with the news that their son not only lived but was a hero of the resistance? How could he bear his family's uncensored derision? And how could he conceal what would exonerate himself—but would endanger them and others?

He could barely lie well enough to fool strangers when lives were at stake, but fooling his parents and sisters would be impossible. And wrong.

Gerrit scraped the last of the sauce from his plate. "How about you, Bauer? Are you sorry not to go home?"

"Ja." His fleshy mouth bent down. "The enemy makes travel so dangerous now, my wife begged me not to take the risk."

Gerrit gave a sympathetic murmur. British and American aircraft ranged deep into German territory, shooting up railways and locomotives. The more the Allies disrupted transportation on the continent, the harder it would be for the Nazis to send reinforcements when the invasion came. And preventing soldiers from taking leave decreased morale.

Yet Gerrit couldn't rejoice at the melancholy on Bauer's jowly face. Although loyal to Germany, Bauer—like Willy Riedel—showed some basic decency. Gerrit didn't trust Bauer or Riedel, but he liked them.

"Did you hear the good news?" Meyer laughed, and bits of food flew from his mouth. "That Jersey cow was sentenced to six months."

Gerrit frowned. "A cow?" Now the Germans were sending cattle to prison?

"A woman," Bauer said. "A Jerseywoman was convicted of throwing manure on German soldiers."

A boisterous laugh from Meyer. "At least it was on soldiers, not OT men."

Laughter flowed around the table. The German soldiers, who had a general reputation in Jersey for "correct" behavior, despised the men from OT, who were known for brutality and drunken brawling.

Gerrit lowered his face so no one could see he hadn't joined the laughter. Six months in prison for throwing manure? A typical sentence for infractions such as owning a wireless set, insulting a German soldier, or spreading news from the BBC.

If the Germans learned what Gerrit was doing, his sentence would be far worse. But with winter weather impeding both shipping to Saint-Malo and construction in Jersey, the delivery of Gerrit's maps and diagrams had slowed.

The British agent had sent Charlie back with another parachute, certainly from the agent's return to France, but no crystals for making ink.

When he ran out of ink, his work would end.

"Lebkuchen?" Hoffman passed Gerrit a tray of little brown biscuits which smelled of ginger and other spices.

"Thank you." Gerrit took one and passed the tray.

Hoffman's close-set blue eyes narrowed as he studied the biscuit in his hand. "My Greta makes the best Lebkuchen."

Meyer hoisted his stein. "Next year you shall eat your Greta's Lebkuchen at home—after German victory!"

Lackluster cheers erupted. Although the Allied offensive in Italy had slowed, the Soviets ground closer to the German border each day. German defeat—not victory—seemed inevitable.

Meyer thumped down his stein, and beer sloshed out. "Let the English come. We're ready."

Indeed, thirty-eight major strongpoints ringed the Channel Islands, and over four hundred thousand cubic meters of reinforced concrete had been poured. If the French coast bore similar fortifications, the Allied invasion would be bloody.

"I wonder how long we'll stay here." Bauer rolled his Lebkuchen in his wide hand. "Most of our workers have been sent to France, but I'd rather stay."

"It's safe, ja?" Hoffman chewed his biscuit. "In France, the terrorists are barbaric. They assassinate our men."

Bauer nodded. "And the English bombers rarely come here."

"Don't be cowards." Meyer's nose shriveled. "I will go where the Führer sends me, die for the Führer if necessary."

To disagree could be fatal, so Gerrit added his half-hearted, muttered agreement.

But he met Bauer's concerned gaze across the table. Gerrit would rather stay in Jersey too.

He'd promised to return to Ivy if he were transferred to France, and she'd promised to wait for him. But leaving her would shred him up inside.

If he left Jersey, he'd have no way to pass diagrams to the Allies. Charlie was his only link to the British agent, and unless Gerrit was sent to the Saint-Malo area, Charlie wouldn't be able to connect Gerrit directly with the agent to continue his work on the continent.

Bernardus knew other contacts in France, but he was confined to the Jouny farm. And how many of his original contacts had been arrested?

If Gerrit were sent to France, he would no longer be able to aid the resistance.

The ginger in the biscuit failed to subdue the nausea filling his stomach. How could he bear to leave?

CHAPTER

30

"Antipyrine!" Joan de Ferrers jabbed a finger at her book.

"For fever and headache?" Ivy leaned her elbows on the dining room table in Joan's home above the chemist's shop—formerly the Carter home. "That's an old drug. Do you have it in stock?"

"It's rarely used, quite toxic. We much prefer aspirin and phenacetin, but if shortages don't improve, we'll use it again." Then Joan sent Ivy a smile. "Yes, I have it."

"It works?"

"According to this." Joan lifted Mr. Carter's book on the role of chemistry in the Great War.

Two weeks ago, Gerrit had run out of secret ink. One week ago, Ivy had worked up the courage to ask Joan for help. Aiding the escapee ring could earn Joan a ticket to prison or a concentration camp, but aiding in espionage would lead to certain death.

Yet Joan had pounced on the opportunity and never asked why on earth Ivy was interested in secret inks. Out of boredom, Joan had been consuming even the dryest of Mr. Carter's books and had recently read the tome in her hands, which concerned the wartime use of medications and poison gas, but also included a chapter on secret inks.

"It's an older book." Joan shifted her mouth to one side. "That means the information isn't secret."

"But if the ink is invisible, the writing might pass unnoticed." It would protect Charlie and Gerrit.

"Let's give it a try, shall we?" Joan sprang up from the table and gestured to the sink. "Never mind the dinner dishes. I can't wash them until the water turns on again tomorrow morning anyway."

Carrying her medical bag and coat, Ivy followed Joan downstairs to the shop. A dry summer and autumn had led to a serious water shortage on the island, and water from the mains was turned off each day from seven in the evening to seven in the morning.

Joan turned on lamps in the laboratory area in the back of the shop and gathered bottles from shelves.

Ivy set her bag on the counter. "How can I help?"

"Stay out of my way." But Joan grinned at her.

Ivy laughed and leaned against the counter. Over dinner, she and Joan had told stories from university, finding commonalities, edging toward true friendship. When they met in public, Joan treated her with cool cordiality, as was appropriate given their involvement with the ring.

Joan set weights on one pan of her scale and spooned clear crystals onto a square of paper on the other pan.

Over dinner, Ivy had learned the ring involved dozens of homes around the island and was loosely run by Dr. Noel McKinstry, Jersey's Medical Officer of Health.

Joan poured the crystals from the pan of the scale into a conical glass flask. "Did you hear about the arrests at West's Cinema?"

"I did." Several employees had been arrested in yet another wireless case, and today the cinema owner had been arrested too. "At this rate, Jersey will have more people in prison than out."

Joan poured water from a jug into a graduated cylinder, then poured the water into the conical flask. "Let's try not to join them."

"I agree. Yet here we are." Ivy waved toward the laboratory bench.

"Here we are indeed. Perhaps this is why everyone tells us not to worry our pretty little heads about chemistry. Apparently, it's a good way to get those heads chopped off, pretty or not." Joan swirled the flask. "Excellent. The antipyrine dissolves easily. Do you want to test it?"

"Yes." Ivy reached into her skirt pocket and pulled out a scrap of silk from Gerrit.

Joan handed her a glass stirrer, and Ivy dipped it in the clear solution and wrote her name on the silk. Nothing showed except dampness, and she waved the silk to dry the ink.

"How do you read it?" Ivy asked. "Heat?"

"Inks developed by heat are the most dangerous sort for a spy to use." Joan slid another book from the shelf. "The earliest secret inks, like lemon juice, were developed by heat, which means heat is the first method tested."

"I see." Ivy held the scrap of silk to a lamp and saw no trace of writing. Unless the Germans suspected the presence of an invisible message, they wouldn't think to search for a developer.

"Ferric chloride is used to develop antipyrine." Joan flipped pages in the book. "Oh good. Ferric chloride doesn't require heat to dissolve."

Very good news, since the gas was already turned off for the day. Joan weighed brownish-black crystals on the scale.

Gerrit didn't let Ivy watch him draw his maps. The less she knew, the better, and she already knew too much. But without her involvement, how would he have procured more secret ink?

A smile rose as she leaned against the counter. She liked knowing she could contribute to resistance work whilst protecting Gerrit and Charlie. Of course, without more ink, their work would cease—which would protect them completely.

Joan poured the ferric chloride crystals into a new conical flask and added a measured aliquot of water. The water turned reddish-brown. "I've received fewer prescriptions from you lately."

Ivy raised a rueful smile. "I'm seeing fewer patients."

"Because of your sister."

"Yes." Gossips like Ethel and Kitty du Puy and Doris Mollet didn't help.

"Ironically, if everyone knew how you help the escapees, you'd be seen as a heroine. They'd flock to your doors."

Ivy chuckled, but she'd rather save the escapees than her practice. "How is your business?"

"Quiet but stable." Joan swirled the flask, and the color of the solution complemented her auburn hair. "Fewer goods and medications to sell, but my work is more interesting. I enjoy compounding from scratch and extracting medications from plants."

"You've made some ingenious discoveries."

"Not my ingenuity. Those who came before me."

Ivy shuffled her thoughts around Joan's humility. "But you did the detective work to find that ingenuity."

"I'm simply stubborn. Shall we see if this works?" Joan held up the flask of ferric chloride. "How shall we apply it?"

"I brought an old paintbrush." Ivy pulled it from her skirt pocket.

Joan laid the silk scrap on a marble slab. "Do be careful. Ferric chloride is corrosive. Don't get it on your skin."

"Thank you." With the brush, Ivy painted the brown solution on the silk. Soon, letters took shape in brilliant red—her own name. "Look at that. It works."

"It does. How exciting. Would you like the ink packaged in a bottle?"

"Crystals would be better." That's what Gerrit had requested.

"I'll make powder papers." On a notepad, Joan scribbled calculations. "It's 0.75 percent, but you'll want household measures. A quarter cup . . . sixty milliliters . . . 0.45 grams. How many doses would you like?"

"How about a dozen?"

Joan set a square of paper on the scale. "Write a prescription, and I'll type labels for the box with the mixing instructions as if it were a headache remedy."

"Brilliant." Ivy pulled her prescription pad from her bag, confirmed the dosage with Joan, and wrote the instructions. If Gerrit fell under suspicion, he could toss the cardboard box and powder papers in the fire to destroy the evidence.

Joan removed the paper and crystals from the scale and folded the paper into a tiny pouch. "Powder papers take time. Do you want to pick it up tomorrow? I don't know if I'll finish before ten o'clock curfew."

"I have a curfew pass. We're fine until the electricity turns off at eleven." Ivy tore the prescription from the pad and handed it to Joan.

Her jaw dropped. "For Opal Jouny? Your aunt?"

Ivy couldn't write a prescription for Gerrit. The Germans had their own doctors, and civilian physicians weren't allowed to treat German troops or men in Organisation Todt. "Don't worry. Aunt Opal isn't a spy." But she housed one spy and hosted another.

With her lips tucked in, Joan set down the prescription and measured another dose of antipyrine. "Your aunt is in the lifeline, sheltering a fugitive." A question lifted her voice.

"Yes." Now Joan knew this was no ordinary fugitive.

Joan's deep-set hazel eyes rounded in shock. Then a smile leapt up. "This is rather thrilling, isn't it?"

Ivy laughed. "It is."

"Ferric chloride, a 10 percent solution in water. Pass that on."

"I will." If she didn't, the British wouldn't know how to develop Gerrit's maps.

Whilst Joan prepared the powder papers and typed a label for the box, Ivy washed the glassware and paintbrush, using the water in the jug. Rinsed the evidence down the drain.

At ten thirty, Joan affixed the label to the box. "Let me know when your aunt needs a refill."

"I will. Thank you." Ivy set the box in her medical bag, to deliver to the farm on tomorrow's rounds. Gerrit would be pleased to return to his mapmaking.

After Ivy put on her winter coat, hat, and gloves, Joan walked her to the front door to lock up behind her.

"Dinner was lovely, Joan." Ivy stepped out into the chilly night. "Thank you for everything."

"It was a pleasure doing business with you." A smile quirked on Joan's lips, but then she frowned toward the west. "Someone isn't heeding the blackout. That will be a hefty fine."

A bright light shone yellow-orange past where Queen Street turned into King Street. The light pulsed.

Ivy's breath caught. "I think it's a fire."

"Oh no." Joan headed down the street.

"Joan, no!" Ivy grabbed her arm. "You don't have a curfew pass. Or a coat. I'll find out what's happening and tell you."

"Thank you." Hugging herself against the cold, Joan returned to her shop.

Ivy jogged down Queen Street, down King Street. The light pulsed harder, and the crackle of flames fractured the night air.

What was burning?

Her breath came hard, puffed white before her.

On the far side of New Street, a small crowd formed around a fire engine. Glass shattered, and flames licked from a window.

The de Gruchy department store.

"Oh no." Ivy came to a stop. For over a hundred years, the people of Jersey had shopped at de Gruchy's for fine goods, strolled through the sparkling glass-roofed arcade, and dined in the lovely restaurant. Although they now carried little for locals and the restaurant held stores for the Germans, de Gruchy's had been part of Ivy's life.

Why was the fire brigade standing there, hoses limp, not doing anything?

"No water." The mutters rolled from the crowd.

Ivy gasped. The water had been turned off at the mains at seven o'clock.

Despite the heat radiating from the St. Helier landmark, Ivy shuddered. Yet another loss due to the war. When would it end?

CHAPTER
31

Bundled in blankets, Gerrit sat beside Ivy in the doorway to the barn. "Aren't you tired of drawing your uncle's cows?"

"Never. See? Today I'm drawing cows in the snow." She lifted her gloved hand and her pencil. On the sketch pad, two cows held hooves to their mouths.

"Are they eating ice cream?"

"Of course. Jersey cows make the creamiest milk and the best ice cream. And in weather like this . . ." She shrugged, rubbing her shoulder against Gerrit's.

"They make their own ice cream, yes? You're adorable." He kissed her chilly cheek.

Ivy murmured her disagreement, only making her more adorable.

In preparation for invasion, OT now required military training on Sundays. Whenever possible, Gerrit made excuses. He'd returned to worshipping at the church in St. Helier, telling his colleagues that his English was better than his German, which was true. He didn't tell them how much it meant to sit in the same sanctuary as

Ivy, even though she had to treat him with her old frostiness and he had to respond with his old stiff formality.

Then every free Sunday he enjoyed lunch with Bernardus, Charlie, and the Jounys. And Ivy. The rest of the day with Ivy.

His sigh floated to the overcast sky. "I wish I could take you somewhere else on the island to draw. Jersey is so beautiful."

"It was more beautiful before your lot came." No resentment colored her tone, only a touch of humor.

Yet he knew what Jersey meant to her. "Someday you'll rebuild everything beautiful and tear down everything ugly. Someday soon." Even though snow dusted the fields before him, spring would come soon. And with the spring, the Allies.

Gerrit was making plans for the invasion. Since the Germans would fight hard to defend the port, St. Helier would be a most dangerous location. He'd advised Ivy and Charlie to meet him at the farm, well inland and far from landing beaches and towns. He and Bernardus had their pistols to protect the family from German soldiers.

Changing out of his German uniform would also protect Gerrit from Allied soldiers, so he'd stashed his civilian suit in Bernardus's room. He didn't intend to conceal his status—only to stay alive until he could reveal it in safety. After liberation, the Allies could sort out the truth of Gerrit's involvement with Organisation Todt and the resistance.

Ivy snuggled closer to Gerrit, and her pencil swooped over the paper.

He didn't want to think about the war. He circled his arm around her well-blanketed waist. "You're drawing the cows. May I draw the house?"

A laugh pushed her round cheeks high. "Are you capable of drawing without a ruler?"

He groaned in mock indignation and smacked a kiss on her lips. "Watch me."

She handed him a pencil, and he went to work, although his

gloves complicated the process. At least the rough texture of the granite walls justified his less-than-straight lines. He outlined the walls and roof behind Ivy's cows, careful not to bump her hand and ruin her art.

Four windows upstairs, three windows downstairs, and a door. "It's easier to draw when I can see what I'm doing."

"Mm." Ivy darkened a hoof of one of her cows. "I can't imagine working with secret ink."

"Working blind in many ways." According to Charlie, the ink Ivy had procured from the chemist had been accepted by the resistance network. "Not only tracing with clear ink, but I don't know whether the Allies are receiving the maps or if they do any good."

"I know they're doing great good."

"Even if they don't, God is still faithful."

Ivy paused with her pencil tip halfway along a tree limb arching over the first cow. "What do you mean?"

Gerrit drew a grid to denote roof tiles. "So often during the war, I've done the right thing but haven't received the expected results. It felt as if I had done my part, and the Lord hadn't done his. It shook my faith."

"Because you couldn't see the results, what you'd hoped for," Ivy said in a thoughtful tone, adding jagged little branches to her tree limb. "It reminds me of the verse the rector quoted this morning. 'Now faith is the substance of things hoped for, the evidence of things not seen.'"

Gerrit's pencil poised at the top of the chimney. "I couldn't see results, so I lost faith."

Ivy turned her lovely dark eyes to him, her cheeks pink from the cold. "What if it's like your maps? You can't see the lines, but someone else can, someone with the right developing solution. You may never see the results of your work, but that doesn't mean they aren't there."

"*She's a marvel, our Ivy,*" Thelma Galais had once told him. He remembered that conversation, the whimsical drawing of a house,

Ivy saying she drew what she saw. And at that tension-filled Christmas dinner, Charlie had said Ivy saw "beyond the seen."

He cleared his dry throat. "You do. You see beyond the seen."

Ivy dipped her head to the side. "I don't know. Sometimes I'm blinded by what I see."

Gerrit understood, blinded as he was by black curls and brown eyes, and he kissed the pink of her cheek.

She nuzzled closer and drew a single leaf clinging to a twig. "You doubted God's faithfulness, and I doubted his goodness."

Something Gerrit had never doubted. "How is that?"

"I always saw his goodness in the beauty of the world and in the people around me, so when those were warped by ugliness and cruelty—well, I could no longer see God's goodness."

Gerrit rested his forehead against her temple. "I'm sorry for the role I played in that."

"Don't be." She melted into his embrace. "Before she died, Thelma reminded me that the cross is the only proof I need of the Lord's goodness."

Gerrit let that thought sift through his head. "Yet what could be uglier or crueler than the cross?"

"Oh, Gerrit." Ivy sat up straight and looked him full in the eye. "Ugly, cruel, and yet so very good. Why didn't I see that before?"

She would have eventually, but his chest felt a bit broader.

A gentle sadness softened her expression. "I miss her."

"I do too."

"She'd be happy to see us together. She was fond of you." Fondness shone in Ivy's eyes too.

Was it too soon? Or the right time? Gerrit swallowed hard, wet his lips.

Ivy added pencil strokes to a cow's ear. "Thelma never saw your uniform. She saw your character. In a way, I did too. The first time I saw you . . ." Her cheeks colored, and she drew with more intensity. "At first my view of your uniform was blocked by people in the pews between us, and I saw something in you—kindness, strength,

235

integrity. Then your uniform came into sight, and I couldn't reconcile what I saw with what I *saw*."

A curl curved around her chin, and he brushed it aside. It was time. "I remember the first time I saw you too. I couldn't stop looking. I still can't."

A wisp of a smile flitted over her lips.

"I've never . . ." His voice came out raspy, and he cleared his throat. "I've never given much heed to the idea of love at first sight. True love takes time. But . . . but I know I started falling in love with you that day. I haven't stopped."

"Oh, Gerrit." She ducked her chin even lower.

"I know. You had the uniform to look past. I didn't. I've had a year and a half to fall in love. You've had only a few months. I don't mind if you don't love—"

"I do." Her chin snapped up, and her eyes rounded with wonder. "I love you so much."

His mind and heart overflowed, pushing all words from his mouth. He had nothing but kisses.

And he gave them to her.

CHAPTER
32

The bright red rash covering little Joey Sanderson's cheeks, his brilliant red tongue and tonsils, and his high temperature confirmed Ivy's fears.

She smoothed the six-year-old's sweat-dampened brown hair as he lay in his bed, and she glanced up to his mother. "It's scarlet fever. No need for alarm, but I'd like him in Overdale Isolation Hospital. Please ring the ambulance."

"Scarlet fever?" Alice Sanderson covered her mouth, and her brow creased. "Joe—my husband had scarlet fever—rheumatic fever. His heart—" Her voice broke.

"Joey's heart sounds fine." Ivy kept her voice low and reassuring, for the child's sake as well as the mother's. "No need to fear. At Overdale, he'll receive excellent care and extra rations." No one had died during the current scarlet fever epidemic, but Ivy didn't want to take chances, not with the risk of complications and with other children in the home.

"Please don't send him away. I'm being careful." Alice gestured to the bottle on the bedside table. "I've quarantined him since you diagnosed him with strep throat last week, and I've given him the medicine you prescribed."

Sulfapyridine from France, past its date of use, the only anti-infective the chemists' shops had in stock. Ivy understood Alice's reluctance to part with her child, so she firmed her tone. "You've cared for him to the utmost, but Overdale is the best place for him—and for the safety of your other children."

A deep sigh. "Very well."

Ivy adjusted the blanket under the boy's chin. "Joey, you're going to have a grand adventure, riding in the horse-drawn ambulance, staying in hospital. Won't your friends be jealous?"

Joey's bleary eyes brightened. "Is it true? They give you chocolate in hospital?"

"It's true. And extra milk." Ivy packed her thermometer and stethoscope in her medical bag.

After the ambulance came for Joey, Ivy reassured Alice once more and left the Sanderson home above their shop on Queen Street, next door to Carter's Chemist's.

Joe Sanderson had little for sale in his shop, save for flowers, which he had in abundance, and Ivy bought a bouquet of daffodils for Easter.

The Sanderson family had remained loyal to the Picot medical practice since Ivy had exempted Joe from deportation a year and a half earlier.

Ivy headed home over streets slick from a spring rain. April already, and yet no invasion. RAF planes frequently crisscrossed the Jersey skies and attacked shipping, which meant fewer trips to France for Charlie. If only the *Ormer* could fly a Union Jack or the flag of Jersey to signal the ship's allegiance.

At La Bliue Brise, Aunt Ruby typed at the receptionist's desk. She gazed at Ivy over the rims of her glasses. "How's little Joey?"

"Scarlet fever. He's going to Overdale, a precaution more than anything." Ivy peeked into the waiting room—empty. At least she'd have time for lunch before rounds.

She fetched a vase from her office, filled it with water, and set the daffodils on the desk in front of her aunt. "Pretty, aren't they? How does my afternoon look?"

Aunt Ruby fingered the yellow blooms. "Four home visits, with two possible cases of scarlet fever. You'll have a lovely ride along the coast—St. Clement, La Rocque, and Fauvic."

Ivy had an escapee to visit in that area as well. She perched on the edge of Aunt Ruby's desk. "How are the finances?"

Aunt Ruby crinkled up her mouth. "Tight. In Monday's post, I'm sending out more bills for payment due."

Ivy riffled through the envelopes, adorned with occupation postal stamps, designed by local artist Edmund Blampied and picturing sights like Corbière Lighthouse, Elizabeth Castle, and Mont Orgueil Castle. "Money is tight for everyone. So many people don't have work, and costs are extraordinary."

"Regardless." Aunt Ruby pulled the sheet of paper from the typewriter. "Our costs are extraordinary as well."

If it weren't for Charlie and Fern, the practice would have failed, and Ivy sighed. "I do wish we weren't beholden to Charlie and Fern. Charlie should be saving for his future, and Fern—her money feels tainted."

"In my opinion, she's simply paying her dues. Finances wouldn't be tight if it weren't for her."

Ivy didn't want to dwell on it, so she raised a smile. "I'm excited to host Easter dinner tomorrow." She'd miss seeing Gerrit, but it couldn't be helped. She'd see him only from afar at church. No kisses, no long talks, no drawing together.

Aunt Ruby leaned back in her chair. "I do find it odd that Opal isn't hosting. It's her turn. She's been rather—well, I hate to say this about my dear sister, but she's been almost inhospitable lately."

On the contrary, Aunt Opal had been extremely hospitable—to Bernardus and Gerrit. "They're under a lot of strain, running a dairy farm with all the German regulations and inspections."

"Constantly changing regulations too." Aunt Ruby gave Ivy a sheepish look. "I shouldn't think that way about my own sister. But I miss her."

Ivy wasn't one to cast blame for thinking ill of one's sister. She'd encourage Aunt Opal to visit the Bissells in town more frequently.

The front door opened. "Hallo!" Fern called in a merry voice.

"Hallo, Fern." Ivy smiled at her sister's good cheer.

Aunt Ruby rose and gathered her handbag. "I'll see you ladies tomorrow for Easter."

"Thank you for your help today." Ivy saw her aunt to the front door. Like Fern, Aunt Ruby had finished her Saturday half day.

When Ivy returned to the receptionist's desk, Fern was peering at the appointment book. "Dear, oh dear. So few appointments. Perhaps now you see how vital I was to the practice."

"I never said otherwise." Ivy closed the book to maintain her patients' privacy.

Fern picked up Ivy's timetable for the afternoon and studied it. "May I?" Ivy held out her hand.

With a little huff, Fern returned the timetable. "Considering how few home visits you have nowadays, you spend an inordinate amount of time on your rounds."

Ivy folded the timetable and tucked it in her skirt pocket. "I give all my patients the time they need." Including the patients not listed on the timetable. And she'd made a habit of using the kitchen timer to stay on schedule.

"I certainly hope you aren't drawing on your rounds. It's illegal, you know."

"I know." How could she forget with Fern reminding her almost daily? In late February, the Germans had banned drawing out of doors, to prevent islanders from sketching fortifications and sending intelligence to the Allies.

Ironically, that very thing was happening under their noses, and Ivy smiled.

Fern gave her a strange look and stroked the appointment book.

"If only it had been banned from the start, we might have saved the practice."

A year ago, such a statement would have devastated Ivy, but now Fern's hypocrisy amused her. "I'm sure that's how you see it."

Fern drew back her chin. "For a failing doctor, you've been rather lighthearted lately, almost giddy. If I didn't know better, I'd think you were in love."

Indeed she was, but her love for Gerrit was too precious a thing to sully before Fern—and how her sister would gloat to know Ivy loved a man in a German uniform.

Ivy let her giddiness lift the corners of her mouth. "It's spring. Haven't you noticed? Everyone's in good spirits. Liberation is coming."

"Liberation? You mean war."

"War came four years ago."

Fern waved a hand east. "When the Germans came, they came as gentlemen. Not a soul was killed."

Eleven had been killed in Jersey in a Luftwaffe attack, but none during the actual landings. "Because the island surrendered."

"And the Germans honored that surrender as gentlemen. But when the English come, they'll come as thugs. How many civilians will die?"

"None, if the Germans surrender—as gentlemen."

Fern shook her head and gazed to the ceiling. "You've been blinded by English propaganda."

And Fern by German propaganda. "Hitler has declared the Channel Islands as fortresses to be held to the last man. If any civilians die, it's the Germans' fault."

"Don't be naïve." Fern strode past Ivy toward the kitchen, then turned back. "You don't know what the English do. English and American bombers are obliterating German cities."

Ivy tipped her head. "As the Luftwaffe did to English cities."

"It isn't the same." Brittle fire flashed in Fern's eyes. "Last summer, the Allies turned Hamburg into an inferno. Helmut's entire family was killed—women, children, the elderly—incinerated. You don't know what he's endured, what millions of decent Germans have endured. The English don't care. They'll do the same here."

Yet fear lashed below the surface of Fern's anger. Someday soon, Helmut would retreat to the continent or be captured—and Bill and the boys would come home.

Last week a Red Cross message had arrived from Dad, stating *"Bill hopes to hear from Fern soon."* He wouldn't have wasted seven of his twenty-five permitted words unless Bill had serious concerns. And when Bill returned to Jersey, the truth would surface, as it always did.

For a woman who was a stranger to remorse, what would it be like for Fern to be held to account?

Sympathy coursed through Ivy's chest. "I'm sorry. Liberation will be difficult for you."

"Sorry for me?" Fern's face twisted in disgust. "You've always been odd."

Fern saw that as Ivy's weakness, but Ivy smiled. "Perhaps that is my strength."

~

ST. PETER'S PARISH
SATURDAY, MAY 27, 1944

Gerrit traced the plan for a Type 606 searchlight bunker at Corbière while Bernardus kept watch by the window at the top of the stairs. Gerrit still wasn't accustomed to Bernardus's shaggy black hair and mustache.

On either side of the fireplace in the bedroom, Arthur Jouny had constructed a false wall. To one side, a wardrobe with a sliding back panel concealed a doorway through the false wall.

Several times, Gerrit and Bernardus had rehearsed hiding, and twice Gerrit had joined his friend in the compartment— once when Fern visited, and once during a German agricultural inspection, even though the inspectors hadn't entered the house.

Gerrit loosened his tie in the heat of the day, and he dipped his pen in the secret ink. Perhaps he should stop this work. Invasion was imminent, and the island was on edge. The islanders elated, the Germans skittish.

OT had recently converted the tunnel complex of Hohlgangs-anlage 8 from an ammunition depot to a giant hospital, ready to receive hundreds of casualties. This time, Gerrit had enjoyed using his engineering skills. Not only was the project humanitarian in nature, but it diverted OT from building yet more fortifications.

Gerrit penned the specifications for the searchlight bunker, even though his diagram might not reach England before the invasion, especially with Charlie making fewer trips to Saint-Malo. Ships could sail only at night, and even then at great risk.

The Germans in Jersey were a monster striking out in its death throes. Two days earlier, they'd arrested a middle-aged woman for harboring a Russian worker, and they were scouring St. Ouen's Parish, just north of St. Peter's Parish, for escapees and helpers.

Had Ivy treated that worker? Would her name arise during interrogation?

He tensed, then sent the tension up into a prayer. No matter what, he didn't want her to stop her work.

Gerrit had far greater concerns for the invasion itself. Protecting Ivy, Charlie, and the Jounys. Surviving long enough to be captured as a prisoner of war. Convincing the Allies that he and Bernardus were on the right side.

To that end, he'd decided that if he received orders to evacuate to the continent, he'd join Bernardus in hiding. Most of the foreign workers had been sent to work on the Atlantic Wall in France, but the staff remained to continue construction with local labor.

That could change at a moment's notice. If Gerrit left Jersey, he'd lose his connections to the resistance—and to those who could vouch for his loyalty. He couldn't allow that.

"Visitors." Bernardus hobbled into the room with his crutch and flung open the wardrobe door. "Germans. Half a dozen. Ran up the drive. Half to the front door, half to the back."

This was no agricultural inspection, and Gerrit flew into action, ticked off his list.

Unplug the lamp. Cap pen and secret ink vial. Stash pen, ink, and rulers in the basket to his side, which already contained his OT cap.

Had an informer told the Germans about Arthur's wireless set or the suspicious new hermit of a farmworker? Or had the scouring of the countryside spread south from St. Ouen?

Either way, they could leave no evidence.

"Arthur!" Opal called in warning to Gerrit and Bernardus. "We have visitors!"

Bernardus stepped inside the compartment, and Gerrit passed the pane of glass to him, with the map and silk clamped in place. His alignment would be ruined, but he preferred that to death.

Loud voices and slamming doors downstairs.

He couldn't panic, couldn't rush, had to follow protocol. He handed his T square and the lamp to Bernardus. If the Germans touched the lamp, the heat might cue them to the men's presence.

Gerrit stacked the books he'd used to elevate the glass, grabbed his jacket and basket, and scanned the room. Had he left anything incriminating? Not that he could see. Bernardus's few personal possessions and Gerrit's civilian clothes routinely resided in the secret compartment.

Footsteps pounded up the stairs, and Gerrit's heartbeat matched the rhythm.

"I can't imagine what you're looking for," Opal said in a loud voice. "We follow all the agricultural regulations. We've never had a single violation."

The loudness of her protests was designed to drown any noise from Gerrit and Bernardus.

As quietly as possible, Gerrit handed the basket and jacket to

Bernardus and stepped through. After he smoothed the linens in the wardrobe, he closed the wardrobe door, slid the back panel into place, and shut the compartment door.

A thump of a door opening, but not too close. Probably Arthur and Opal's room. Two male voices, barking questions.

"I guarantee, you'll not find a cow in my bed." Opal's polite indignation pierced the walls. "We register all calves at birth as required."

Gerrit pressed back against the wall in the narrow space, and his blood whooshed loud in his ears. Bernardus's heat radiated beside him.

Something rested on the floor where his right foot wanted to be. He didn't dare scoot it lest it made noise. But he didn't dare lose his balance, so he fumbled with his toes for a foothold.

Clipped Bernardus in the ankle. A tiny groan. The bad ankle, but Gerrit's apology would have to wait.

Loud thuds arose. Furniture being overturned?

Gerrit grimaced. The wardrobe was too heavy to move, wasn't it?

A door banged open. Bernardus's room, and Gerrit willed himself as invisible as his ink.

"Traitors in the area are hiding our workers," a man said in a gruff voice. "What do you know of this?"

"Only what I read in the *Evening Post*," Opal said.

But they were hiding someone worse than a slave worker—a saboteur who was presumed dead. If Bernardus were found, he'd be executed, and Gerrit for being with him. What would happen to Arthur and Opal? To Ivy? Charlie?

He prayed in a long, disjointed, incoherent string.

Metal scraped on wood—a bedframe? And a soft thud.

"Who lives here?" the man said.

"This is our sons' room. They're in England."

"Someone lived here recently."

The wardrobe doors opened. Soft light penetrated the back panel and the compartment door, and Gerrit shrank back.

Opal huffed. "If you must know, my husband snores. Sometimes I come in here to sleep."

Fabric rustled mere centimeters from Gerrit's knees.

"I just folded those linens," Opal said. "And look what you've done to the beds. Are you going to put this house back to rights before you leave?"

Her tone sounded irate enough for how any sane person would feel in her circumstances, but not irate enough to earn harsh treatment.

"I think not." The German sounded just as irate. "If we find nothing, your reward is sleeping here tonight, not in prison."

"As I told you at the door, there is nothing for you to find. Now, if you're done, I suddenly find myself with a great deal of housekeeping."

Two sets of footsteps pounded away, but more bangs and bumps resounded from downstairs.

Dust tickled Gerrit's nose, and he pinched his nose shut. A single sneeze would be fatal.

Beside him, Bernardus didn't stir. They'd remain hidden until the Germans left and Arthur or Opal gave them the signal.

Gerrit took long, slow breaths through his open mouth. Liberation couldn't come soon enough.

CHAPTER
33

Mrs. Le Huquet and Ivy sipped parsnip coffee in a drawing room crammed with stacks of books and papers.

Since Mrs. Le Huquet's leg had been mangled in the accident a year ago, walking to La Bliue Brise with a cane was difficult for her, but Ivy didn't mind visiting her charmingly cluttered home and listening to the widow describe the novels she was reading. Mrs. Le Huquet needed company more than care, but company was a form of care Ivy had the luxury of providing nowadays.

"Do you think this is it?" Mrs. Le Huquet stared up at her ceiling.

Airplanes droned overhead as they had without stop since late the night before. Hundreds of aircraft bound for France.

A mixture of excitement and fear raced through Ivy's chest. "It must be. The Germans shut down the telephone services this morning, and they've posted guards throughout town."

Mrs. Le Huquet fingered the coil of silvered black hair at the nape of her neck. "Finally this nightmare will come to an end."

"Yes, finally." Much of the danger to the men she loved had

247

already come to an end. After the German field police raided Uncle Arthur's home the week before, Gerrit had stopped drawing maps and Charlie had stopped sending them.

If the invasion had indeed come, it was too late to provide the Allies with more intelligence. Gerrit had only to avoid evacuation and lie low until the Allies came. Somehow.

The rumble of aircraft engines spoke comfort to her.

Ivy's kitchen timer dinged, and she gave Mrs. Le Huquet an apologetic smile and packed her timer in her bag. Thank goodness, her patients had accepted her new habit as an eccentricity. "I'm afraid I must be on my way, but it was lovely visiting with you. I would love to borrow that book when you've finished."

"I'll set it aside for you." Mrs. Le Huquet scooted forward in her chair.

Ivy held up one hand. "Please don't rise. I'll see myself out."

Mrs. Le Huquet settled back with a relieved smile. "Happy Liberation Day."

"We can hope." Outside, Ivy mounted her bicycle and pedaled up Roseville Street under a cloudy sky throbbing with airplane engines.

Her next appointment was one she'd made herself—at the farm for the BBC news broadcast at noon. Surely Uncle Arthur had been listening to his wireless set since dawn. When listening to the BBC was no longer a crime, the secret of how he hid his set so well could emerge.

Elation overrode fear. A laugh erupted, and she pedaled faster. All around, people waved to each other, wearing red or blue— although not enough of both to incite German ire.

Along Hill Street, German soldiers behind sandbag barriers guarded States buildings with machine guns, and on the Esplanade, two German ambulances parked in front of the Pomme d'Or Hotel, ready for casualties. Soon the hotel would no longer be German naval headquarters, adorned with a swastika flag, but would return to hosting sunburnt English tourists on holiday.

"Oh, the joy," she said. She couldn't help herself.

A familiar auburn-haired woman approached along the Esplanade, and Ivy waved. "Good day, my friend!"

Joan swept her hand skyward with the biggest smile Ivy had ever seen on the chemist's face. "A magnificent day, my friend."

More laughter flowed, and she stood on the pedals to gain speed. Soon to have open and honest friendships.

And an open and honest love. No more meeting Gerrit clandestinely on the farm, and he could burn his detested uniform. Wouldn't he be handsome in a civilian suit? Dark blue to bring out his eyes, a homburg at a slight angle.

What must he be feeling today, knowing the Allies would soon use his maps? Yes, he'd be interrogated after liberation, but he'd be interrogated by the Allies with civilized methods. The truth would quickly surface.

Gerrit had hidden his last dozen or so silk maps in Aunt Opal's scrap bag. Once the Allies developed the maps and compared them to those he'd sent earlier, Gerrit's story would be validated.

When Ivy arrived at the farm, she knocked. "It's Ivy."

Aunt Opal flung open the door and wrapped Ivy in a giant, laughing hug.

"It's true, then?" Ivy said. "The Allies—"

"They call it D-day, but there's been little in the way of news yet." Aunt Opal shut the door behind her. "Your uncle and Bernardus and Charlie have been listening to the BBC all morning. The Germans sent the ship and dock workers home."

They feared invasion and rightly so.

"They're in the kitchen. Go on through. I'm on sentry duty." Aunt Opal snapped up a military salute.

Ivy laughed and opened the kitchen door. "Good—"

"Hush!" Three hands raised in her direction. Three heads tucked in close to the wireless set on the kitchen table.

Ivy pulled up a chair.

"D-day has come," the BBC announcer said. "Early this morning the Allies began the assault on the northwestern face of Hitler's European fortress."

"Opal!" Uncle Arthur called. "You can't miss this."

Aunt Opal rushed in and leaned over Uncle Arthur's shoulder.

"Under the command of General Eisenhower," the announcer said in polished tones, "Allied naval forces supported by strong air forces began landing Allied armies this morning on the northern coast of France."

"The northern coast of France," Ivy murmured. Brittany? Normandy? The Pas de Calais? The Channel Islands lay in the gulf between Brittany and Normandy.

The announcer continued: "No details have yet come in from the Allied side of the progress of the operations. The Germans, who have been broadcasting news of the attack on all their services except their own home service, say that the points assailed extend from Cherbourg to Havre, with the main weight of the attack in the area of Caen."

"Normandy," Uncle Arthur said.

So close. Ivy's eyes tingled, and she blinked away tears of hope and grief. The hope of everyone living under Nazi occupation—of prisoners in concentration camps and forced labor camps, and of civilians in the constant strain of scrutiny and scarcity. All soon to be free.

And grief for the cost. What were those soldiers enduring today?

Charlie bolted to his feet and whooped for joy, and Ivy laughed and wiped her eyes.

Her brother pulled her to her feet and swung her around the kitchen floor. With much laughter, Uncle Arthur and Aunt Opal joined them in their dance, whilst Bernardus clapped in time to the imaginary music.

As they danced, Ivy studied Charlie. At almost seventeen, he stood several inches taller than she. His labor had added breadth and depth to his shoulders, and his resistance work had added breadth and depth to his character.

Charlie whirled her past the stove, his mouth wide with laughter. He had grown in character more—far more—than if he'd spent the past two years at Victoria College.

If he should return to school or remain on a ship's crew, he would be better for it all.

Her throat thickened, but a smile loosened her words. "I'm proud of you, Charlie."

His dark eyes glinted. "And I'm proud of you."

"You threw a party?" A woman's voice came from the doorway to the kitchen. "And you forgot to invite me?"

Fern. Smiling, but in a stiff sort of way.

Ivy and Charlie froze.

Uncle Arthur clicked off the wireless.

"*Extchûthez-mé*," Bernardus said in Jèrriais, and he hobbled out the back door, his head low. His cover as a local farmworker would be blown if Fern recognized Bernardus Kroon behind the black mustache.

Uncle Arthur and Aunt Opal stood blocking Fern's view of the wireless, their faces long.

Fern's gaze flicked amongst the four of them. Her mouth puckered, and hurt swam in her brown eyes. "Do you think you're in danger—from me?"

"Fern . . ." Aunt Opal said, apologetic and soothing.

Fern hugged herself, and her eyelashes fluttered. "I've always known about your wireless. I—I've never said a word." Her voice cracked.

"We thank you," Uncle Arthur said.

"You think . . ." Fern clapped one hand over her mouth. "Do you honestly think I'd denounce my own family?"

"Of course not." Ivy stepped closer to her sister. "You simply startled us."

Charlie let out a little huff. "And we know where your *affections* lie."

"Charlie." Ivy gave him a stern look. She might agree, but he wasn't helping.

Fern sniffed, lowered her hand, and raised her chin. "I came to hear the English side. The German broadcasts say the Allies are landing near Caen with heavy casualties. We expect to throw them back into the sea."

"General Eisenhower is being more circumspect," Uncle Arthur said. "He said *we* are landing with strong forces."

Ivy held her breath, and Fern's mouth tightened. Surely she noticed her "we" referred to the Germans, and Uncle Arthur's to the Allies.

"This is good news, dear Fern," Aunt Opal said. "The war will soon be over."

"And our family will come home." A challenge lit in Charlie's eyes.

Fern's gaze swept the room and drilled into Ivy. "This is your doing. You've poisoned my family against me."

Like a kick to Ivy's chest. "I—"

"Fern!" Uncle Arthur said. "That isn't—"

"You have." Fern sharpened the drill. "All this time, I've been supporting the medical practice, contributing my wages, and you've been spreading poison behind my back. Well, no longer. Since you don't appreciate my contributions, I'll keep my money for myself."

Ivy gasped for breath. "I never . . ."

Fern spun for the door, then waved toward the wireless. "Don't worry, Uncle Arthur. Unlike some people, I don't betray my family."

As Fern stomped out of the house, Aunt Opal put her arm around Ivy's shoulder. "Don't mind her. It isn't true."

"I know." Ivy breathed hard, and with each breath, the pain reduced to a sting.

Fern used words to her advantage. But now the pit she'd dug herself into was collapsing upon her, and she had nothing to shore it up but words.

Words weren't enough.

CHAPTER
34

A loud yawn defied Gerrit's will and stretched his face as he and Ernst Schmeling marched across the parade grounds of the lower ward of Elizabeth Castle.

Schmeling shot him a derisive look. Despite the early hour, the man's discipline prevailed. "Coming early is the best way to conduct a surprise inspection. Our flak guns aren't doing enough, and I want to know why."

"Not nearly enough." Gerrit feigned a concerned expression. All day, all night, Allied aircraft passed over Jersey, often strafing and bombing German positions on the island, and German antiaircraft guns had yet to bring down prey.

Inspecting gun crews fell far outside Organisation Todt's jurisdiction, although inspecting the structures themselves might be justified. Of course, guard duty also fell out of OT's jurisdiction, but on D-day, Gerrit and all other uniformed OT staff had manned gun positions.

Along the walls of the parade grounds, men piled sandbags. Elizabeth Castle served as a penal colony for OT workers who

253

had escaped the labor camps or stolen food or committed other infractions. Did they know their liberation was near?

Gerrit and Schmeling stepped through a gate out of the lower ward. To the left, a staircase led down to a breakwater capped by a medieval hermitage high on a rock and by a modern cubical gun position. Under a blue sky, a handful of patrol vessels and cargo ships plied the aquamarine waters.

The men passed the staircase and continued down a walkway alongside the castle wall.

The Allies had a strong foothold in Normandy on the far side of the Cotentin Peninsula, close enough that the rumble of bombing reached Jersey, even cracking windows on the east coast.

Although some of the Germans in Jersey believed the Allies would strike next in the Pas de Calais region of France, the rest believed they would come to the Channel Islands.

Then Gerrit's work, the danger he'd risked, the scorn he'd endured—all would be vindicated.

Gerrit and Schmeling mounted a stone staircase back through the castle wall.

Schmeling's arms swung hard as he climbed. "We need to make sure our defenses are strong before we leave for France."

Gerrit's chest clenched. Only a few hundred of the forced and volunteer workers remained, but the evacuation of staff had been delayed. "Do you think we'll leave?"

"I'd rather stay—this is my responsibility. But we have a greater responsibility to the Reich, and there is much work in France."

Gerrit fought to control his face. No matter what, he couldn't leave Jersey. Not only would retreating with the Germans through France be deadly, but he'd be required to work for the enemy without the satisfaction of also aiding the Allies. He'd be cut off from the people and from the secret ink maps that could prove his loyalty.

He'd be cut off from Ivy. If he left, he couldn't protect her and her family. He wanted to stay with her, see Jersey's liberation with her, celebrate with her.

And propose to her. He would be in custody for a while, but before that, he'd ask her to be his wife.

Gerrit's breath came harder as he climbed. He kept his duffel packed so he could flee to the Jouny farm at short notice.

At the top of the stairs, the rising sun illuminated the open space of the upper ward, crowned by a cylindrical gun tower and a flak gun.

Shouting rose from the tower. Metal gears cranked.

A whine built to the west, a roar.

An air raid!

"Take cover, Herr Oberbauführer!" Gerrit dashed back into the stairway and lay flat on the stone steps under the rocky arch. "Take cover!"

A whistle, and something silver plummeted through the air. The flak guns thumped as they thrust steel skyward.

Gerrit pressed his hands over his ears. *Lord, let the flak gunners miss.*

The steps bucked beneath Gerrit. The stone wall across from him quaked. A plume of earth arched high on the far side. But the walls remained intact. As did Gerrit.

More whistles. Splashes far below.

The RAF would aim for ships. For ships like Charlie's, and Gerrit grimaced. Lately, the *Ormer* had made only a handful of trips and had turned back several times under fire.

Even though Gerrit's pulse thudded in his ears, even though his breath skittered in his lungs, a strange grin rose.

The Allies were prevailing. They would come soon.

Gerrit just had to survive until victory.

∼

ST. HELIER
FRIDAY, JUNE 30, 1944

After dinner, Gerrit relaxed on his bed with a library book. Since the sun wouldn't set until after nine o'clock, he didn't need to use electricity.

"Van der Zee!" A man knocked on his hotel room door. "Van der Zee!"

Book in hand, Gerrit ran to the door.

Ernst Schmeling stood in the hallway. "We have orders to sail to Saint-Malo. Meet in the lobby with your luggage in fifteen minutes."

"Fifteen minutes?" Panic and exhilaration wrestled inside him. "The Allies have landed in Jersey?"

"Nein. We have more important work on the continent."

Panic won. How could he escape to the farm? "Why now? Why so soon?"

"We have a break in the weather. Hurry." Schmeling knocked on the next door.

"No, no, no," Gerrit muttered, and he threw on his uniform jacket. He'd expected a day's notice. At least an hour's notice. But fifteen minutes?

"Lord, help me escape." Leaving his library book behind and unfinished, he tossed his shaving kit into his packed duffel and raced downstairs. If he beat the other OT men to the lobby, he could slip away.

Gerrit threw open the stairway door on the ground floor.

Half a dozen officers stood in the lobby, including Willy Riedel, who waved Gerrit over.

A gaping pit formed in Gerrit's belly, but he worked up a pleasant expression and joined the men. Schmeling must have summoned the officers before the noncommissioned men like Gerrit.

As the officers talked in low tones about the dangers the Allies posed to ships and the necessity of continuing their work in France, Gerrit's gaze drifted to the front door. A lorry parked outside with an armed guard.

How could Gerrit sneak past so many eyes, so many pistols? All the men were armed.

"Come along." An officer ushered the group—now a dozen men—outside.

Trapped in the group, Gerrit had no choice but to climb into the back of the lorry, to sit there, paralyzed, as the lorry drove through St. Helier.

Two years earlier, he hadn't wanted to come to Jersey. Now he didn't want to leave.

How could he leave? He couldn't. He couldn't keep up the charade of being loyal to the German cause. He couldn't build and fight for everything he hated while his true comrades fought for everything he loved.

That pit in his belly seethed. He couldn't leave Ivy. He hadn't said goodbye, couldn't send her a message to tell her he was departing.

Pressure built around his throat. Did she know how much he loved her? Did she know he'd do everything in his power to return to her? If he survived.

The lorry halted at the harbor entrance to let another lorry pass, and Gerrit gripped the metal edge of the bed. He could jump out. Run.

If he did so, he'd be shot.

The lorry rumbled into the dock area and stopped at the foot of Albert Pier, where half a dozen ships docked. Gerrit climbed out. He had one last chance, not to escape, but to let Ivy know he was leaving. If he could find Charlie, even catch his eye, Charlie would understand. Charlie would tell her.

A guard motioned for the OT men to wait, and more guards led two dozen civilians onto the pier.

Gerrit's chest caved in—ordinary men and women of all ages. Prisoners convicted of crimes such as spreading English news or harboring escaped workers or stealing food from the Germans, off to serve sentences in horrific prisons or concentration camps.

Ice tingled in the cavern in Gerrit's chest. Rumors of atrocities in those concentration camps had spread around the island, more so in the last two days.

The source of those rumors now trudged down the pier, dozens of wraiths in rags, with sunken eyes and protruding cheekbones, herded by black-clad guards.

Two days earlier, these slave workers had arrived on their way to France from Alderney, one of the Channel Islands. From all accounts, conditions for the forced laborers in Alderney made conditions in Jersey seem mild. And this group of Jews and political prisoners had been supervised by the notorious German SS.

An officer to Gerrit's right grunted. "I'm glad we're sending these workers to the continent. We need as many as we can get."

Gerrit clamped his tongue between his molars so he wouldn't speak. They'd have far more workers if they didn't work the ones they had to death.

The swastika armband burned on Gerrit's arm. If only he could rip it off, shred it. By wearing it, wasn't he defending the very nation that perpetrated such crimes, that murdered good men like Demyan Marchenko and countless others? Wouldn't it be better to take a bullet?

Gerrit squeezed his eyes shut and breathed hard, prayed hard. What would that accomplish? Would it stop the atrocities? Would it bring an Allied victory? Would it help the people he loved?

In a way, it would be a purely selfish—if principled—act.

"Come along, van der Zee." Riedel nudged him.

Gerrit pried his eyes open, shoved his feet down the pier.

Charlie—he had to find Charlie. But he didn't see the *Ormer*, didn't see his friend.

The OT men filed on board a cargo ship and crammed onto the deck. Gerrit and Riedel found a spot at the rails.

"I don't want to leave." Riedel cast a rueful gaze over the town. "But we're in danger of getting trapped here."

"True." The other day, the Americans had taken the port of

Cherbourg at the northern tip of the Cotentin Peninsula. Would they now drive south toward Saint-Malo?

Still no sign that the Allies were coming to the Channel Islands. Surely they wouldn't bypass the islands—their own soil, their own people.

Yet that soil was covered by the heaviest defenses on the Atlantic Wall, and those people would be endangered in battle. The British had abandoned the islands in 1940 due to the lack of strategic value. Would the Germans come to the same conclusion and evacuate their troops? Or follow the dictates of the military commander of the Channel Islands and fight to the last man?

If the Allies even came.

A frown tugged at Gerrit's lips. If they never came, his work was for nothing. All those maps, all those diagrams—a waste of silk and secret ink and lives risked.

Loaded with OT men, the cargo ship rumbled away from the pier and into the gray bay in the gray evening.

A cool breeze buffeted his face, and Gerrit closed his eyes and prayed. He had no control over any aspect of his life right now—probably never did. He had to trust God with the results, trust God to protect Ivy and Charlie and Bernardus and the Jounys, because he couldn't—probably never could.

His breath stilled, and a strange sense of peace filled him. On Sunday, the rector had preached from Habakkuk: "Although the fig tree shall not blossom, neither shall fruit be in the vines; the labour of the olive shall fail, and the fields shall yield no meat; the flock shall be cut off from the fold, and there shall be no herd in the stalls: Yet I will rejoice in the Lord, I will joy in the God of my salvation."

Gerrit prayed out his own version. Even if he were marched all the way to Berlin. Even if he were never exonerated. Even if he never saw Ivy again. Even if he died—even if executed as a traitor—yet he would rejoice in the Lord.

"Oh, Lord," he whispered into the wind. "Show me how."

A murmur swept the deck, built to cries.

Gerrit's eyes flew open. Low over the water, a large aircraft approached the far side of the ship, propellers spinning in four shiny discs. Twin projectiles plummeted from the plane's wings and slapped the water, and the bomber roared past over the ship.

"Torpedoes!"

With wild faces, men surged to Gerrit's side of the ship. Some scrambled over the rails and into the water.

Gerrit stared down into the gray waves. Stay on a ship about to be torpedoed? Or swim to safety? To an escape even?

His left hand stretched and coiled once. He had no time to deliberate, and he looped the strap of his duffel over his head and vaulted over the rail.

Cool water slapped the breath out of him, rushed over his head. He paddled to the surface, gulped in air, and swam hard for shore. His duffel served as a brake, but he'd ditch it only if necessary.

More splashes in the water, and a dozen men swam alongside him.

A shuddering crash.

Gerrit glanced over his shoulder.

The cargo ship lurched to one side but didn't explode.

Riedel leaned over the rail, his broad face frantic. "I can't swim, van der Zee! I can't swim."

Gerrit paused and treaded water. He was a strong swimmer, but could he save another man? How could he not try?

"Stay there, Riedel," he yelled. "You're safer on board. If the boat sinks, I'll help you."

"Yes, stay there." Ernst Schmeling treaded water not far from Gerrit, his wet hair glistening silver. "Patrol boats are coming."

Two small vessels zipped through the bay toward the cargo ship.

"Swim to shore, van der Zee." Schmeling paddled toward land. "The patrol boats will rescue our men."

Gerrit raised one hand to Riedel in farewell, then swam toward the beach, his breath coming hard, shuddering in the cold.

He couldn't escape from OT, even now, not with Schmeling and a dozen others in sight.

But he'd have another day in Jersey.

A chance to say goodbye.

CHAPTER
35

"If sketching outdoors was still allowed, I'd have plenty of time for it." Ivy set her afternoon timetable back on the receptionist's desk.

"True." With a rueful smile, Aunt Ruby rose from the desk and gathered her purse. "I'll see you tomorrow."

"Thank you." Ivy walked her aunt to the front door.

She had no afternoon appointments in the surgery, only two home visits, and no visits to treat fugitives. With most of the foreign workers evacuated to France, no new escapes had occurred, and the men in hiding were medically stable. Although another round of arrests in a wireless case had sent islanders into hiding to avoid prison, none of them needed medical care.

If only the Germans let the Jersey doctors help in their portion of Jersey General Hospital. Then Ivy would have something to do, a way to help the suffering. Since D-day, hundreds of wounded German soldiers had been evacuated from France to Jersey, but the Germans had run out of anesthesia and refused all assistance. The cries of the wounded haunted the halls.

At the door, Ivy waved goodbye to Aunt Ruby. A quartet of aircraft roared past to the south, over the harbor most likely.

Few ships braved the trip to France lately, and Charlie complained of boredom. However, that particular danger had kept Gerrit in Jersey.

Ivy closed the door and hung up her white coat, now yellowed from the lack of good soap. For the first fortnight after Gerrit's evacuation ship had been damaged, he had rejoiced to stay. He even had work to do, with the Germans constantly shifting guns around the island.

But yesterday at the farm, Gerrit had been troubled.

Ivy unlocked the supply room and slipped the key back into her skirt pocket.

The Allies pressed forward in Normandy, slowly, ponderously, unstoppably, but they hadn't come to the Channel Islands. The exhilaration in Jersey had disintegrated into bewilderment, Gerrit's joy into frustration.

Ivy sorted through her dwindling stock of medications, bandages, and supplies. Little to nothing came from France anymore, and even if supplies became available, how could Ivy afford them? Fern no longer contributed her wages, and Ivy's income fell lower each day.

A few weeks earlier, Gerrit had offered to help, but she'd dismissed the idea. Taking money from a Todt would drive away her remaining patients, who saw Ivy as above reproach.

She locked the supply room and went to the kitchen to prepare lunch. She'd had to let the housekeeper go, but at least Ivy had time to cook and clean.

After she chopped up a small potato and a carrot, she lit the stove and cooked them without butter or salt. If nothing changed, the island's supply of gas for cooking would run out by September. Each household had registered to use communal kitchens.

Pressure built behind her temples, and Ivy rubbed them. Yesterday, Gerrit had been preoccupied by his problems, and she'd failed to comfort him. And how she'd longed for comfort herself.

Ivy turned off the gas, scraped her bland lunch onto a plate, and sat at the table.

How could she continue to live with a sister who despised and blamed her? Ivy had hoped for some wisdom from Gerrit, some understanding, some support. She'd received none.

Perhaps Gerrit was an imperfect foundation. Not a sandy foundation like Fern, but more like Dad and Mum.

Ivy bowed her aching head over her tiny meal and prayed for God's rock-solid foundation, his wisdom, and his comfort.

Footsteps pounded down the hall and into the kitchen. Charlie grabbed the loaf of bread on the cabinet and sawed off a slice. "I lost my job."

"No! What happened?"

"The *Ormer* was damaged in yesterday's air raid. They don't have the supplies to repair her, and it isn't safe to sail anyway. They let the whole crew go." The knife shook in Charlie's fist. "All morning I've looked for work. Nothing."

"Oh, Charlie. I'm so sorry."

He thumped the knife down onto the cabinet. His head bowed, and his shoulders hunched. "I've failed you."

Ivy stood and took a step toward her brother, but he wasn't a little boy in need of a hug. "You haven't failed me. You never could."

"What am I to do?" He braced his hands on the cabinet. "I can't find work. I can't go back to school. We couldn't afford the fees, and I don't want to go to school anyway. I want to help. I need to help. How will we make do?"

How would they indeed? "I don't know, but we will."

"How?" Charlie wheeled around, his eyes wild. "Fern's being selfish and petty. Your patients can't pay their bills, so we can't pay ours. How will we buy wood this winter so we don't freeze? How will we buy food?"

Ivy didn't know, and words wouldn't come.

Charlie groaned and brandished his piece of bread. "I'm not

helping the Allies, not supporting my family. I'm a useless mouth. That's all I am."

"You—you're not."

Charlie tossed the bread back onto the cabinet and stomped out of the kitchen.

Ivy sank into her chair. She couldn't help Gerrit, couldn't help Charlie. They couldn't help her either. "Lord, help us all."

～

ST. PETER'S PARISH
SUNDAY, AUGUST 20, 1944

Gerrit poked at the vegetables in the soup Opal Jouny had prepared for Sunday lunch.

Beside Gerrit, Charlie sagged back in his chair, his own soup untouched. "Even if it were safe for ships to sail, they have nowhere to go. We're completely cut off."

Grim nods circled the table. Three days earlier, the Allies had taken Saint-Malo. From Jersey, Gerrit had seen the fires in the port city.

"The war will be over soon." Arthur sipped his blackberry leaf tea. "The Allies are almost in Paris, they're sweeping through Brittany, and they landed in southern France last week."

Opal frowned as she stirred her soup. "It seems cruel to pass us by."

"It's sound military strategy." Bernardus tapped the table. "The Channel Islands are essentially serving as an Allied prisoner of war camp for over twenty thousand German soldiers. The entire 319th Infantry Division is trapped here, plus all the naval forces."

Ivy swallowed a spoonful of soup. "But if they'd left, we'd be free."

"Bernardus is correct." Arthur nodded in a confident way. "If the division had left, the Allies would have had to fight them in France. This hastens the end of the war."

Gerrit's rations had been reduced, along with those of all the besieged civilians and German soldiers, but he had no appetite. "Please excuse me."

He rose and left through the back door. The heaviness of coming rain pressed in the air, pressed his raw heart.

"Gerrit?" Ivy said from behind him. "What's wrong?"

Hadn't she heard the conversation? "We're cut off."

"It was coming."

"Now it's final."

Standing two meters away, Ivy clasped her hands in front of her stomach. "You're frustrated because you can no longer help the Allies."

By the open kitchen window, Gerrit rapped his fist on the granite wall. "I never helped." His voice climbed and sharpened. "What good are maps of Jersey if the Allies never come here? And the diagrams I sent—they were for structures we modified from the standard models. They're unique to Jersey."

"I'm sure—"

"They're useless." Gerrit whacked the wall again. "Lately I've drawn diagrams of standard structures—structures found throughout France and Germany. Those would be useful. But they're stuffed in your aunt's scrap bag. I have no way to send them to France."

"I know, but . . ."

In the open window, the kitchen curtains fluttered in the breeze. "All my work is in vain, a mist in the wind. Why—why hasn't God done anything?"

A look crossed Ivy's face—a look he'd never seen before. A twitch near her nose, a furrow in her brow, a tightening of her mouth. "My sister is a notorious collaborator. My brother lost his job. My medical practice is failing. I have no idea how I'll pay for medical supplies or food or wood. But I'm trying—I'm determined to remember God's goodness. He *is* good, and he's good to me. He's helping me through. Thank goodness, because he's all I have."

She'd left him out. Because he'd left her out, and his mouth and heart fell open.

She folded her arms across her well-worn dress, and she blinked too many times. She looked so small, so thin. So alone.

"Ivy . . ." His voice grated over his throat.

She shook herself and pulled tall. "I don't understand. The Allies are winning. Isn't that enough for you?"

It should have been. Why wasn't it? Was he working for Allied victory? Or Gerrit's victory?

A groan ripped through him. "I'm sorry."

He shoved his feet toward her and gathered her in his arms. She stood stiff in his embrace, and he kissed her hair. "It is enough. It will be. I'll get through this. I'm sorry, *mijn geliefde.*"

Ivy relaxed, and her arms wound around him. "What does that mean?"

"'Mijn geliefde' means 'my beloved.' That's what you are." He kissed her hair again and rocked her. "I'm sorry I didn't treat you that way. I'll never leave you alone again."

She pressed her face to his chest and rubbed circles on his back. "Nor I you."

CHAPTER
36

To Ivy, silence had always meant peace, but not now.

Without a word, Ivy and Fern prepared their breakfasts at opposite ends of the kitchen. The gas supply had ceased on the fourth of September, so Ivy stirred oats she'd soaked in cold water the night before and added a handful of the blackberries she'd picked whilst on her rounds the other day.

On the kitchen table sat dinner for her and Charlie—a crockery dish of potatoes and vegetables she'd take to the Picots' assigned bakery to cook all day. Since Fern always ate out for dinner now, she took no responsibility for the evening meal.

No sounds had yet arisen from Charlie's room. After losing his job, he'd looked for work each day and taken odd jobs when he could find them. Recently he'd spent evenings with old school chums, which had cheered him.

Someone banged on the front door, and Ivy frowned. The surgery didn't open for another hour and a half, and medical emergencies went to the casualty department at General Hospital.

She strode to the door, wiping her hands on her apron as she went, with Fern behind her.

"Open the door!" a man yelled.

Ivy's blood crystallized, and her breath hitched. Germans? Had they learned she treated escapees?

A quick prayer, and she opened the door.

Five men in overcoats and trilby hats stood on the stoop. "We're looking for Charles Picot."

What had Charlie done? He hadn't served as Gerrit's courier for several months. Ivy struggled for composure. "Charlie? He hasn't come down for breakfast yet."

The leader, a man around forty, motioned for the other two men to enter the house. "Find him."

"I beg your pardon." Fern stepped in their way with a beautiful smile and an outstretched hand. "My name is Fern Le Corre, and I work for the Feldkommandantur—rather the Platzkommandantur now. Charles is my brother. You are Hauptwachtmeister Karl-Heinz Wölfle of the Geheime Feldpolizei, yes? How may I help you?"

The man known as the "Wolf of the Gestapo"? Ivy's breath snagged on her throat. Thank goodness Fern was using her charm to intervene.

"You may help by telling us where your brother is hiding." Wölfle spoke fluent English with a Canadian accent.

Fern added a sweep of eyelashes to her smile. "I assure you, Herr Hauptwachtmeister, my brother has no need to hide."

"Then you have no need to fear a search." He brushed past her into the hall.

Ivy stumbled backward as the men shoved inside. One man flung open the door to Ivy's office, another marched toward the back door, two men pounded up the stairs, and Wölfle slammed a leather satchel onto the receptionist's desk. Papers fluttered from the desk to the floor.

"Do you recognize this?" Wölfle asked.

With the engraved nameplate on top of the satchel, proclamations of ignorance would be most unwise. But her voice bounced, silent, in the depths of her gut.

"It's Charlie's." Fern fingered the nameplate. "Where did you find it?"

"On the beach at La Rocque where a group of cowards tried to desert to France last night."

To desert? To escape? Charlie? Ivy's hands clenched together.

A man shouted in German from the back of the house and rattled a doorknob.

"The door is locked." Fern snapped her gaze to Ivy. "The supply room. Quickly, before he breaks the lock."

She would never be able to replace the lock that protected medications and foodstuffs and her bicycle, and she ran down the hall, wrestling the key from her pocket. "Please! Please stop. Wait. I have the key."

Fern called out a translation as Ivy ran.

Despite shaking hands, Ivy inserted the key in the lock. She opened the door for the field police. "See? No one is hiding here."

The man shoved things around on the shelves, and bottles crashed to the floor.

"Please don't," Ivy said. "Please. We have shortages of medicines."

Fern translated in a longer version, and Ivy used the break to catch her breath. When it mattered, she could count on Fern and their mutual love for Charlie.

"Come here, ladies," Wölfle called from the receptionist's desk. "I'm not finished questioning you."

Without glancing at Ivy, Fern strolled to Wölfle wearing a sedate smile.

Ivy's feet tangled with each other, and she fumbled for the wall, fumbled for breath. "What do you mean—Charlie *tried* to escape?"

"A party of youths deserted by boat." Wölfle patted the satchel. "Our men shot one of them. He dropped this bag."

Ivy clapped her hand over her mouth and gasped.

"Shot?" Fern flung out a splayed hand and braced herself against the wall.

"Last night the patrol found this bag but no other trace of the injured man, so they assumed his comrades had rescued him. But this morning, we found blood leading away from the beach."

"Oh no." Ivy's voice came out muffled. "Charlie."

"You're a doctor." Wölfle's gaze carried both restraint and intimidation. "He came to you for treatment."

"No. No, he didn't."

"Where did you hide him?"

"I didn't." Ivy's head swung back and forth. "Oh no. Where is he?"

Thumps arose upstairs, and Ivy sent a fractured plea heavenward. What if Charlie had indeed come home last night? What if he was hiding in the house? No, if he was injured, he would have awakened her.

He was somewhere else. But where? How badly was he injured? Was he even alive?

Wölfle unbuckled the satchel and pulled out a pile of silk squares. "What are these?"

"I don't know," she murmured, not even a lie. Although she knew they were Gerrit's sketches, she didn't know what he'd sketched.

Fern fingered the maps. "It's silk. Where did Charlie get silk?"

"I can't imagine." The words pulsed moist heat into Ivy's fingers. In truth, she had no idea how Gerrit obtained the silk.

Wölfle's gaze sliced back and forth between sisters. "We believe it's a parachute from an English spy."

"A spy?" Fern jutted out her chin. "I assure you, no Picot has any doings with English spies."

Ivy could only shake her head in confusion.

Upstairs, furniture thudded and scraped.

"We will find your brother." Wölfle stuffed the silk into the satchel. "When we do . . ."

Fern teetered, leaned back against the wall, and pressed her fingers over her mouth. "I read the notice in the *Evening Post* the other day. Desertion to the enemies of the German forces shall be treated as espionage."

"Correct." Wölfle slid the bag off the desk, and the appointment book tumbled to the floor.

Ivy's fingers dug into her cheek. If the Germans realized secret ink adorned that silk and they developed the maps, they'd discover both Charlie and Gerrit were truly guilty of espionage.

Footsteps descended the stairs, and two Germans marched down the hall, joined by their colleagues who had searched the ground floor, each holding armfuls of papers.

Ivy winced, but she'd never put any of her work for the ring down on paper. Surely Charlie hadn't written about his exploits either.

Wölfle thrust a finger at Fern and Ivy. "Harboring spies will lead to severe punishment. If you hear anything about your brother, you must report it to us immediately."

"Of course, Herr Hauptwachtmeister." Fern hoisted her chin high. "I would never defy German orders."

Ivy had already defied orders, and she'd do so again if it meant her brother's life, but she nodded. "I understand, sir."

The five men strode outside and slammed the front door.

"What did you do to Charlie?" Fern spun to Ivy. "What did you get him involved in?"

"Me?"

"Don't play innocent." Fern's hands formed claws and shook in front of her. "You were lying to the Feldpolizei. I can always tell when you're lying. This is your fault. You turned Charlie against me, turned him against the Germans, and now he's breaking the law."

Heat built in Ivy's chest. With one sweep of her arm, she swiped away the blame. "Charlie has a mind of his own, eyes of his own. He sees the Germans for who they are. He's seen them beat their workers. He's seen his friends arrested for nothing more than listening to the BBC. Heaven forbid they hear the truth."

"Your fault." Fern's mouth formed the words with precision, and her gaze seared. "Now he's tried to desert to the enemy, and he's hurt, bleeding. Where is he? Where would he go?"

Ivy closed her eyes to Fern's accusations, to think. Where would he have gone? To the farm? St. Peter's Parish was at least five miles from La Rocque, and Charlie would have passed through St. Helier on the way. He would have come home for care, for help hiding.

"Where is he?" Grief shredded Fern's voice. "Where's my little brother?"

"I don't know." Ivy pried wet eyelashes apart and met her sister's gaze. "I don't know, Fern."

Fern's chest heaved, and she brushed tears from her cheeks. "Thank goodness I have influence with the Germans. I'll go to Helmut and smooth things over. I may not be able to save Charlie from prison, but I might be able to save his life."

Fern stormed out of the house, leaving the front door wide open.

With halting steps, Ivy went to close the door.

In the street, a man in a coat and a trilby pushed away from the house across the way and followed Fern. Another man, similarly clad, read a newspaper outside the house next door.

Ivy shut the door. She leaned back against it and clutched the sides of her head. They were being watched. If she searched for Charlie, she'd be followed.

Her breath came hard, in erratic bursts. In recent weeks, many had escaped by boat—or tried to. When they did, the German field police searched homes of family members.

"Oh no. Aunt Opal." If they searched the farm, they'd find Bernardus—and Gerrit. Gerrit had little work lately and spent Saturdays at the farm.

She had to warn them, and she spun to the doorknob. No, she'd lead the Germans straight to the farm.

The telephone. Two steps, and she slammed to a stop. The farmhouse didn't have a telephone. She'd ring Joan, give her the code to move a patient straightaway.

273

"No, no." If the Germans were watching the house, they were certainly listening to the telephone line. The code might be secure, but the fact that Ivy rang so soon after a raid would raise the alarm and place Joan under scrutiny. And using the Jouny name might lead them to unravel their codes.

"Oh, Lord." A sob rent its way up Ivy's throat. "Lord, what do I do?"

～

ST. PETER'S PARISH

"Oh, Gerrit." Opal Jouny grabbed his arm, drew him into the farmhouse, and shut the door behind him. Red rimmed her eyes and stained her cheeks. "Charlie's escaped."

"Escaped?"

"By boat. We found a letter on the kitchen table this morning." Opal dashed to the kitchen, and Gerrit followed.

She thrust a piece of paper into Gerrit's hands.

Dear Uncle Arthur, Aunt Opal, and all,

By the time you read this, I'll be in France! I've left with three of my friends from Victoria College. Now that we're seventeen, we're old enough to serve in the British forces. I'm no longer able to help the Allies in Jersey, but I can once I arrive in France.

My departure will also help Ivy, since she'll no longer need to support me.

In addition, I'm taking Gerrit's diagrams. After overhearing Gerrit's argument with Ivy, I know how important it is that his new diagrams land in Allied hands. By doing so in person, I'll be able to verify the source of previous deliveries and assure them of Gerrit's and Bernardus's good work and loyalty. I left one sample behind for Gerrit to show upon liberation.

Please show this letter to Ivy, Bernardus, and Gerrit, and then promptly burn it. You all have my deep love and affec-

*tion, and I look forward to seeing you upon the liberation of
this island.*

By leaving now, I hope to hasten that day.

Yours sincerely,
Charlie

Gerrit's mouth flopped. What had Charlie done? Over the past
few weeks, many young men and women had tried to escape. Some
had succeeded. Some had been arrested when their boats blew
back to Jersey. Some had drowned when their boats were dashed
on rocks.

Opal stuck wood into the oven. "Radio-Paris announces the
names of those who arrive in France. In the meantime, you need to
leave straightaway. When men escape, the Germans always search
homes of family members. They'll certainly search the farm."

"Bernardus." Gerrit's gaze sprang to the ceiling.

"He's packing, destroying evidence." Opal grabbed the letter
from Gerrit and tossed it on the fire in the oven. "Arthur is asking
a neighbor if he can hide Bernardus temporarily."

Bernardus swept into the kitchen with a bag over his shoulder
and a pile in his arms. He dumped the pile on the table. "Burn it
all."

Gerrit snatched out his civilian clothes and the last silk map.
"I'll keep this map. It's our only proof in case . . ."

Bernardus's gaze crept up to him, stark and gaunt. In case Charlie was arrested. In case he didn't survive.

And if the Germans captured Charlie with Gerrit's maps?

He'd heard hushed tales of torture at the field police headquarters at Silvertide in Havre des Pas. If the Germans suspected the use
of secret ink, they could develop the images, and Gerrit, Bernardus,
the Jounys—even Ivy—would be in great danger.

"I'll do one more search, make sure I didn't leave anything."
Bernardus set his bag on a chair and rushed out of the kitchen.

Opal fed the remaining evidence into the fire—the chemist's box of secret ink crystals, Gerrit's wooden ruler and T square, and the unused scraps of parachute silk. "I need to run to the telephone box and ring Ivy, tell her about Charlie, warn her that the Germans will search her home, and tell her Bernardus must be moved straightaway."

"Wait." Thoughts careened through Gerrit's head. "Ivy uses codes on the telephone in case the Germans are listening. If they know Charlie escaped—"

Opal gasped. "They'll listen to her line. I'll go in person."

"No, I'll go. Stay and help Bernardus."

Opal squinted at him. "Change into your civilian clothes."

"Yes." He'd be less conspicuous, do less harm to Ivy's fragile reputation.

"Quickly." Opal shooed him out of the kitchen. "You mustn't be here when the Gestapo comes."

"Yes, ma'am." In the washroom, he removed his jacket and slipped his civilian jacket over his uniform shirt.

What would he tell Ivy? She'd be overwhelmed with worry for her little brother. Until they heard his name on the radio, they'd live in uncertainty.

Gerrit wrenched off his boots, stuffed his uniform cap inside one and the silk map inside another, and changed trousers. What would Ivy say when he told her why Charlie had escaped?

Guilt smacked into his grief. Charlie had overheard Gerrit's selfish rant about his maps, his work, his self-importance. Now Charlie had braved a beach planted with mines, a coast lined with guns, and a perilous crossing.

Gerrit couldn't take the blame for Dirk's death or Cilla's, but if anything happened to Charlie, Gerrit could indeed take part of the blame.

"Lord, forgive me." He rolled his uniform around his boots and stuffed the bundle into his satchel.

His chin fell to his chest. The Lord would forgive him, but Ivy never would. Even if Charlie arrived safely in France, he'd risked his life because of Gerrit's foolishness.

Gerrit would lose the woman he loved.

Regardless, he would tell her the truth.

He gritted his teeth and strode back to the kitchen.

Bernardus was slipping on his jacket, and Opal was filling a basket with bread.

Arthur tossed papers into the fire. "Take my hat, Gerrit. You look too Dutch." He gestured to a gray homburg on the table. "Give Ivy our love."

"I will." He clapped the hat on his head and shook Bernardus's hand. Would he ever see his friend again? Then he shook Arthur's hand and accepted Opal's peck on his cheek. He wouldn't return to the farm until liberation, and he strode out of the house, mounted his bicycle, and pedaled away.

For so long, he'd complained that he'd done the right thing and no good had come of it.

Now he'd done the wrong thing and something horrible had come of it.

CHAPTER
37

ST. HELIER

With her hands pressed to her cheeks, Ivy wandered in circles in the hallway.

She couldn't help Charlie. Not at all. Even if she knew where he was, she couldn't go to him, couldn't treat him, or she'd lead Wölfle to him.

She couldn't warn her aunt and uncle, couldn't tell the ring to move Bernardus. "I can't do anything, Lord."

And Dad and Mum—with Red Cross messages now cut off, she had no way to tell them.

Her wooden-soled shoe bumped the appointment book on the floor, and she picked it up. She had three appointments this morning, and the office was in disarray.

That's what she could do.

Ivy gathered the papers from the floor and stacked them on the desk. Poor Aunt Ruby would have to straighten the mess when she arrived.

Aunt Ruby! Ivy pulled in a breath of refreshing air. Her aunt might be able to help in some way, get a message to someone.

"Joan!" Ivy grabbed a piece of paper and ran to the supply room.

The shattered medicine bottles needed to be replaced. If Aunt Ruby went to the chemist's to make a purchase, she could also deliver a message.

Ivy plucked out shards of glass, read the labels, and wrote down the contents. Then she scooped up tablets and brushed them off. Before the occupation, she would have thrown them away, but not now. Not when these might be the last medications she'd have until liberation.

The front door opened, and feminine footsteps came down the hall. "What on earth?" Aunt Ruby cried. "Ivy? Are you all right?"

Ivy set a handful of tablets on the shelf and joined her aunt. The horror of the morning and her relief at seeing Aunt Ruby jumbled together. "The field police came searching for Charlie. He tried to escape by boat last night, and the Germans shot and injured him."

"No!" Aunt Ruby collapsed into her chair.

"He evaded arrest somehow. They don't know where he is. Neither do I. He didn't come here." Ivy's voice cracked, and she sank to her knees on the wooden floor.

Aunt Ruby fumbled for Ivy's hand. "Poor Charlie."

Ivy squeezed her aunt's hand. "They may search your home. Do you have any contraband? Do you need to warn Uncle Leo?"

"No, no." She gasped. "Arthur! His wireless."

And Bernardus and Gerrit and the mapmaking materials. "I need your help to send him a mess—"

"I'll go straightaway."

"No, the Germans will follow you. They're watching the house. I have another idea." Ivy pushed to standing. "They made a mess in the supply room, broke medicine bottles. I'll send you to Carter's Chemist's with a list. If the Germans follow you, you'll have an excuse."

"All right." Aunt Ruby followed Ivy to the supply room.

"Take the list to Miss de Ferrers. Many of the medicines will be out of stock, but it'll give you a reason to talk to her." Ivy resumed sorting through the broken glass for labels. "I have a message for

Miss de Ferrers. You must wait until no one else is around, and you must repeat it word for word."

"Oh my. This sounds rather hush-hush."

"Tell her I need a prescription filled for Arthur Jouny for fifty grains of aspirin."

"Fifty grains? You mean five."

"Fifty. You must say fifty." Ivy scribbled another medication on her list. "If Miss de Ferrers corrects you, as she will, say Dr. Picot insists on fifty grains."

"Is that some sort of—"

"Please don't ask questions." Ivy wrote down one more medication, stood, and handed her aunt the list. "Go now and quickly."

"Not too quickly, or I'll look suspicious." Aunt Ruby's brown eyes widened behind her glasses. "Fifty grains of aspirin for Arthur Jouny."

"Yes." Ivy pecked her on the cheek. "Thank you. Be careful."

"I will." She frowned at the mess. "Then I'll come back and clean."

After Aunt Ruby left, Ivy took a deep breath. What next? Patients could arrive within the hour.

Her office, overlooking the street, was strewn with papers and folders that would take hours to sort.

She sighed and checked the first examination room, where she'd see patients, her top priority. Cupboards and drawers had been emptied, and she gathered supplies from the floor and tucked them out of sight. She'd set them to rights later.

"Ivy? Ivy, are you all right?"

"Gerrit?" Ivy dashed out.

He stood by the receptionist's desk in a gray civilian suit and homburg, gaping at the overturned chairs.

"Come." She pulled him into the examination room and shut the door in case patients arrived.

"The field police?" His face contorted, and he reached for her.

She fell into his arms. "It's Charlie. He tried to escape last night, but the Germans shot and injured him. He evaded them, but we don't know where he is or how badly he's injured or if he's even alive."

"Oh no." He pressed his cheek to the top of her head. "He left a note at the farm."

"He did? I wanted to warn Uncle Arthur. The police may raid the farm."

"They realized that." His chest rose and fell under her cheek. "They burnt all the evidence, sent Bernardus to a neighbor. You'll need to tell the ring to move him straightaway."

"I sent Aunt Ruby with the message." Her breathing slowed in the warmth of Gerrit's embrace. "I'm glad Uncle Arthur recognized the danger."

"I am too." He settled a kiss on her forehead. "Charlie—do you have any idea where he might have gone?"

"No. I can only imagine him coming here or to Aunt Ruby's or to the farm, but he didn't. The note—what did he say?" She raised her head.

Hesitation swam in his green-blue eyes, and his Adam's apple dropped to his collar and rose again. "He went with three of his friends from Victoria College."

Ivy groaned. "That explains why he's met with them lately."

"They're all of age. They want to serve in the forces. Do you know—were the others captured? Shot?"

"They escaped by boat. Only Charlie—" Her throat clamped off. Her brother—her bright, lively, compassionate, clever brother.

"If they didn't capture him," Gerrit said, "how do they know it's Charlie who was shot?"

"He dropped his bag. It has his name on it. Oh, Gerrit, your maps were in the bag. The Germans have them."

Gerrit grimaced and scrunched his eyes shut. "I was afraid of that."

She clutched at his back. "What if they figure out how to develop the ink?"

His eyes inched open, just enough to meet her gaze. "The maps—that's one of the reasons Charlie tried to escape."

"Yes . . ." Charlie must have wanted to deliver them to the British.

Gerrit's jaw shifted forward and back, and his eyebrows bunched together. "His escape attempt is partly my fault."

"Your fault?"

"A few weeks ago at the farm, I was upset and walked out. You followed me. We were by an open window. Charlie heard me."

The conversation grazed through her mind. Gerrit had called his work a mist in the wind. He'd mentioned diagrams of use to the Allies, trapped in Aunt Opal's scrap bag. And Charlie, always thoughtful, always generous, had heard Gerrit's rant.

Her breath puffed through her nostrils. "He did it for you."

"He did." Gerrit's words came out choked. "Yes, he also went so he could fight for Britain, but I accept full responsibility."

Ivy tugged on his suit jacket. "Now he's bleeding somewhere, in pain, dying, maybe already dead. My little brother."

His face crumpled, but he kept his gaze on her. "I'm so sorry, Ivy."

Her hands clenched fistfuls of gray wool. For the first time in her life, she wanted to hit someone. She wanted to hit Gerrit.

And yet behind the blinking blond eyelashes, something flickered in the narrow band of green-blue. Concern for Charlie. Acceptance of the consequences of his words. Acceptance of losing her.

The front door opened. "Ivy? I'm back."

Aunt Ruby! Staring at Gerrit's tortured face, Ivy fought to control her breath and signaled for him to stay silent. She slipped out of the examination room, shut the door behind her, and stood in front of the door to keep her aunt out—and so Gerrit could hear. "Did you pass on the message?"

"I did, and I received one in return." Aunt Ruby set a little box of medicine bottles on the desk, and she gripped Ivy's hands. "Charlie is in hiding, and Dr. Tipton treated him."

"Thank you, Lord." Ivy sagged back against the door, and it rattled.

"Miss de Ferrers said he was shot in the side and lost a lot of blood. He's still in danger." Aunt Ruby leaned close. "We are not allowed to know where he is. Miss de Ferrers said the Germans will follow you, and you must keep that in mind when making home visits. I don't know why she made me promise to tell you, but she insisted."

"She's being considerate." Ivy raised a watery smile. She would no longer be treating patients in the ring.

Aunt Ruby's gaze sharpened. "We need to promptly forget we heard this about Charlie. We know only what the Germans know, understood?"

"Understood." She'd let Uncle Arthur and Aunt Opal know when she saw them next, but no one else. "You can tell Uncle Leo, but we mustn't tell Fern."

"No." Her lips folded in, then she shook her head and glanced at her wristwatch. "Your first appointment is in twenty minutes. Is the examination room ready?"

"Almost." As soon as she shooed away her visitor. "Why don't you inspect the damage upstairs?"

Aunt Ruby clucked her tongue. "The waiting room."

"I'll take care of that." Ivy set chairs upright as Aunt Ruby ascended the stairs. When she reached the top, Ivy would escort Gerrit out. Thank goodness he was wearing a civilian suit rather than his uniform—the field police would assume him to be a patient.

The front door banged open and shut, and Fern hurried into the waiting room. Her face was red, and tear tracks marred her high cheekbones. "Any news on Charlie?"

None that she could repeat, but Fern's concern for her brother softened Ivy's spine. "I don't know where he is."

Fern let out a fierce grunt. "This is your fault. You filled his head with nonsense, but all he had to do was obey the rules."

Ivy's spine hardened again. "I never told him to break any rules.

And if he'd told me he planned to escape, I would have begged him not to."

Gerrit would have too, and Ivy's breath caught. He was no more to blame for Charlie's actions than she was.

"You and Charlie." Fern thrust a finger in Ivy's direction. "You don't even care how your actions affect me."

A laugh erupted. The hypocrisy, when Fern didn't care how her actions affected Ivy and Charlie. "You? Charlie has been shot, and you're concerned about how this affects *you*?"

"I lost my job." Fern's mouth shrank into a tiny dot. "I went to Helmut to ask for his help, to ask for mercy for Charlie when they find him. But he said he can't trust me, not with the family under investigation. He—they think I might be a spy."

Ivy gave a sympathetic murmur. "He won't see you anymore, will he?"

Sparks flared in Fern's eyes. "It's your fault. You couldn't bear seeing me happy, and you ruined it."

Ivy gritted her teeth so she wouldn't speak the truth. Again.

"Is this your revenge?" Fern's nostrils flared. "You're jealous because I'm in love, and you—you know nothing about love. You never will."

"I know more about love than you ever will." Ivy let out a little gasp. Why had she said that? She'd all but admitted to being in love.

The sparks quenched, but the nostrils flared even wider, and Fern released a scoffing sound. "I pity you." She whirled away and marched upstairs.

As soon as Fern's bedroom door slammed, Ivy rushed into the examination room. "Did you hear Aunt Ruby?" she whispered.

"I did." Gerrit leaned back against the examination table, gripping the edge, his expression taut. "Trust your friends to treat him, to hide him."

"I do." She leaned back against the table beside him so they could speak quietly.

"I heard your sister too," Gerrit said. "I'm sorry. I'm sorry about everything. I accept full responsibility."

With long, slow breaths, she blew the blame away. "Did you tell Charlie to do this? Even suggest it?"

"No, but . . ."

Ivy stroked his hand on the table between them, so stiff and tense. "Charlie chose to escape without asking us, without informing us. He is responsible for his decision."

Gerrit heaved out a sigh. "Yes, but if I hadn't—"

"He still might have gone with his friends. He's seventeen." She pried Gerrit's hand off the table and massaged it as if she could massage away his guilt. "If you must blame someone, blame the Germans. They came uninvited, they've caused hardship and suffering, and they refused to leave when they should have done. That's why so many are trying to escape."

Gerrit stayed silent. Stayed stiff. "You're very kind, but I understand if you never want to see me again."

Ivy studied the fingers she held, the fingers she stroked, the fingers she loved. "To sketch you, I have to see you, to look at you. Isn't that what you told me? And I love sketching you."

Gerrit said nothing, but he gathered her into his arms.

Her nervous chuckle ruffled his necktie. "You must think me rather odd."

"Oh, mijn geliefde." He kissed her forehead. "I think you're a marvel."

CHAPTER
38

Gerrit stepped out of the hotel garage, where he'd parked his bicycle and changed back into uniform.

Corralling his thoughts along the way had been difficult due to his concerns for Charlie, the maps in German hands, the investigation of the Picot family—and due to Ivy's forgiveness. But corralling those thoughts had been necessary to avoid violating any of the petty orders governing the island. If he'd been stopped along the way and asked for his papers, and he had presented his OT paybook while in civilian clothes, he would have been in grave trouble.

With his satchel over his shoulder, he straightened his rumpled uniform jacket and entered the hotel lobby.

Ernst Schmeling rose from a chair by the window. "Where have you been, van der Zee? We've been looking for you."

Two other men rose as well, one in a German Army officer's uniform and the other in a black civilian suit.

Something tilted inside him, threw him off-balance, and he took a step to the left. "Pardon me, Herr Oberbauführer. I was told I had no work today, so I bicycled around the island."

"Come with us, Haupttruppführer." The officer—a captain—gestured to the front door, to a car waiting outside.

"May I ask what this is about?"

"You do not ask questions. We do." One more gesture, firmer this time.

Gerrit glanced toward Schmeling but received only steely silence. Organisation Todt would not be rising to his defense, not when the Nazi Reich was threatened.

"Ja, Herr Hauptmann." Gerrit pulled himself tall, marched outside, and slid into the backseat, joined by the man in the civilian suit.

The car drove north into town, and Gerrit forced himself to keep calm, to think, to pray. Was he under arrest? Would he be tortured? Would he crack? He was a horrible liar, and the Nazis were experts at exposing lies.

The town flashed by outside, and Gerrit measured his breaths and prayed for wisdom to know when to speak and when to stay silent. Prayed for protection of those who could be hurt by what he knew.

If he were innocent, what would he know? He wouldn't know Charlie had tried to escape or had been injured. He wouldn't know about the raid on the Picot home. He certainly wouldn't know anything about scraps of silk.

Hemmed in by granite walls, the road climbed a hill under a cloud-streaked sky.

Gerrit gripped the satchel in his lap. If only he'd left it in the garage. What if they searched his bag? How could he explain the civilian suit inside? OT regulations required wearing a uniform at all times, even on leave. And the map. Oh no. When he changed, he'd transferred the silk map from his boot to his civilian shoe. The map would match the ones in Charlie's bag. Infractions of uniform codes paled in comparison to espionage.

The car parked outside an elegant white building, probably a hotel before the occupation.

The army officer opened Gerrit's door. "Come with us."

Surrounded by the three men, Gerrit proceeded inside. He'd heard of resistance fighters throwing themselves from windows to avoid revealing information or incriminating their friends, but the officer ushered him into a ground-floor room.

Just as well. Gerrit doubted he could do such a thing.

"Sit down, van der Zee." The army officer pointed to a chair in front of a steel table, and he removed his cap, revealing his balding head.

"Yes, Herr Hauptmann." He obeyed.

"I am Hauptmann Klein, and this is Hauptwachtmeister Wölfle of the Geheime Feldpolizei."

The military police and the secret field police, but Gerrit saw no torture implements. Klein and Wölfle sat across from Gerrit, and Schmeling sat behind Gerrit in the corner.

They had told him not to ask questions, so he stuffed his satchel under his chair and waited.

Wölfle raised a sardonic smile. "Are you nervous, van der Zee?"

Gerrit tried to mirror that smile. "Wouldn't you be in my place? No one has told me why I'm here."

Klein leaned bony elbows on the table. "Do you know a man named Charles Picot?"

"Charlie? Yes."

"How do you know him?"

Gerrit rested his hands on his thighs, out of sight of the interrogators. "He worked on a cargo ship which transported supplies for OT. He showed us around the island—my friend Bernardus and me. We've become friends. Why do you want to know about Charlie?" Honest worry lifted his voice.

Wölfle tugged at the sleeves of his well-cut suit. "He tried to desert to our enemies last night. A patrol shot and injured him, but he's evaded capture so far."

Gerrit's breath rushed out. "He tried to—he's hurt? Oh no. Poor Charlie."

Klein grunted. "You feel sorry for a man who defied Germany?"

"I feel sorry for a boy I know as a friend." He kept his voice firm but calm.

"Do you know where he is?" Wölfle asked.

"No. How could I?"

"Where might he have gone?"

They'd already searched the Picot home. Gerrit tucked in his lips as if deep in thought. "His sister is a doctor. He'd—"

"Where else?"

"He has aunts and uncles here." They were already expecting raids.

"Why would he desert?"

Gerrit puffed up his cheeks with air and blew it out. "He never said anything to me about desertion. He did lose his job after his ship was damaged in an air raid, and the food situation is rather bleak. I don't understand. I thought he was on our side. Remember, Herr Oberbauführer? Charlie is the one who warned me when Bernardus tried to commit sabotage." He glanced back at Schmeling.

Schmeling's jaw shot forward.

"Ah, you see, van der Zee." Klein smoothed his ring of graying blond hair. "That makes us rather curious. Kroon was a traitor, now Picot. Both known associates of yours."

"You don't think I . . ." Indignation cramped his voice, and he sent Schmeling a frantic glance. "Haven't I always done good work for Organisation Todt?"

One silver eyebrow rose in affirmation, but his jaw remained set.

Wölfle fetched a brown leather satchel from under his chair and set it on the table. "Have you ever seen this?"

It had to be Charlie's bag, filled with Gerrit's maps. A sudden flash in his mind—instead of answering their questions with lies, he could anticipate the questions. "No, I haven't."

"Picot dropped it." Wölfle opened the bag, pulled out the silk maps, and laid them on the table.

"Is that silk?" Gerrit fingered the cloth. If only he could rub away the secret ink. "Where would Charlie get silk?"

Klein sniffed. "We believe it came from an English parachute."

"From a crash site?" Gerrit frowned at the army officer. "It's against the law not to report downed airmen. By penalty of death."

Tiny eyes grew even tinier in Klein's round face. "Why would he take it to France?"

Gerrit shrugged. "Silk would have great value on the black market, ja? Do you think he planned to sell it to ladies in France?"

"You can imagine our curiosity," Klein said with an acidic smile. "Why would he risk the death penalty to make a few francs?"

Gerrit huffed. "He's seventeen. What boy of seventeen expects to be captured?"

Klein brushed his hand across the top map. "Very curious."

If these men even suspected the presence of secret ink, they'd search for a developing agent. Although they couldn't send the maps to Germany for analysis, they still had radio contact with Berlin.

If they developed the ink, Schmeling would recognize the maps and recognize Gerrit's hand.

Gerrit cleared his throat. "Very curious indeed."

⌁

ST. HELIER

Behind his locked hotel room door that evening, Gerrit finished his sketch of the St. Helier Parish Church in black ink.

Tomorrow morning in church, he'd drop the folded sketch beside Ivy's pew and ask her if she'd dropped it.

Since his secret ink had been burned at the farm, he had to write plainly. But he could try to conceal his words from casual scrutiny.

After he shaded the edges lightly in pencil, he wrote in the smallest possible letters within the shading.

Mijn geliefde,

Today I was interrogated. Don't worry—I wasn't hurt, nor was I arrested. However, with both of us under investigation, it's best that we do not meet, and I will no longer visit our favorite spot. Also, burn this letter after reading it.

Please know I love you dearly. When all this is over, I will come to you as soon as I'm able. Then no one and nothing will keep us apart.

I will pray for you and your family, and I will trust the Lord. He is good and he is faithful, even when we can't see it.

Gerrit leaned back in his chair and raked his hands back into his hair. If only he'd proposed. Then she'd know he meant every word of his promise.

CHAPTER
39

Ivy removed her stethoscope from Mr. Whistler's stocky chest. "You gave us a scare with that heart attack last week, but you're recovering well."

"Too well." The nursing sister pulled the blanket back into position. "He won't stay in bed."

"How can I when there's work to be done?" He gave Ivy a significant look. He was sheltering an escaped Russian worker.

"I'm sure your wife can manage." Ivy maintained a breezy manner. "From now on, you mustn't let yourself run out of digitalis. The chemists can make it from the foxglove on the island, so you have no excuse."

Unlike patients who needed other medications, like insulin. Before the siege, occasional shipments of insulin had arrived from the continent, but none since June. All but one of the diabetics in hospital had died.

The shortages grew worse each day. Recently the Department of Public Health had printed appeals in the *Evening Post* for thermometers and for materials that could be used as bandages.

Heaviness pressed on her lungs, so she drew a long breath, smiled for her patient, and stood. "I'll see you tomorrow, Mr. Whistler."

"She's a good doctor, our Dr. Picot." He patted the nursing sister's arm with the back of his hand. "No one could ever tell me otherwise. Now everyone knows."

Ivy's smile faltered, and she left the ward. The news of Charlie's escape attempt had been printed in the *Evening Post*, along with a German demand for information on the fugitive. She would have rather remained a pariah and have her brother home safe and sound.

Although she came to Jersey General Hospital to see Mr. Whistler and her other patients, her reason for daily visits now stemmed from her thirst for information on Charlie.

She peeked into the surgical ward and caught Dr. Tipton's eye, and he jerked his head to the side, toward the physicians' office.

At the end of the hallway, Ivy entered the small room used by several doctors as an office. Thank goodness no one else was present, because she hadn't been able to meet with Dr. Tipton for several days.

Charlie was healing well from the surgery for his gunshot wound, but he'd lost a lot of blood. Since he'd hidden in the ocean under the pier and medical care had been delayed, the risk of infection loomed large.

The window looked toward Gloucester Street and the prison next door, full to overflowing. Those convicted of minor infractions now had to wait to serve their sentences. At least no one could be deported to prisons or concentration camps on the continent anymore.

Ivy crossed one arm over her empty stomach and pressed one hand to her empty heart. The danger to Charlie and Gerrit hadn't diminished. The Germans could still execute prisoners, especially those guilty of espionage.

She missed Gerrit. She'd stashed his sketch with the concealed letter in the apothecary jar he'd given her, high on the office bookshelf. How could she burn something of such great beauty? How could she destroy the only token she had of his love?

The door opened, and Dr. Tipton entered.

"How is he?" she asked.

Dr. Tipton rounded the table in the center of the room and leaned against the wall by the window. A frown crinkled his freckled face. "I'm afraid infection set in. He isn't responding to sulfapyridine."

"Do you need more? I have some in my bag. It's past its date of use, but—"

"He's receiving the maximum dosage. He isn't responding, Dr. Picot."

Ivy clutched at the fabric of her white coat. "He's young. He's strong."

"Yes." Doubt flooded his light eyes.

"No, no, no." Ivy clapped her hands over her eyes. How could this happen to her brother, her brilliant, tenderhearted, funny little brother?

"Charlie has made a suggestion. To escape to France."

"Escape?" Ivy peered over the tops of her fingers. "That's how he was injured in the first place. He could have been killed."

"Many have succeeded in escaping." Dr. Tipton spoke in measured tones. "The British and Americans have a broad array of anti-infectives, including new drugs we can only dream of. But if Charlie is to escape, it must be soon. The more the infection progresses, the less likely he'll survive the journey."

"He might not survive the journey anyway." Her voice rose, and she tamped it down. "He could be shot again or he could drown or be arrested."

Dr. Tipton kept a steady gaze on Ivy. "If he stays in Jersey . . ."

He would definitely not survive. Her chest contracted, curled her shoulders in, expelled a groan.

Dr. Tipton scooted over a chair and guided Ivy into it. Then he squatted in front of her. "Charlie has the name of the man who helped with his previous attempt. He's known in our circles and trusted. But Charlie is too weak to go alone. He'll need help. He wants you to accompany him, as well as Benny and Gary. Benny, I know, but not Gary."

Bernardus and Gerrit, and Ivy nodded. "I know both men and trust them completely. They'll take good care of Charlie."

"Benny would be a tremendous catch for the Germans. I assume Gary is as notorious? At times when Charlie is feverish, he mentions losing maps, worries about them falling into German hands."

Ivy winced. Charlie might be able to withstand torture, but not delirium.

Dr. Tipton pushed up to standing, and he paced the length of the room and back to Ivy. "We don't mind aiding escaped workers. They're only trying to survive. We don't even mind fugitives wanted for infractions that weren't illegal before the occupation. But saboteurs? Spies? Harboring them, helping them could land us in far greater trouble than a prison sentence."

"Then allowing Benny to leave the island might benefit the ring."

Dr. Tipton huffed, but in a resigned way, and he crossed his arms. "We suggested sending Charlie with other men trying to escape, but Charlie refuses to go with anyone but Benny and Gary."

Her brother might be gravely ill, but his spirit remained strong. "Would it be any worse for Charlie if he were caught with Benny and Gary than with someone else?"

Another resigned huff. "Probably not."

"I can't think of anyone I trust more to accompany Charlie. Benny and Gary are good men who have risked their lives to aid the Allies. They're fond of Charlie, and I know they'll take good care of him."

Dr. Tipton raised one eyebrow. "As will you."

Outside the window, the blue sky stretched over Jersey and France and England. What would it be like to live in freedom again? To not live in constant dread of arrest? The Germans hadn't returned to La Bliue Brise or arrested anyone in connection with Charlie's disappearance, but they were still watching her. Following her.

If she escaped to France, she'd have plenty to eat, and she wouldn't be separated from Charlie and Gerrit. Wouldn't that be wonderful?

"Dr. Picot?"

A sad smile rose. "I can't leave. My patients need me. You understand."

"I do. Charlie will too."

"What next?"

Dr. Tipton pulled up a chair and sat. "Do you know how to reach Gary?"

"Yes."

"Then we must both make arrangements with the gentlemen Charlie named. I know where Benny and Charlie are hiding. You do not, nor should you, nor should I know how to contact Gary."

Ivy frowned. "I can't go to this man. The secret police are following me."

"I'm aware. I brought my car. I'll pull behind the hospital, and you'll lie down on the backseat. We'll drive to the gentleman's home and back. Then you'll leave the hospital for home as always. We should go at once."

"Now?"

"The sooner we can arrange an escape, the better. If we wait too long . . ."

Not even the most modern medications would save Charlie's life.

296

ST. PETER'S PARISH
SUNDAY, OCTOBER 8, 1944

Gerrit shouldn't have come. He cycled down a quiet lane on the far side of the Jouny farm in case the Germans were watching Arthur and Opal or had followed Ivy.

Tension had defined the past two weeks. Although he hadn't been interrogated again and a search of his room had yielded nothing, Schmeling didn't trust him. Claiming that he no longer required Gerrit's engineering skills, Schmeling had assigned him to manual labor with the few dozen volunteer workers remaining in Jersey, ripping up a railway line along St. Ouen's Bay for firewood for the coming winter. Ironically, a railway line laid by OT.

After looking in all directions, Gerrit dismounted, hoisted his bicycle over the hedgerow, and clambered over into the pasture. His arms and legs ached from twelve hours of labor a day, six days a week.

A pair of Jersey cows chewed their cud and eyed him.

"Good afternoon, ladies." He rolled his bicycle toward the farmhouse, thankful as always for the hedgerows and granite walls that shielded the farm from sight of the main road.

The note from Ivy crinkled in his uniform pocket. After church, she'd passed his pew, and a piece of paper had fluttered down beside him.

A sketch of a puffin with a note concealed in the shading, telling him to meet her at the farm at one o'clock on a most urgent matter.

Urgent indeed if she'd risked writing to him and meeting with him. Was it news about Charlie? Gerrit had no way of learning of his welfare.

In case the secret police watched the front door, Gerrit went to the back and knocked.

Arthur threw open the door and pulled Gerrit and his bicycle inside, and then he left the kitchen.

Drawing the curtains at the kitchen window, Ivy looked pale

and haggard, not unexpected after a fortnight of worry for Charlie and scrutiny by the Germans.

But beautiful. So beautiful. "Ivy?"

"Oh, Gerrit." She dashed into his arms and kissed him.

Never had they kissed with such fervency, such hunger, and he longed to keep kissing her that way forever.

But he couldn't. He pulled back. "What's wrong?"

"It's Charlie." Her brown eyes shimmered with worry. "He's developed an infection, and he isn't responding to treatment. He needs medications we don't have in Jersey."

"Oh, darling." His chest constricted, and he gathered her closer.

"His only hope for treatment is to escape to France."

"France?"

"It's all been arranged, and he wants you and Bernardus to come too."

He drew back his chin so he could look her in the eye. "Me?"

"He's weak. He must be carried. Bernardus may be strong, but he needs a crutch to walk. He can't carry Charlie alone. And Charlie is worried about you, about the maps. How long until the Germans figure out what's on them?"

Behind Ivy's back, Gerrit's hand worked. "I need to think."

"It's tonight."

"Tonight?"

"It must be tonight. The helper has a boat and an outboard motor, and he says the moon and tides favor an escape. And Charlie—his doctor doesn't know how long—" Ivy's face crumpled, and she leaned her head against Gerrit's chest.

His hand and his mind worked in tandem. What remained for him in Jersey? Manual labor, no ability to aid the Allies, and a possible appointment with a noose.

Escape would be exceedingly risky and a declaration of guilt. If he were captured, he'd be executed.

But helping his friend was the right course of action, regardless of what happened. Charlie's injury might not have been his

298

responsibility, but Gerrit would take responsibility for helping him survive.

"I'll go," he said, his voice rough. "I have my satchel, everything I need."

"Thank you." She gave him a sweet little kiss, a tender look, and then she stepped back and removed a scrap of paper from her skirt pocket. "This is a map to the embarkation point in Fauvic in the southeast corner of the island. You need to memorize the directions, then I'll burn this."

Gerrit studied the hand-drawn map. The location was well chosen. Since the Germans had expected an Allied invasion on the broad, gentle beaches to the west and south, the east coast was poorly fortified.

The Germans had coastal artillery three kilometers north at Gorey and resistance nests one kilometer south at La Rocque and one kilometer north at Fort Henry, but near Fauvic only an "action point" at Le Hurel, which was manned only during alerts. And no mines or barbed wire protected the beach.

Ivy pointed at two squares on the coastal road. "You'll see an attractive white two-story house. Directly north is a one-story granite barn, your meeting place. Please arrive at nine o'clock tonight. Charlie and Bernardus will arrive separately. The Bertram family will help you. Tell them your name is Gary."

"Gary?"

"Yes, and Bernardus is Benny. You must wear your civilian suit. We told the Bertrams you and Bernardus are Dutch, but they don't know you're in Organisation Todt. We told them you were Dutch only to explain your accents."

Gerrit murmured and memorized the sequence of turns. La Grande Route de Saint-Clément to Rue de Fauvic to La Grande Route des Sablons.

"Take your pistol," Ivy said in a soft voice.

To protect her little brother, and Gerrit gave her a solemn nod. But how could he leave her? Why should he have to? "You should come too. They're investigating you, and the food shortages grow worse each day. It isn't safe here."

Ivy gazed down at her clenched hands, and her cheeks twitched. "I thought about it. I could help Charlie on the journey. But my patients need me as well. The health of the islanders is in great peril, and the doctors are spread so thin."

Gerrit's throat clamped shut, and he gripped her forearm. "How can I leave you? If you escaped, we could be together." He could propose to her, marry her.

Her face turned red, and she shook her head and let out a little sob. "Oh, this is just like at Oxford. I'm choosing Jersey over love. Again."

Gerrit stilled. Her boyfriend had forced her to choose. Gerrit didn't want to do that, not at all. "This is temporary, mijn geliefde. When all this is over, I'll come to you, to Jersey."

"Oh, Gerrit." She wobbled. "I'll miss you so much."

He pulled her hard into an embrace and kissed the top of her head. "I love how you care for your patients. I love your conscientiousness. I love your loyalty to your family and community. I would never ask you to choose me over all that."

Her shoulders shook, and he rocked her until the shaking stopped.

How long until he could hold her again? Would he ever?

CHAPTER
40

Since a mere slit of light emitted from the shield over her carbide headlamp, Ivy had cycled home with great care.

She pulled her bicycle into the garden in the moonless night. She'd stayed late after dinner with Uncle Arthur and Aunt Opal. Any secret police watching the farm and following Ivy wouldn't be free to follow the men to the beach.

By now, the Bertram family would be instructing Gerrit and Bernardus, and soon they'd take Charlie and the boat to the beach. Deputy Wilfred Bertram—Ivy still couldn't believe a States deputy was involved—had told her the party would row to sea under cover of darkness. Later, the three-quarters moon would help them navigate east to the Cotentin Peninsula of France.

Ivy's green coat grew thinner each year, and she shivered. If liberation didn't come before the winter, she'd need to patch the seat again.

Her shiver became a shudder. German patrols, coastal guns, patrol boats, tides, rocks, rough seas, Charlie's weakness and delirium—would he even respond to medication in France?

The dangers piled high, so she chipped away at the pile with faith. "'Now faith is the substance of things hoped for, the evidence of things not seen,'" she said in the blindness of night.

After Ivy unlocked the back door and the supply room, she pushed her bicycle inside the supply room and removed her medical bag from the basket.

The light in the hallway flicked on behind her, and Fern stood silhouetted in the supply room doorway. "Did you have a pleasant evening?"

Ivy couldn't see her sister's face, but her tone hinted at insincerity. Regardless, she'd treat it as a friendly question. "Quite pleasant. I spent the evening with Uncle Arthur and Aunt Opal."

"Is that so?" Fern held up a piece of paper. "You weren't with 'mijn geliefde'? Did I pronounce that correctly? It's Dutch, yes?"

All the blood rushed from Ivy's face, tingling, dizzying, pooling in her gut.

Fern leaned back against the doorjamb, and the lamp illuminated a smug smile. "I thought it curious this morning in church when you dropped a piece of paper into the pew beside Gerrit van der Zee, and he failed to return it to you."

Ivy fumbled for a shelf for balance, and the keys in her fingers tapped the wood.

"Do you want to know why I found it curious?" Fern said. "Hmm? A few weeks before, he handed you a paper you'd dropped. So why didn't he return today's piece of paper?"

Words dried out in Ivy's open mouth, but words would be of no benefit. Not when Fern knew the truth.

A chuckle from Fern. "I always knew he was smitten with you. Then I remembered that nonsense when you insisted you knew about love, and I realized you two were exchanging notes like silly schoolchildren. So I looked around."

"My office." The words shot from Ivy's mouth. "My private papers."

Fern shrugged one shoulder and glanced at Gerrit's letter. "'Please know I love you dearly. When all this is over, I will come to you as soon as I'm able. Then no one and nothing will keep us apart.' Well, he certainly won't win awards for poetry, but you don't provide much in the way of inspiration."

How many times had Ivy born the sting of such barbs? But she couldn't bear the insult to the man she loved. "Poetry is a poor measure of love."

"Love? You little hypocrite. Looking down on me for loving a German officer, all whilst you were in love with a Todt? They're the bad ones."

"Not Gerrit."

"Of course not." Sarcasm rippled in Fern's voice. "Your scruples. You could never love someone who supported Germany."

Ivy's hand coiled around the handle of her medical bag. In case anything went wrong tonight and Gerrit had to return to his duties, she couldn't incriminate him any more than she already had.

Fern clucked her tongue. "I remembered his friend Bernardus, the man who died trying to commit sabotage. What if Gerrit had been a fellow saboteur, then deserted Bernardus when things went awry? They turned Charlie to the other side, didn't they? Is that why Charlie tried to escape? Because he's a traitor like they are? Like you are?"

Ivy's breath came hot and fast, pulsing with the truth that there was only one traitor in the family. But some truths were best silenced.

Fern straightened up. "Thank you for this opportunity."

"Opportunity?"

"To prove myself. Now Helmut will know I've been loyal all along."

"What does that—"

"Didn't I mention? The police are coming. I rang as soon as I saw your bicycle approach. They're on their way to Gerrit's quarters as well."

Ivy's knees buckled, and she braced herself against the shelves. Gerrit wasn't in his quarters—but now they'd send out a search immediately rather than in the morning when Gerrit didn't report for duty. What if the boat were delayed for some reason? He'd be captured.

Even if he escaped, Ivy would be interrogated, beaten. She couldn't let that happen. Couldn't risk betraying the men she loved. Her aunt and uncle. Joan and Dr. Tipton and the ring. The helpers and escapees.

"No," she whispered.

"Yes," Fern said in a satisfied tone. "Your treachery caused me to lose the man I love, so now you'll lose the man you love. And so much more. Just to be sure, I'll lock you in here until the police arrive."

Fern stepped back. The door creaked. The light diminished.

"No!" Ivy charged forward, wedged her shoulders into the doorway, swung her arms through. Her bag thumped to the floor beside her with a great rattling of glass. The keys tinkled onto the hallway floor.

"Get inside!" Fern shoved at Ivy.

"No, no, no." Ivy gripped her sister's upper arms, lunged forward, pivoted. Her back banged against the doorjamb. She couldn't let herself be locked inside, couldn't be arrested.

"You won't get away." Fern's fingernails dug into Ivy's shoulders, and she wrestled her toward captivity. "You won't."

"No!" With all her might, Ivy threw her sister to the side.

A scream. Fern tripped sideways over the medical bag and tumbled inside the supply room. She flung out her arms, and the bicycle toppled over, fell on her. She screeched.

No time to think.

Ivy kicked her medical bag out of the doorway and slammed the door shut.

"Ivy! You can't do this! You can't." Thumps resounded inside.

Breathing hard, Ivy staggered backward. The keys glinted on the floor. Could she? Should she lock up her own sister?

With Charlie's life at stake?

Ivy snatched the key, thrust it into the lock, and turned it. "I'm sorry, Fern."

"It's no use." Fists pounded on the door from down by the floor. "The police will be here any minute. They'll let me out. They'll find you. Where do you think you can go?"

France.

Ivy clapped her hand over her mouth. She'd promised to stay, to care for her patients.

But if she were arrested, she couldn't care for them, nor could she if she went into hiding. No matter what happened tonight, the practice was lost.

And if she were arrested, she'd risk the lives of dozens.

She had to escape from Jersey. And now.

Fern screamed and kicked at the door and called down curses.

A pit formed in Ivy's stomach. No matter what happened tonight, her relationship with her sister was lost forever.

"Goodbye, Fern," she said softly.

With her bicycle locked inside, she'd have to drive and pray the remaining drops of petrol would take her to Fauvic. She scooped up her medical bag and ran into the garden, to the garage.

Prayed she didn't arrive at Fauvic too late to join the men.

In the distance, police sirens whined.

Prayed she wouldn't be captured.

"Lord, please." She unlocked the garage and slid into the car. "Please start. Please."

CHAPTER
41

FAUVIC

Inside the granite barn, a young lady served hot carrot tea to Gerrit, Bernardus, and Jack, a youth who would be escaping with them.

Gerrit studied the navigational charts on the barn floor as an elderly fisherman instructed them how to avoid the many rocks, reefs, and currents in the waters.

Jack and three of his friends had planned an escape for tonight and had secretly moved a twelve-foot dinghy from storage in St. Helier to Fauvic and had gathered supplies for the voyage. But his friends had been arrested earlier in the week for stealing food, stranding Jack without companions and opening room for Gerrit, Charlie, and Bernardus.

By the door stood their contact, Bill Bertram, around fifty years old, bespectacled, with thick silver hair receding above the temples.

Charlie lay on a stretcher beside Gerrit, covered with blankets, his face red and sweaty, his eyes bleary. And too quiet. Between the gunshot wound and the infection, he was too weak to walk.

The carrot tea tossed in Gerrit's stomach as he memorized the instructions. He didn't dare correct the men's information on the coastal defenses. For islanders to knowingly help uniformed members of Organisation Todt to escape would be a grave offense in German eyes. It was best if these men assumed Gerrit and Bernardus were forced workers—and forced workers would be ignorant of military information.

"Do you understand?" the fisherman asked.

"Yes, sir," Gerrit said with the others.

Bill tipped his head to the dinghy. "It's ten fifteen. German patrols pass at ten o'clock and again at midnight. If you move quickly, you'll have plenty of time before the moon rises."

Gerrit warmed his hands on the cup. He alone didn't wear an overcoat or hat. His greatcoat and cap bore OT insignia, and he refused to take clothing from his friends in Jersey when replacement was impossible.

In his satchel, he carried his last silk map, provisions, his canteen, pistol, shaving kit, and the few personal items that had survived the drenching when he'd jumped overboard in June. And not one item to remind him of Ivy. Not one item to point to her in case he was captured.

"Are you ready?" Bill asked the men.

"Yes, sir." Gerrit swigged down the last of his tea.

The young lady who had served tea knelt beside Charlie and wiped his forehead. She gave Gerrit a worried look. "Will he be all right?"

Only the Lord knew the answer, and Gerrit gave her a small smile. "We'll do our best to get him to France. Thank you for your help."

"Wear this." Jack removed a black knit cap from his thick swatch of black hair, and he handed it to Gerrit with a glare. "Your hair's so bright, you'll get us all shot."

"Thank you." Gerrit pulled it down over his hair and looped the strap of his duffel crosswise over his body.

"I want it back."

Gerrit raised a bit of a smile. "As soon as we're out of range of the German guns."

"Godspeed." Bill shook hands all around, and he waved in a group of men, ranging from youth to middle age.

Some of the men lifted the boat, and others carried a large wooden sled used to maneuver boats down the seawall. Gerrit lifted one end of Charlie's stretcher and Jack the other.

With Bernardus following on his crutch, the company maneuvered the boat, sled, and stretcher out of the barn into the inky night.

About thirty meters to the east, they reached a concrete walkway along the shore. A seawall built of stone sloped four meters down to the beach at a steep angle. Light waves lapped at the sand.

Gerrit peered into the night. Grouville Bay made a gentle curve between La Rocque at the southeastern corner of Jersey and Gorey. At Gorey stood the medieval Mont Orgueil Castle with its modern German weaponry.

"Clear," Bernardus said in a low voice.

Gerrit nodded. He saw no patrols.

With practiced efficiency, the helpers set the sled at a shallow angle from the top of the seawall down to the beach, spanning the narrow band of rocks rimming the shoreline. Then they guided the boat down the sled.

An ingenious method. With great care, Gerrit and Jack walked the stretcher down the sled and rested the stretcher inside the boat.

Gerrit stashed his satchel in the boat and tucked the blankets around Charlie. "Ready?"

Charlie nodded and shivered. "So cold."

The sooner they got him to France, the better.

While Gerrit, Bernardus, and Jack removed shoes and socks, set them in the boat, and rolled their trousers above the knee, the helpers and their sled disappeared up the seawall.

It was time.

Jack took the bow of the boat, and Gerrit and Bernardus took the stern.

"One last look," Bernardus said in a low voice.

Gerrit squinted around the bay and listened hard, but no motion or sounds caught his attention. "Clear."

"Let's go." Jack splashed into the light surf and climbed into the bow. Gerrit and Bernardus pushed the boat knee-deep into the chilly water and boarded one at a time.

A small wave raised the boat, and Gerrit and Bernardus shoved off with the oars.

Once free, Gerrit passed his oar to Jack, and Jack and Bernardus—the strongest two of the men—set the oars in the rowlocks and rowed hard.

Gerrit would have his turn at the oars, but for now he'd man the tiller and serve as sentry. He crouched in the stern by Charlie's head and held the tiller firm. In his breast pocket, he had a compass to use after the moon rose. The Cotentin Peninsula lay fifteen miles to the east, and they had the tide in their favor. And a few more minutes of darkness.

His calves tingled as the seawater evaporated, and he shivered, but he needed to wait until his feet dried before donning socks and shoes.

To the north, the dark mound of Mont Orgueil distorted the line where sky and land and sea intersected. Gerrit had seen the defenses built on the ancient castle, the powerful rangefinder, the large guns, the searchlights.

If the alarm sounded, the little boat wouldn't be safe.

The oars slapped the water, and the boat rose and fell on the slight waves. Overhead, bands of clouds smudged the stars, and a faint glow formed to the east as the moon neared the horizon.

A moan from Charlie, and Gerrit leaned close. "Quiet."

Another moan, this time in affirmation.

Gerrit scanned the shore behind him. A figure ran along the beach.

"Get down." Gerrit motioned to Bernardus and Jack.

The men tucked in the oars and ducked low.

"What do you see?" Bernardus whispered.

Gerrit peeked over the gunwale. "A man."

The cresting moon spilled revealing light on the man.

The silhouette was wrong. Delicate, shapely. Wearing a skirt. A woman—a woman carrying a square little bag—a medical bag?

Ivy? The woman ran to water's edge, waving hard. Had she come to say goodbye?

"It's Ivy."

"What's she doing?" Irritation grated in Bernardus's voice. "She shouldn't be here."

No, she shouldn't. She wouldn't. Ivy would never risk their safety and her own for a romantic gesture.

Gerrit saw beyond what he saw. "She wants to join us, to escape."

"Too late," Bernardus said. "She knows the contact. She can come another night."

Ivy waved her arm in a wide arc, tiny and distant. She did indeed know the contact. So why would she come now?

Gerrit swallowed hard. "She'd come only if it were vital. If her life depended on it."

"We're not going back for a girl." Jack glowered at Gerrit. "The moon's rising, the tide's going out."

"Gerrit," Bernardus said in a soft tone. "We can't go back. Our lives depend on it. Charlie's life."

Far back on shore in the growing moonlight, the woman he loved waved frantically.

Gerrit's hand opened and flexed. How could he convince the others?

CHAPTER
42

FAUVIC

She was too late.

A cry built in Ivy's lungs, and she swallowed it, absorbed it, so she wouldn't endanger the men at sea.

To avoid leading the police to the Bertrams, Ivy had abandoned her car a mile from Fauvic amongst some trees, and she'd run to the beach, unsure of the actual embarkation point.

Her chest heaved from the run, from the terror.

She'd missed them. They couldn't see her.

By now, the police would have released Fern and realized Gerrit wasn't in his hotel room—but his uniform was. They'd be searching for both of them.

Clamping her mouth shut so she wouldn't scream, Ivy waved again. Even if they'd seen her, they couldn't turn back, could they? The moon was edging over the French coast, and the boat needed to get far from land, far from sight.

Everything in her strained toward the boat, toward Gerrit, toward her brother. She plopped onto the sand, untied her shoes, stuffed her socks in her medical bag, and tied her shoelaces to the handle of her bag.

She'd swim to them. But how could she catch a boat rowed by

grown men, in the dark, in the cold water? She'd have to leave her coat behind, her bag. When found, her belongings would point to her actions as surely as Charlie's bag had.

A sob ripped up her throat, and she clapped her hands over her mouth to contain it.

If she swam, she might incriminate Deputy Bertram and his family by her proximity. If she stayed, she'd be captured and might incriminate the Bertrams and numerous others. To go into hiding would require contacting Joan or Dr. Tipton—in St. Helier, where the German field police were searching for her.

"Oh, Lord." The words pummeled her fingers.

What had her father told her the day he evacuated to England? "In times of peace, we choose amongst many good and pleasant paths, but in times of war . . ."

Ivy had replied, "No path is good or pleasant."

"Not pleasant, no. But you can still choose the good. You must."

Sitting on the damp sand, with a chilly breeze ruffling the hair at the nape of her neck, Ivy stifled another sob. "There is no good path. None."

Her only path was to evade arrest as long as possible and to bear up under interrogation and torture. "Lord, help me stay silent. Protect Charlie. Protect Gerrit. Protect Bernardus."

The boat's silhouette appeared larger, and she frowned. Between rowing and the tides, they should be moving farther away each minute. They weren't. They were coming to shore.

For her!

She sprang to her feet and stifled a cry—of joy this time, of relief, of life.

When the boat pulled closer, Ivy sloshed into the water to meet them. She clambered over the side, and Gerrit helped her, embraced her, kissed her.

"No time for that," Bernardus said in a low, sharp voice. "Get down."

Ivy crouched low, and Gerrit shoved off, the oar scraping the sand below.

Gerrit passed the oar over Ivy's head to a dark-haired stranger, and the stranger and Bernardus rowed hard.

The waves bumped beneath her, and Ivy knelt beside Charlie and smoothed his hair. "Hallo," she murmured.

"Missed me so much, you couldn't stay away?" A teasing tone lit his feeble voice.

She pressed a kiss to her brother's burning forehead and squeezed her eyes shut. When they were farther out to sea, she'd give him some aspirin.

"Oh no." Gerrit squatted in the stern with his hand on the tiller. A black cap covered his fair hair. "A patrol."

A curse from the stranger, and the pace of oars on water quickened.

Shouts arose to the west. Pops—gunfire?

"They spotted us," Gerrit said. "Ivy—take the tiller. I'll start the motor."

"Not until we're three miles out," the stranger said.

Bernardus pulled hard on his oar. "Doesn't matter anymore. They've spotted us. They'll sound the alert."

Ivy crawled to the tiller and held it firmly.

Gerrit stretched one arm over the stern—a pistol in hand.

Ivy clapped her free hand over her ear and ducked her other ear to her shoulder.

The shot slapped her eardrums.

"What did you do that for?" The stranger cussed again.

"To make them take cover," Gerrit said.

"To delay them." Bernardus dug the oar into the water. "Show them we'll fight back."

"We don't have much time." Gerrit dragged over the outboard motor. "The nearest resistance nest is a kilometer away—they'll have heard the gunfire."

More gunfire from shore, and Ivy kept her head down, not that the wooden hull would protect her.

"Let go, Ivy." Gerrit removed the tiller and clamped the outboard motor in place.

"Stay low, darling." Ivy scooted back and curled up beside her brother.

A bright light arced overhead.

"Get down!" Gerrit said.

"No, don't!" Bernardus said. "Row. Start the motor."

Ivy peered up. A beam of light swung back and forth above them.

The outboard motor coughed. Coughed again. Hiccupped. Roared.

The boat surged forward.

"Thank you, Lord," Ivy whispered.

Bernardus and the other man drew in their oars and lay flat in the boat.

A deep boom to the northwest. Another. Another.

"Hold on." Gerrit crouched by the motor.

Loud splashes in the distance, each louder than the first. The boat rocked. Water sloshed inside.

"They're getting their range," Bernardus said.

Gerrit shifted the boat's course a bit to the south. "I'll zigzag, throw them off."

More booms, more splashes, more rocking, more course changes, and Ivy hunkered low, one arm across Charlie's chest, praying hard.

In time, the booms receded. Stopped.

Ivy's respiration and heart rate settled down, and Bernardus and the other man sat up.

"How are you doing, Charlie?" Ivy asked. "Would you like some aspirin?"

Charlie murmured his agreement, and Ivy rummaged in her medical bag—in great disorder from the night's mistreatment.

"Why'd you come, Ivy?" Charlie asked in a weak voice.

She chewed on her lips as she slipped two tablets from a bottle and into her brother's mouth. Only the truth could explain her actions, but the truth would inflict pain. "Fern found out about Gerrit and me. She saw the connection between Gerrit and Bernardus and your escape attempt. She decided we're all traitors."

"Traitors?" Charlie huffed. "We're loyal to the Allies."

Ivy's gaze slid to Gerrit. "She denounced me to the secret police. You too, Gerrit. The police were on their way to my house—and to your hotel. Fern and I—we fought. I locked her in the supply room and escaped by car."

Gerrit's jaw dangled.

Ivy's gut heaved, over and over, and she clapped her hand over her mouth. Her sister. Her own sister.

"Ivy." From his position manning the motor, Gerrit reached for her.

She sagged into his embrace, and sobs released, freeing, cleansing.

"I was right," Gerrit said in a fierce tone. "I knew you wouldn't risk our escape unless it was vital. I saw, Ivy. I saw."

"He fought for you." Charlie's voice strengthened. "They didn't want to go back."

"With good reason." The stranger huffed, his eyes dark. "We could have been blown to pieces."

"No, Jack," Bernardus said. "Gerrit was right."

"You should have heard him, Ivy," Charlie said. "'Think of the names Ivy knows,' he said. 'Deputy Bertram, Uncle Arthur, Aunt Opal, Dr. Tipton, all the people who helped Bernardus hide.'"

"You saved my life that night I was injured." Bernardus gave Ivy a sheepish look. "Gerrit said I owed it to you to go back. You risked your life to save mine. The least I could do was risk my life to save yours."

Ivy wiped her eyes with her coat sleeve and twisted to see Gerrit's face better. He'd fought for her, and she pressed a kiss to his chin. "Far better than poetry."

CHAPTER
43

Fire burned in Gerrit's shoulders and biceps. How many years since he'd last rowed?

Right before sunrise, they'd run out of petrol and had taken turns rowing. Through the night and morning and into the afternoon, Charlie had slept fitfully and the rest of them had snatched bits of sleep and nibbled the provisions of bread and apples.

Sweat needled Gerrit's scalp under the bandage Ivy had tied about his head in lieu of a hat. He looked ridiculous, but he preferred to avoid a sunburnt scalp.

In the stern, Ivy used a bucket to bail the seawater that slopped inside or leaked through.

Behind Gerrit, Jack raised a Union Jack on the mast to identify them to the Allies as a friendly vessel. "We're getting close. I see houses. That had better be France, not Jersey."

"It's France." Gerrit leaned forward to start another stroke.

"A lot of boats have blown back to Jersey. What if—"

"We have a compass." Gerrit kept his tone patient, although Jack had raised the concern a dozen times in as many hours. "We've held an east-southeast course as instructed, and we have a westerly wind."

Jack grumbled. "You'd better be right, because I see men on shore. They have guns. They've spotted us."

Gerrit glanced at Bernardus, and his friend nodded. They paused with their oars out of the water, fished their pistols from their suit jackets, and handed them to Ivy. "Drop these over the stern."

Her brown eyes enormous, Ivy held the pistols by their handles. "Don't!" Jack cried. "We might need them."

Bernardus gave Gerrit the signal to resume rowing. "Those are Allied soldiers. We don't need them."

And German pistols would only cause trouble. Gerrit yanked the bandage off his head, tugged on the oar, and gritted his teeth against the pain in his shoulders.

"What if they're German soldiers?" Jack's voice rose. "If that's Jersey?"

Gerrit's oars left a glittering trail of droplets on the sea. "Then two pistols won't do us any good."

Ivy's gaze bounced between Gerrit and Bernardus, and she dropped the pistols over the stern. Then she crawled back to kneel in front of Gerrit, and her brow furrowed. "We'll have to say goodbye soon."

"We will." Gerrit had his OT paybook for identification, and Bernardus had his false Jersey papers. Both suspicious. "Bernardus and I will be in custody awhile."

"We'll tell the truth." Bernardus huffed out a laugh. "But the truth is rather unbelievable."

"They'll see." Although Ivy smiled, her brow remained furrowed. "I know they will."

"Since we're telling the truth, we have consistency in our favor." Gerrit leaned back, and the sea fought his oar. "I have one last map as proof."

Ivy set her hand on his knee. "Ferric chloride, a 10 percent solution in water. Don't forget."

"I won't." Would the map help if no other maps had arrived in England for comparison? If none of the French resistance contacts had survived to corroborate their story?

Gerrit blew out a breath as he drew the oar through the water. Regardless, he'd done what was right and he didn't regret it.

Ivy spun away to her medical bag, and she pulled out her sketch pad and pen. "I'll give you my grandparents' address in England. Memorize it in case they take it from you during interrogation." She ripped off a corner of paper and held it out to him.

Bernardus paused rowing so Gerrit could too. After he memorized the address, he tucked it in his breast pocket. "If I can come to you, I will. If I can't, I'll write."

Ivy pushed up on her knees, took Gerrit's cheeks between her hands, and pressed a kiss to his lips, so sweet, so passionate, he almost dropped the oar.

"Row," Bernardus said in a stern voice, but then chuckled. "You'll have time for that later."

"I *will* come to you." Gerrit sent her a firm look and scooped his oar into the ocean.

"Who goes there?" a man shouted from shore.

An American accent, and Gerrit grinned at Bernardus and glanced over his shoulder. Half a dozen men in olive drab pointed rifles at them.

"We're from Jersey!" Jack yelled. "We're escaping."

"New Jersey?" another man said in a deep bass. "You rowed all the way—"

"Not New Jersey, you numbskull," the first American said. "Old Jersey. Over there in the Channel Islands. The Jerries are still there. Haven't you heard?"

"Old Jersey?" Ivy said in a low voice. "The original Jersey."

"How many of you?" a soldier shouted.

"Four men and a girl," Jack said.

That girl—a grown woman—rose to standing, and she waved.

"I'm a physician. My brother has an infected gunshot wound. He needs to go to hospital straightaway. Please fetch an ambulance."

One of the soldiers jerked his thumb over his shoulder, and two men ran off.

The boat's hull scraped on the sand.

"You in the bow," an American shouted. "Get out, hands where I can see them. Pull the boat in."

Jack splashed down into the water, and Gerrit shoved with his oar.

"Get out, one at a time, hands up."

"My brother's too ill to walk," Ivy said. "He's on a stretcher."

"Yes, ma'am." A soldier sloshed into the water and offered her a hand. "She's right. Got a kid on a stretcher back here."

Gerrit laid down his oar and lifted his hands, as did Bernardus. After all they'd been through, the last thing he wanted was to get shot because he made a wrong move.

When a soldier gestured with his rifle, Gerrit stepped out, drenching his shoes and socks. Yet he grinned. On free soil for the first time in over four years.

"Papers?" The soldiers kept rifles and glares trained on the escapees.

"I'm from Jersey." Jack handed a gum-chewing soldier his identification papers. "So is the girl and her brother on the stretcher. The other two are Dutch."

"Dutch?" The soldier guarding Gerrit flared his nostrils. "How'd you wind up in Jersey?"

Gerrit exchanged a look with Bernardus and Ivy, and he drew out his paybook. "We're with Organisation Todt."

"Forced laborers," Jack said. "The Germans grab men off the streets and make them build for them."

"We weren't forced." Gerrit handed over his paybook. "We were volunteers."

Jack's face distorted, and his hands coiled into fists. "Volunteers?

You're Todts? They're the worst of the worst. I never would have shared a boat with you." He charged at Gerrit.

"Hey, now." A soldier stepped in front of Jack with a rifle.

"We're with the resistance." Gerrit kept his hands high. "We joined OT so we could send maps of German fortifications to the Allies."

Bernardus handed over his papers. "These are false papers. I was injured committing sabotage and went into hiding."

"Liars." Jack stayed back, but poison laced his gaze.

"It's true." Charlie's voice warbled as two soldiers carried his stretcher out of the boat. "I was their courier."

The Americans gaped at the group.

"Hey, look at this." Gerrit's guard showed his paybook to the soldier beside him. "It's this same guy, all right, in a Nazi uniform."

The second soldier snorted. "We got ourselves a couple of Jerries trying to sneak in."

"It isn't true." Ivy twisted her hands together, and her chin quivered. "They're good men. They're on the Allied side. They risked their lives to help us."

"It's all right, mijn geliefde." Gerrit gave her a soothing look. "The truth will come out. No matter what, God is good."

She nodded, and her face crumpled. "And he is faithful."

"Even if," he murmured. "Even if."

CHAPTER
44

"This is the best food ever." Sitting up in his cot in the US Army hospital, Charlie closed his eyes in pure bliss.

"It's just beef broth." Wearing a waist-length olive drab jacket and matching trousers, Lt. Norma Kincaid set her hands on her hips and laughed. "In all my years, I've never had a patient who loved hospital food."

"You've never had a patient from Jersey." Ivy sat in a chair at Charlie's bedside, wearing a similar outfit, loaned to her by the nursing sisters—no, *nurses* in American English.

"Only four ounces of meat a week, you said?" Norma's eyes stretched wide.

"Every other week." Charlie sipped more beef broth. "In meatless weeks, we have two ounces of butter."

"But only when meat and butter are available." For the first time in four years, Ivy's stomach felt full.

"Wait till I tell the folks back home, grumbling about twenty-eight ounces a week," Norma said.

Charlie took a large spoonful of broth.

"Do be careful," Ivy said. "You aren't used to rich food, and you've been very sick."

"Not anymore." Charlie glanced up to the glass bottle hanging by his bed. "The BBC said this new penicillin was a wonder drug. They were correct."

"No kidding." Norma adjusted the rubber tubing that poured the medicine into Charlie's veins every four hours around the clock. "It's saved countless lives since D-day. If the boys survive long enough to get to the hospital, we have a good chance of saving them. Even crazy boys playing hide-and-seek with German beach patrols." She winked at Charlie.

He winked back and grinned.

Ivy smiled at her brother's good cheer, but tears threatened. Captain Reed, the American medical officer, said her brother had arrived just in time. After two fretful days, Charlie had rallied. As soon as he was stable, he'd be sent to a hospital in England to complete his recovery.

After American Army officers had questioned Ivy, they'd sent her to Cherbourg to be questioned by the British. Since nothing in her story or papers aroused suspicion, they'd allowed her to stay with Charlie so she could accompany him to England. The nurses welcomed her to their quarters and begged for her stories.

But every story reminded her of Gerrit, and she'd heard no word about him or Bernardus since they were transported from the beach in separate lorries.

At least she'd been able to send telegrams to Mum, telling of the escape and of Charlie's progress. Soon she might have a response.

"Excuse me, Dr. Picot?" Captain Reed approached with a civilian in a dark gray overcoat, and he beckoned to her. "May I have a word?"

"Yes, sir." Ivy joined the two men.

Captain Reed gestured to the civilian. "This is Hugh Collingwood with the BBC. Mr. Collingwood, this is Dr. Ivy Picot."

The radio correspondent had golden-brown hair and a bright smile, and Ivy shook his hand. "It's a pleasure to meet you."

"And I you."

"Mr. Collingwood would like to interview you and your brother."

"With your permission," Mr. Collingwood said. "I'm broadcasting a story about escapes from the Channel Islands. The evacuees in England are eager for stories from home, and what I've heard of your story is quite intriguing."

Ivy glanced back at Charlie, who peered with interest at the newcomer. "I don't know. We have family and friends who listen to the BBC at great risk. Even owning a wireless set is cause for imprisonment."

"They might be reassured by news of your escape," Mr. Collingwood said with concern in his voice. "But if it places them in danger . . ."

Ivy turned back. "We can be discreet. We have four years of experience."

"Very well," Mr. Collingwood said. "I'll ask preliminary questions now, and we'll record afterward. If you'd like anything removed from the recording, let me know."

"Thank you." After Captain Reed departed, Ivy led the correspondent to Charlie's bedside. "Mr. Collingwood, this is my brother, Charles Picot. Charlie, this is Hugh Colling—"

"Of the BBC! I've heard you—" Charlie's eyes stretched wide in alarm.

Mr. Collingwood pulled up a chair. "It's quite all right, Mr. Picot. It's no longer illegal for you to listen to the BBC."

"Mr. Collingwood would like to interview us," Ivy said.

Charlie grinned. "Smashing."

Mr. Collingwood pulled a notepad from his coat pocket. "I was told five of you escaped."

"Yes." Charlie handed his tray to Norma. "Three weeks ago, I tried to escape with three school chums, but a German patrol shot me."

"Oh dear."

Charlie patted his side and winced. "I managed to hide whilst my friends escaped."

"He developed an infection." Ivy cut in before Charlie could mention Dr. Tipton or the family that sheltered him. "We haven't the medications in Jersey to treat him, so we arranged for his escape."

Mr. Collingwood scribbled on his notepad. "You accompanied him to care for him, Dr. Picot?"

"That wasn't the original . . ." Grief pinged at her heart. She could still see the rage in Fern's eyes. But telling that story would publicly implicate and humiliate her sister, and she wanted to keep the path of reconciliation open, should Fern ever choose to walk it. Ivy swallowed. "Yes, I accompanied him."

"With three other men?" Mr. Collingwood said.

"One was a stranger to us," Ivy said, "but the other two are good friends."

"The best." Charlie gave a firm nod. "Gerrit van der Zee and Bernardus Kroon."

Mr. Collingwood jerked his head up from his notes. "Gerrit van der Zee? From the Netherlands?"

"Yes, sir." Charlie's eyes lit up. "Gerrit and Bernardus are in the resistance, and they joined Organisation Todt so they could draw maps of German fortifications. Gerrit traced them on silk in secret ink, and we sewed the maps inside my jacket. I was their courier. I worked on a ship and took the maps to my resistance contact in Saint-Malo. I can say that now that Saint-Malo is liberated, yes?"

Ivy's head swam at the speed of Charlie's speech. "I think so."

Mr. Collingwood hadn't written a word. He kept gaping at Charlie. "Gerrit van der Zee? Did he ever mention cousins named Aleida and Cilla?"

Now Ivy gaped. "Why, yes. How did you . . ."

Mr. Collingwood sat back with a giant grin. "Aleida happens to be my wife. She and Cilla will be overjoyed. They've been quite worried about Gerrit."

"Cilla?" Ivy frowned. "Gerrit said she'd died."

"Cilla? Heavens, no. Aleida and I dined with her and her husband not a fortnight ago."

Ivy and Charlie exchanged looks of wonder. Wouldn't Gerrit be thrilled to learn Cilla was alive—and both she and Aleida were safe in England?

The correspondent's grin broadened, and he laughed. "Where's Gerrit? I simply must meet him. And what a fantastic story."

Ivy gripped her hands in her lap. "Perhaps too fantastic. I'm concerned the Allies might not believe them. I haven't heard a word about him or Bernardus since we landed. I have no idea where they are."

"But it's all true." Charlie sat forward, then grunted, pressed his hand to his side, and leaned back. "Gerrit and Bernardus are heroes of the best sort. I owe my life to them. The Allies must believe them. They simply must."

Mr. Collingwood's gaze swept between Charlie and Ivy, his expression graver with each sweep, and he tucked his notepad into his pocket. "It's routine for refugees to be questioned by security and immigration to prevent German spies from entering Britain. I'll make inquiries for you."

"Thank you." Ivy gave him a grateful smile. If only inquiries could prove Gerrit's loyalty.

CHAPTER
45

Once again, Gerrit sat in an interrogation room.

Over the past ten days, he'd been interrogated by American and British Army officers in France. Then they'd shipped him to England, where he'd been interrogated by a varied stream of officials, both uniformed and civilian. No torture, no intimidation, and plenty of good food, but tiresome.

Most recently, his companion had been Capt. Andries Romijn, a Dutchman in a British uniform, who asked friendly questions about Amsterdam schools and shops and restaurants, concerned questions about conditions in the Netherlands, and intrigued questions about Gerrit's work in the Dutch resistance. All a ruse to determine whether Gerrit actually came from Amsterdam and to confirm his statement with details provided by other Dutch refugees. That part, Gerrit knew he'd passed.

Gerrit's head flopped back, and he rubbed his sore neck. He'd have to tell his story again this morning. Each time, it sounded more ludicrous. If he hadn't lived it, he wouldn't believe it himself.

Was Bernardus undergoing the same tedious questioning?

Gerrit hadn't seen him since their capture, most likely so they couldn't coordinate their stories. At least the British had been kind enough to inform him that Charlie was responding to treatment and was expected to make a full recovery.

The door opened, and Captain Romijn entered with an army officer Gerrit hadn't met.

"Good morning, Captain." Yet another round of questioning would begin, but Gerrit smiled, stood, and extended his hand to the new man. "I'm Gerrit van der Zee."

"Col. Rupert Hargrave." He stood tall and trim with a dark pencil-thin mustache. "Please have a seat."

Gerrit did so. "Shall I start at the beginning?"

Hargrave opened a portfolio and slid a rumpled piece of paper across the table.

Gerrit hadn't seen the paper for almost two years. A crude map in brown on one side and Bernardus's familiar handwriting on the other. "That's the first map we sent. It arrived! Bernardus wrote a pretend love letter to his contact in Saint-Malo. I drew the map with the lemon Charlie brought us from France."

"Lemon juice." Hargrave's nose wrinkled above his mustache.

"The resistance contact told us not to use it again."

"I'll say. It's a most indiscreet method."

But Gerrit couldn't help smiling. At least one map made it to England. "That's why the British agent sent secret ink crystals concealed in a pen."

Hargrave pulled something white from the portfolio and spread it before Gerrit.

He gasped. "One of my silk maps. So that's what it looks like developed. The lines aren't very straight, are they? And look at the gaps. It's difficult enough to draw on fabric. Even more so when you can't see the ink."

"Tell me about this map," Hargrave said.

"These are the German defenses on St. Aubin's Bay—anti-tank walls, resistance nests, bunkers." He guided his finger along the brownish-black lines and guided his mind over the new information. "It arrived in England. Well done, Charlie."

"It did indeed arrive."

Gerrit sighed. "Too bad it was of no use to the Allies."

"On the contrary." Hargrave tapped the map with a narrow finger. "We've conducted extensive aerial reconnaissance of Jersey, and your maps confirmed—or explained—what we viewed from above. This aided our photographic interpretation techniques. When we studied aerial photographs of the coast of Normandy, intelligence such as this helped us interpret those photographs correctly."

Gerrit's jaw hung slack. "I never thought . . ."

"How about this?" Hargrave whisked the first piece of silk aside and laid out another—a diagram of a bunker in bright red.

Gerrit traced it with one finger. "That must be the secret ink the chemist made when we ran out of the British ink. Red—wouldn't Ivy like to see?"

Hargrave glanced at Romijn, who nodded.

"Describe this diagram," Hargrave said.

Gerrit pointed out the features. "This is Strongpoint Verclut on St. Catherine's Bay. A Type 670 casemate for a 10.5-centimeter gun, a tunnel extending behind, two heavy machine-gun bunkers, a searchlight position."

"When our lads landed in Normandy, they encountered similar casemates. Intelligence like this helped them capture the positions." A shade of pink flooded Colonel Hargrave's face, and he poked out his chin. "It is an honor to meet you, Mr. van der Zee."

"Not so hasty, Colonel." Captain Romijn's mouth rumpled, and he stood and opened the door. "Mrs. Mackenzie, would you please bring the tea tray?"

Hargrave's gaze solidified. "It is indeed an honor. You did this at great personal risk and with great skill."

Gerrit stared at his diagram, and his breath stilled, his throat cramped. His labor had not been in vain. It hadn't achieved the results he'd intended but had achieved perhaps even greater good. God had seen all of this, known all of this.

Gerrit slammed his eyes shut. *Oh Lord, why did I doubt you?*

Even if none of the maps had been received, even if Gerrit had been tried as a traitor, his work had merit because he'd done what was good and right—even if no one else had ever known.

"Gerrit?" a woman cried. "It *is* you."

His eyes flew open, but his mind—what was he seeing? The woman with the tea tray looked like his cousin Cilla, sounded like Cilla. But Cilla was dead.

"Ci—Cilla?"

"Ja, you blind and silly man," she said in Dutch, laughing, and she tugged him to his feet and embraced him. "Organisation Todt? Jersey? I can't believe my cautious cousin had a grand adventure."

He wouldn't call it an adventure, and he pulled back to study her face. Yes, Cilla's bright smile and the van der Zee green-blue eyes. "You're alive."

Captain Romijn cleared his throat. "I do hate to interrupt, but I need to verify—"

"Yes, Captain." Cilla hooked her arm through Gerrit's. "This is my cousin Gerrit van der Zee, a long-standing member of the Dutch resistance, along with our good friend Bernardus Kroon. I already identified Bernardus. I advised him to shave off that ridiculous mustache and told him black hair most definitely does not suit him." She grinned at Gerrit.

"Thank you. We'll leave you to your family reunion." Romijn headed for the door.

Colonel Hargrave gathered Gerrit's maps, pumped his hand in a firm handshake, and departed.

Gerrit's head swam, and he braced one hand on the table. "You're alive. In England. How did you get here?"

Cilla released Gerrit's arm and fiddled with the hem of a green-blue suit jacket. "By boat."

How unlike Cilla to give a short answer to what could only be a long story.

"That's all in the past." Cilla grabbed both of his hands. "You'll need to be questioned by a few more people. But then what fun we'll have. Aleida's here in England too."

A four-year-long sigh escaped. "Thank goodness. We knew she and her husband had tried to escape to England, but we'd heard no word, of course."

"She made it, but her husband was killed in the exodus. She's married again—to an Englishman. And I married a Scotsman."

"Mackenzie," Gerrit murmured. The captain had summoned a Mrs. Mackenzie.

A light grew inside, illuminating his vision. As soon as the various British agencies released him, he planned to marry a Jerseywoman.

CHAPTER
46

Standing at the rails of the hospital ship, Ivy held on to her ratty old green hat and scanned the pier for Dad and Mum. A stream of ambulances awaited to transport the wounded soldiers and sailors from the ship to hospitals.

"Do you see them?" Charlie said from his wheelchair beside her. He would have a few more weeks in hospital, but his color had returned.

"Not yet." Ivy peered through the morning haze. Telegrams had flown between Ivy and her mother in the past fortnight. In the telegram Ivy had received before the hospital ship sailed from Cherbourg, Mum said Dad had received leave and they'd both meet the ship.

The medical officers promised Charlie a half hour for the reunion, then they'd shuttle him away.

Hugh Collingwood had generously arranged for Ivy and her parents to stay overnight at his wife's cousin's house in Portsmouth. In the morning, Ivy and her mother would take the train to Ivy's grandparents' home, and Dad would return to duty with his regiment.

Charlie chuckled and stretched to see over the rails. "Won't Dad and Mum be surprised to hear our story?"

"Most definitely." In her telegrams, Ivy could communicate only the barest details.

"I'm glad I didn't evacuate in 1940."

"You are?" Ivy stared down at her brother, ill and wounded and malnourished.

Charlie lifted his eyebrows. "Aren't you?"

So much had happened. So many good people lost—Thelma Galais and Demyan Marchenko and too many others. So much oppression and deprivation and fear.

Yet she'd gained friendships and love, and she'd grown in confidence and capability and faith—even in discipline and punctuality. Most importantly, by remaining in Jersey, she'd been able to save lives and relieve suffering and provide a dose of humanity to the oppressed.

"I am," Ivy said. "I'm glad I stayed."

"Ivy!" Dad's deep voice rose from the pier. "Charlie!"

"There they are," Charlie said. "Dad! Mum!"

Dad stood on the pier in his officer's uniform and Mum beside him in a dark blue coat and hat, both waving. "Ivy! Charlie!"

A joyous pain squeezed Ivy's chest, and she waved too, even as the vision of the people she loved blurred before her. She'd longed for this day and dreaded it—dreaded disclosing the news she bore.

A crewman removed a gate at the top of the gangplank, and an orderly approached. "Welcome to Old Blighty, Mr. Picot. Half an hour with your family."

"Half an hour is more than I've had in four years." Charlie grinned at the orderly and wheeled toward the gangplank.

The orderly grabbed the wheelchair handles. "Not so fast."

Ivy followed her brother and the orderly down the gangplank to free British soil.

Dad and Mum rushed over, both grayer, but alive and well, and they took turns crushing Ivy and Charlie in embraces.

"You're so thin." Mum took Ivy's cheeks between her hands. "But so, so beautiful. My sweet girl."

Ivy's smile quivered beneath her mother's warm hands. "I've missed you so much."

"Look how you've grown." Dad shook Charlie's hand and patted his shoulder, and his cheeks worked. "We missed your entire youth."

Charlie smiled. "Most parents would pay for that privilege."

Mum laughed and swiped away tears. "Your voice—I scarcely recognize it."

"Wait until you see him standing," Ivy said. "He's taller than you, Dad."

The orderly cleared his throat. "Let's move this happy family."

"Oh yes." Ivy looped her arm through her mother's and led the way down the pier to make way for the other patients to disembark.

"A crewman on a cargo boat," Dad said without contempt.

"He did it for the family," Ivy said. "To support the practice."

"It was entirely my idea," Charlie said. "Ivy tried to talk me out of it. My education, you know."

"We know." Mum glanced at Ivy with resignation and sadness in her medium-brown eyes, so like Fern's. So unlike Fern's.

"You needn't fear," Charlie said. "I am determined to return to school and join the long line of Doctors Picot."

Ivy spun to her brother. "You are?"

"You shan't dissuade me." Charlie waved her along. "I've spent the past fortnight in hospital, watching what doctors do, watching what penicillin does. That's what I want for my life. I want to join the family practice."

In the infrequent and short Red Cross messages, Ivy hadn't been able to convey the damage to the medical practice. Her smile wavered. "If we have a practice to return to."

"Nonsense. We shall be absent only a few months more." Dad

gestured to an open spot on the docks. "The war shall be over by Christmas."

Charlie tucked in a dragging corner of blanket. "After Jersey is liberated, the truth will come out about Ivy and what she's done, and the patients will return."

"Truth?" Mum frowned at Ivy.

Oh dear. She hadn't wanted to discuss this on their first day together, and she smoothed the front of her threadbare green coat, bearing fresh scars from the escape. "I told you about Fern's job."

"With the Germans?" Dad clucked his tongue. "What was she thinking?"

"She thought her wages would help the family." Ivy drew in a long breath. "But her reputation as a collaborator tarnished me and drove patients away."

"You two aren't getting on," Mum said.

Ivy's throat swelled, and she shook her head.

"We've been quite worried about her," Dad said. "Even before the Channel Islands were cut off, Bill hadn't received a Red Cross message from her in over a year."

Ivy might never tell her parents about her final confrontation with Fern. Honesty mattered, but so did her parents' love for their eldest daughter. Knowing Fern had denounced Ivy to the secret police . . . it would wreck them.

Instead, she raised a watery smile. "This isn't a day for worry. Haven't we all done enough of that?"

"Indeed." Mum hugged Ivy's arm. "This is a day to rejoice."

Dad gripped Charlie's shoulder as if he never wanted to let go. "Tell us how we came to receive an invitation from none other than Hugh Collingwood of the BBC. To stay with—who was it, dear? A cousin?"

"Of his wife's, I believe." Mum gave Ivy a quizzical look. "And a friend of yours?"

Despite her own resolution, a fresh wave of worry crashed over her. Where was Gerrit? Would the British ever believe him?

"Yes," Charlie said. "She's a cousin of Gerrit van der Zee."

Ivy nodded. "The man I love."

⟿

PORTSMOUTH

In the waning light, Gerrit and Bernardus stood outside their hotel in brand-new clothes. Gerrit's dark blue suit needed tailoring in the waist and sleeves, but it was far better than his much-abused gray suit.

Bernardus had shaved off the mustache that so offended Cilla and had gotten a haircut, but the black dye would take weeks to grow out. "Free men in a free country."

"At last." In the morning, Gerrit and Bernardus would depart to visit the War Office in London for yet more questioning—but as free men. Behind the scenes over the past week and a half, the competing British intelligence agencies had exchanged notes until a picture of Gerrit's and Bernardus's work had emerged from the mist.

Leaning on his crutch, Bernardus adjusted the rim of his new homburg. "We can't go home yet."

"Not yet." In German-occupied Amsterdam, their families considered them the worst sort of collaborators and believed Bernardus and Cilla were dead. If only the Allied offensive north into the Netherlands in September had succeeded. It had not.

A black car pulled to the curb, and Cilla bounded out of the car and hugged Gerrit and Bernardus. Again.

A naval officer stepped out from behind the driver's seat, a tall man with red hair and a cane.

"My husband, Lachlan," Cilla said. "Lachlan, my cousin Gerrit and friend Bernardus."

"It's an honor to meet you." Lachlan spoke with a Scottish accent. "Cilla told me what you did in the Netherlands and Jersey. But is it true? Was Cilla actually in the resistance?"

Cilla spun to him, her blond hair flying about her shoulders. "Lachlan Mackenzie!"

Her husband laughed and pulled her to his side. "Welcome to Portsmouth, lads."

After everyone climbed into the car, Lachlan drove away. "Now that you are free, what are your plans?"

"Plans?" For the past fortnight, Gerrit hadn't thought beyond escape and release.

"We can't go home yet," Bernardus said. "Who knows how long?"

Gerrit had only one plan established. "I'll return to Jersey after liberation."

Bernardus chuckled. "With the fair Ivy."

"Oh?" Cilla glanced over the seatback with delight in her eyes. "Tell me more."

In the afternoon, Gerrit had sent a telegram to the address Ivy had provided. Perhaps he could see her in a few days. "Later."

"Later?" Cilla huffed. "Men being men, it's a wonder marriage ever happens."

"Aye, lass." Lachlan smirked. "A wonder indeed."

"Excuse me, Lachlan." Bernardus leaned forward. "I can't help but notice that you use a cane, and yet you serve in uniform. Is there any hope for me? I want to serve."

Lachlan exchanged a glance with Cilla. "Aye, I'll make inquiries."

Cilla waved toward the scenery around them. "If not, look at the bomb damage. Surely a geologist and a civil engineer could find employment."

"True." Gerrit frowned at a vacant lot they passed. Jersey had endured many calamities in the past few years, but not the devastating bombing seen in Britain and continental Europe.

On the outskirts of town, Lachlan pulled up to a modest but handsome house of red brick. A blond woman flung open the front door and waved.

"Aleida!" Gerrit ran up the walkway and swung his cousin into his arms. How long since he'd seen her? He gripped her shoulders.

Her face had changed, but she still had the same gentle smile. "It's good to see you."

"And you." Tears filled her blue eyes, and she turned to Bernardus. "And Bernardus. How good to see you."

"It's been many years."

"Too many." Aleida ushered them into a sitting room. "Come, meet the children. My son, Teddy."

A blond boy of about seven approached with a shy smile, and he extended his left hand to shake. He kept his right hand stuffed deep in the pocket of his little jacket.

Not wishing to embarrass the boy by calling attention to the error, Gerrit extended his own left hand. "I'm glad to meet you, Teddy."

"That's my sister, Caroline." Teddy pointed to a little blond girl toddling toward a baby sitting on a blanket. "And my baby cousin, Magsie."

"Her name is Margaret." Cilla scooped up the baby and kissed her cap of strawberry-blond hair.

Gerrit met Aleida's teary gaze. "What fine children. And your husband? Will he be joining us?"

"Oh yes." A squawk from the toddler, and Aleida swung the child up to her hip. "Hugh will want to interview both of you. He's with the BBC. That's how he—"

"Aleida!" Cilla nudged her.

Gerrit frowned. "That's how he what?"

Both ladies turned huge, fake smiles to him.

Gerrit groaned, rolled his eyes, and sank onto a sofa.

The front door opened and shut, and a man with brown hair entered the sitting room, followed by a middle-aged couple. They looked familiar, reminded him of—

"Ivy!" Gerrit stumbled to his feet.

It was her. It was his own beloved Ivy.

She stopped in the doorway, her brown eyes huge, and she edged forward. "Gerrit? Gerrit! You're free!"

He dashed toward her, banged his ankle on a chair leg, pulled her into his arms, kissed her, hugged her, kissed her, hugged her.

"I knew they'd believe you," she said between kisses. "I knew it."

"Charlie?" He kissed her again. She was too sweet not to kiss. "How is he?"

"He's fine. He'll finish his recovery here in England." She laughed, turned to the side so his kiss landed on her soft cheek, and righted her hat. "Gerrit, I'd like to introduce my parents."

The parents of the woman he was mauling with kisses.

His face warmed, and he turned to the couple he recognized from Ivy's drawings.

But they were smiling, and her mother looked misty-eyed.

Her father extended his hand. "It's an honor to meet you, Gerrit. Ivy has told us many wonderful things about you."

His right hand accepted the handshake, while his left opened and flexed in absolute certainty. "Dr. Picot, may I have your daughter's hand in marriage?"

"Gerrit!" Ivy gasped and clutched his arm. "You might want to ask me!"

He might indeed. His jaw hung open. His cheeks flamed.

Her eyebrows lifted high above her big brown eyes, and her mouth hung open too.

Was it too soon? What if she didn't want to marry him at all?

Ivy shut her mouth and gave the slightest of nods. "Yes."

"Yes, what?"

"Yes, I'll marry you." A glow built in her gaze, a glow of hope and joy and forever.

"You will?" He gathered her close and reaped another crop of kisses.

Her parents! Gerrit sprang back, one arm about Ivy's waist, and he addressed her father. "May I?"

The elder Dr. Picot laughed, big and hearty. "You don't seem to need my permission to kiss her."

"To marry her, sir, ma'am." Gerrit held Ivy close to his side. "I love her dearly, and I want to make a home with her for as long as the Lord gives us. In Jersey."

"In Jersey?" Ivy's eyes rounded even more.

"Where else?" Gerrit gave her a teasing smile. "You belong there, and I belong with you."

A soft sigh, and Ivy leaned her head on his shoulder. "And I with you."

Her love was a result he hadn't tried to obtain and hadn't earned, which made it all the more beautiful.

CHAPTER
47

In the summer sun, Ivy descended the gangplank of the mail boat with her husband, her parents, and her brother. The German forces in the Channel Islands had held out to the end, not surrendering until May 9, the day after Victory in Europe had been celebrated in England. At least the surrender had come without bloodshed.

The damage to her beautiful island struck her fresh. The wind-blown oaks around St. Aubin's Bay chopped down for firewood. The concrete bunkers studding the beaches. The railway lines slashing through the hills.

"We'll rebuild," Gerrit said from behind her, carrying their suitcase. "And restore."

With her medical bag in hand, she smiled over her shoulder at him, so handsome in his dark blue suit and homburg. After helping repair bomb damage in England, now he'd work for the States of Jersey to undo what Organisation Todt had done.

The medical practice would also be rebuilt. Charlie had completed a year with the evacuated version of Victoria College in

England, and he would now complete his final year in Jersey, in the hope of studying medicine at Oxford.

At the Weighbridge, Uncle Arthur and Aunt Opal stood waving and crying with Uncle Leo and Aunt Ruby, and much kissing and embracing and laughing ensued.

Aunt Opal gave Gerrit a particularly long hug. "You dear boy. Now you're family."

Aunt Ruby lifted her nose as if offended. "Leo and I are rather hurt to have been left out of all the excitement."

Ivy squeezed Aunt Ruby's arm. "You did deliver a clandestine message, remember?"

"Yes." Aunt Ruby turned a mock glare at Charlie. "Because of you, you cheeky lad."

Charlie laughed and marched away with his suitcase in hand. "Come on. I want to go home. Look! The Pomme d'Or—the Union Jack is back. And over Fort Regent. Glorious."

"It is indeed." Uncle Arthur fell in beside Gerrit as they walked up Mulcaster Street. "Any news on Bernardus? And your family?"

"Bernardus went home a few weeks ago, and I've been able to write my family. Ivy and I plan to visit next month. My family all survived but are much thinner. There was a severe famine in the Netherlands, the *Hongerwinter*, they call it. Many thousands died of starvation."

Uncle Arthur grumbled. "We had a similar winter here. Almost nothing to eat, no heat, no electricity, no gas. If the Red Cross ship hadn't brought supplies, we would have starved too."

"The SS *Vega*," Aunt Opal said. "The Red Cross parcels saved our lives."

Ivy passed a shopfront. "We have goods in the shops again."

"Yes." Aunt Ruby's eyes lit up. "Still rationed, but we can actually buy tea and sugar and salt and soap and clothing."

"And we have electricity and gas," Uncle Leo said. "And we'll have coal this winter."

"How lovely." Ivy slipped her hand inside Gerrit's as they passed

St. Helier Parish Church, where they'd met. If only they could have married there, but it had been a blessing to marry at her grandparents' church.

"Ruby?" Mum asked from behind Ivy in a quiet tone. "Did you tell Fern we were coming home?"

"I did. She rarely goes out, not since Liberation Day."

Ivy winced, and Gerrit squeezed her hand. Fern's denunciation of Ivy had indeed won back Helmut's heart. But on Liberation Day, mobs had attacked women who had consorted with Germans—including Fern.

Uncle Leo and Aunt Ruby had taken Fern into their home to protect her, and Helmut and the rest of the German forces had been deported to prison camps in England.

"I think we've convinced her to go to England," Aunt Ruby said. "Have a fresh start."

"That would be best. Bill and the boys will come home soon." Mum let out a little sob. "I want to see her."

"Give her time," Aunt Ruby said. "She may want to see you someday, but not . . ."

Not Ivy. But she drew herself taller. She'd done everything in her power to allow reconciliation, but reconciliation would require contrition and remorse on Fern's part.

Gerrit slipped his arm about her waist and kissed her cheek. "Even if."

"Even if," she said. Even if she never saw her sister again, she'd praise God for his goodness and praise him for revealing glimpses of his goodness in clouds and flowers and rabbits, and in people like Gerrit and Charlie and Thelma.

And in her home. La Bliue Brise looked tired, the blue paint on the door and on the window trim faded and chipped. But paint could be replaced, and Ivy stroked the door as she passed through.

Joan de Ferrers and Dr. Tipton stood in the waiting room. "Welcome home."

Ivy rushed forward and hugged Joan. "Oh, it's good to see you."

"Miss de Ferrers and Dr. Tipton kept an eye on the house after Liberation Day," Aunt Ruby said.

"Not Miss de Ferrers." Joan returned Ivy's hug. "Mrs. Tipton."

"Mrs. Tipton?" Ivy pulled back to study her friend's face, and she laughed. "Why didn't I see it? You're perfect for each other."

The two redheads beamed. Her two dear friends.

Dad shook Dr. Tipton's hand. "Thank you for watching our home, Harold."

"It was an honor. And I have a proposition." Harold glanced between Dad and Ivy. "A partnership between our practices. As people learn how Ivy helped the foreign workers and how you served in the Army, your patients will return, but . . ."

But gossip was easier to spread than to gather.

"A brilliant idea," Ivy said. "A partnership would not only help us rebuild but would also lighten the burden during epidemics and make it easier for each of us to take holidays."

Dad looked at her with his eyebrows raised in surprise and admiration. She hadn't asked his opinion first. "I agree with Dr. van der Zee. The three of us can discuss this soon."

Joan tugged on her husband's arm. "We should leave you to settle in."

"Yes, we should." Aunt Opal gave Mum one more hug. "Come to the farm for dinner."

"Thank you. That sounds lovely."

The family carried their luggage upstairs, and Ivy brought Gerrit into her room—their room.

"We'll need a bigger bed." Gerrit patted the bed and grinned at her.

"We will. And soon." With a little smile, Ivy set down her medical bag and pulled out her sketch pad, which would be a permanent part of her equipment, along with Charlie's timer.

Gerrit removed his hat and lounged on the bed with his hands behind his head. "I never imagined myself in your bedroom."

"It is a logical result of our love." She perched on the side of the bed and opened her sketch pad as bubbles danced in her chest. She handed the book to Gerrit. "So is this."

He studied the sketch with a blank expression. Sat up. Swung his legs over the side of the bed. Stared at the sketch. "Is this . . . ?"

"Don't you see?" Ivy patted her belly. "Oh, you can't see. Not for another seven months. You'll need to have faith."

Gerrit held aloft the drawing of a tiny round face, tiny hands, sweet eyes painted a shade of aquamarine, the same shade as the waters in St. Aubin's Bay, not far from shore. Although their children would surely have brown eyes.

Gerrit turned to Ivy with a look of joy and wonder and gratitude.

That morning in church almost three years earlier, she'd captured his likeness on paper. His goodness. His kindness.

Ivy had seen this and was seeing it, and she'd see it for the rest of her life.

AUTHOR'S NOTE

Dear reader,

I hope you've enjoyed this journey with Gerrit and Ivy. For years, the story of the Channel Islands in World War II has fascinated me. The four main islands of Jersey, Guernsey, Sark, and Alderney had widely different experiences during the war. For example, Jersey's tradition of potato farming meant they didn't experience the severe potato shortages that plagued Guernsey.

The five-year sweep of this novel allowed me to show many aspects of occupied Jersey, but not nearly as many as I would have liked.

On June 19, 1940, reeling from the recent evacuation of Dunkirk, the British decided to demilitarize the Channel Islands. Evacuation was offered to the population, with priority for children, mothers, and men of military age. In Jersey, an appeal by Bailiff Alexander Coutanche headed off panic, and only 6,600 evacuated, while 41,000 remained.

After a single, but devastating, air raid on June 28, the Germans took the surrender of the island on July 1 without further bloodshed. A deluge of German orders and regulations followed, governing every aspect of life for the islanders. Cut off from their traditional trading partner of England, the Channel Islands had to establish new ties with France. Rationing was strict and grew stricter throughout the war, and prices for food and clothing soared.

Shortages hit the medical community especially hard, with few commercial medications available. Joan de Ferrers is fictional, but island chemists did indeed do wonders with local plants and seaweed. Tragically, the shortage of insulin was real, and all but one of the island's insulin-dependent diabetics died during the war. The epidemics of diphtheria, whooping cough, and scarlet fever mentioned in the story were also real.

Armed, active resistance wasn't seen in the Channel Islands for a variety of reasons. The islands are small, with close-knit communities and no places for bands of fighters to hide. At the peak, Jersey had one German soldier for every three islanders, a far higher ratio than in any other occupied nation. And most men of military age evacuated before the occupation.

Regardless, the people of Jersey did resist. When the Germans ordered the confiscation of all wireless sets in June 1942, thousands of islanders hid—or made—their own sets. Since listening to or spreading news from the BBC was illegal, this required courage and dedication to the truth, and many paid for this with their freedom—or their lives.

During the occupation, about four thousand people in Jersey were convicted of infractions against German orders, mostly for possessing a wireless set, spreading English news, sheltering escaped foreign workers, or stealing food, supplies, or weapons from the Germans. About twenty-two of those men and women died or were killed in prisons or concentration camps. Four of those who perished were arrested in the St. Saviour wireless case mentioned in the novel, including Canon Clifford Cohu. In another notorious case, Louisa Gould was killed at

Ravensbrück for the crime of taking an escaped Russian worker into her home and treating him like a son.

Dr. Noel McKinstry was the real-life Medical Officer of Health and the organizer of a loose ring that helped escaped workers. The character of Dr. Harold Tipton is fictional as are the codes Joan and Ivy used to communicate, but these characters represent dozens of ordinary people who took great risks and showed compassion for the unfortunate.

Over the course of the war, about one hundred fifty men and women succeeded in escaping from Jersey by boat, especially in the autumn of 1944 during the "siege" after the Channel Islands were cut off from France. Twenty-four who tried to escape were arrested, nine drowned, and one young man was shot and killed by a German patrol. The "Fauvic Embarkation Port" was real, run by Deputy Wilfred "Bill" Bertram, his family, and dozens in his community.

Other real-life people mentioned in the story include the Very Rev. Matthew Le Marinel of St. Helier Parish Church, surgeon Mr. Arthur Halliwell, artist Edmund Blampied, and Hauptwachtmeister Karl-Heinz Wölfle of the German secret field police.

Organisation Todt was a quasi-military unit responsible for most German military construction. Uniformed personnel—all Germans or "Aryans"—worked directly for OT or for contracted construction firms. OT's need for labor exceeded the willingness of locals in occupied nations to work for them. The Todt workers included volunteers attracted by high wages—or Spanish Republican "volunteers" offered a choice between working for OT or returning to Spain. Other workers were conscripted in France, the Netherlands, and Belgium, but were paid and were treated moderately well. However, thousands of slave workers from the east, especially Ukraine, Russia, and Poland, were forced to work without pay, under appalling conditions, and with cruel guards. An estimated seventy-three "Russian workers"—as all the slave workers were called regardless of nationality—died or were killed in Jersey during the war.

In the story, Gerrit longs to tear down the hundreds of fortifications built by OT. In reality, the solid construction of reinforced concrete proved difficult to remove. This is a boon for modern tourists, who can visit the Jersey War Tunnels museum at the tunnel complex of Hohlgangsanlage 8 and the newly opened St. Catherine's Bunker (referred to in the story by its wartime name of Strongpoint Verclut), run by Jersey War Tours. I was privileged to take a tour by this outstanding organization and to visit this bunker before its official opening.

Words fail to describe the beauty of Jersey, and I long for Ivy's gift with sketching. If you ever have a chance, please visit. St. Helier is charming, Elizabeth Castle and Mont Orgueil Castle are extraordinary pieces of history, and the views are outstanding.

I hope you enjoyed this glimpse into life in Jersey in World War II.

ACKNOWLEDGMENTS

When writing acknowledgments, I'm always reminded how much I depend—in the best sense—on others.

A writer's world can be confined and solitary, and sometimes my introverted self enjoys that too much! Yet novels are born from people and life and the stories of others. So I'm thankful for my "real-life" friends from church, the "Estrada Girls" from my neighborhood, and a host of friends in the writing community. You keep me grounded.

I'm also thankful for the support and encouragement from my children, my daughter-in-law, my parents, and my sister—who is kind and humble and very un-Fern-like! And gratitude overflows for my two *precious* grandchildren, who provide delight and joy.

Extra thanks to my husband, who bears the brunt of living with a writer. Sometimes he gets perks like research trips to Jersey. We had an amazing time exploring so many of the sights in this story.

Once again, I'm thankful for my critique partners, Sherry Kyle and Judy Gann, and for my outstanding publishing team—my agent, Rachel Kent, my editors, Rachel McRae and Kristin

Kornoelje, and Karen Steele and Rachael Betz in publicity and marketing.

And a special thank you, my dear reader, for choosing to read my stories. Please visit me at SarahSundin.com to leave a message, sign up for my email newsletter, read about the history behind the story, and see photos of my research trip to Jersey.

DISCUSSION QUESTIONS

1. Which historical events in *Mists over the Channel Islands* were familiar to you? Which were unfamiliar?

2. At the beginning of the story, Ivy and Charlie decide to remain in Jersey—and the majority of the population did indeed remain. What do you think of their decision? What would you have done?

3. What do you think of Gerrit's decision to join Organisation Todt? What factors came into play? What would you have done in his place? What do you think of his willingness to sacrifice not only his life but his reputation for this work?

4. Both Gerrit and Fern have a deep desire for control and for recognition of their work. How does this desire change Fern? How does Gerrit change this desire?

5. Ivy struggles with time management. How do others help her grow more disciplined? How does she change? Can you relate to this struggle?

6. Gerrit wants his work to matter. How is this positive? How does this turn negative? Have you ever struggled when you feel your efforts don't receive appropriate recognition or produce the results you want? How do you handle this?

7. Ivy is said to "see beyond the seen." How does this come out in the story? What are her blind spots? Are you intuitive like Ivy—or more like Gerrit, "seeing what you see"?

8. Early in the story, Ivy comes to doubt God's goodness and Gerrit doubts God's faithfulness. Have you ever had similar concerns? How did Ivy and Gerrit overcome this? Did this show you anything new about the Lord?

9. Gerrit and Bernardus have a deep and long-standing friendship, and Ivy slowly develops a friendship with Joan. What stood out to you in these friendships? How is each person good for the other? What qualities do you admire most in your closest friends?

10. Ivy has always depended on others. How is this good? When can it be bad? How does she change during the story? Are you more likely to lean on others or go it alone?

11. Charlie makes many decisions that drive this story—from dropping out of school to helping Gerrit and Bernardus to his choice at the climax of the story. What do you think of Charlie? What do you imagine for him in the future?

12. Ivy wants to preserve family harmony. How does this benefit the Picot household? How does this create problems for Ivy? How does she grow? Are you someone who avoids conflict to preserve harmony? Or one who thrives on conflict?

13. Thelma Galais and Demyan Marchenko represent the types of people caught up in the tragedy of Nazi occupation. What do you think of these—very different—people?

14. In Jersey, many ordinary people made dangerous decisions to harbor escaped workers. What would you have done?

15. Ivy's drawing brings joy to herself and others. How do you see this in the story? Do you have any hobbies that bring you joy?

READ ON FOR A SNEAK PEEK
AT SARAH SUNDIN'S NEXT BOOK,

A WWII CHRISTMAS NOVELLA.

AVAILABLE SEPTEMBER 2026.

On the first day of Christmas my true love sent to me . . .
a partridge in a pear tree.

SAN DIEGO, CALIFORNIA
MONDAY, OCTOBER 18, 1943

Soft sunshine, a sea breeze, and a shining new opportunity. Maggie Oliver paused to savor the Italian Renaissance façade of San Diego's USO-Army-Navy YMCA building. Then she climbed granite steps and swung open the door.

A senior hostess sat at the front desk, her cherubic face crowned by silver hair.

"Good morning." Maggie mirrored her bright smile. "I'm Margaret Oliver, and I'm—"

"Late." All resemblance to a cherub disappeared in a great pinching of features.

A clock above the woman's head indicated Maggie was five minutes early, but she knew better than to argue. "I do apologize. The trolley—you understand."

The woman rose, barely taller standing than sitting. "Miss Perkins, please watch the front desk."

"Yes, Mrs. Laverne." A redheaded young lady scampered over.

Mrs. Laverne marched across the red-tiled lobby under a wood-beamed ceiling. "I serve as one of the directors of this USO club. I'll show you to your office, Mrs. Oliver."

"Miss Oliver."

"Miss?" She cranked her gaze back to Maggie and almost stumbled. "When will USO-Camp Shows learn their lesson and stop placing responsibility in the hands of single young ladies? After the unfortunate situation with Miss Holmes . . ."

Unfortunate? Bernard Anderson, the Camp Shows regional director, had hired Maggie after Miss Holmes married.

Maggie trotted after the club director. Perhaps kind words would help. "Mr. Anderson told me about the important work you do at this club. He said you have over five hundred beds for servicemen and offer lots of services and recreation."

"We do. We've had five million visitors since January. Do you see this tile floor? It was supposed to last ten years, but we had to replace it after only one year."

"Oh my."

Mrs. Laverne passed through an arched doorway and waved toward a gymnasium. "You can imagine what an imposition it is to sacrifice space for Camp Shows personnel, but sacrifice we must."

Maggie lifted an eyebrow as she followed the woman up a staircase. Mrs. Laverne wasn't her supervisor, but she was indeed opening space in her busy club to a separate branch of the USO. "Thank you for making room for us."

On the second floor, Mrs. Laverne gestured to a room with an open door. "Here's your office. Your assistant arrived fifteen minutes ago. Now, if you'll excuse me."

"Thank you." But Maggie's smile landed on the club director's retreating back.

Inside the office, a middle-aged woman strode up to Maggie, and her dark eyes pierced like an obsidian knife. "Get to work. You have a show to run."

Well, that was an unusual way to be welcomed, but Maggie found a smile. "Good morning. I'm Miss Oliver—"

"San Diego's new Camp Shows director." The woman spread out manila folders on the larger of the two desks. Gray streaked her neatly rolled black hair. "The Navy wants a Christmas show, but Miss Holmes waited too long. The Camp Shows troupes are already booked, and you'll have to start from scratch. Only two months till Christmas, and we've got nothing."

Maggie's head spun, so she removed her hat and straightened the jacket of her dark blue suit, the one Grandpa said made her eyes look as blue as Grandma's.

Sweet Grandpa. He was so proud of her, but this job was on a trial basis. If she couldn't pull a show together, she'd lose this job. And he'd lose his home.

"I've organized this for you." Miss Nameless slapped her hand on a folder. "Let's go."

So, Maggie had a hardworking assistant, and she joined her at the desk. "Your name is . . . ?"

"Ria Fernandez." She held out a folder, and a golden band sparkled on her ring finger.

Maggie set her hat and purse on the desk and took the folder. "Ria? That's pretty."

"Ria is short and fast." She flicked the folder. "The show, Miss Oliver."

Maggie settled into the wooden chair, and Mrs. Fernandez pulled over a chair beside the desk.

Putting on a show would be a thrilling challenge, and Maggie could do it. After over ten years dancing in Hollywood, she'd danced with USO-Camp Shows, then choreographed, then directed. This was the next step.

She opened the folder. "What do we have, Mrs. Fernandez?"

"Call me Ria. Save a lot of syllables."

"Is that so? Call me Maggie and save a few more."

Ria snapped up her gaze, and a smile burst out. "I like you."

Maggie laughed. "So, what do we have?"

"Nothing." Ria pointed to the folder in Maggie's hand. "List of venues, contacts, phone numbers. An *X* means they aren't available."

Maggie whistled. "That's most of them."

"You have appointments this afternoon at the three best options.

Here's your schedule, your contacts, where to meet them, the trolley route." Ria handed Maggie a neatly typed list.

"Oh my." Very efficient.

Ria slid over another folder. "Mr. Anderson gave me a list of Hollywood stars, but we'd better book them fast."

Halfway down the list, Maggie gasped. "Prescott Duke? He's my favorite star. I danced in three of his movies. Not with him, of course. Just in the ensemble. With his dark good looks, they always paired him with blondes, not brunettes like me. But, oh my. He's so handsome and such a gentleman and that voice. It's like midnight blue velvet."

Ria cleared her throat, and the obsidian returned to her gaze.

Maggie gave her an apologetic smile. "Too many syllables?"

She tapped the list. "See the *X*? You don't want Mr. Duke. He was burned in an accident. Really bad scars."

"I—I'd heard." Prescott Duke's story had been the talk of the town. He'd been one of the first stars to enlist after Pearl Harbor, but his bus to the training camp had crashed and burst into flames. Mr. Duke had escaped but then returned to the inferno to save other men. He'd been discharged from the Army due to his injuries, and he hadn't made a film since.

The man was a hero, and Maggie slid her finger over the *X*. "I want him in my show. Scars and all."

<hr />

Yeoman Third Class Frank Sebastian led Maggie toward the Old Globe Theatre in San Diego's Balboa Park. Modeled after Shakespeare's Globe Theatre in London, the circular building had half-timbering near the roof and Old English lettering.

With all her visits to the park, why had Maggie never been inside the theater? "I love it. I absolutely love it."

"We're mighty fond of it." The square collar of the sailor's navy blue tunic fluttered in the wind. "It was built for the California Pacific International Exposition in '35. It was supposed to be torn

SARAH SUNDIN

down afterward, but the city rallied, raised money, and had it built to code."

The squawk of seagulls, the rustle of palm trees, and the scent of eucalyptus trees added a California layer to the charm. "Now the Navy runs it."

"Yes, ma'am. After Pearl Harbor, we took over most of the buildings in Balboa Park to expand the naval hospital. We use the theater for lectures and entertainment. We use the Museum of Man over yonder for a hospital ward."

Holding back her hair, Maggie turned in a circle. To the left of the theater, the Spanish-inspired museum raised an ornate stucco tower and a colorful tiled dome to the blue sky. "It's perfect."

"Don't get too excited, ma'am. The theater only seats about five hundred. You'd need multiple showings for all the sailors in San Diego, and the theater will rarely be available for rehearsals."

She followed the handsome blond sailor toward the theater. Frank Sebastian . . . the name was familiar, but the face wasn't. Since he was from the South and easily ten years her junior, she couldn't imagine where she might have met him.

He opened the door and led her through the lobby and into the theater.

Maggie strolled down the aisle. The stage was small, but she liked how the wall encircled the floor seating and how balconies stacked up that wall like bunk beds.

She could practically see actors in Elizabethan garb calling out lines. "Too bad Shakespeare wouldn't fit for a Christmas show. I can't see our boys sitting through a play in Ye Olde English anyway."

"That's what they thought for the Exposition too, so the Globe Players performed short versions of Shakespeare plays. They were a big hit. The scripts are in the office. Want to see?"

"Why, yes." Maggie followed the yeoman up the aisle. "Short versions?"

"Yes, ma'am. About an hour."

"An hour . . ." The men might sit through that, especially if it were a comedy, especially if supplemented by song-and-dance numbers and plenty of pretty girls.

Frank Sebastian entered an office off the lobby, shoved aside boxes in the crowded room, and opened a file cabinet. He riffled through the contents. "Here we go. *The Taming of the Shrew, Hamlet, Twelfth Night, Macbeth*—"

"*Twelfth Night*? May I see?"

"Yes, ma'am."

Maggie took the thin script. "I played Olivia in this play in high school. I loved it. Full of comedy and mistaken identities. And . . . and Shakespeare wrote it for Christmas."

"Huh." The sailor screwed up one eye. "The fellows always like a good laugh."

Maggie clutched the script to her chest, and a plan danced in her head like a Busby Berkeley spectacular—the venue, the program. All she needed was a star.

◦∽◦

LOS ANGELES, CALIFORNIA

Prescott Duke sat in a leather armchair in front of Melvin Underwood's shiny desk, and his foot jiggled. "Anything for me? Anything at all?"

Melvin rested his big hands on his big belly. "You know the answer, Press."

Prescott tugged at his shirt collar. "I know I'm done in movies. I know that. I mean, I'll do anything. A charity gig, a—"

"What are you worried about?" Melvin's thick gray eyebrows fused. "You have a fancy house, a fancy car, and enough money for life if you manage it well. And you do."

"It's not the money. It never was. I'd work for free."

"Never say that to your agent."

Prescott cracked a smile, then sobered. "I mean it, Mel. I'm going stir-crazy. It's been almost two years since the accident. I'm tired of doing nothing all day."

"What're you going to do? Get a job?"

Modern art hung on the paneled walls, a far cry from the tar-papered walls of the tenement where Prescott had grown up. "I've been thinking about it."

Melvin sighed and leveled his gaze at Prescott, hard but not unkind. "With those hands?"

He flinched and rubbed the gnarled skin. In the agonizing weeks in the hospital, he'd lost four of his fingers, two on each hand. Even holding a pen was difficult.

"Listen, kid. I'm not being mean, just realistic. You've got a sixth-grade education and no job skills. What're you going to do? Go back to the boxing ring where I discovered Joe Prescott and turned him into Prescott Duke?"

Heaviness filled his chest, and he shook his head. He had nothing but his voice. But with a mangled face, acting and singing were out of the picture.

Melvin fished a pear from the fruit bowl on his desk. "A lot of men would be happy to be retired."

"I'm only thirty-five. I shouldn't be retired."

"It's not too late to take up drinking." Melvin flashed a mischievous smile and bit into the pear.

Prescott was in no mood to play along. "Never."

"Wish I'd discovered you before you found God in that rescue mission. Would've made my job easier."

A tiny smile for old time's sake. If he'd played the bad boy role, he might have made the jump from B movies to the A list a lot earlier. But at what cost?

Melvin waved his pear in a little circle. "Find a hobby. Take up bird-watching or something."

"I've been reading a lot."

A quiet cuss, and Melvin's head drooped. "Whatever you do,

promise you won't take up writing. Every actor thinks he can write. Every actor is wrong."

Melvin's secretary leaned in the door. "Mr. Underwood? Call for you from a Miss Margaret Oliver with the USO regarding a Christmas show for the Navy boys in San Diego."

"Put it through, Edna." He glanced at Prescott. "You don't mind?"

Prescott shook his head and waved his agent toward the phone.

Melvin set down the half-eaten pear, sandwiched the phone between shoulder and ear, and slid open a desk drawer. "Melvin Underwood here. How many dancing girls you need?"

Then Melvin's gaze shot to Prescott. "You want Prescott Duke?"

Prescott sat up straighter, his mouth hanging open.

Melvin held up his hand to stop him. "I'm sorry, Miss Oliver, but you must not have heard. Mr. Duke was badly burned in an accident. He—he has scars."

Prescott's face burned on the left side. Burned. But it was better for the woman to find out now than when he showed up for the first rehearsal.

Melvin ran his hand through his silver hair. "Yes. Yes, I understand stage is different from film . . . No, his voice wasn't affected, but lady, you don't know what you're asking."

No, his voice wasn't affected, and Prescott edged forward in his chair.

Melvin slapped his folder onto the desk. "I don't care if his name is on your list. He isn't available."

What? He'd been available for well over a year. Prescott sprang forward and snatched the phone right out of Melvin's hand. "Miss Oliver? I am very much available. I would be honored to be in your show."

A feminine gasp. "Is that—Mr. Duke?"

Melvin groaned. "Press, you don't know what you're doing."

Prescott jabbed a finger at the phone. "The lady invited me to be in her show, and I want to do it. What else do I need to know?"

"Mr. Duke?" The woman's voice quivered. "I—I'm so sorry. I didn't know you were there. How much did you hear?"

"I heard that I have a chance to do something worthwhile with my sorry life for the first time in almost two years. What would you like me to do?"

"Oh. Well. Serve as the emcee and sing a song or two, dance perhaps. I hadn't thought that far. And we're doing a short version of Shakespeare's *Twelfth Night*. I thought—with your name—I thought maybe you could play the role of Duke Orsino."

"Anything. I'll be a stagehand, water boy, whatever you want. I'm yours, Miss Oliver."

"Oh." She gave a nervous little laugh. "Thank you."

Melvin rolled his eyes.

Prescott hadn't meant to sound flirtatious, and he raised a sheepish smile.

"Fine." Melvin grabbed his gold pen and took back the phone. "All right, Miss USO. Where does he need to be and when?"

Prescott settled back into the armchair.

This wouldn't solve his problem, not by a long shot. But for two months, he could fill the void of his life.

Sarah Sundin is the bestselling and Christy Award–winning author of eighteen World War II novels, including *Midnight on the Scottish Shore* and *Embers in the London Sky*. Her novel *Until Leaves Fall in Paris* won the 2022 Christy Award, *The Sky Above Us* received the 2020 Carol Award, and *The Sound of Light*, *When Twilight Breaks*, and *The Land Beneath Us* were finalists for the Christy Award.

During WW II, one of her grandfathers served as a pharmacist's mate (medic) in the US Navy, and her great-uncle flew with the US Eighth Air Force. Her other grandfather, a professor of German, helped train American soldiers in the German language through the US Army Specialized Training Program.

Sarah and her husband live in Southern California and have three adult children and two adorable grandchildren. Their two rescue dogs make sure she gets plenty of walks and fresh air. Sarah enjoys teaching Sunday school and women's Bible studies and speaking for church, community, and writers' groups. She also serves as co-director of the West Coast Christian Writers Conference. Visit SarahSundin.com for more information.

GET TO KNOW

SARAH
SUNDIN

To Learn More about Sarah,
Read Her Blog, or See
the Inspiration behind the Stories,
Visit

SARAHSUNDIN.COM

Be the first to hear about new books from Revell!

Stay up to date with our authors and books by signing up for our newsletters at

RevellBooks.com/SignUp

FOLLOW US ON SOCIAL MEDIA

  @RevellFiction